SINISTER VOWS

A.M. MCCOY

COPYRIGHT

This book is intended for mature audiences.

CONTENTS

Warning   V

1.   About Sinister Vows   1

2.   Chapter 1 – Arianna   2

3.   Chapter 2 – Arianna   6

4.   Chapter 3 – Arianna   28

5.   Chapter 4 – Nico   44

6.   Chapter 5 – Arianna   51

7.   Chapter 6 – Nico   60

8.   Chapter 7 – Arianna   76

9.   Chapter 8 – Nico   84

10. Chapter 9 – Arianna   94

11. Chapter 10 – Nico   105

12. Chapter 11 – Arianna   115

13. Chapter 12 – Nico   126

14. Chapter 13 – Arianna   134

15. Chapter 14 – Nico   146

16. Chapter 15 – Arianna   155

17. Chapter 16 – Arianna   166

18. Chapter 17 – Nico   180

19. Chapter 18- Arianna   192

20.	Chapter 19 – Nico	209
21.	Chapter 20 – Arianna	218
22.	Chapter 21 – Nico	232
23.	Chapter 22 – Arianna	243
24.	Chapter 23- Arianna	251
25.	Chapter 24- Nico	259
26.	Chapter 25- Arianna	265
27.	Chapter 26 – Nico	275
28.	Epilogue – Arianna	279
29.	What's Next	289

WARNING

Sinister Vows is a dark romance with elements that may be disturbing to some readers.

Triggers include but are not limited to:

CNC/Dub Con

Detailed Sex on Page

Profanity

Murder

Violence

Assault

Child Abuse

Arranged Marriage

Smoking

Alcohol

Drugs

Blood

Pregnancy

Emesis

Animal Abuse

If you have any concerns or questions ahead of time, please do not hesitate to reach out to A.M. McCoy's team at a.m.mccoybooks@gmail.com to discuss.

ABOUT SINISTER VOWS

I was sold to the Don of the Italian mafia when I was twelve years old. Now, at twenty, I've been summoned to Nicolas Capasso's home, a man I've never even met, for my wedding day. No wiser of what it means to be a wife to a man like him.

Let alone what goes on between a husband and wife in the dark.

Nonetheless, I was assured it was all part of the *plan*.

Step one, marry the Don. Got it.

Step two, provide him with as many children as he requires. Gross.

Step three, live silently and dutifully as the wife to the most powerful man in history. Oh, come on.

The only thing standing in the way of completing such a simple plan, you ask.

The blessing ceremony on the eve of my wedding.

The most outdated form of torture imaginable on a pure bride like me, and something my family had been doing for centuries.

Yet, when I found myself dressed in white, laid atop a ceremonial bed-spread, and offered up to the deviant priest as a sacrifice, the man that walked into the room wasn't at all what I expected.

Don't even get me started on what he did to my body during the ceremony, or what carnal things he made me feel while he did it.

My future marriage was supposed to be blessed by the ceremony, paving the way to a peaceful union between our families.

If that was the case, why was it the man from the night before that consumed my every thought as I walked down the aisle the next day?

CHAPTER 1 – ARIANNA

"Ari!" My father snapped his fingers from the seat opposite mine. "Are you listening to me?"

"Yes, Papa." I answered on autopilot, the phrase was simply muscle memory at this point in my life. I forced myself to look at him and my mama sitting on the leather bench seat of the limo as it drove through the unfamiliar countryside.

"Good. Because we do not have much time left before we get to the estate and you need to be on your best behavior when we do."

"She will be, dear." My mother's calm and melodic voice assured my father as she patted his knee, "This is what we've spent her entire life preparing for."

My father smiled at my mother and put his hand on top of hers before looking back at me with a pointed stare. "You are the future of this family Arianna. If you do not fulfill your duty to this family, we will go extinct."

The future of the Rosetti Family rests upon my shoulders.

Yeah, I've heard that same bull shit line since I was old enough to process the words he spit my way.

Arianna, the dutiful and docile daughter of Emilio and Mina Rosetti, the third child out of five, was going to be the saving grace of the entire familial line.

Puke.

I let my eyes fall away from his to look back out the window at the vibrant red and orange leaves on the trees mixed with the green ones as we drove by.

I'd never seen fall foliage in the north before.

Perhaps living here wouldn't be so bad after all.

The limo slowed and I craned my neck for a glimpse of the estate as we rolled into the massive gatehouse. Armed men with menacing glares and even scarier guns strapped to their chests circled the limo as our driver spoke to them. The windows in the back rolled down and my father nodded to a guard as he looked first at him, then my mother, then across the space to where I sat on the bench seat facing backward. He was massive, far over six feet tall, and nearly as wide as he was tall with dark eyes and a strong jawline. He was the absolute definition of scary and I fought not to wilt under his stare.

The man's eyes traveled from my head to my toes and back before he nodded to me and stood back up. I shivered from the brute power I felt rolling off the men surrounding us as the limo started rolling up the driveway again.

I blew out a silent breath and deflated into the seat, trying to steal my resolve again.

Seconds on the infamous Capasso property, and I was already balking with fight or flight urges. I felt like with each foot of the driveway that the limo ate up, I was getting closer to my execution.

My mother smiled brightly as she commented on the expansive grounds with the immaculate landscapes and designs and my father smirked into his scotch glass.

Everything was falling into place for them.

Yet for me... I was doomed.

The car stopped and staff from the massive mansion walked down the steps, lining up to receive us as my parents got out of the car and signaled for me to join.

I took a deep breath and smoothed my hands down my light pink dress and forced my body to slide off the seat and follow them.

I tried to make my face relax and look more approachable, standing next to my mother as the eyes of all the staff fell onto me in morbid curiosity. I hated being the center of attention. Not once in my life had I been the important one in the room, and I didn't like that I was now.

"Mr. Rosetti," A man in a suit stepped forward with a slight bow to my father, "Mrs. Rosetti, my name is Manny, I am the head butler here at Armarow Estate." He didn't acknowledge me as he stiffly turned, "If you'll follow me, I'll show you to your rooms so you can freshen up before dinner, and your meeting with Mr. Capasso."

"That would be wonderful," my father said, placing his hand on the small of my mother's back leading her forward to follow the butler, leaving me with no choice but to dutifully follow after them.

The staff lining the many steps up to the front of the mansion were mostly maids in traditional black and white uniforms and butlers in crisp black tuxedos. Some looked above the heads of everyone, and some looked at me with curious glances, but every single one of them bowed their heads when I walked past.

As we stood in the front foyer, I looked for the face of the man I was to marry tomorrow. I'd never met him before and knew absolutely nothing about him, but soon he was supposed to be the most important person in my life. Out of the men in the room, I could tell he wasn't one of them. I knew that when I did see him for the first time, I'd know it was him.

Men with power like Nicolas Capasso, were hard to miss.

I followed my parents up the large, curved staircase to the second floor and then down a series of halls and corridors until we came to a wing of the house that seemed devoid of any other guests.

"Mr. and Mrs. Rosetti, your rooms are to the right, and your room," he finally looked at me, "Ms. Rosetti, is to the left." He indicated two separate hallways across from each other with ornate carvings in the archways. "Dinner will be served at seven in the west dining room. Your meeting with Mr. Capasso, Mr. Rosetti, will be at six. The rest of your family should arrive shortly."

"Thank you," my father smiled and nodded to the man as he walked back down the way he came. When he was gone around the corner my father's smile fell and he raised his lip in a snarl as he glared at the halls over his shoulder. "Of course, he gave us rooms in the East wing of the house," he hissed, "There'd better be drapes thick enough to cut out the morning sunlight."

My mother slid her hands down his arms as she walked past him towards the hallway that Manny indicated as mine. She nodded for me, "Go on in now, dear," she sang, "I'll have your luggage brought up and laid out in the closet for you." She ran her hand down the back of my head over my hair as I passed by her. "Perhaps you should take a bath or something to relax and pass the time. I have a glam team coming in an hour to dress and prepare you for tonight." She looked down at her watch, "Do not leave your room. I'll be by with them when they get here to start getting you ready to start your future as the new Mrs. Capasso," she cheered happily.

I went down the hall to the only other set of doors at the end and walked in. I looked around the room and sighed as I took in the white and feminine furniture fit for a fairy princess in a tale as old as time.

"Lucky me," I whispered and sat down on the padded bench at the end of the bed.

If only my knight in shining armor would swoop in and rescue me from the terrifying dragon holding me hostage in the tower of his castle before it was too late.

Who was I kidding?

The dragon was my soon-to-be husband and the rumors of his ferociousness and terror were known across all the land, ensuring no one even tried to slay him.

And I was being offered to him as a sacrificial lamb at sunset tomorrow.

Chapter 2 – Arianna

"Y ou're so lucky," my little sister Anita whined from her prone position on my bed as she watched the glam team fuss over me. She was twelve and didn't understand everything that was happening today and tomorrow, so I tried to not take my anger and frustration out on her.

My other sister Amelia, the middle daughter, rolled her eyes from her seat at the large makeup vanity along the wall, "She's lucky to be sold off like cattle?" She was eighteen and facing her own impending doom soon, so she had a different opinion than our little sister.

"She gets to marry one of the most powerful men in our time and gets all of this," Anita flung her hands out around the room, "And it doesn't hurt that he's really cute."

"You've seen him?" I asked, finally mustering enough energy to speak. "When?"

Anita paused and swallowed, shrinking under the stares of Amelia and I, "Well, I haven't seen him personally, but Mama said he was handsome." She said guiltily as I deflated into my chair.

"She also thinks Papa is handsome," Amelia rolled her eyes again and then shuddered, "You're doomed." She said to me with a shrug of her shoulders. "I heard he's old. Like grey and old. He is probably wrinkly too."

"That's enough," I sighed and looked at the reflection of a prim and proper princess in the mirror above the dresser I was seated at. I had large rollers in my dark chocolate hair making it look like I was four inches taller than I was, and thick makeup that made me look ten years older than I was.

Because it was true, my soon-to-be husband was much older than I was. I was turning twenty-one soon, and if I did my math correctly based on being promised years ago, he was in his mid to late thirties. Not as old as Amelia tried to make him sound, but much older than me.

The glam team my mother hired was the best money could buy because the Rosetti family had no shortage of that. So they stayed silent as my sisters and I spoke about such inappropriate things. I didn't silence Anita and Amelia because I was worried about them talking badly about one of the most powerful and dangerous men in the Italian mafia. I ended the conversation because my heart couldn't stand the pain and despair that acknowledging my predicament brought.

And my tonic was wearing off, leaving me raw and susceptible to rogue thoughts as the fog lifted from my brain and my limbs.

My parents had been drugging me for months now as the wedding date got nearer. I didn't know if they knew that I'd figured out that my mother's holistic tonic was full of sedatives and mood suppressors or not. Perhaps they didn't even care if I knew I was being distorted into the silent and obeying daughter they had always hoped for.

I had no choice in the matter.

So I dutifully took my tonic and let the numbness push me into silence as they mapped out the entire thing for me. It wasn't like I hadn't tried to stop the whole sordid thing before though, when I was young and brave.

One time, a few years ago as I started to realize what an arranged marriage meant for a girl like me, I told my father that I refused to be a part of his plans and that I wouldn't marry a man he picked for me.

In response, he backhanded me so hard that he broke my jaw and left me bedridden with my mouth wired shut for months. It was at that point that I realized; I was nothing more than a pawn on a chessboard to him. He didn't love me; he didn't care for my happiness. He only cared about the deals he schemed with his allies and enemies to ensure that he stayed rich and content for the rest of his merry life.

To hell with everyone else.

So numb was better than miserable in my book.

Right on cue, my mother floated into the room wearing an elaborate dressing gown, with a juice glass of the magic fog and handed it to me like it was a sweet glass of orange juice. "You look breathtaking dear; Nicolas won't know what hit him when you meet him tonight."

"Hmm." I hummed like I agreed and swallowed the tart liquid down.

My mother turned to my sisters and clapped her hands, "Girls, go to your rooms and get dressed in the gowns I've laid out for you. Be back out in the hallway in fifteen minutes to go down to dinner together."

"Yes, Mama." The girls replied in unison. Anita skipped from the room in glee and Amelia gave me a look of silent support as she left, leaving me alone with the glam team and my mother.

"Now," my mother said, sliding her fingers over the nape of my neck affectionately, "After dinner, the blessing ceremony will take place."

My blood froze at the mention of the archaic torture ceremony that my family had been doing on the eve of weddings for centuries. Violent waves of nausea bubbled in my gut, and I prayed for the tonic to work quickly so I could handle the conversation without letting my anger or fear escape. I could almost feel the panic coursing through my veins at her words.

I didn't reply, my acknowledgment wasn't needed. It was happening without my agreement either way.

"Remember what we discussed," she said lightly, but I could feel the threat behind her words. She was keeping her mask in place because of the other people in the room, but I could read between the lines. "You will be on your best behavior, both for dinner and the ceremony, and then tomorrow you will be wed," she sang, "And you will be the most envied woman in the world."

I didn't want to be envied by anyone in the world.

I just wanted to be safe and happy.

But my hopes and dreams didn't matter.

"Are you listening to me, Ari?" She snapped her fingers in front of my face. Her and my father's favorite form of *pay the fuck attention, Ari.*

Which I would be far better at if I wasn't so dead inside thanks to their drugs.

"Yes, Mama," I replied, "I'll be the image of obedience." I even managed a smile at her as she patted my cheek.

"Good girl," she smiled back, pleased with my response. "I'm going to get dressed, so get in your gown and take your hair out and then I'll meet you in the hallway in ten minutes."

"Yes, Mama."

She left and the silent women working on me took my hair down and spritzed it with setting spray and then helped me into the gown I was going to meet my future husband in.

It was rose gold and probably one of my favorite gowns that I'd been forced to wear in my lifetime, even though I had no choice in picking it out. It had thin straps and was surprisingly low cut, showing off a large amount of my cleavage above the jeweled bodice that hugged my waist tightly. The skirt was fitted with the same rose beading from the bodice and accentuated my hips before pooling around my legs.

I felt surprisingly mature and attractive in it, compared to the modest gowns I usually wore.

I suppose when one was being dangled in front of a grown man as bait, some tits were necessary.

Even if I didn't have a clue what to do with them to be seductive.

I spared myself only a short glance in the floor-length mirror before walking out to meet my family where they congregated in the hallway outside of our rooms.

My older brothers, Carmine and Cristian leaned against the wall with their fitted suits and bored expressions on their faces. They were the real *heirs* to the Rosetti line and the weight of continuing on the name was usually on their shoulders, specifically Carmine's as the oldest Rosetti sibling. But the joining of the Rosetti and Capasso families was decades in the making, and I think they were happy to not be responsible for something for once.

"Ah, darling," My mother cheered, "You look fabulous!" She touched my hair again, "Nicolas is one very lucky man." She nearly squealed with glee as my father walked out of their rooms, adjusting his tie. My sisters joined as well, both dressed in modest long sleeve white gowns adorned with lace. I felt exposed compared to them, but I guess that was the point. Heaven forbid my future husband focus on anyone else but his child bride.

Even if I wasn't a child anymore, I still felt obscenely lacking compared to the grown man who commanded entire countries worth of men and businesses.

"You look beautiful, dear," my father added, "A prize fit for a king." He mused and my stomach rolled at the lascivious look in his eyes as he addressed me. "Speaking of the king," he paused, "I've just met with him, finalizing everything for tomorrow. So, just be a good girl until you're wed, and then you're his problem to bear."

I stayed silent, knowing nothing I could say to that comment would please him. He turned away and tucked my mother in against his side to walk to dinner.

I took a deep breath and Carmine stopped at my side, giving me one of his infamous playboy winks as he held his elbow out for me to take.

He was always my favorite sibling if I had to be honest. With his dark features and charismatic charm, he was also the biggest thorn in my father's side.

Which was why we got along so well, I suppose.

Or at least we had before my *conditioning* started a few months ago. I'd spent most of my time since then, locked away and silenced. Learning all I would need to know as a wife to a powerful man like Nicolas Capasso.

"Let's go meet the old goat, shall we?" He whispered as we walked down the steps. He was only twenty-five years old, so my future husband was around a decade older than him even.

"I think I'd rather not," I whispered back, breaking through the fog.

Sadness crossed his eyes briefly before he looked away. He was as helpless as I was to this whole thing. "I know," he sighed, "If there was something I could do-"

"I know." I cut him off, patting his arm. "We're all just pawns in the game."

"Maybe you'll be better off here," he said and I could hear the hope in his voice. "Maybe he'll be..." he paused like he was searching for the right word, "Kind to you. Or good at least."

"Maybe," I whispered and leaned my head against his shoulder as we got to the bottom of the stairs, "I guess we're about to find out one way or another." I took a deep breath and followed my parents through the house, looking at the expansive and meticulously cared-after home.

It was breathtaking, in reality.

It had the ancient charm of a mansion that had survived world wars and revolutions, with the comfort and beauty of modern upgrades. If I was being honest, I was kind of excited to explore it as my home.

Or one of them.

Mother had said that Nicolas was only in residence at Armarow Estates a few times a year, which left me wondering if I'd be with him when he moved around his different homes. Or if I'd be put up in a place like this, and kept like a possession on a shelf in a formal living room that no one ever sat in.

I couldn't decipher if being ignored by a man I didn't want was more appealing than being the object of his attention.

I guess I needed to lay eyes on him to figure out what I felt towards him.

Besides the feeling of anger at being told I had no choice but to marry him.

That pissed me off.

"Arianna," my father called as we entered a lavish dining room, decorated with candles and flowers elegantly. "You sit here, across from me," he nodded to a seat to the right of the head of the table. He took the one to the left of the head and my mother sat next to him. Carmine took the seat next to me, as my other siblings filled in the empty seats until only the one at the head of the table remained empty.

Nicolas' seat.

Where was he?

Did I think he'd be here waiting for me? Excited to meet his young bride? Probably not.

But the version of him in my head that had haunted my dreams, was always a grey-haired unattractive fat old man who drooled and pawed at me crudely. Though, he'd have to be present to do any of those things.

"Dinner is served," Manny, the head butler spoke from the entrance as men and women walked into the room with platters of food and started serving.

I eyed the empty chair next to me as my plate was filled with all kinds of delicious-smelling foods that I hadn't been given in months. My father thought I needed to lose weight before my wedding, so he made me follow a strict low-calorie diet to shave off the pounds.

My family dug into the meal, and I took a few tentative bites as I looked up under my lashes. The food was phenomenal, but my appetite was off from the tonic and before long I was full.

"Papa," I questioned cautiously, "Where is Mr. Capasso?"

My father huffed around a mouthful of lamb and waved his hand at me. "He's busy."

"Busy?" I asked, forcing my tongue to move in my mouth to form words through the fatigue of the tonic. Even chewing the food had tired me out.

"Yes," he snapped, drawing a few looks from the waiters lining the wall behind him. "He's a busy man."

"When will I meet him then?" I questioned, against my better judgment, knowing he was not interested in talking to me. But he had assured me that we'd meet tonight, given that my wedding to the man was tomorrow.

For fucks sake, was it too much to ask to meet your groom before the altar?

"When he feels like it!" my father snapped, slamming his fist down on the table and clattering the silverware. My eyes rose to more cautious glances from the staff that were seeing the side of my father he rarely ever showed to anyone outside of our household. "He doesn't have time to be bothered with the inconsequential woes of a blushing bride." He glared at me. "Now eat your meal and stay quiet," He picked up his wine and polished off what had to be his third glass since we sat down. "Besides," he smacked his lips together, "The blessing ceremony will commence after the meal is finished, you'll need substance in your belly for it."

My stomach rolled at the mention of the ceremony taking place tonight. I think I would have dreaded it more than the actual wedding if I was allowed to be honest. I put my fork down and pushed my plate away defiantly. It was the first glimpse of disobedience I'd shown in a long time.

My father took it as well as I thought he would. He slammed his fists down on the table and leaned across it to grab me in anger. Carmine put his hand on my arm and pulled my seat back out of my father's reach hastily, nearly toppling me over onto the floor, but it kept his hands from striking me. "Papa!" My brother hissed, nodding his head to the now-open stares from the staff in the room. "Remember why we're here," He whispered.

I panted in my seat as fear and anxiety burned my spine.

It felt good.

Well, stupid.

Because who willingly pokes a bear with a toothpick just for fun?

But still, good.

"The sooner you're married off, the better!" My father hissed and sat back down in his chair, flinging his hand forward for a repour on his wine. "Eat or don't eat, whatever. But regardless, this evening and tomorrow will go as planned." He glared at me, "Don't make me remind you who is in charge here."

I shuddered, but held his stare in silent appraisal as he looked away and went back to eating. Carmine relaxed at my side and slid my chair back into the table and let out a weighted breath. "Eat," he whispered. "Please."

I held off for a few more minutes as the rest of my family cautiously went back to eating in silence before I picked up my fork again.

The food *was* really good.

The meal passed with only my parents and Carmine speaking of things pertaining to business back home as I watched the minutes tick by on the grandfather clock in the corner. The more time that passed, the closer to doom I got.

When the food was gone and my father and mother were well into the later stages of being drunk on wine, I felt like I was crawling out of my skin.

I couldn't do it.

I couldn't. It was too... repulsive.

But I didn't have a choice. I wasn't in charge. "Come," My mother said, standing from her chair and walking to my side, "Let's get you ready for the ceremony." She turned and spoke to my father, "Get the priest ready."

My father nodded to her and then looked at me with a smirk on his thin lips. "You'll be on your best behavior, or I'll make you regret it." With that he stood up, wine glass in hand, and walked from the room with a slight tilt to his frame.

I looked over to my brother Carmine, but he wouldn't meet my gaze. His hands were on the table in fists as he stared down at his plate in silence. He wasn't going to stop this for me.

And my future husband hadn't even shown up to dinner before I was being sent to the priest as a sacrifice.

"This is bullshit," I cursed under my breath and then my mother's fingers wrapped around my upper arm and dragged me out of my chair aggressively.

"Silence." She hissed and hauled me after her to my room.

As we left the dining room, curious glances and concerned looks burnt my skin as we passed the staff. Some looked almost appalled by the open display of force against me, but it wasn't like any of them were going to step in. I knew that.

It almost helped that at least some of them felt a bit of outrage from the entire situation.

Like solidarity of some sort, even if it was in silence.

When we got inside my room she shoved me forward, before grabbing a bottle of the tonic off my dresser, pouring a hefty amount into a cup, and pushing it at me.

I took the glass but hesitated before putting it to my lips to drink like I normally would. My mother paused as she held up the nightdress I was supposed to wear for the ceremony.

"Drink it," She ordered, "Believe me, you'll want it."

I watched her as the first glimpse of a woman who'd been through the same arranged marriage traditions that I was going through surfaced. "Will it hurt?" I whispered and tipped the tonic to my lips, giving in to my fate. Because she was right, I would want the numbness for what faced me.

"Yes," she said firmly, and then sighed, "Though far less than it would if it was your new husband I'd guess."

I set the glass down and felt the tingling of the tonic dance across my tongue. "Why do you say that?"

She shrugged her shoulders before coming around my back to unzip my dress and help me out of it. "I don't suspect your husband is a gentle type of man," she replied as I crossed my arms over my bare chest and turned towards her.

She nodded to the basin of water that was left on an antique table in the center of the room. Next to the basin were linens with golden crosses embroidered on them and I fought the revulsion that rolled through my body at the blatant lie they represented to me.

"The ceremony will-" she paused as she hung the dinner gown up and I grieved that it went wasted, "Take away most of the pain for the first time you're with your husband." She said and then held the new white gown out for me to slide my arms into. It was like a robe, with long flowing sleeves and ties at the throat, the breast, and the hips.

The soft fabric burned my skin because of what it represented.

"Please don't make me do this, Mama." I tried, letting my fear surface. "Marrying a stranger is one thing, but letting an old priest-" I couldn't finish the sentence and shuddered violently.

"You will allow the priest to bless the marriage and prepare you for your husband," she snapped with an exasperated sigh, "It's how it's done in the Rosetti family, and how it's been done for *centuries* before. We aren't going to suddenly change the tradition because you request it." She yawned and then stepped back, looking at me in the gown. "You will do this, just as I did, and just as every Rosetti woman before you did. By tomorrow, you will forget it happened and you will have a blessed union with Nicolas Capasso because of it." She pushed my shoulder towards the bed that had been turned down in my absence to dinner. "Now get in." She pushed me again and I clamped my jaw shut to stop the whimper that wanted to break free.

This was barbaric.

She arranged the ceremonial bedding around me and pulled a white sheet up and then paused, looking down at me. "You will be fine Ari, it's a moment of pain and then it's done."

"It's rape." I retorted.

I didn't even see her hand move, though I should have expected it. Searing pain radiated across my cheek from her slap. I gasped and covered it with my hand in shock and shrunk back into the bedding.

My mother had never hit me.

That was my father's favorite form of affection towards me, not hers.

"Shut up!" She hissed, and then clicked off the bedside light and glared at me through the shadows as she adjusted her dress like she hadn't just assaulted her daughter. "You'll be thankful it's an impassive priest performing a religious ceremony. He gets no pleasure out of it, only when it's done will you understand what it could have felt like if it was your brutish husband looking to empty himself at your expense." I couldn't believe the words coming out of her mouth. It was like she was brainwashed by old creepy men from the church into believing they didn't enjoy deflowering virgins on the eve of their weddings in the name of their God. "Thankfully it will be dark in here when the priest arrives, so he doesn't have to see the proof of your disobedience." She indicated to my cheek where the skin burned with pain. I knew I wore the imprint of her hand. "He will be here sometime in the next hour after he meets with Nicolas and your father. Stay here and be *good*. I will see you in the morning." She gave me a curt nod once again and then walked from the room.

Locking the door from the outside on her way out.

I let out a shuddered breath and looked at the dark ceiling as my world started to darken from the tranquilizers. It normally took longer for the tonic to start lulling my senses.

But I suppose tonight the drink was heavy to *help* me endure.

I waited for what felt like hours, hardly breathing every time a noise echoed down the long hallway outside of my bedroom door until I was near tears. Shadows danced around the dark room thanks to the soft glowing candlelight that came from the table where the basin of holy water lay in the center of the room. It was a guiding light for the monster to cleanse his hands after his *duty* was done.

Fucking puke.

The tonic deepened after a while, leaving me in a steady lull of numbness and indifference and my eyelids started to close from boredom and fatigue. I hadn't slept soundly in what felt like weeks because of this entire thing and it was catching up with me.

But then, I heard the sound of the key sliding in the lock and turning, before light filled the doorway as the door opened, and in walked my tormentor.

I snapped my eyes shut and forced myself to take deep steady breaths as I listened to him turn the lock from the inside and then the soft tap of his shoes as he slowly walked across the room towards the basin.

My heart raced in my chest, and I felt lightheaded like I was going to faint from the sound of him in my room alone. The woes I had about marrying the most feared man in the world shrunk away as I faced this obstacle to even get to that one.

I cracked one eye open and tracked the man to the basin and sucked in a quick breath when I saw how large he was. He stood quartered away from me, looking down into the basin.

I wasn't sure what I expected to see when I looked, perhaps a small old man wearing black robes of holiness. But what I wasn't expecting was to see shoulders the size of a mammoth covered in a tight white button-down shirt that tapered where it tucked into a pair of black suit pants that hugged his narrow hips and long legs. It was dark, and I had trouble seeing anything else about him because he stood between me and the light. At my gasp, he looked over his shoulder far enough to glance at me before turning his attention back to the bowl.

Holy fuck.

And I meant that in the most disrespectful way possible.

There was nothing holy about this priest except for how badass he looked. His hair was short on the sides and with wavy dark strands on top, and in the warm glowing light, it looked like it had some salt and pepper to it around his temples.

He looked like a hot silver fox model on Instagram.

He scoffed and brought me back to reality, and poked his finger into the bowl of holy water, watching it ripple before standing up to his full height and turning towards me.

I shrunk back into the bedding further, hoping to disappear completely under his predatory gaze as he stalked closer. When he was at the end of the bed, he stood there, silently watching me with his face encased in shadows as I felt something prickling my skin through the haze of the tonic.

But I had no idea what the hell it was.

"Arianna." He said with a thick purr and my chest caved in on a sigh before I took a deep breath, clutching the sheet to my chest.

"Yes," I whispered as he slid his fingers over my toes and gathered the sheet in his hand, and slowly pulled it down. I clutched at it under my chin, and we had a quick game of tug-of-war over it before he pulled harder and it slid from my fingers, whispering down over my gown into a pile at his feet.

"This ceremony is to prepare you for your husband, and to bless your marriage." He didn't phrase it as a question, so I didn't reply, instead I just laid there and watched him. His eyes were a green color that seemed to glow in the shadows. I watched them travel from my head down my body to where my bare toes peeked out from under my gown and a predatory smile pulled his lips back, showing off his bright white teeth.

"You're the priest?" I voiced the doubt swirling around in my head. I'd never seen a priest look like this before. His shirt sleeves were rolled up on his forearms, and I was pretty sure I could see the dark swirls of tattoos on his skin, but in the dark, it could have been shadows.

"Were you expecting someone else?" He raised one harsh eyebrow at me.

"No," I whispered and then took a deep breath, fighting the tonic to form more words. "I don't know what to do."

That snarly smile graced his face again and he ran the back of his finger over the pads of my toes on one foot, then fingered the hem of my gown. "What do you want to do?"

His question surprised me, and I opened and closed my mouth repeatedly as I tried to form an answer. "Get this over with, I guess."

I'd never admit it, but his gentle touch on my toes was making things stir inside of me. He wasn't at all what I expected, and the pure... *dominance* of him and his presence was making me, warm.

Like all over.

Warmth filled my limbs and worked its way to my torso and then lower as he watched me with his silent stare.

"Then let us get on with it then." He said putting one knee on the bed next to my legs and leaned over me until his face was only a foot away. "First, let's get this off," reaching up before gently pulling the bow loose on the tie at my throat. I could feel my pulse racing in the skin right below his fingers.

"Why?" I whispered, "Why take it off?"

"Because I want it off," he said firmly and reached down to the tie between my breasts and pulled that one free.

I looked past his head to the ceiling and tried not to moan when the fabric brushed against my nipples. They were hard and ached to be touched, though I couldn't figure out why.

He slid the third and final bow free and the gown I wore opened, sliding off my body to reveal all of my skin to his eyes as he looked down at me.

I was going to pass out.

My heart was racing far too fast for my own good and I was going to faint.

"Look at me, Arianna," He commanded in a low voice and my eyes snapped to his, "Don't look anywhere else but at me. Do you understand?"

"No," I admitted, "I don't understand anything right now."

He smirked again and ran the back of his hand down my stomach and the skin quivered under his touch. "I'm the only thing in this room that matters to you right now," he spoke as he ran his warm palm over my hip and thigh before hooking it under my knee and pulling it wide, opening my legs to him.

I bit back a groan of embarrassment as he stared at my most private area like he was the wolf in a little old lady's clothing. His expression was pure *hunger*.

That should repulse me. The man that was entrusted by parents to perform... never mind.

This man wasn't honorable, and neither were my parents or any other parents who willingly allowed a stranger to rip through their virgin daughter's hymen in the name of tradition.

"Just do it," I panted. Desperate for the man to get it over with and leave me alone so I could think straight again. Because there was something about him that clouded my senses far worse than any dose of tonic ever did. "Please."

"Are you wet for me?" he asked and I shivered at the repulsiveness of this question.

My eyes rounded and I shook my head quickly. I was a virgin, but I wasn't innocent of the arousal of women and what happened to our bodies when it occurred. I was twenty years old, not five.

"Then we need to get you wet, or I'll rip you open when I take you." He said, pushing my legs open wider and kneeling between them.

"Isn't that the point?" I asked, closing my eyes.

"Maybe to some, but not to me," He answered quickly.

"How noble of you," I said before I could stop myself, and then I flinched when his hand moved, expecting to get hit. When it didn't come, I cracked one eye open to see him bent over me still, staring down at my scrunched-up face.

His fingers slid under my chin, and he tilted my head to the side, showing the side of my face that my mother had hit before she left. "They hit you?"

"Does it matter?" I challenged, "Just do what you came here to do, please." I closed my eyes again and forced myself to keep them closed even though I knew he was staring down at me.

Why did he care? It wasn't like the church ever cared about parents disciplining their children before, why start now?

Because this man was not like others I'd ever met before.

He was an enigma of sorts.

"If you insist," he said and then moved down the bed, hooking his hands under my knees and pushing them towards my chest.

I hated this.

But I couldn't deny the way the air felt cold against my wet lower lips as he spread me open, revealing the lie I'd told earlier when he asked me if I was wet for him.

I was so fucked in the head.

I opened my eyes again and looked down at my body as he settled on his stomach with his head right above my exposed vagina.

I'd never admit it, but with his face so close to it, I was glad my mother had forced me to get waxed a few days ago.

"What are you-?" I asked and froze as he locked eyes with me and lowered his mouth to my wet center. "Oh my God!" I gasped when he ran the flat of his tongue up the length of me and ended with a twirl of it around my clit. He tilted his head and kept his eyes locked on mine.

"Sweet, sweet cunt, Arianna." He growled before lowering his lips to me again. This time he sucked in like he was slurping liquid off a spoon and I saw stars in my vision and fell back onto my pillow.

This wasn't right.

He wasn't supposed to do this.

My mother said the man would come in, lay on top of me, break through my hymen, and then be done. She insisted that it wasn't sex because he wouldn't thrust or finish. He would simply push himself into me to break the barrier for my future husband.

But this.

This felt so much more personal.

"You can't-" I panted, staring at the ceiling as he gently shook his head back and forth with my clit sucked into his mouth, stimulating every centimeter of my vagina with his thick stubbled jaw. "You're not-." I broke off again and covered my mouth with the back of my hand when he let my clit go with a pop before he pushed his tongue into me and hummed, "Fuck!" I hissed and he chuckled.

Chuckled!

"You're so sweet," he said with that thick gravel in his voice that vibrated his chest against my thighs. "And innocent." He flicked my clit again. "Hearing the word fuck fall from your lips is intriguing to me."

"This is wrong," I cried, but before the words were even out of my lips, I rocked my hips forward against his face like a slut and moaned into my fist when he sucked on my clit again. "It's cheating or *something*!" I panted.

"Cheating on a man you've never met, who couldn't even be bothered to join you at the dinner table tonight?" He asked and then he ran the pads of his fingers against my outer lips before gently pushing one into me, stopping when we both felt the resistance an inch or two in. "It's not cheating. It's *tradition*," he said, but the way he spoke the last word, was like he hated it as much as I did.

But that couldn't be right.

He was the priest for fucks sake.

"I want you to come, so you'll be relaxed when I fuck you," he demanded and I gasped at his crude words. He sucked on my clit again and then rocked me back and forth onto his face like I was riding a horse and within seconds

I was cresting over the edge of my first-ever assisted orgasm. Were my parents down the hall while I enjoyed this torture? Could they hear my moans?

I was so ashamed of myself and of them for even making me do this. But that didn't stop the pleasure.

"Oh my God," I hissed and arched my back until only my hips and my scalp touched the bed as he pushed me through it and into a spontaneous second orgasm. "Stop," I cried, pushing at his face, "Please, it's too much," I begged, he popped my clit again and then slid off the bed, leaving me in a puddle of wetness and pleasure.

I watched him get to his feet and stare down at me, confused as to why he was stopping if he hadn't even done what he came to do. But then he reached up and slid the top button of his shirt free before moving down and undoing them all, and then pulled it free of his slacks.

His jaw glistened in the low light from my orgasms, and I watched in silent euphoria as he stripped his body right in front of me.

Good God, he was magnificent.

The darkness on his arms was ink, and it didn't stop there. Black swirls and words covered every inch of his upper body, across his chest and stomach, and under the fabric of his waistline.

I pressed my knees together as he loosened his belt and undid the button of his slacks revealing the bare skin beneath.

Commando.

"Why are you getting naked?" I whispered in fear and trepidation.

He smirked that same predatory snarl at me and pushed his pants down, revealing the biggest dick I'd ever seen before.

And while I had never seen one in person, I'd watched more than a few videos online to know that he was larger than most.

Even bigger than the paid actors.

"Would you rather I stay clothed when I take your virginity?" He asked, kicking off his shoes and pants to stand naked at the end of the bed. He ran his hand over his abs, rubbing his stomach before pushing it lower to grab onto his erection, and slowly stroked it while I watched.

I groaned, closing my eyes and covering them with my hands for good measure as he crawled back up the bed, pushing his thigh between mine until his large body lay cradled against mine.

It was too intimate like this, naked and touching from toes to sternums.

"Look at me, Arianna," he commanded and I obeyed, dropping my hands to my chest in fists because I couldn't fight my body's instant reaction to him. His green eyes glowed right above mine and I licked my lips in apprehension, and he tracked the movement. "I want you to look at me, the entire time."

"Okay," I whispered.

"Good girl," he said and reached between our bodies to rub the head of his massive cock through the wetness he drew from me. "Dripping for me." He smirked and I shuddered in embarrassment. I kept my hands on my chest, as I prepared for the invasion, but he didn't surge forward like I expected him to. He just kept sliding himself through my wetness in a teasing manner.

"Do it," I said, "Please, just get it over with."

He lifted one side of his upper lip, slowly pushing into me.

I gasped and my fists left my chest, digging my fingernails into his strong shoulders as he met that same resistance inside of me. He pulled back out and ran the underside of his shaft up through my wetness, against my clit again and I moaned, unable to stop it before it left my lips.

I felt the blush of embarrassment that had been on my face since he walked in the door deepen even more as I admitted that I wanted him with sounds alone.

He pulled back and did it again, but when my lips parted to moan again, he lowered his to them and absorbed it before running his tongue against mine in a seductive dance.

I'd never been kissed before.

And somehow, the way he kissed me, slowly rubbing his tongue against mine until I started to reciprocate, felt more intimate than the way he ran the length of his cock against my vagina.

One of his hands left the mattress and slid under my neck to anchor me to him as he tilted his head and deepened the kiss even more. I slid my hands up his shoulders, unable to keep them still and he groaned into my mouth when I raked my nails over the back of his scalp.

I clung to him as he continued rubbing my clit with the entire length of his cock and fucked my mouth with his tongue, losing myself to the erotic taboo that he was spinning around me like a web. I was so lost to him, I didn't notice when he shifted his hips and lined back up with my entrance until he surged forward, ripping through my virginity and pushing his entire cock into my body.

"God!" I screamed against his lips as waves of pain and nausea rolled through my body from the abruptness of it. He stayed still, buried deep inside, and watched me as tears filled my eyes from the stinging burn.

But he stayed still and waited for me to get over the shock of it. I blinked rapidly as I rode out the waves of pain until my breathing finally returned to normal and I removed my nails from the back of his neck where they'd dug in. I swallowed and tried to relax my muscles to prepare for him to pull out and end this torture of pain and pleasure that he inflicted on me like my mother had said he would.

But instead, he tilted my head back towards his with the hand still cradling the back of my neck and stared down into my eyes. "Tonight, I am your god," he growled and rolled his hips, rubbing my clit with his hard pelvic bone until I moaned again. "Good girl," He praised me with that same smirk.

"That's it, right?" I panted, taking my hands off of his shoulders to lay against my chest again, "It's over?"

He rolled his hips again and hitched my thigh up around his waist before slowly pulling out of me. When only the thick bulbous head of his cock remained inside of me, I held my breath, waiting for the empty feeling I imagined would come when he pulled free. But he licked his lips and slammed into me again, rolling his hips on the forward thrust and pulling out again, before repeating the motion over and over again. "I'm not anywhere near done with you, Arianna." He growled and pressed his lips against mine again, silencing the next line of moans that fell from them as the pain gave way to intense pleasure with each rock of his hips and the glide of him pushing and pulling from my body.

"I don't," I gasped, "I don't understand."

"Don't," he answered before taking one of my hands and sliding it back up around his neck where they had gone when he first kissed me. "Just enjoy."

"Enjoy?" I cried like the thought was barbaric, even as I moaned on the next breath.

"So tight," he growled, biting my bottom lip, and sucking it into his mouth, "This cunt is so good."

"Oh, my God." I groaned, pushing my head back into the pillows further to get away from his mouth even as I lifted my hips and tightened my leg around his waist, adding my other to cling to him.

"Take your pleasures from me," he demanded, reaching between our bodies to grab one of my breasts, squeezing it and pinching the nipple into a hard bud before dropping his mouth to it as he continued to thrust into me.

"Fuck!" I cried out, digging my nails into the back of his scalp to hold him to my breast as he sucked on it like he had my clit. "Don't stop," I moaned, ignoring the shame that tried to burn in my belly.

He rewarded me by sucking it deeper into his mouth and thrusting harder, pressing against my clit with more force on each down stroke as I panted in his arms.

"I want you to come for me." He said, letting my nipple go to lean back over my face. "I need to feel your body convulsing around my cock, Little One."

My eyes rolled in my head, and I dragged my nails down his shoulders as his words flew through my hazed brain like heat-seeking missiles, on their way through my body to the nerve receptors responsible for my orgasms. Because moments later, the switch flipped inside of me, and I exploded around him.

"Yes!" I cried, lifting my head off the pillow as my body tightened from nose to toes, "Yes!" He fucked me harder still, slamming into me until his chest was above my face and I bit his pec in ecstasy as my orgasm took over.

"Fuck," he groaned, slamming his palm to the headboard of the bed as he used his hips to grind against me. "That's it. Harder," He added, "Bite harder."

I was fucked in the head, unable to stop my teeth from tightening even harder around the thick corded muscle of his chest as he roared my name. I felt the heat inside of me swell and thicken as he thrust twice more before stilling. His cock jerked and spasmed with the warmth, and I realized he was filling me with his come.

My teeth popped free of his chest and my head fell back on the pillow in shock.

What the fuck did I just do?

He flexed his hips, over and over again, like he was trying to push even deeper into me as my inner walls continued to clench around him on their own, with aftershocks of my orgasm.

When he finally stilled, he pulled his hand from the headboard and rested both elbows on the pillow under my head, and stared down at me. I didn't know what to say, as disbelief and shame coursed through me.

Was it like this for every virgin?

Or at least the ones forced to perform this ancient act?

It couldn't be.

No way.

This was all him.

"Hmm," He growled deep in his chest, vibrating against my own and my nipples hardened against him even more. His green eyes glowed before a look of indifference passed over his handsome face.

Handsome?

Did I really just call this... *torturer* handsome?

And did I really just call it torture?

Because if I had to be honest, it wasn't. I didn't want this, but somehow he still managed to make me want him, and to enjoy it like he demanded I do. He was twisted and so was I.

He pulled his hips back and slid from my body, watching me wince as he pulled free. I could feel the wetness of his orgasm and mine mixed together drip out of my body in his absence and clamped my legs closed as he crawled off the foot of the bed to stare down at me.

"Let me see," He ordered, pushing my knees apart to stare at my vagina. He growled again, "Virgin no more." He nodded with a tilt of his lips and released my knees.

That's when I noticed the smear of red covering his dick and pubic bone. He walked over to the basin in the center of the room and soaked one of the cloths in water and then wiped my blood from his body. He soaked the other cloth and walked back to me, without another word.

He pushed my knees wide once more and wiped away the mess we'd both made, watching my face intently as I winced again at the burning pain left in his wake, but offered no condolences or comfort. When he was done, he stood back up and stared upon me with the same indifferent look on his face.

It was like he wanted to say something but forced himself to stay silent.

What would he say after a moment like this?

Sorry, I took advantage of you.

Glad you came all over my cock like a good little slut though.

I snapped my knees closed and clutched my gown closed over my chest, hiding myself from him even though he had already seen and tasted most of it.

He smirked at me with that threatening snarl and then ran one of his large hands across his abs again.

I don't know why, but the motion made me feel... feral.

It was such a turn-on.

And I hated myself for that.

He got dressed, slowly, like he didn't care that I lay before him watching. I felt the tonic fog start to descend on me again, now that the adrenalin and fear were gone.

My eyelids fluttered closed and my body relaxed into the bed fully until I heard the clink of the glass on the dresser top and my eyes popped open.

The man stood there, taking the glass off the top of the tonic before lifting the bottle to his nose to sniff the yellow drink.

"Don't drink it," I whispered and then cleared my throat to try to add more volume to it. "It's drugged."

He put the bottle back down on the dresser and looked at me out of the corner of his eye. His eyebrows were pinched tightly over his eyes and his face was no longer impassive or indifferent.

Now it was enraged.

"Drugged with what?"

I shrugged my shoulder and turned over on my side to face him, unable to keep my eyes open any longer so I let them close. "Something to keep me obedient."

When I finally opened my eyelids again, he was still staring at me with that angered look on his face. He put the glass back over the opening of the bottle and returned to the bed, bending down to pick up the sheet and blanket that had been set on the floor before the *ceremony*.

He flicked his wrists and fanned them both out over the top of my curled-up body and stood over me, "Your marriage has been blessed," He said. "Good luck with your new husband."

Then he turned and walked back out of the bedroom, tossing the key down on the table next to the door and flipping the lock from the inside before closing the door.

He locked the rest of the world out and gave me what was hopefully the only key.

That was a gift I'd never been blessed with before.

And I fell into a deep dreamless slumber knowing no one could get to me and interrupt it.

CHAPTER 3 – ARIANNA

The next afternoon, I sat in a silk dressing gown at the vanity, much like I had last night, as my mother's glam team dried and curled my hair. I was in a daze, but it wasn't from the tonic this time.

It was from the memories that kept swirling through my head of the mysterious priest last night and the things he made my body feel and experience.

And how I ached to feel them again.

I couldn't even be bothered to think about my future husband and worry over what kind of man he would be towards me anymore, because I only had enough brain capacity for the man from last night.

"Ari!" Anita yelled from across the room. "I said, can I wear this?" She held up a white silk dress that I'd brought for wedding activities, though I hadn't needed to wear it given that I didn't have any activities to attend besides the dinner last night.

The same one that my future husband hadn't bothered to attend.

That was what the priest had said anyway.

"No, you cannot wear white silk to your sister's wedding, Anita." My mother huffed from her seat across the room. She held her forehead in her hands and nursed a mimosa.

"Mama, are you well?" I asked, surprising almost everyone in the room, because I usually didn't have it in me to speak, thanks to the sedatives in the tonic. But I was bright-eyed and bushy-tailed today.

Perhaps it was because I had slept all night long and well into the late morning.

Which was usually never allowed of me, but when I finally did wake up and forced my tender body from the bed, I opened the door to the hallway and found two giant men standing guard outside.

The bigger of the two guards, Saul, as he introduced himself, told me that they were under strict orders to keep anyone from disturbing me while I slept. Even after I woke up, they stood guard inside of my room when anyone else was inside with me.

"Fine, dear," My mother said with a glare, "Your father and I enjoyed ourselves a little too much last night and realize we are not as young as we once were." She drank the mimosa down and held the glass up for another one.

A maid stepped forward from the wall and took her glass and headed out of the room to get another one made.

"Well, what am I supposed to wear then?" Anita pouted and flopped backward on my bed. "I don't want to wear the plain dress you and Papa picked out for me," she wined, "It looks like a shapeless potato sack."

"It's about protecting your modesty, dear," Mother droned, sounding less than interested in the conversation, especially since Anita had argued the same point for every event she'd attended in the last year.

Which was also her first year in the marriage market, as Amelia and I called it. It was sick really, given that Anita was only twelve and my parents were parading her around at events in the hopes that a family may see her and desire to join in alliance with ours through marriage. But it was exactly what happened to myself and my middle sister.

It was how I landed here.

In a mansion tucked away in the mountains, on the day of my wedding to a man I'd never met before, simply because his father had desired to make a deal with my father eight years ago at some soiree.

It was archaic and barbaric and I couldn't believe there weren't laws out there to stop people like my father from doing such things.

But I guess when you're one of the richest men in the world, you can get away with more than your average Joe.

So I sat back in my seat and allowed the team to continue to prep me to get pimped out for the rest of my life to a man that was rumored to be the worst villain in any story.

"Ari," my mother called from her slumped-over seat, "do get up and get yourself a glass of tonic dear, I don't remember getting you one yet today since you slept in like a lazy-boned dog."

"Give her a break, Mama." Amelia argued for me, "After enduring the ceremony last night with no major hiccups, I think she was due a bit of rest on the day of her wedding." My sister winked at me, and I felt my face bloom red.

Did she know?

That I... *enjoyed* myself last night.

No, there was no way.

Not unless she heard my cries of pleasure.

"Ari!" my mother yelled, "Tonic. Now." Cutting through my internal worries. I stood up out of the seat, brushed off the glam squad, and walked to the dresser.

But the glass decanter of tonic was gone, as was the glass. "Mama, it's not here."

"What do you mean it's not there?" my mother snapped in irritation, "Where did you put it?"

"I didn't move it," I stared at her with wide eyes.

I tried to outsmart my mother a few times when the tonic was involved in the past. Once I poured half of it down the drain and filled it the rest of the way with lemonade to dilute the drugs, but she'd smelled the difference the instant she took the lid off. Another time, I'd poured the entire bottle down the drain and broke the glass decanter into a million pieces inside of a pillowcase and flushed them all down the toilet in defiance.

She locked me in my room for twelve days for that one and I was only given three meals that entire time.

I knew better than to mess with the precious mind-control drink anymore. I was never going to win the war against her and my father as long as they had that in their arsenal.

My mother stood up from her chair and the room fell silent as my sisters watched the scene unfold in front of them. She walked across the room slowly, with the gentle power of a female lion stalking her prey and I fought the fight or flight coursing through my veins, screaming at me to run.

This was going to hurt.

"I didn't move it, I swear." I tried once more, as she neared with menace in her dark brown eyes. "I didn't."

"You lying cunt," she whispered in anger.

"I moved it." A small voice called from the other side of the room. The maid that had been fetching my mother's mimosa stood in the doorway, with two cocktails on her tray and a frightened look on her face.

The guards from earlier were also there, and at some point, they had moved closer to us unnoticed while my mother stalked me.

My mother turned on the poor girl, throwing daggers from her eyes. "Why would you move something that didn't belong to you?" she snapped.

"Mr. Capasso insisted that the only food and drinks that Ms. Rosetti be served today come directly from the kitchen through me to her," the maid said firmly, no doubt brave enough to face off with my mother because of the hundreds of pounds of muscle on each side of her.

"That's absurd!" My mother screeched. "She is my daughter and I know what is best for her, I want her tonic back. And I want it back right now!"

"I'm sorry, Ma'am," The maid said but held firm, even while I shook like a leaf, "Mr. Capasso instructed me as well as Saul and Dio, that if there were any issues with his order, to take it up directly with him."

"Fine," My mother snapped, turning back towards me with fire in her eyes. "I'll be back, and when I return, I expect you to take your tonic without complaint."

I nodded with wide eyes and watched as she stormed from the room before I collapsed into one of the chairs nearby.

"Miss," the maid stepped forward, setting one glass down on the dresser and handing me another before kneeling in front of me. "Are you okay? I'm sorry if that upset you." She was young, probably around my age, maybe a few years older. Her bright platinum blonde hair was tied back in a fancy knot at the back of her head and her eyes were crystal blue as she lifted my hand from my lap and tucked the glass between my fingers. "Drink," She instructed. "You are pale."

I lifted the glass to my nose and sniffed, unable to catch the hint of anything bitter or medicinal, and then took a small tentative sip. "Mmh," I smiled at her and took another drink, "This is delicious."

She smiled brightly at me and looked over her shoulder to the guards. Saul sank back against the wall like he could blend in with the cream-colored wallpaper in his black suit and dark features, and Dio, the other one, left the room, locking it once again from the inside on his way out.

"What is your name?" I asked the young maid as she stood up and smoothed her hands over her straight black skirt.

"Molly, Miss," she said with a quick bow of her head. "I'll be your new personal attendant during your time here at Armarow Estate, now and in the future. Anything you need, will go directly through me and I'll make sure your every need and want is met."

"What a life," Amelia quipped from across the room with a smirk and I waved her off.

"Thank you, Molly." I nodded back to her and took another sip of my drink, "I'm sorry you met that side of my mother," I grimaced, "Though to be honest with you, I'm glad it was you and not me. You handled her far better than I ever have."

She patted my shoulder and picked up the other glass, handing it to Amelia with a wink before she started straightening out clothing that my sister Anita had torn out of my closet and left in a pile. "I have only one person to answer to while inside of this estate miss," She said with a small smile, "And after this evening's ceremony, so will you."

"Mr. Capasso?" I asked, ignoring the questioning looks from my sister at the mention of their soon-to-be brother-in-law.

"Yes, Miss," Molly said hanging up the dress that Anita had requested to wear. "Mr. Capasso is in charge of everything in this area. Even over your parents when they visit after today."

I snorted into my glass and smirked, "I don't think they'll be visiting me when this is all said and done." I looked out the window behind her and once again, admired the landscape and fall colors outside. "Though I don't feel all that torn up over it, as you can imagine."

Molly smiled and nodded her head knowingly as she continued her task.

"Wait," I said with a pause, "How did Mr. Capasso know about the..." I paused to think of a more appropriate name for the drugged drink but came up short, "tonic?" I shook my head, "Why did he place guards here at all?"

Molly shrugged her shoulders as she worked, "I'm not sure, Miss, he was waiting for me this morning when I was preparing for the day and gave me my instructions. Saul and Dio were already stationed outside of your door when I arrived."

"Hmm," I hummed and took another sip of my drink, "Interesting."

I made my way back over to the vanity and allowed the team to resume their task of making me bridal-ready as a comfortable chatter commenced between my sisters again.

I listened to them, but my thoughts went back to last night and everything that transpired in the very room I was sitting in.

I closed my eyes and remembered the way he stared down at me with such power in his eyes. But for once, I didn't feel fear from the power he held over me.

I remembered the way his mouth felt when he kissed me. And when he licked my breasts and my...

A blush crawled up my cheeks at the memory of him lying between my legs, pleasing me with his tongue like he had nothing else in the world to worry about at that moment.

"Are you well, Miss?" Molly asked, and I snapped my eyes open to find her standing next to the mirror with worry in her eyes.

"Quite," I said and swallowed away the tingles that were building in my body from the arousal that the memories of that man brought back.

God, I was so twisted in the head to think back on that ceremony fondly.

"Well," Molly said with a smile as she laid a platter of delicious-looking snacks down on the table in front of me, "Mr. Capasso asked me to bring you these. He said to make sure you had your fill today."

I fought the smile that tried to tilt my lips up at what seemed to be a kind gesture from my future husband. If only he'd taken the opportunity to join me at dinner last night so I could have met him.

"Is he a... kind man?" I asked Molly in a quiet voice. I didn't want Saul or my sisters to hear the vulnerable question, and I hoped that if she was quiet in her response, she might feel comfortable giving me an honest answer.

"Mr. Capasso is-" She paused and fussed over the food, "Intentional," She grimaced like that word wasn't the right one. "He never does or says anything that he doesn't mean to. He's always two or three steps ahead of everyone else in the world."

"But that doesn't speak of his kindness," I said with a sigh.

"It does," she whispered. "In the five years that I've worked for him, I've never once been given direct instructions from him for one of his guests as I have with you," Molly winked. "He even hand-plated this food for you, Miss." She smiled, "I've never seen him do that before. I won't lie and say he's gentle or kind to anyone, at least not in my presence. He's a powerful man, and I suppose to an extent if he were gentle and kind, that would diminish his control over the world."

"Hmm," I hummed, looking down at the array before me. "Thank you."

"Of course, Miss."

"Please, call me Ari," I said with a smile, and she smiled back and bowed her head, but didn't agree to it before walking away to clean up other plates and dishes around the room.

Before long, I was all done up with perfect hair and makeup, as were my sisters and it was nearing sunset.

Which meant my wedding had arrived.

I stepped into the wedding gown I'd had no say in choosing, which matched the decision-making of my hair, makeup, and even my nail color. I would admit that the gown was beautiful, even if it wasn't my style.

It was lace, with a sweetheart neckline and fitted bodice around my body with a heavy long train of the ornate design. The veil I wore was nearly as long, draped down my back to add to the effect of the entire ensemble.

"You look beautiful, Miss," Molly said with her hands clasped in front of her heart. "Like a queen."

I smirked and took a shuddered breath as I tried to fight through the nerves. My talk with Molly earlier, and the little 'gifts' that Mr. Capasso, Nicolas, had delivered to me throughout the day had eased a bit of apprehension in my stomach about the entire event. But it didn't remove it completely, and going off the tonic cold turkey had left me feeling on edge and raw because I was forced to feel things for the first time in forever.

To be honest, there was excitement at the prospect of adventure underneath the fear and anger over the entire situation.

I just hoped he wasn't old and ugly.

Or mean.

Or vile.

Or... any number of other disgusting traits.

"Wow." My brother Carmine walked into my room in a sharp black tux. "Sunshine, you look beautiful."

I smiled at him and gave him my cheek when he leaned down to kiss me. "Thank you, Car."

"I've been sent to fetch you," he said putting his elbow out for me, and I didn't miss the way his easy-going smile slipped a bit.

"Does it feel like you're leading me to the firing squad?" I asked him, "Because that's kind of what it feels like to me," I said quietly as he led me from the room. Molly carried my veil and train silently behind us, but I felt comfortable talking freely in front of her. However, Saul and Dio trailed down the stairs behind her, though, so I didn't feel as free.

"If I could stop this, Ari, I would," Carmine said firmly and I hated the way I could feel the anger aimed at himself from that statement. He blamed himself for not being powerful enough to end it yet. "When I lead this family, these sick traditions will stop."

With a sad smile, I patted his arm. "We both know, even in the grave, Father will pull the strings of this family for years to come."

"Maybe," he sighed, but I believed that he wanted to try to change things. I just hoped that maybe he'd get to that place before Anita and Amelia faced the same fate as me.

"There you are!" my father hissed as we approached him. He stood by the doors to the backyard pacing back and forth. "I was nearly on my way up to drag you down here by your hair, you insolent child."

"She's not late, Father!" Carmine snapped, but I pushed his arm away before my father could retaliate against him for speaking out of line.

"I'm sorry, Papa," I said, looking down at the ground. "I wanted to look perfect for the ceremony."

I lied.

He knew I lied.

But it appeased the predator in him the slightest bit to see me trying to go along with his elaborate plan. Especially because I wasn't drugged anymore. He probably envisioned me coming downstairs in a flurry of chaos and re-fusals.

I knew my fate wouldn't change, even if I made it a difficult process.

And I'd never admit it, but a small part of me didn't want my husband to meet me for the first time while I threw a tantrum like a child.

I kind of wanted him to be proud of the woman he was being married off to.

As I said, I'd never admit that to anyone. Especially not my brother.

"Let's just get this done," I said firmly, nodding to my father and giving Carmine a glare that hopefully would spur him into behaving. I couldn't bear the thought of him receiving punishment on my behalf.

In a few minutes, I wouldn't be his problem anymore.

"Go to your seat, Son," my father commanded, and Carmine nodded to me before walking out onto the patio.

Curtains covered the doors, to hide me until I made my walk down the aisle if I had to guess, but I caught a glimpse of the crowd gathered outside.

There were probably fifty people outside on the lower patio, and I was hit with a wave of nerves again.

"Are all of those people his?" I asked my father as my feet froze under me.

"Don't worry about that, just smile that pretty smile of yours, and let's be on our way," He said and wrapped my arm around his, squeezing it almost painfully. "Be on your best behavior," He stared down at me, "Or I promise you, I'll make Amelia and Carmine pay dearly for it. Just like I plan to do for your disobedience with the blessing ceremony last night."

"What?" I gasped in surprise. "What are you-" I gasped, "God!" I cringed as his hand tightened around my fingers so much that they popped and lightning bolts of pain shot up my arm. "Please!" I cried, bending to try to remove my hand from him. "I'm sorry! Please!"

"Mr. Rosetti," Saul snapped from behind us, and my father glared at him. They stared at each other for a few tense seconds more as nausea from the pain nearly consumed me before my father released my hand and placed it back on his arm like he hadn't just tried to dislocate twelve different knuckles at the same time.

I sagged and swayed on my feet as my vision darkened. My father said something and then the doors opened, revealing me to the grand affair waiting outside.

I swallowed back the sob that tried to rip free as he stepped forward and dragged me after him.

I'd been willing to go through with the entire thing, resolved to simply accept my fate. Of course, he had to go and tip the scales once again, exerting his power over me as he dragged me down the aisle.

I fought to keep my face impassive and devoid of the pain I was feeling as I passed by strangers who looked me up and down with criticism written all over their faces. Most of the guests were men, in fancy suits, with women dressed in elegant ball gowns on their arms.

Tears welled in my eyes as I tried to focus and keep my poker face in place. I didn't want anyone to see the weakness on my face as I walked down the aisle. I'd accepted my fate and wasn't balking at that.

My vision blurred from the tears as my father led me to the alter and I vaguely made out the silhouette of my future husband standing there waiting for me.

I tried to blink again to clear my view of him, but it was impossible to see through the haze.

"Here you go, darling," my father said in a sickly sweet voice, passing my hand to the man before leaning over to kiss my cheek. I flinched when his lips touched my skin as my soon-to-be husband held onto the hand I was sure was broken in multiple places.

"Thanks," I whispered with a tight smile, looking down at my feet as my sister Amelia took my bouquet and Anita fixed the train of my dress to lay perfectly.

The tears fell to the ground at my feet and my vision cleared enough to see things again and I looked at the man's feet, almost afraid to look up at him now that we were so close, and on display for so many people.

I forced myself to be brave, and let my eyes travel up his body.

He was tall, really tall.

And his legs were thick and muscled in his tight-fitting black suit pants.

When my gaze landed on his large hand, still holding my injured one, I gasped out loud.

Tattoos. They covered each of his fingers and the back of his hand, disappearing under his suit jacket.

I recognized them.

My eyes snapped up to meet the electric green eyes that had haunted my every thought since last night when they stared down at me as the mysterious man had pushed into my body. Now they stared down at me with amusement and something else burning in them.

"No," I whispered taking a step backward. His hand tightened on mine, and I winced in pain, recoiling from his touch.

His eyes darkened and the crowd watched on silently as things got uncomfortable.

What did they expect to see at the wedding of an arranged marriage?

"Quiet now, Little One," Nicolas commanded in a deep voice. "Father, get on with it." He turned to the priest standing next to us and I tore my eyes away from my future husband and jumped when I looked at the little old man.

"What?" I asked, shaking my head in confusion. I was silenced when Nicolas stepped forward, eliminating any space between us, and took my other hand in his as well, tightening his hold on both. I winced again and clenched my teeth to keep from outright screaming in agony.

He was intimidating me with his size and power.

A move I recognized from my father's catalog and a piece of my soul broke.

Every hope and a small bit of warmth that I'd felt today at the arrival of each of his small, kind gestures wilted away as I realized I was marrying a man who was so much like my father.

So much so, that he'd somehow beat the century-old tradition of the Rosetti family and was the one to steal my virginity last night, while letting me believe he was the priest.

The real priest, an old man twice the age of my father started his rambles about marriage and unions, but I couldn't focus on what he said. I stared down at my hands still held tightly in Nicolas's and tried to stay conscious.

My body rebelled against the idea that I'd laid with my soon-to-be husband last night without even knowing it. I couldn't wrap my head around why he would lie and trick me when he couldn't even bother to attend the dinner before that.

He had even talked about my future husband like he was someone else entirely.

"I do," Nicholas snarled, staring down at me when I forced my head back to look up at him.

The priest went on and then paused, waiting for me to agree as well. But everything swarmed around in my head at lightning speed, leaving me breathless and confused.

A hiss from the front row caught my attention and my head snapped to my brother Carmine. His face was red and tense as he stared at me, and veins on his temple and neck bulged, but he didn't say anything.

I saw my father move just slightly in the seat next to him and I caught the glint of the metal torture device he carried around in his pocket where it was pressed against my brother's ribs. It emitted electric shock like a taser though it looked like a small fork, designed to replicate the divot repair tool that golfers used to fix the grass when they dug it up. It was inconspicuous until he used it.

And then it was gruesome. Only once had he stabbed me with it, and it had been the worst pain of my life.

"I do." I gasped, "I do!" I didn't even bother to try to act like I was saying it to my husband, I stared directly at my father until he released his hold on my brother, who sagged in his chair as the electricity stopped pulsing through his body.

Nicolas followed my stare down to my father, who just raised an eyebrow at him with a smirk.

"I now pronounce you husband and wife," the priest said, and it permeated through the fog of panic in my brain. "You may now kiss your bride."

I whipped my head back to Nicolas as fear and uncertainty rushed through me.

He wouldn't.

The man let go of my hands as he stared down at me with intensity burning on his handsome face.

I didn't just call the man handsome, did I?

"Wife," He said with a sneer and slid his large hand around the back of my neck and tilted it back further as he lowered his face to mine.

No.

He pressed his warm lips to mine roughly, exerting his power over me with a simple move and I froze into solid stone at his touch. The crowd clapped and cheered like they were actually happy at the union that was just created through the entire bizarre situation.

I expected him to pull back, now that the marriage was sealed, but he didn't. He growled against my closed mouth and then bit my bottom lip, making me gasp in outrage. When I did, he deepened the kiss, pushing his tongue in and possessing my mouth like it was now his. The cheers got louder, and rowdier as men catcalled and jeered at his possessive display.

Worse yet, my body melted to his touch, giving into the desire that he created inside of me just like last night when he pressed into my body.

"Please," I panted against his lips, begging for reprieve as everyone watched.

"You'll be begging again soon enough, Little One," he growled, and then lowered his lips to my ear, "I wear the imprint of your teeth over my heart and your nails down the back of my neck." I could feel his smirk against my skin as he dropped his lips to my neck. "I wonder what your dear old daddy would say if he knew I could still taste your sweet cunt on my tongue?"

I gasped and then clenched my teeth to keep myself from rising to his bait as he pulled back to look down at me, waiting for... an outburst?

Rage?

I didn't know. But he wasn't going to get it from me.

I'd been beaten down way too much in my life to rise to his challenge just because he wanted me to. Instead, I pushed my shoulders back and kept my mouth shut as the crowd waited for us to walk back down the aisle as husband and wife.

He raised one of his dark eyebrows at me and then smirked, taking my left hand in his and turning away to lead me down the steps and back towards the house silently.

He shook hands with men along the way and got more than a few claps on the back as the men stared at me with wild looks in their eyes and the women glared daggers like I'd taken something of theirs.

I felt like I was living in some faraway reality that didn't make any sense, where everyone was in on a joke except me.

And it was about me.

I kept the same impassive look on my face through the entire bizarre parade until we were inside where Molly, Saul, and Dio waited for us. As soon as we cleared the threshold Nicolas dropped my hand and walked over to the lavish bar to pour himself a tall glass of liquor and threw it back without even a wince.

"Ma'am," Molly said gently, catching me off guard. I suppose now that I was married, I was no longer a Miss. "Put this on it to stop the swelling," She wrapped a bag of ice in a linen cloth and gently pressed it to my sore hand. I'd almost forgotten that she was behind me when my father crushed it.

"Thank you," I whispered in complete dismay.

"Swelling?" Nicolas barked from his spot across the room as he stared at us. "What are you talking about?"

I ignored him and put the ice on my hand gently, hissing when even the weight of it hurt against my knuckles.

Two of them were dislocated. I could tell from just looking at them, purple bruises were starting to form under the skin. Once again, my father had managed to disfigure me.

"I asked you a question, Wife," he hissed the last word like an insult, and I hated that he was so angry with me for some reason.

I was the one that was tricked, forced, and injured into this marriage.

For fucks sake, I'd spent the last six months comatose because of this entire affair.

"It's nothing," I replied, not looking up as Molly fussed over the cloth, holding it closed over the ice.

I heard his heavy footsteps as he crossed the room and I closed my eyes and took a deep breath, fighting the urge to run. I had nowhere to go anymore, this was my life.

Molly stepped back when he neared with a small smile and a nod to her boss. He lifted the bag of ice off my hand and looked at it where I cradled it against my chest. I refused to look up at him and instead stared at the floor as tears burned the back of my eyes.

"What happened?"

"Nothing," I answered out of habit. He was an outsider, and I was taught at a very young age to keep family things inside the family.

He shifted and I dared to take a glance up at him in time to see him look over his shoulder to Saul, who stepped forward.

"Her father broke it as he walked her down the aisle," Saul said evenly, "To keep her from acting out."

I risked a glance at my husband and regretted it instantly.

A fire burned in his green eyes when he looked back down at me, and I wilted under the power of it.

Nicolas stayed silent and clenched his jaw as he gently placed the ice back on my hand. I stared down in submission and hated how I felt so weak to all of these men all of the time.

"That's why you flinched during the ceremony," Nicolas said, "Because I squeezed your hand to get your attention."

"Yes," I whispered because the truth was I wanted him to know I was in pain. I stupidly hoped that maybe he'd care.

Maybe someone would finally care.

"And when you said, 'I do'?" He asked firmly, "Why did you look at him as you said it?"

I took a deep breath and looked back up at him. "Because when I hesitated, he stabbed Carmine with an electric shock device that he carries around."

His jaw clenched again and the muscles in his cheeks popped and rolled under the pressure. "To keep you obedient," he repeated my words from last night when I told him about the tonic.

"Yes."

He looked over his shoulder to Saul who nodded his head grimly.

"Take her upstairs," Nicolas looked at Molly, "I'll be up shortly." He turned back to Saul as Molly took my arm and gently pulled me towards the stairs. "Bring me, Carmine."

"Don't hurt him," I begged, drawing my husband's eyes back to me. "Do whatever you want to me, but please don't-" My voice cracked, "don't hurt my siblings. Please!"

His scowl deepened and he swallowed before nodding to Molly again, who pulled me along after her with more force until I was obliged to follow.

My heart and my head were at war as I followed Molly upstairs blindly. When she opened a heavy wooden door, I finally realized we weren't outside of my room. I looked up and down the hallway in confusion.

We weren't in the wing that my family was staying in at all.

Molly smiled at me knowingly and nodded for me to follow after her, "Your new room, Ma'am," she said gently, "In Mr. Capasso's private wing."

I took a tentative step inside the room and looked around. I originally thought the room I'd stayed in last night was luxurious, but this room topped it exponentially.

Cream-colored bedding adorned a beautifully crafted wooden king-sized bed with four posts on the corners. Above the bed, cream linens were draped, creating a billowed look that reminded me of a princess bed from my childhood.

Windows on the far wall showed off the back lawn where the wedding had taken place and doors lined two other walls.

"Would you like to get out of the dress now?" Molly asked and I sagged with relief. The thing was heavy and hot and given how the entire ceremony and marriage had come to be, I wasn't sentimental towards the gown and wanted to be rid of it.

"Yes, please," I nearly whimpered as she started undoing the buttons and zipper. When I was free of it, she slid a long white satin robe over my naked body and took away the offensive dress.

I collapsed into a reading chair near a fireplace that was lit and curled my legs underneath me and reflected on what happened in the last twenty-four hours.

The blessing ceremony that I'd been forced to participate in was all a sham. My husband was the man that showed up and took my virginity, lying to me that he was the priest. While that should give me some sense of relief, given that he didn't just break my hymen, but instead fucked me through multiple orgasms before enjoying his own; it gave me only more anxiety.

Because knowing that I was not only attracted to but craved my new husband was almost scarier than being repulsed by him like I had imagined I would be. He knew I enjoyed myself last night, and he knew he had power over me because of it.

He'd already proven he was so much like my father, which meant he would use my attraction to him against me if I let him.

So, I sat there in the chair, with a bruised hand, and a broken spirit, planning all the ways I was going to protect my heart and my body against the man who had stolen so much from me already.

Chapter 4 – Nico

"I want to know exactly what happened!" I barked, pouring more alcohol into my glass as I listened to my new wife's heels click across my marble foyer on her way upstairs to our bedroom.

Ours.

What a fucking oddity.

Saul sighed and Dio threw himself down into the chair at the table.

"She came downstairs with no problem; her brother Carmine brought her down. She seemed almost..." Saul paused searching for the right word.

"*Hopeful*," Dio added with a raised brow.

"Yeah," Saul nodded, "She was upbeat like the wedding was something she could handle and was optimistic about." He sighed again with a slight shake of his head. "Each time something from you was delivered throughout the day she'd smile and sigh a little like it was helping warm her up to the idea of it. But then her father met her at the door downstairs and lit into her without a second of hesitation."

"What do you mean?" I asked, forcing myself to walk away from the liquor I'd been nursing constantly for the last few days so I could approach this entire situation with a somewhat clear head.

"He commented on the ceremony last night. And how he'd make her pay for it. Then he crushed her hand as he dragged her down the aisle so she couldn't cry out."

My blood ran cold when I realized he broke her hand because I decided to break his fucked-up tradition last night. How did he even know?

Over my dead body was I going to let my new wife get fucked by some old man just because Emilio Rosetti's family was twisted in the head enough to allow it for years.

"And the taser thing with Carmine?" I asked Saul, remembering the way my tiny bride had stood up to me, begging me to spare her brother like she thought I meant some harm to him.

"I never saw it," Saul shrugged.

"I did," Dio said, who was usually silent, but he had spoken up twice now in the matter.

"What happened?"

"Emilio pulled something from his pocket and pushed it into his son's ribs when you said your part, and then when Arianna paused, Carmine jolted stiff as a board. Emilio used it to get her to do her part and when she was done, he released his son."

"His fucking heir!" I snapped, "Why the fuck is he dangling his heir in front of his middle child like a bargaining chip? Why does he care so much about this union taking place? It makes no sense," I scrubbed my hand over my face and paced.

"Something is at play here," Saul added, "You think the girl is in on it?"

"No," I said firmly because I knew it in my bones. "She had a handprint on her face last night when I got to her, and she was nearly unconscious from the drugs when I walked in. Then add the broken hand today," I shook my head, "No, she's just a pawn in their game like I am."

"Well, they picked the wrong family to try to control," Saul said with menace and Dio nodded his agreement.

"Sure as fuck did," I said, lifting my glass to my lips. "My father was lenient with Emilio Rosetti over the years, that's how I got shackled to his child. But my father is gone now, and I'm going to eradicate Emilio's pathetic existence from this earth," I sneered, "Starting with him and working my way down his bloodline."

Saul and Dio looked at each other but remained silent. My father had made the deal with Emilio a decade ago for me to marry his daughter Arianna. And I had no intention of going through with it after my father passed away last year. I intended to tell the Rosetti family to go fuck with someone else's family line because I had no desire to be linked to the vile man.

But then, eight months ago, I saw the grown up Arianna Rosetti, in passing at an event in Milan.

To say I'd been entranced was a fucking understatement.

Which led me to where I was currently.

Married.

With the plan to be a widow before the year was over.

I stood in my office watching the party take place outside on the back lawns with a sour mood threatening to pull me under into an even more terrible one.

It wasn't because I'd planned on being a bachelor my entire life yet now stood as a married man either. Marrying Arianna Rosetti hadn't been any real hardship on my part, to be honest, it wasn't as if my lifestyle needed to change just because of the change to my marital status.

Arianna was breathtakingly beautiful; I'd realized that in Milan and that alone had spurred me into allowing the union to take place. But more than that, she was... entrancing.

I watched her at the gala from across the room and witnessed her charm diplomats and businessmen firsthand who hardly ever batted an eye at anything that wasn't cold hard cash. Though for her, they not only paused, they also hung onto her every word.

She drew them in dutifully with her mother or father at her side pulling her strings, and she was outstanding.

She looked like a goddess and played the part of a god. It was captivating to watch.

At that moment, I knew I needed her at my side, and luckily for me, we were already engaged in a way. I already held a claim to her, but I wasn't dumb enough to think that Emilio Rosetti wouldn't entertain other offers if they came along. That night I contacted him and set the wedding into motion, no longer hiding from my future.

Now, I was married and rethinking everything I'd planned, with the dynamics of the Rosetti family revealing themselves to me minute by minute. Nothing was as it seemed before last night when I laid eyes on Arianna Rosetti again and then helped myself to her innocent body.

My dick stirred in my pants for the hundredth time since leaving her bed from thinking about the stolen moments with her.

Even if I'd lied my way into her bed, it was worth every single second. Because when I gave her the attention she so deserved, she opened up underneath me like blooming flower petals in the spring sunshine.

It had been life-changing to watch firsthand. Even though I was supposed to hate her, and hate everything she represented, I found myself longing for another taste.

"Nico," Saul said as he opened the door drawing me out of my thoughts, "Mr. Rosetti." He motioned for the young man to enter ahead of him before closing the door and standing guard outside of it.

"Carmine," I said walking around my desk to offer my hand to shake.

"Mr. Capasso," the younger Rosetti man said firmly while shaking my hand. He was my new brother-in-law, and though I hated his father, I could admire the differences in their personalities already.

Emilio was a slimeball, all the way around.

But Carmine-

I could see a lot of strength and honor in his eyes, and I appreciated that.

"Call me Nico, please," I said with a nod toward the lounge chairs by the fireplace, "Since we're related now, after all."

"Hmm," he said, but took the offered seat and watched me closely. He was young, around twenty-six or so, but wise.

I could see it in his eyes.

"I wanted to speak with you, freely," I added with an influx to my voice, "About your father and your sister." He raised one eyebrow at me but didn't say anything, so I continued on. "Arianna's hand is broken." I watched his face for any ques, and I got exactly what I expected.

Shock.

Anger.

And then indifference.

"Is it?" He asked.

"Yes, a couple of her knuckles are dislocated as well. My doctor is on her way here to place it."

"Thank you for seeing to her care," He said impassively and I could see his father's teachings shining through.

"You aren't interested in asking how it happened?" I challenged.

"I figured you'd tell me either way."

I stared at him knowing bigger and worse men would have wilted under the glare I'd perfected at a young age. But not Carmine.

I leaned forward to rest my elbows on my knees and cocked my head. "Did you know your mother and father beat her? Drugged her? And did God knows what else to her that I'm sure I'll find out in the coming days."

He swallowed and watched me back with the same intensity. "I'm aware."

"Yet you did nothing to stop it!" I snapped, hating that the topic had any power over my emotions. I shouldn't give two shits, but last night when she told me the drink on her dresser was drugged, saving me before I took a sip, I started to care.

"What would I have done?" he hissed back, leaning forward on his own elbows. "I have three other siblings I'm trying to protect as well. I did what I could for her," He challenged, "Believe it or not, marrying you was the best thing for her."

"I'm the worst kind of monster there is. Surely you know that she won't be better off with me, The Wolf."

"Will you feed her?" he countered, "Because they didn't. For weeks now they've withheld food from her to keep her dependent on them. Will you allow her to walk around your lavish estates freely as it pleases her as long as she is safe and within your boundaries? Because they locked her in her room for months at a time, sometimes even in a small closet with no windows or fresh air. Will you see that she is healthy and relatively happy in what will no doubt be your numerous absences from the home for business and other women?" He accused, "Because, for the last twenty years, they've tortured her!" He stood up in anger, rising to meet my own and I let him stand over me in a move that most men wouldn't dream of doing. "They starved her. They beat her. They drugged her. They locked her away in isolation when she served them no purpose and then paraded her around at events like a horse at a meat market when she did! They threatened her safety to keep me in line and they threatened mine and our other siblings to keep her in line. Don't think for one second that I don't know how terrible her life has been, because she's my little sister and I love her, and I burdened what I could for her. But I couldn't do anything to stop it! Not without jeopardizing my other sister's safety." His chest rose and fell with exertion and redness blotched his face with anger.

I unfolded myself from the chair and stared him in the eye as I took a step forward to close the distance between us. "He will never touch her again. She's mine."

"Good," he replied with as much strength, "It's about time someone had enough power to do something against him." I quirked an eyebrow at him, and he rolled his eyes and shifted on his feet. "Don't act like I don't know about your disdain for my father. Half of his allies can't stand him and only keep him in their circle because of his obscene wealth. The other half only keep him around for their entertainment." He scoffed, "It's despicable and embarrassing to share his name."

"I understand the burden of being the oldest son of a powerful man, better than most," I acknowledged, and held my hand back out to him again, "As long as your intentions for my wife are always good, you and I will be friends." He wearily took my hand and I held onto him and stared down with dominance. "And with my friendship, comes great power and even more powerful allies." His eyes squinted marginally as he tried to understand what I was saying, "Great power and allies are what turn princes into kings, Carmine."

He took his hand from mine, "What are you saying? The Capasso family has been in my father's pocket for decades."

I shrugged my shoulders and tossed back the rest of the drink in my glass. "Those decades have passed and the need for your father's money ended when I took over and took care of my own financial stability in ways my father never could. That generation of Capasso rule has changed, and I think it's due time that the Rosetti household turns over as well."

"Are you proposing to help with that?" He watched me.

A knock at the door interrupted my need to respond and Saul stuck his head in. "Doc's here." I nodded to him and then looked back at Carmine.

"I'm going to go see to my wife now. Go home with your family and I'll be in touch," I said with a slap on his shoulder as I passed.

I didn't linger to explain anymore of my plan to the man, simply because I didn't trust him yet. But I did trust his affection for his little sister, that much was clear to see.

While I didn't need to assist the doctor with treating Arianna, I ached to see her again. The same way I had all day since leaving her bed last night, which was why I'd sent small tokens to her. Even if I poised it as simply trying to take care of her, the truth was I wanted to win her affection.

Even if I hated her entire existence.

CHAPTER 5 – ARIANNA

A knock sounded at the door and Molly entered with a woman behind her. "Mrs. Capasso," Molly said with a small curtsey, "This is Dr. Travis, she's here to look at your hand."

"Hmm," I hummed because I knew I didn't get a say in it. And being called Mrs. Capasso had thrown me for a loop long enough for the doctor to cross the space and set a black leather bag down on the coffee table between my chair and the fire. She was middle-aged, with brown hair that had started turning grey at her temples and something about the natural look of age made me feel comfortable with her. Like she was authentic instead of fabricated like everyone else I ever interacted with.

"Mrs. Capasso," The doctor sat down on the coffee table and looked at my swollen hand where I cradled it in my lap. "I'd like to take a look at your hand and re-place the joints. I believe the sooner I get them re-placed, the sooner the swelling and tenderness will go down." She said directly before cocking her head, "But I'd be lying if I said it wasn't going to hurt a bit."

The door to the bedroom opened again and I looked over as my husband walked into the room with an indescribable look on his face. His black tux had been dismantled, leaving him in only a white dress shirt that was rolled up at his forearms, revealing the black ink underneath and unbuttoned at the throat, showing off the muscles that I bit my teeth into last night.

"Ma'am?" The doctor said, drawing my attention away from my sinfully sexy new husband and back to her. I felt the red flush crawl up my cheeks from being caught ogling him and unfolded my legs from underneath me, trying to gain my composure.

"Sorry." I chanced a look back up at Nicolas as he rounded the chair and stood behind the doctor, noticing how his gaze was trained on the length of my bare leg through the opening of my robe, and my skin burned under his touch. "I can take the pain."

"Very well, Ma'am." The doctor said and held her hand out for mine. I held it out and she gently ran her fingertips over the swollen knuckles, sending jolts of pain up my limb and I knew it was going to really suck when she reset the joints.

"Molly," Nicolas said, without taking his eyes off of me as I glanced up at him, "Go see to the Rosetti's things being packed. Use whoever you need, to get it done quickly, I want them gone as soon as possible."

"Yes, Mr. Capasso," Molly bowed her head and gave me a small smile before leaving the room.

"You're kicking my family out?" I asked him, daring to tilt my head back and stare up at him directly as the doctor continued her examination.

"Your father's childish actions will not be tolerated in my home." He answered plainly, and then added, "Your body won't be brutalized by them any longer." As he said that, there was a spark of recognition in my brain, reminding me of the way he looked last night when he turned my face and saw the handprint I wore from my mother. He had been angry last night, and he was angry now too.

"And my siblings?" I looked back down at my hand, "Are they to be lumped into the same unfortunate group as my parents?"

"Your siblings' nature and intentions do not interest me, Arianna." He said with finality in his tone, so I didn't bother asking anything else.

"Okay, Mrs. Capasso," Dr. Travis interrupted our tense conversation, "I'm ready to begin,"

I nodded to her and took a deep breath, trying to relax my muscles as she popped my first knuckle back into place. A scream ripped through my lips and I barely covered it with the back of my good hand in time to muffle it as blinding pain burned up my limb.

"I'm sorry," The doctor grimaced, "Two more to go."

I panted and tried to fight the anxiety crawling up my throat at having to feel that two more times.

"Hold on." Nicolas interrupted her and when I opened my eyes he was sliding his hands under my legs and around my back.

"What are you-?" I asked but he just sat down with me in his lap in the chair I'd been in and turned it so I was still facing the doctor head-on.

"Continue," He nodded to her as I panted in... fear?

Uncertainty?

No, it was excitement from feeling his body pressed to mine again, but I'd never admit to it.

I didn't have time to wonder about it for long though because the doctor pulled my hand back into her space and I tensed up, anticipating the pain before she even started probing the swollen joint.

"Relax, Little One," Nicolas said, sliding his warm palm against my cheek and forcing me to turn to look at him. "If you tense, it may not go back into place correctly, and then she'll have to do it again."

"How am I supposed to relax?" I argued in a whisper, not clarifying that it was from the proximity to the man underneath me and not the pain that caused my discomfort.

"Like this." He lowered his face to mine, using the hand along my cheek to hold me still as his lips kissed me. I gasped and he absorbed it, using the startled reflex of mine as his chance to swipe his tongue between my parted lips. "Relax," He commanded me again and I sagged into his chest as he deepened the kiss.

"Fuck!" I hissed against his lips when the doctor placed the second knuckle seamlessly thanks to my distracted state, but tensed yet again when she moved to the third and last dislocated knuckle.

"Almost there." She affirmed and my body trembled in Nicolas' lap.

"Relax." He repeated, kissing me still and laying his other hand down on my thigh, pressing his fingers in the open slit of the robe until they found their way between my thighs. He was only a couple of inches from the fabric of my panties, and I cringed knowing the doctor was seeing his permissionless exploration of my body.

Then I remembered that I was his wife now, and to those looking in, this perhaps looked normal. Even if our union was anything but.

His hand on my cheek slid around my neck and anchored around my nape, pulling me even tighter against his chest as something vibrated under the soft fabric of his button-down shirt.

"Good girl," he whispered against my lips and pushed his tongue into my mouth again, nibbling on my lips with each leisurely pass. "Relax."

Even as he said the words though, I could feel how tense his body was underneath mine and I shifted against him. That's when I felt it.

His erection.

Pressed tight against my ass as his hand wandered higher between my thighs. A small whimper left my lips and his turned up into a snarl I recognized from last night when he looked at me before dropping them to my vagina.

Snap.

The third and final knuckle slid into place as I flinched and hissed, biting down on his bottom lip so fast I didn't have time to tell myself not to do it until I felt him flinch and tasted the metallic blood on my tongue.

"That should do it. You'll be sore and tender for a few days, but take some ibuprofen and put ice packs on it a couple of times a day and you should be right as rain. I'll check back in on you in a day or two," Dr. Travis said, and I tried to pull back away from our intimate embrace but my husband's hold on my neck tightened as he in turn pulled back just enough to create sufficient space between our lips to address the doctor.

"Thank you, you can see yourself out."

"Yes, Mr. Capasso." She answered demurely as I opened my eyes and found his staring directly into mine. I listened to her footsteps on the thick carpet and then the click of the door closing behind her as he continued to hold me immobile.

"You bit me," he said firmly, running his tongue over the small nick in his bottom lip. "Twice now you've latched those pearly white teeth into my flesh."

"I'm sorry," I answered impulsively, having apologies ingrained in my brain from years of fear of recourse.

"I didn't say it was a bad thing," he relaxed his hold on my neck, finally letting me put an appropriate distance between our faces even as I continued to sit on his lap. "How does your hand feel?" His thumb on the hand nestled between my thighs gently stroked back and forth over the inner part of my leg, weaving a dizzying spell of arousing sensations over my confused brain.

"Hurts," I answered truthfully and then looked down at my hand which was turning more purple.

"I suspect today and tomorrow will be the worst of it, and then it will start to feel better."

"You sound like you speak from experience."

He lifted one side of his upper lip in a sort of smirk and leaned back into the chair, "I've dislocated my knuckles more times than I'd care to remember."

"From punching things?" I asked curiously, trying to figure out the man I was now wed to.

"From punching people," He answered plainly and I shivered at the strength behind the statement.

"Thank you for your-" I paused and swallowed audibly as his hand between my thighs twitched moving higher still, "help."

"Hmm." He mused with an amused glint in his eye like he was enjoying the way my body responded to him.

Though he couldn't pretend he was unaffected by our bodies touching, because I could feel the hard ridge of him under my ass still.

"Why did you lie to me last night?" I asked, finally speaking to the deceit between us.

"I never lied."

"You weren't the priest either," I rebutted instantly, already prepared for his response somehow.

"Your family's tradition is..." He paused, tightening his lips.

"Archaic?" I offered, "Barbaric?"

"Repulsive," He finally answered, and I felt like it was a personal depiction of his opinion of me as well.

"You're not telling me anything I don't already know." I scoffed, "I wasn't willingly participating."

His green eyes bounced back and forth between mine like he was trying to detect a lie in my response, except there wasn't one to find.

"We both agree it's repulsive, but that doesn't answer why you intervened," I argued, making my spine stiffen with strength and his eyes darkened at my audacity to question him. "You couldn't even be bothered to show up to dinner," I added, "Something you said by the way, not me."

"I was there, you just didn't see me." He countered and I scowled at his riddle.

"Fine," I swung my legs off his knees and went to stand. If he wasn't going to offer any more information to me, I wasn't going to just lounge in his lap all day while he continued to play with me like a pet.

"Stop!" He barked and tightened his hand around my upper thigh, "I haven't dismissed you."

"Haven't you though?" I countered, clutching at the front of my gown as the top gaped around my twisted torso revealing the swell of my lace-covered breasts. "You won't answer me, that seems pretty dismissive."

"Choosing what answers to give you when I feel like it, isn't dismissive, but it is how our interactions will proceed for the foreseeable future." He argued, letting his eyes drop to my chest, "It's something you're going to have to get used to."

"My father broke my hand while leading me down the aisle to you on our wedding day. Something I had actually come to terms with and had accepted before that moment, because of something you did. A decision you made to interfere with a century-old tradition. While I'm not going to lie and say it doesn't offer some sort of relief knowing I wasn't raped by some stranger last night; it doesn't just let you off the hook for what you did." I stiffened my spine, "I deserve an explanation if nothing else, regardless of what you believe I should just accept or not."

He watched me as I laid into him, letting his eyes rove over my face as I argued my point until I huffed in silence and waited for some sort of reply from him, given that short of physically fighting him for my freedom, I was stuck.

"I wasn't going to let some old fucking creep take something that belonged to me." He answered easily before running his tongue over his bottom lip, drawing my eyes to it and I could feel his anger growing inside of his tight body. "Your body is mine, which meant your virginity was mine to take, whether you like it or not. You are mine to use and to play with as I see fit. On days I feel generous I'll allow you pleasures like I did last night when you were moaning and clawing at me in ecstasy. On days that I don't, I'll take what I want, how I want, when I want it regardless of your feelings on the matter." He stood up and pushed me to my feet. "I need sons." He stared directly into my eyes, "That is your purpose. Anything more than that is to be determined."

"I'm just to be a broodmare for you to breed?" I snapped at him angrily. "Maybe you should have just purchased a thoroughbred horse then and fucked it to get your jollies off, you animal."

He moved so quickly that I didn't have time to cower as his hand tightened around my throat and pulled me flush to his chest. I clawed at his hand, but he didn't budge on the tight grip he had around me. "I can be an animal if you want me to be, wife." He hissed the title angrily before reaching for the tie on my robe and pulling it free.

Cool air stimulated my overheated body as he pushed the silk off my shoulders to bare my wedding lingerie to his hungry eyes. "I hate you." I sneered, feeling the anger inside of me burn to a boiling point. I'd been held captive my whole life, and I had hoped this would be different. That somehow this man would be better than my father had been.

Clearly, I was wrong.

"Wrong," He tsked, shaking his head, "You don't even know me yet, Little One." He pushed me backward by my throat until my legs bumped into the back of the chair and then he twisted me around and folded me over the tall back, keeping his hand around the back of my neck. My bare feet hung uselessly above the ground as fear raced through my body. "But if you insist, I'll give you a reason to hate me."

His hands gripped the thin lace of my panties, and he ripped them from my body with absolutely no effort at all. "No!" I kicked, trying to right myself over the back of the chair as his hand came down on my ass cheek in a thundering slap, stilling me in pure shock as my fear turned into adrenaline.

He pushed my thighs apart and then dipped his thick fingers between them, rubbing against my entrance and then down to my clit, pinching it almost painfully. "Tell me, Little One," He chided with almost mirth to his evil voice, "Is this wetness, my come from last night dripping out of your tight cunt still or from your arousal right now?" He held me tighter as I squirmed harder while he pushed his fingers into my vagina, before growling and thrusting them in and out a few times. He pulled them free and then I heard the telltale sound of him licking them clean above me and I groaned at how it made me feel to know he was tasting me again, even indirectly. He moaned theatrically, "Mmh, that's all you baby. Sweet cream from inside of you coats your pussy, readying your body for my cock, doesn't it."

I hissed as his hand connected with my already burning ass cheek again and screamed in frustration into the cushion of the chair, angry at my useless body.

He chuckled and pushed his fingers in deep again, making obnoxious sounds with my wetness to further shame me as more gushed out of my traitorous body. Memories from last night assaulted me, reminding me how good it felt when he used his mouth to make me come before running the length of his cock through my lips over and over again to prepare me for his girth. The way he grunted and praised me while he fucked me and stole my virginity even as I tightened my legs around him and pulled myself closer with each thrust.

"That's my good girl," he praised me again, twisting his fingers inside of me. "I should be punishing you."

"This is punishment!" I screamed.

"This is pleasure," he countered instantly and then I stilled to stone when I heard him pull his zipper down.

"Don't!"

"Don't what, Wife?" He asked, before slapping the head of his cock against my upturned ass. "Don't fuck my property?" He pressed the head of his cock against my wet entrance and pushed in. He growled as he pushed deeper, and I bit the cushion under my face to remain silent as the burn of his size and the tenderness from last night mixed with a weird pleasure from being filled with him. "Fuck, your cunt is so tight," He let go of my neck and wrapped both hands around my waist. "Your body was made to take me, Arianna, it was built to be used like this."

"Fuck you." I hissed and he chuckled before slamming the rest of the way into me, forcing the air from my lungs. "Fuck!" I bit my lip and moaned, hating my traitorous body.

"If you insist." He spanked my ass again and then started doing exactly that. He fucked me mercilessly, slapping his body against my thighs as he repeatedly forced his giant cock into me.

I was fucking warped in the head because, within a dozen punishing thrusts, I was exploding around him. I fought the sensations of my orgasm, biting the cushion and forcing myself to remain silent as I came but I didn't fool him, not for a second.

"Good girl," he growled, "That's a good fucking girl, Little One. Milk me dry." His dirty words were repulsive, yet arousing at the same time and I hated the effect he had on me. His thrusts sped up even more and then became so much deeper before he roared out loud, exploding inside of me. Last night he had been quiet when he came, but today, he didn't care who heard, which only brought me more shame.

His cock jerked inside of me, and he grunted again before pulling out, leaving an empty feeling inside of me before backing away.

I slid from the chair onto the floor and brought my knees to my chest as I hung my head in shame, staring at his pristine black shoes and pants.

What the fuck was it about this man that turned me so rabid for his pleasure?

He panted above me, and I heard him put himself away and zip his pants back up, but I didn't look up at him. I couldn't because he'd see that I wasn't as angry with him as I was with myself for letting him get me off. I was so stupid and pathetic.

"Take a bath, to ease your body," he said finally, "I'll have Molly bring you ice for your hand." Then, he turned his back and walked out of the room without a backward glance like we hadn't just had a giant game of tug of war, where I clearly lost.

I tried to tell myself that I hadn't wanted it, and that's why I had told him to stop. But I knew deep down, and so did he, that I only said stop to make myself feel better. I knew I shouldn't have wanted it. But I did.

I wanted Nicolas Capasso more than I had ever wanted another man before in my life. He was my husband. And my villain.

And I was totally and utterly fucked over it.

CHAPTER 6 – NICO

Two days.

It had been two days since I laid eyes directly on my new bride. I had been watching her constantly on the security cameras I had throughout my estate, but I hadn't faced her since I brutalized her over the back of the chair in our bedroom.

I told myself that was because I didn't want to deal with her anger over it. However, I was pretty sure I didn't want to deal with my indignity over it. I couldn't quite put my finger on what exactly about our few encounters had led me to feel like an animal for taking her the way I did and then ignoring her for two days straight, but something did.

I was a monster, that wasn't a secret. I'd been called 'The Wolf' my whole life. I took what I wanted and didn't apologize for it, in all things in life. And women were included in that. Most of the time I never had a problem getting a willing woman in my bed. But bending Arianna to my will on our wedding day left me feeling... no better than her father.

She had been brutalized at his hand, in the name of parenting. And it enraged me to imagine all of the ways she suffered over the years because of Emilio and Mina Rosetti, especially after Carmine had described some of the things to me in our impromptu chat.

Then I'd gone and used her attraction to me and my power over her as her husband, to take her when she challenged me on why I intervened on the eve of our wedding.

"*Capa*," My second, Matteo, interrupted my thoughts as he walked into my office calling me the Italian nickname for boss that sounded like my last name.

"What?" I snapped angrily thanks to the sour churning in my gut, and it wasn't even nine am.

"Molly has an update for you," He replied with raised eyebrows, bristling at my tone and no doubt wanting to challenge me on it. Only, he kept his mouth shut, using his facial expressions to get his point across.

Message received, old friend. Though not headed.

"See her in," I nodded to the door and then took a deep breath as my wife's personal maid walked in to give me her daily update on the mysterious woman living in my home.

"Mr. Capasso," Molly curtseyed at the door, then walked to the center of the rug and folded her hands in front of her. She'd been employed here at the estate for years now and she was always reliable and respectful, which was why even at a young age, she was promoted to head maid and my wife's right hand.

"Tell me, how is Arianna?"

"She's not improving, Sir," she voiced her concern sternly and I respected her for it, even if the news was unsettling.

"Explain."

"She hasn't eaten since yesterday morning. Her hand is still tender and ailing her, and she just sits in the chair by the window and stares out at the grounds, Sir. I think she's depressed or in shock or something worse."

I felt that familiar tightness in my chest that had taken root since meeting Arianna and bristled at the implications of it. "The doctor will return this evening to check on her hand again," I said in avoidance of the emotional update and Molly stiffened at my brush off. "I'll go see her in a moment."

"Very well, Mr. Capasso." She nodded again and then walked out of my office, obviously finding my response lacking. She cared for my wife, and not just because she was employed to physically see to her needs. My wife had wormed her way into the young maid's heart, in the few days that she was here.

"*Capa*," Matteo walked back in as Molly left. "The shipment has arrived at the warehouse; it needs to be verified."

I slid my hand into my pants pocket and walked towards him, "Then go see it's verified." I slapped his shoulder as I passed him. "I'm needed here today. Report back as soon as you arrive and take inventory."

He cocked his head a bit but decided agreeing was better than arguing and nodded. "Yes, Sir."

He was more than capable of taking the shipment in, I had just never allowed him to do it without me being present. Not because I didn't trust him or anything, but because I was simply a control freak that needed to have my hands in every pot all at once.

But right now, I needed to get to the bottom of my wife's unhappiness. And maybe laying eyes on her firsthand would ease some of the anxiety inside of me. It felt like I was a teenager who had their first taste of a high and couldn't think of anything else but when they were going to get that rush again, even if they knew it was bad for them.

And Arianna was very, very bad for me.

I didn't knock; it was my bedroom after all.

My wife paid me no attention as I walked into the space she had occupied since saying her vows. I locked the door behind me and watched her small frame curl around itself at the window where Molly had said she'd be. She wore a pink silk robe that only came to mid-thigh and her pink painted toenails matched almost perfectly where they poked out in front of her.

I didn't allow Molly to bring Arianna's luggage in from the guest room that she used the first night she was in residence at Armarow Estate. Because I was the worst kind of bastard that only intended to use Arianna Rosetti to serve my own selfish needs. I handpicked a handful of lingerie from her room and a few silk robes for her to wear. Nothing else.

Again, because I was a bastard. I wanted her uncomfortable and to know that I was in control of everything, including her comfort. I wanted her to know I was the boss.

First, I needed to see to my own needs that were building inside of me. Unfortunately, they were directly connected to her and her well-being.

So I came bearing gifts with my visit. I had a platter of food in my hands and set it down on the table next to the window cushion before sitting next to her.

She finally turned her eyes in my direction and then looked at the platter before looking back out of the window without a word.

"Why haven't you eaten?" I asked her, trying for calmness I didn't feel.

"I'm not hungry," She replied.

"It's been nearly thirty-six hours since you've eaten last Arianna."

"I didn't realize you were a nursemaid." She rebutted and I smirked at the sass in her tone.

"I didn't realize you were pathetic enough to starve yourself just to get my attention." She turned on me with fire in her eyes and her mouth open ready to flail me up one side and down the other with her sharp tongue, but she stopped when she saw the smirk on my face. "Well now that I actually have your attention." I raised one eyebrow at her, and she clenched her teeth, "Tell me the real reason you aren't eating."

"I told you-" She argued and I held my hand up silencing her.

"No lies, Little One. Ever." I stared pointedly at her, "Lies are one thing I will not tolerate from you."

"Is that so?" She tilted her chin up and looked down her nose at me, "Because the list of things I can't stand about you is at least as long as my arm."

"A truth, I'm sure." I mused and picked up an elegantly sliced strawberry off the platter before holding it out between us. "How about this, for every piece of food you eat, I'll give you something."

Her nostrils flared as she looked at the ripe berry clutched in my fingers, and she swallowed.

She was hungry.

So she was mine.

"What will you give me?" She asked, tearing her warm brown eyes away from the strawberry.

"What do you want most right now?"

"To go-"

"Don't you dare say home." I cut her off with a harsh tone, "Because we both know you don't want that."

"Outside," she whispered.

"You want to go outside?" I repeated, admitting to myself that had not been what I expected her to say.

She looked back out the window, "I've never seen fall foliage so vibrant before."

I glanced past her at the scenery outside, something I'd experienced every year of my life, and tried to see it through her eyes. I also knew she had seen it before, but she was pretending that she hadn't.

"Then clothing," I responded, "Each bite will give you a piece of clothing better suited to go outside in." I let my eyes roam over her bare skin exposed to my eyes around the small robe. "Deal?"

She tilted her head back towards me, and chewed on her bottom lip in a way that made me want to taste it myself, and then shifted to face me more directly. "Clothing, and answers. One and then the other."

I dropped my hand to my lap with the berry and glared at her, "Now you're pushing it."

Her full lips pulled up into a tentative smirk, almost like she wasn't used to smiling, "Take it or leave it." She nodded towards the platter, "I'm used to going far longer than one day without eating. I can outwait you."

I growled in my chest, "You won't use food as bartering chips with me, Arianna." I warned, "After today, you'll eat a healthy amount of food, any food you desire. I won't have you putting your health in jeopardy to play a game."

"Aren't our lives just one big game of chess?" She wondered out loud with a cocked eyebrow. I didn't answer her, because she was right, and I didn't want to give her that satisfaction. She sighed and reached for the strawberry in my hand, "Fine. Give me."

"Nu-uh." I pulled my hand back before she could grasp it. "Allow me." Her eyelashes flared wide as I put my hand over hers that she tried grabbing the strawberry with, pinning it on my leg as I lifted my other and placed the berry right in front of her lips. "Open."

"I can feed myself." She argued, her eyes jumping back and forth between the berry and my own.

"Open," I repeated and she sighed but obliged, parting her full pink lips slightly as she stared at me. "Good girl." I put the juicy strawberry against her bottom lip, and she opened further, allowing me room to place the entire thing into her mouth before closing her lips around the tips of my fingers and taking the fruit.

I doubt she meant it seductively, given that she had no experience with men before we met days ago, but the action sent electric bolts of desire straight through my body, though my face remained impassive.

I watched her chew and run her tongue over her lips when she was done. "Another," I picked up a block of cheese and held it out for her, but this time I didn't reach as far forward, making her lean to me to get the offered food.

She rewarded me by using her teeth to grasp the food instead of her plush lips and nipped my thumb in the process before pulling back and smirking again, proud of herself.

I smirked too, simply because I couldn't help it.

"The strawberry was for a pair of pants, and the cheese for an answer."

"Hmm." I hummed, leaning back against the wall behind me and nodding for her to continue.

"Why did you take my mother's tonic and station your men to intervene on our wedding day?"

I clenched my jaw at the memory of that bitterly drugged beverage her parents used to control her with and answered. "Because it wasn't right of them to do that to you." I said plainly, "And I wasn't going to allow it to happen inside of my home."

"And what you did to me after our wedding *was* right?" She snapped and I chuckled at her dismissively.

"It's not your turn." I rejected her and picked up a rolled piece of ham off the platter. "It's mine, now open those pretty lips and eat."

Her nostrils flared at my words, but she obeyed, leaning forward once again and taking the offered food. When she was done chewing, she simply said, "Socks."

"Fair." I took a piece of pineapple off the platter and lifted it, "Be careful, it's juicy." I taunted her and she rolled her eyes, leaning forward and defiantly taking a bite.

I watched the sweet yellow juice flow over her lips and down her chin before running down her neck. She tried to wipe it away, but I had anticipated her move and grabbed her wrists, pinning them in her lap with one hand. "Allow me," I growled and leaned forward, dropping my mouth to her exposed collarbone and pulling her robe open to reveal where the juice had run down the crevice between her lace-covered breasts.

"Nicolas," she whispered but didn't fight me as I dipped my tongue between her full breasts, capturing the sticky sweetness before trailing it up her chest and neck. She tipped her head back, exposing more of her neck to me and I smiled against her skin at how affected she was by my tongue before collecting the last of the juice on her chin. When I reached her lips, I didn't even pretend to be there for just the mess, I wanted her lips for selfish reasons, and I took them.

I kissed her, letting the sweet taste of the fruit fill my tastebuds as I pushed my tongue into her mouth. She groaned and pulled her face back, closing her lips to me. "No," she shook her head as I slid my fingers into her dark hair and pulled her back.

"Are you so quick to end our game?" I said against her lips, licking them and catching her sweet moan as it fell from her lips. "So quick to deny yourself pleasure."

"I don't want pleasure if it's part of your game." She rushed out. "I don't want to be played with."

"Then just enjoy, because I'm in a giving mood today." I kissed her again and she opened for me instantly. "Good girl."

A fire burned between us, and I knew she was as affected by it as I was, even if I was more in control of expressing it than she was. "I need clothes," she whined, "And answers."

"Do you want either of those things more than you want orgasms?" I challenged and slid my lips around the side of her neck to bite her ear and suck on the lobe as she moaned.

"I-" She panted and fought the hold I had on her hands, and I let her go, fully intending to feel them push me away as her good sense overtook my desirable ones. But instead of pushing me away, she wrapped both hands around the back of my neck and dug her nails in, pulling a growl from my lips as she tilted her head and kissed me deeper.

Naughty girl.

"Reward can come in many ways," I said after a while and lifted her to stand on her feet in front of me. "Do you want one?"

She chewed her lip and played with the sash on her robe uncertainly. But then she took a deep breath and nodded, "Yes."

"Take your robe off," I commanded.

Her eyelids drooped slightly, and she tilted her head back defiantly, "And what will you give me if I do?"

"A sweater. To go with your pants and socks."

She mulled that over for a moment and then slid the sash free before letting the silk robe glide off her shoulders and pool in a pile at her feet. I leaned back on the window seat and gazed at her sinfully sexy body, curved and delicate in such a feminine way it called to the primal side of me. Her lace bra was baby blue and see-through, barely cupping her generous breasts and there was a navy-blue bow in the center that I ached to tear off with my teeth. Her panties were matching lace, with a navy blue trim edge that I knew ran up between her ass cheeks in a thong cut because I had picked it out for her to wear.

"Run your hands down the front of your body, starting at your neck," I commanded next, "Slowly caress your breasts as you go."

"What will I get if I do?" she countered and I smirked at her ability to do business when my brain was short-circuiting from the sexual need burning inside of me while she acted unaffected. But I knew better.

"Shoes." I raised an eyebrow at her and scratched my bearded jaw. "Kind of hard to go outside without shoes, am I right?"

"Right." She took a deep breath and I watched in rapture as she lifted her hands to her dark chocolate hair, tossing it over her shoulders and grazing her fingertips over her shoulders to her neck. Her lush lips were parted and her warm chocolate eyes closed as she tipped her head back and traced the graceful lines of her neck and collarbones.

"Sway your hips," I instructed and she didn't miss a beat, gently swinging them with a silent song of seduction as her nails traced over the visible hard peaks under her lace bra.

She sighed as she circled her nipples and my cock twitched in my pants. Her fingers drifted lower over her soft stomach and to her hips, before gliding to the center of her waistband where a matching blue bow lay.

"Take them off," I growled, clearing my throat as my desire turned my voice into sludge. "Bra and panties."

"I want answers," She hummed, continuing the sway to her hips as her painted white nails slid under the band of her panties. "Two."

I would have given her my left leg to see her fingers slide inside the lace, but I didn't tell her that. "Ask them."

"Will you answer them?" She challenged, opening her eyes and staring directly at me.

"Ask them, and we'll find out. But do it quickly or you'll lose your chance." I palmed my erection and her eyes glowed as she watched me squeeze the length.

"Why do you hate me?" She asked, bringing her hands back up her stomach to her chest and circling her nipples again. "And don't for one-second try to say you don't. I've spent my whole life being hated by the people around me, so I know it when I see it."

She was trying for indifference, but I could hear the anger behind her words, even as she tried to distract me from it.

So I answered her honestly. "I hate what you represent." Her nostrils flared but she kept her mouth shut so I continued. "You represent the choice I didn't get to make for myself. Your father and mine made the plans for me without a care in the world for what I wanted. And I hate that you're the piece in the game they used against me."

Her body stilled as she watched me, mulling it over. "I didn't get a say either." She swallowed and put her hands by her hips. "You represent the same thing for me."

"Wrong." I leaned forward and rested my elbows on my knees. "I represent an escape for you. You may not have chosen me personally but marrying me got you away from your father and his cruel treatment. I'm your bloody prince charming if you think about it long enough."

She scoffed but forged on, "Why didn't you dissolve the agreement once your father died? I may not be privy to a lot of knowledge about how these things work, but I've heard enough whispers about you over the last few years to know you're powerful enough to break a contract like this with my father and there would be nothing he could do about it." She reached up and undid the clasp of her bra and slowly slid it over her arms and tossed it into my lap. "So, why marry me?"

My wife knew how to conduct business. She was cutting and wise and I'd be sure to keep that in mind. "Milan," I replied, watching her face as her eyes squinted in confusion before I let mine trail down to her perfectly pink nipples, standing hard on the tips of her tanned breasts. God, they were beautiful fucking breasts. "Eight months ago I saw you in Milan at the Amoroso Gala." I looked away from them to her face again, she swallowed as realization dawned on her. "I knew then that I had to have you, simply because I didn't want anyone else to." I leaned back in my seat and nodded to her lace panties which were the last barrier between me and what I wanted. "Even if I hated the idea of you." I waited for her to mention the time before that, here at Armarow when we met. But she didn't, and it just further instilled what I already knew.

She didn't remember the first time that we met when she was so young and naïve.

She opened her mouth to say something and then snapped it closed, clenching her jaw to keep her thoughts inside. Then without another word she slid her delicate fingers into the band of her panties and pushed them down her thighs, seductively twisting her hips with each shimmy until they pooled on the floor around her ankles. She lifted one dainty foot and stepped out of them and picked them up, ready to toss them aside.

"No," I commanded, halting her move. "Bring them to me."

She lifted her chin to look down her nose at me defiantly but eventually walked the few steps forward and held the blue lace out pinched between two fingers. I took them from her as she stood naked in front of me and ran my fingers over the fabric until I found the dampness I knew would be there.

I smirked up at her and her face bloomed with a blush that made a small part of the monster inside of me settle and relax. "Such a sweet reward."

Her chest rose and fell quickly as she watched me. "Game over." She tossed her hands out at her sides. "I'm all out of bargaining chips."

I tsked at her and slid her panties into my pocket, keeping them for later. "That's a shame, because I had so many more rewards to give you."

She chewed her lip in contemplation. "How exactly do you expect me to earn them?"

I grinned at her, and she swallowed audibly. I made my way to the bed and sat down. The bed I hadn't slept in the last few nights because I'd been avoiding her and desperately missed. "Crawl to me."

"What will I get?" She asked over her shoulder, crossing her arms over her chest.

"Depends on how good you are once you get to me."

"What does that mean?"

"Do it and find out." I shrugged, "Decisions need to be made though because I'm running out of free time to spend entertaining you Little One. I have responsibilities to see to."

She sighed and glared at me, but I knew I had her. Even if the reward was only the pleasure I was undoubtedly going to give to her when she came to me, she was going to do it.

She wanted me just like I wanted her. If she used the guise of this bartering game to hide her longings behind, I didn't care.

We both knew the truth.

I watched as she slowly lowered herself to her knees and tenderly crawled across the carpet to me, swaying her hips with each move. "Eyes on me," I commanded when she tried staring at the floor. "I want to see you when you obey me."

She swallowed and pursed her lips but continued on her way to me. Like such a good girl. When she got to my feet she sat up on her heels and looked at me for her next instruction.

"Take my socks and shoes off."

Her eyelashes flared in anger, but she kept her mouth shut as she untied my shoes and pulled them off, stuffing my socks into them when she was done.

This lesson wasn't about degradation, it was about trust. Even if she didn't know she was even learning anything at the moment. I wanted to know how far she was willing to go. "Now what?" She asked, barely veiling the sass in her tone.

"My shirt." I spread my arms wide and waited as she climbed to her feet and hesitantly touched the first button of my shirt, sliding it through the opening. I brought my hands forward and laid them on her flared hips, hooking them on the God-made handles there, and smirked as her breath caught in her throat at the contact. "What's the matter, Little One?" I prodded her.

"I'm not used to touches being... *gentle*."

Any arousal I'd been feeling dried up inside of me as I watched her face as she stared down at the task of undoing my buttons. Her eyes misted over, but the tears didn't fall as she blinked them back and clenched her jaw.

"You thought I was going to hurt you?"

"You weren't exactly gentle last time." She countered and aggressively pulled my shirt from the waistband of my pants before pushing it open. She pulled one hand from her waist and undid my cufflink and pulled my shirt free of that arm and then put it back, before taking the other one off and repeating the process. When she was all done, she finally raised her eyes to mine and held my stare. "What now?"

I hated that she was gentle with me when she obviously wanted to be anything but. I stood up from the edge of the bed, keeping my hold on her hips, and pulled her flush to the front of me. However, before I could answer her, a knock came at the door.

"*Capa*." Saul's voice rang from the outside. "We need to leave soon if we're to get to your meeting on time."

Arianna's eyes held mine as she listened to my man, and I couldn't tell if it was relief or disappointment in her eyes at being interrupted. But I intended to find out.

"Cancel it." I barked back, "And get the fuck out of my wing."

"Yes, Sir." He called, and Arianna sucked a quick breath in.

"I'm not the kind of man to not finish what I started," I informed her as I turned her until her ass was resting against the edge of the bed and I lifted her up to sit on it. "And I'm far more invested in this than anything else I had planned for the day."

"Nicolas." She whispered as I pushed her further up the bed and placed my hand on my belt.

"Nico." I corrected her. "You will call me Nico when we're like this."

"What exactly is this?" She asked, crossing her legs as her eyes watched me open my belt and pull at the closure of my pants.

"Anytime you aren't angry at me I suppose." I joked, "Though I don't think that will be very often."

"You think I'm not angry with you right now?" She challenged, quirking an eyebrow at me.

"I think your need to orgasm outweighs any anger you may have felt toward me earlier." I countered and she licked her lips.

"You're going to give me an orgasm?"

There was almost a challenge to her question, like she doubted my abilities and I grinned at her as I pushed my pants and boxer briefs to the floor. Her eyes instantly dropped to my hard cock, and I fisted it as I stepped out of my pants, hungrily seeking pleasure for me and torture for her.

"Even when I was a bully with you the other day, you still came on my cock like the perfect little wife." I chided and she bristled at the tone, "But I'm not feeling very violent right now."

She swallowed and licked her lips as I slid my hands up her knees and pulled them apart, exposing her pretty pink pussy to me and she leaned backward as I leaned in. "And what are you feeling right now?"

"Like I'm in the mood to drag orgasm after orgasm from your body long before I sink inside of you." I slid one hand under her ass and picked her up and dropped her further up the bed, so her head lay perfectly on the pillow in the center. She gasped and panted as I looked down at her and grabbed an extra pillow and shoved it under her hips. "And I'd be lying if I said I wasn't aching to taste your sweet pussy again and make you cream on my tongue like you did the first night I had you."

"Nico." She moaned when I pushed her thighs wide for emphasis and slid to my stomach between them. "Please."

"Please what, Wife?" I asked, lowering my lips to hover directly over her swollen clit. Her scent was intoxicating and I wanted to feel her pretty thighs tremble around my head while I ate her out. But I wanted to hear it from her lips first.

"Do it." She whispered, rolling her hips, "Please do it."

"As you wish, Little One," I smirked and then spit on her pussy before diving in for my fill. She squeaked and moaned as I did everything I could to force an orgasm from her body as quickly as possible. Because I'd been telling the truth earlier, I wanted to make her come multiple times before I fucked her, but with the noises, she was making and the way she clawed at my head and rocked her hips under my face, I was on the fast track to losing my resolve to hold off on fucking her. "That's it, baby." I purred against her clit and pushed a finger inside her tight pussy. It was insane how tight she was, even with taking me twice now.

"Yes." She moaned, throwing her head back and arching her back, "Right there, don't stop."

I smiled against her clit as she begged for what she wanted and rewarded her with the same combination of sensations. I wasn't a fucking tool bag who changed things up when a woman told him exactly what she wanted. Women weren't rocket science after all, they were very direct if men took the time to care.

Before Arianna, I hadn't exactly cared for a woman's pleasure, as long as it meant I got mine. Except, right now I wanted to feel her convulse under me and beg for me to fuck her.

"I'm-" She gasped and her mouth hung open as she started trembling underneath me.

"Good girl." I praised her and felt her body tighten even more at it as her orgasm took over.

"Yes!" She screamed, covering her mouth with the back of her good hand and biting her knuckle as she came hard, "Oh, my God!"

I chuckled against her and slowly let the pressure of my attention up until my touches and licks were gentle and teasing as she sank back into the bed. "I already told you, I'm your god."

"Hmm." She panted, "Prove it."

I bit the inside of her thigh and rolled her over onto her face and crawled up her body, pressing my thigh between hers and pushing it wide. She lay on her stomach with her knee brought up high against her side and I laid half on top of her. I wrapped my arm under her neck and grabbed her shoulder, hitching her head and chest up as I pushed two fingers into her pussy from behind.

She gasped and clutched at my arm as I fiercely rocked my hand front and back with my fingers buried inside of her. "You shouldn't have done that baby." I hissed into her ear as she moaned and mewed underneath me, unable to move as I tormented her body. "I'm going to make you do something you never even knew was possible." I bit her shoulder and she hissed, "And you're going to thank me for it when I'm done."

"What?" She gasped. "I don't understand."

"I know you don't." I rocked my hips forward, rubbing my cock against her ass as I tightened my hold on her throat. "And that drives me absolutely feral, Arianna."

"Fuck." She whined as I picked up my speed, the wet noises my fingers were making inside of her made me want more. "It's too much."

"Too bad." I scolded. "You wanted me to prove to you who owns you." I slid my hand from her shoulder to her breast and palmed the weight of it before pinching her nipple and pulling on it. "So I'm going to show you."

"Oh fuck." She moaned, "I'm going to." She shook her head as a cold sweat covered her body. "I can't!" She screamed, "Stop."

"Come for me," I demanded.

"I'm going to pee!" She argued, clawing at my arm as she kicked her legs madly.

"You're going to squirt. There's a difference." I bit her shoulder again and moaned when she tightened around my fingers. "I'm going to fuck you so hard after you soak this bed with your orgasm." I flexed my hips again, desperate to relieve the ache inside of my balls. "Come for me," I demanded.

"Please!" She screamed and then she gave in to the pressure building inside of her and bit my forearm as she coated my fingers and my hand with her orgasm.

I roared as her teeth cut through the skin on my arm and her pussy clamped down so hard on my fingers. Before she was even done convulsing, I lined up and buried myself inside her soaked hole, drawing another scream from her lips. I fucked her hard, slamming into her body as she pushed back into me with each thrust greedily. "Take it, Arianna," I growled in her ear, as she clawed at me. "You don't want my gentleness, do you?"

"No." She panted, arching her back even more and pushing back into me. "I want this. I want you like this."

"Little One," I hissed and spread her thighs even wider to accommodate my legs and then pulled her hips up in the air so I could get the depth I desired. "You've got me." I spanked her ass and watched it ripple with each thrust.

"Oh, my God." She groaned, "I'm so close again. How is it this good?"

I chuckled and picked her up to press her back against my chest as I held her up with a hand around her throat and my other one buried between her thighs, rubbing her clit. "Come on my cock again Arianna." I commanded, "Milk my come straight from me."

"God." She moaned and I felt her body stiffen against mine seconds before her pussy clamped down on me again and I couldn't hold back anymore.

I rumbled with my head thrown back as I filled her up, grunting and spasming like a man being electrocuted as pleasure like no other wracked through my body thanks to hers. I sagged, letting her go as she fell forward onto the bed in a heap, panting and gasping and I followed her and rolled to my side to avoid crushing her.

"Holy fuck." I grunted, rubbing my hands over my abs as I sucked air.

She lifted her head off the bed slightly with a smirk on her face and rolled her eyes. "It was alright."

I swatted her ass, still exposed and available to me and she yipped and then giggled.

"Naughty Little One."

"Hmm." She hummed with closed eyes. "I kind of like being naughty."

Fuck. That was not good.

I cringed inwardly, imagining all the trouble she was going to give me with her newfound naughty streak and confidence.

Then I smiled because I knew I'd enjoy the fuck out of correcting her behavior.

CHAPTER 7 – ARIANNA

"**M**a'am," Molly called from the door of the bedroom with a wide smile. "I have a delivery for you."

She stepped aside as other maids dressed in simple black dresses carried armfuls of clothing through the large bedroom and into the master closet.

"All of them?" I asked surprised, clutching the robe closed around my body. I'd been laying on the couch by the fireplace watching the flames dance as I replayed my morning with Nicolas. And now I was even more confused.

We'd bargained for an outfit, painstakingly bartering piece by piece of it so I could go outside and here he was giving me everything. After once again, turning me into a sex crazed lunatic that would willingly give him anything for the pleasure he delivered. He told me the other day that he'd only give me pleasure when he felt like it, and the other times he'd use my body to please his own. But I was pretty sure he lied.

He was this brute scary man that controlled thousands of people with fear and power, yet he hadn't shown that side to me. Not really, anyway.

The time over the back of the chair was just a taste of his power, I was sure.

Except it hadn't scared me like when my father used to wield his power around; instead, it had aroused me. And in response to that arousal, I came for him like a needy little slut.

What a weird freaking life mine was turning out to be.

"Yes, Ma'am." Molly nodded, drawing my attention back to her. "And he's arranged for a personal shopper to deliver even more tomorrow. You'll get to pick whatever you want out of the collection she brings."

"Wow." I mused as the maids all curtseyed on their way back out of the room after arranging the clothes in the massive master closet. Next to all of his clothes.

Molly walked over to the platter that Nicholas had brought with him earlier and smiled when she found it mostly empty before picking it up and holding it on her hip. "How is your hand feeling Ma'am?"

"Molly," I sighed smiling at her, "Please call me Ari. Everyone else is so formal and I feel like you're my only friend here, please use my name."

She smirked and bowed her head, "If you insist."

"I do." I nodded, pleased with myself for getting something else to go my way today. "My hand feels-" I looked down at it and flexed it, "Better. Still tender but not painful like before."

"Good. Dr. Travis will be here this evening after dinner, which Mr. Capasso has requested you join him for in the dining room."

"I'm allowed to go downstairs too?" I questioned, trying to wrap my head around it all.

"Mr. Capasso never instructed me that you couldn't go down before." Her eyebrows pinched together in confusion, "You just didn't have any clothes, and well," She paused like she was trying to find the right words, "You didn't seem interested in exploring either."

I grinned at her and shrugged my shoulders, "I suppose you're right, I wasn't in the mood before. But I am now." I walked past her to the closet. "Can I go outside now?"

"Yes," She followed me in and watched as I perused the clothing that my mother had purchased for me before moving here. I'd never seen most of it, but it didn't matter. Even if my mother was a terrible parent, she was a great shopper. "Saul and Dio are in the hallway, ready to escort you wherever you please to go."

"Fantastic." I mused, grabbing a pair of forest green skinny jeans and a cream-colored sweater, and tossing them on the counter in the center of the room before turning back to find more comfortable underwear and shoes, seeing as how my panties were smuggled out in my husband's pocket when he left hours ago. "I can almost taste the fall air from here."

"It's a beautiful time of year here in the mountains. Though it doesn't last nearly as long as I wish it would before the snow comes."

"Does Nicolas spend his winter's here?" I asked innocently, hoping for a glimpse of information into my future and my mysterious husband as I began dressing in front of the woman. She'd already seen me naked, having dressed me on my wedding day so it didn't matter. I dropped my robe and started pulling on a cotton bra when she gasped and I looked at her over my shoulder, "What is it?"

"Ma'am," She slipped back into formality as she stepped closer, "Your shoulder. Did you injure yourself?"

I tried seeing what she was talking about but couldn't, so I turned in front of the floor-length mirror and looked at my back. I instantly understood why she was so worried.

Teeth marks.

Three sets to be exact.

A flush of arousal and embarrassment warmed my skin as I turned away from the bites Nicolas had left on me earlier. "I'm quite well Molly." I smiled to myself as I dropped my face and let my hair curtain it as I continued clasping my bra and pulled on the warm sweater to hide the marks that surprised her so.

"Are you sure?" She looked concerned, wringing her hands together in front of her as I shimmied into the jeans.

"Yes, Molly," I chuckled and took pity on the girl. "Turns out Nicolas has a fascination with biting. That's all."

"Oh." Her face turned a bright shade of red and her mouth popped open and closed, "Oh." She composed herself and shook her head, "I'm so sorry for sticking my nose where it's not needed. I just wanted to-"

"Don't worry about it. I understand why you'd be concerned but I'm just fine." I walked over to the shelf of shoes that the maids had quickly organized and pulled out a pair of black booties and slid them on. "But we must leave this room before he changes his mind or something and traps me here for good." I grabbed her hand and pulled her with me from the room. "Now I'll need your help," I opened the door and looked up and down the hallway, "finding my way out of this elaborate maze."

She chuckled and pulled me alongside her as she walked to the right. "This entire wing is the private rooms for Mr. Capasso and yourself." She described as we walked, "This afternoon he gave strict instructions for no one but myself and employees I see fit to step foot off the top of the stairs into the private wing."

"Hmm." I nodded, remembering the way he threatened his man earlier when he interrupted us right outside of the bedroom door.

"In the wing, there is the master suite and three more bedrooms as well as a sitting room for you to use for whatever pleases you. These stairs lead directly into the main living room off of the kitchen downstairs. Had we gone to the left out of your bedroom, you would have found another set of stairs that lead to the back of the house towards the garage."

I nodded trying to visually remember everything as she talked. At the bottom of the stairs, my two large bodyguards Saul and Dio stood as though they were waiting for their next task from me, but I wasn't sure what I was allowed to do or worse, what I had to ask permission to do.

Luckily, Molly took pity on me and addressed them for me when I didn't.

"Mrs. Capasso would like to go outside and enjoy some fresh air."

Saul nodded and Dio spoke into his wrist like an undercover spy, and I let the formality of it all roll off my shoulders. I was too eager to get outside to laugh at the ridiculousness of it all.

"Thank you," I said to both her and the guards as I stepped down onto the marble floor.

"I'll be around when you return." Molly said, "Make sure you go check out the pond, it's magical this time of year." Patting my arm once, before walking off with a smile to Dio.

"Can one of you show me the pond?" I asked in uncertainty, "Or at least how to get to an exterior door-," I murmured as I looked around the massive living area. There were large windows, showing off the grounds outside, but no doors.

"This way Ma'am." Saul nodded his head to the side and led me through the house and into the kitchen that I recognized from before my wedding. "These doors will take you to the entertaining space outside." He informed me as we walked out onto the pristine patio, I was married on a few days ago.

"Thank you," I murmured as I took it all in.

Flowers had been hung on the railings and I vaguely remembered a white carpet laid down the aisle but everything else about the event was blurred.

I didn't remember hardly any of my own wedding, and even though it was arranged and should have been repulsive, I still regretted not taking it all in when it was happening.

Behold another thing my father managed to rob me of thanks to his cruelty.

I walked down the steps to the lawn and noticed that Saul and Dio followed at a distance close enough to reach me quickly if needed but not close enough to hover, and I tried to ignore them as I walked through the lavish landscape.

Fruit trees lined a walkway, and I knew in the spring they would be beautiful with their blooming flowers and sweet scents. I didn't know if Armarow Estate was where I'd live full time, or if Nicolas would stay here with me if I did, but I knew it'd be hard to find another place to live that topped the regality of this home.

I followed the brick path through more bushes and trees that were blooming with bright reds and oranges as the plants prepared for winter sleep. Tracing my fingertips over the leaves, collecting the dew on them as I went reminded me of a memory from my childhood, but the more I tried to remember it clearly, the more it evaded me.

I focused on it where it sat right on the edge of reality and daydream, lost to the chase, when the path ended and I realized I had found the pond. "Wow," I whispered and took a deep breath as I looked around the expansive grounds.

The pond itself was large and in the center was a great fountain that sprayed an intricate design of dancing water onto the calm body below before spraying it up into the air again.

Benches and seats lined the grassy edge around the perimeter but what caught my attention the most were the wooden rope swings hung at a couple of different points. Tall wooden structures held up the swings with dreamy vines covering the length of the ropes and on the one closest to me, a wide plank seat beckoned me to take a rest on it.

I walked over to it, looking around to see if my henchmen had followed me or not, and found them lingering at the path's end like they were trying to blend into the shrubbery in their black suits and ominous size.

I shook my head and gently sat down on the swing, praying it wasn't old and frayed so I didn't end up with my ass on the ground.

Much to my surprise though, the ropes hardly groaned with age or fatigue as I let my weight settle into the seat. I kicked myself backward, gently swaying as the cool Autumn breeze swirled around me.

I watched the fountain perform its magical dance and swayed timelessly, enjoying the peace that the area loaned me as my reality drifted away with the breeze.

When warm hands slid over the tops of my shoulders though, I shrieked, nearly toppling off the swing, and looked behind me to find Nicolas smirking down at me.

"You scared the daylights out of me." I gasped, righting myself on the swing so I didn't fall off.

"You've been out here too long. You must be cold." He said in place of an apology, and I rolled my eyes as I faced the fountain again. I didn't know how long I had been resting on the swaying paradise, but the cool ache in my body told me probably longer than I should have.

"Well, I didn't win a jacket in the barter earlier so-." I shrugged my shoulders impassively as he chuckled.

"I figured that'd be your excuse." He said, running his fingers under my hair against my neck. The move was intimate and foreign for us, yet not unwanted on my part either. It was odd. "Jesus, Arianna," He groaned, "You're freezing."

"I'm fine," I said, flexing my stiff fingers around the ropes and ignoring the way they ached when the blood started returning to the cold limbs.

"Come here." He walked around the front of the swing and picked me up, ignoring my protests before setting his weight down onto the swing with me in his arms.

"If this thing breaks under your big butt I'm going to be really upset." I chided him as he turned me on his lap until my head was tucked under his chin with his warm arms around my body. He wore the same button-down shirt that I'd stripped off his body earlier and I could smell our sex on his skin, which made my head dance.

"I would hate to do anything to draw your anger Little One." He teased and I poked his chest, drawing a grunt from him. "Where did you get this scar?" He asked, running his thumb over my cheek where a faint white scar ran down the flesh like a tear trail. Most people never noticed it thanks to my father's highly esteemed plastic surgeon who promised to fix it the best he could.

"I don't-," I paused and shook my head. "I don't remember. It's kind of fuzzy."

"What do you remember?" He asked, staring at me like he was waiting for me to crack some massive code that held all of the world's dark secrets.

"A cat." I smiled and rolled my eyes. "That's it."

"A cat?"

"Yep," I shrugged. "I remember an orange cat, and my parents being so pissed at me when they saw the scratch on my cheek."

He stayed silent and then looked back out over the water fountain. "What do you think of the grounds?" He asked after a while, "Do the fall colors live up to your expectations up close?"

"That and so much more," I admitted wistfully, and his arms tightened around me. "I thought you weren't a gentle man?" I leaned back to look up at his face, "This doesn't feel like the man that I married a few days ago."

He sighed and pursed his lips. "Give it time. I can't hide him forever."

"Hmm." I mused, "A little Dr. Jekyll Mr. Hyde?"

"Mr. Hyde would be nicer than I am, I assure you." He looked away from me and then rose, setting me down on my feet in front of him.

"I suppose I should run away then," I stated, staring up at his strong jaw and perfect green eyes.

"You should." He said but didn't make any move to walk away from me.

"Okay." I dropped his gaze and turned to walk around him towards the path that was now empty of my guards, but Nicolas' hand wrapped around my arm, pulling me back to his chest.

"I don't understand you." He said with a scowl, and I could see the real bewilderment in his gaze.

"Are you supposed to just simply understand me without even knowing me?" I questioned.

"Yes." He replied instantly. "I know people. I've spent my entire life studying everyone that I've been near, learning them, calculating their moves before they make them. Always staying ahead," He shook his head, "But with you, I can't figure you out."

"Hmm." I hummed again, smiling softly up at him, "Then my plan is working flawlessly."

"Careful Little One." He called as he followed me when I walked away from the swing towards the warmth of the house.

"Or what?" I joked with a false sense of braveness, "You'll spank me?" I looked over my shoulder and caught the way his eyes darkened, and his jaw ticked, "Because we both now know that I enjoy that." I stopped walking and turned to face him, and he didn't stop until he was pressed flat against my chest again, "Or at least I enjoy it when *you* do it."

"Ari," he growled and slid his hands around my waist. "I don't have the time to discipline you right now."

"Then why did you come out here?" I challenged and ran my fingers over the bitemark I knew he still wore on his peck.

"I'll let you know when I figure it out." He said and then lowered his lips to mine. I didn't fight him or pretend it wasn't exactly what I wanted him to do and instead, I wrapped my arms around his neck and clung to him as he growled and deepened the kiss until we were both panting and clawing at each other for more.

"*Capa*." Someone called from above us on the path and Nicolas groaned and bit my lip to soothe his frustration.

"Your bites do something to me," I admitted in a whisper before trying to pull back away from him.

He tightened his hold on me and sucked on my bottom lip soothing it with his touch, "I'll have to remember that."

I chuckled and pulled away from him, enjoying the feeling of being on top of the situation for once in my life. "You do that, *Capa*."

CHAPTER 8 – NICO

My men stood around my office, drinking my liquor, smoking my cigars, and enjoying my space. It wasn't every day that I allowed such meetings to occur inside my home, but truth be told, I hadn't left the estate in days.

Since my wedding to be exact.

Something was holding me here, and the more I tried to act like it wasn't the enticing presence of my new wife, the harder it was to come up with excuses to stay. In reality, I could conduct most of my business from my office at Armarow, I just never had. I hardly stayed on the country property for more than a few days at a time to recharge and relax, because my penthouse in the city was far better suited for business.

But here I was, summoning the darkest and most depraved men on my books from all over the country to my private home and entertaining them so I could maintain my reign without leaving Arianna's side.

Because I wasn't ready to let her leave this place and share her with the rest of the world.

Tonight she would stand at my side, as my wife.

As the most important woman in the *Cosa Nostra*.

It was her coming out in a way, as the wedding had a very short guest list of only family and captains that could be considered family. The dinner being put on tonight would serve as her time to take her throne.

And she didn't even know it.

I took another drag off my cigar and let the familiar taste of the smoke fill my lungs and dance across my tongue as I pretended to listen and care about what my men were trying to share with me.

But my mind was stuck on the beautiful brunette due downstairs any moment now. I had gone up and picked out her dress for the evening, even going as far as laying out the lingerie I wanted her to wear and paired it with sexy new shoes and jewels I had delivered for her as well while she was in the shower.

My body physically ached to see her wearing all of my gifts.

I was fucked in the head over her already, which shouldn't have been surprising considering I made the knee-jerk decision to go through with the wedding after seeing her across the room at a gala last year.

I guess in a way I had been fucked over her since then.

Except, it was worse now that I had tasted her.

Taken her.

Marked her and claimed her as mine.

Even going as far as purposely trying to impregnate her with my child to cement the link between us forever.

Like I said, *fucked in the head*.

"Boss," Saul pulled my attention from my dance down daydream alley into the present with a quiet nod, "Mrs. Capasso is on her way down."

"Thank you." I snubbed my cigar out and tossed back the rest of my drink and watched the double doors across the room for her arrival.

"Anxious about something, Capa?" Luca Farone, a goodfella that had been a part of the Capasso family organization since before I was born, harassed me.

"Hmm." I hummed, trying to ignore him as the other men around me chuckled, enjoying my obvious distraction. "The only ones here that should be anxious tonight are the lot of you." I pulled my eyes away from the door and faced them down, "Because if any single one of you steps out of line in my wife's presence, I'll gut you right in front of her and keep your still beating heart for her collection."

Luca held his hands up and chuckled, "We'll be true boy scouts this evening," He looked around the group, "We all got the warning with the invitation."

"Good," I said as the double doors opened, and Dio stood to the side to let my wife enter the room. Suddenly no one else in the room existed.

Her step faltered slightly when she saw the packed space, but before any of the eyes turned to her, she caught herself and the mask of duty slid over her features as she searched for me in the room.

When her liquid chocolate eyes found mine, I tried to tell myself a veil of comfort or familiarity passed through her, but I was probably lying to myself.

I watched with rapture as her slender body moved through the crowd, as my men parted and bowed their heads to her as she passed. I also noticed how their eyes took generous gazes at her sensual body wrapped in the rose gold-colored lace dress I picked out for her.

The lace almost matched her skin tone and while the dress covered her from collar bones to the top of her thighs, the fabric was sheer everywhere that wasn't covering her breasts and waist, giving off the sexuality of my wife's body without exposing her completely to the men's hungry eyes.

"Arianna," I held my hand out to her as she neared and she took it, sliding her dainty fingers through mine as I pulled her to my side. "You look ravishing this evening."

She looked up at me as a blush covered her cheeks, "You have nice taste, I'll give you that much." She gently brushed her fingers over the diamond choker wrapped around her throat before she looked away to the men staring at her.

But all I could think about was how she would look later, laid out beneath me with her dark hair fanned out around her wearing only that diamond necklace as I fucked her deep.

"Capa," Leo, one of my other captains, whistled, "I see why you haven't been overly anxious to return to the city." When I finally pulled my eyes away from Ari, I found his panning back up her body appreciatively.

Normally I didn't care if my men lusted after the woman on my arm, more times than I could remember I gifted a woman to my men when I was done with her.

But not Ari.

Not my wife.

"Careful, Leo," I warned, sliding my hand over Ari's back and down over the swell of her ass, resting the weight of it against her. "Or you'll find yourself served at the next meal."

"Ach," He scoffed with a gold-toothed grin and a chuckle with his men, "Just admiring the surprising beauty that came from Emilio Rosetti's loins."

Ari stiffened slightly against me, but offered him a gentle smile. "I'll take that as a compliment given my father is one of the ugliest men I know."

His grin widened as did the ones on the men around him as she surprisingly aligned herself with the Capasso family in place of her own.

"Hmm." Leo winked at me, "Smart too."

"Very." I agreed as Manny, the head butler for the estate, entered the room and announced that dinner was ready. "Let's save any more compliments for my pretty wife until we get through the doorway into the dining room." I joked and pulled her along with me to lead the party in for the meal.

When we were in the hallway she leaned in further and hissed, "Why didn't you tell me there were going to be... guests? I look like a whore."

"I think you look like a Goddess." I countered and her jaw fell open in surprise. Perhaps she wasn't used to getting compliments, or perhaps she just wasn't expecting one from me, but it excited me to know I managed to render her speechless. "Be a good wife and hostess for the rest of the night like I know you were raised and taught to be," I leaned down until my lips were pressed against her ear, "And I'll reward you for your good behavior."

She swallowed audibly and pursed her lips before pulling away from me when we got to the table. "And what will my reward be?" She countered expertly, which I expected.

I pulled the chair out to the left of the head of the table and motioned for her to sit but when she slid between me and the chair to take her seat, I slid my fingers up the back of her short dress until they pressed against her satin covered pussy and she gasped. "You get to pick one of three rewards, so be good." She fell into the chair, effectively pulling my fingers free of her thighs, and glared at me with flushed cheeks.

If any of my men saw my move, they weren't dumb enough to bring attention to her embarrassment.

But the way her cheeks and chest bloomed with a blush made my cock hard. I had a fetish for exhibitionism, and if I wasn't careful, I would let my lust for her get out of hand and I'd end up fucking her right in the center of the table for my men to watch her come undone.

Which wouldn't serve me at all, because then I'd have to kill every single one of them for seeing her in such a situation.

"Lavish event, Capa," Luca signaled from his seat next to Ari with his wine glass, "Us lowly soldiers could get used to being invited to such spoiled meals."

I scoffed, taking my seat and lifting my glass. "None of you have been soldiers in decades, Luca." I pointed my finger at him and raised an eyebrow, "But test my patience tonight and you can be again if you so choose."

He chuckled and then fell silent as the butlers brought in the meal, plating delicious food in front of everyone.

I watched Ari as a plate of lobster bisque soup was sat down in front of her and her eyes rounded before, she pushed it away, turning to her butler. "I can't have this." She whispered to the man who quickly picked it up and walked away.

"Why can't you have soup?" I questioned as she awkwardly sat with an empty place setting in front of her. My men began digging into their meals happily, chatting merrily, and enjoying my hospitality. "I thought we talked about you eating more often."

"I'm allergic," she said under her breath, "To shellfish."

"How allergic?" I asked, pausing with my spoon above the delicious-smelling liquid.

"Enough to make you a widow if I ate that soup." Her butler reappeared with a green soup that looked and smelled far less appetizing and apologized in hush tones for his blunder. "It's fine, just please tell me what's in each dish that is served, and we'll avoid any big dramatics this evening."

"Yes, Ma'am," He bowed and backed up, but I caught his elbow.

"Take mine as well and have Chef Alec adjust my meals to ensure I don't accidentally expose my wife to any allergens." I handed him the bowl of bisque my chef had gotten his fame for and waited for a bowl of whatever my wife was served.

Several eyes were on us as the men realized something was going on at the head of the table while they ate.

"Exposed how?" Ari asked, dipping her spoon into her new soup and taking a bite.

"From my lips to yours."

Her eyes lifted to mine and rounded before looking back down at her soup, "It's not necessary to go without for me."

"It is." I halted her argument before she could finish it. "I won't put you at risk for something simple like this. Drop it." I nodded to her green soup. "What is that anyway?"

"Gazpacho." She hummed as she took a bite, "Delicious too."

My bowl of soup was delivered, and I took a large bite, trying to show solidarity with my wife even if I'd never bent my wants to someone else's needs before.

"So, Capa," Leo called from his seat down the table, "You have us here." He left the statement open, and I wiped my mouth as all of the eyes turned to me.

"Can't a Don just invite his men over for a family meal?" I questioned and smirked at their knowing glances. "Fine, you're right. There's business to attend to. Business in the West Shores that I've left unchecked for too long."

"Fuck yes!" Leo agreed with a toast of his glass. "How are you planning on attending to it now?"

"Swiftly." I acknowledged, "Harshly and without mercy."

I watched as eyes fluttered to Arianna and then to me in uncertainty before Luca spoke up. As one of the longest Goodfellas with the Capasso family, he was allowed more freedom to speak without restraint than some of the younger captains.

"West Shores is notoriously pro-Rosetti, *Capa*." Luca said pointedly, "If you plan to swiftly handle them the way you have others in the past, aren't you worried about..." He shrugged his shoulder deliberately, "Repercussions."

"If you mean, don't I worry that my wife will be angry with me," I took a sip of my drink and sat forward resting my elbows on the table as I looked to where he sat next to Arianna, "I don't worry about that at all. Arianna has no interest in her father's dealings. There's..." I shrugged the same way he had a moment ago, "Bad blood there. My wife is now a Capasso and therefore she aligns herself with me and my decisions, regardless of her father's opinions on the matter."

"That's not entirely true." Arianna rebutted, drawing the full attention of every man in the room as she sipped her wine with an impassive look on her face. "I wouldn't say I won't take my father's opinion on matters into account, just like I always have, now that I am a married woman." She set her wine glass down and turned to face the men watching her with scrutiny, "But I would say that I will now automatically favor the decision most likely to piss him off entirely. And something tells me," She looked at me, "That my husband has a plan in mind to piss him off as much as possible. And I thoroughly look forward to witnessing it."

Luca roared with great laughter as the other Captains joined in, "Well, well, well." He lifted her hand in his and toasted his wine glass in the air with his other, "To adding some much-needed excitement to the boring life *Capa* has had us all leading for the last bit of time."

"Hmm," She smiled, lifting her glass again, "I can't wait to enjoy the show."

Hours later the meal had wrapped up and my wife, my guests, and I were all relaxing in the lounge when the real business started being discussed.

"How exactly are you planning to ascertain West Shores?" Luca questioned at a quiet moment. "They won't go down in silence."

"You're probably right about that," I said, sliding my hand over the back of Arianna's neck as she sat in the wing-back chair next to where I stood. "Dr. Travis is here to see to your hand," I said, gently squeezing the tight muscles underneath the curtain of her hair draped elegantly. "Go upstairs and I'll have her seen up."

She looked over her shoulder at me and I half expected her to fight me on it, but she simply pursed her lips slightly and rose from her chair, "Thank you all for a lovely evening." She said politely to the group and then faced me. "Have a good rest of your night." She said dismissively and I smirked down at her.

"I'll be up shortly." I leaned down to kiss her cheek, "Put on the outfit I've laid out for you and be ready to pick your reward. The jewels stay put."

She eyed me suspiciously before walking out of the room, drawing the gazes of my men like moths to her flame. And I understood the pull she had on the male species, letting my own eyes trail after her as she seductively walked down the long hallway like it was a runway.

"I'm not sure if you're a lucky man or a damned one." Leo grinned from behind his whiskey glass near the fire and others chided in with their agreeance.

"I'm a damned man," I clarified, "everyone knows that." I smirked and cocked my head to the side, "I'm just enjoying the finer things in life while I have the opportunity, that's all. But back to West Shores." I cleared my throat and stood in the center of the room, commanding attention. "To be honest, West Shores is simply the smoke and mirrors to my real plan."

Murmurs floated around the room and quickly gained volume, so I held my hand up to silence them.

"Emilio Rosetti has seen the end of his power and position. I plan to use West Shores to facilitate the shift of power over to his oldest son, Carmine."

More murmurs and side-eyed glances filled the space.

"That's a bit..." Luca shrugged wisely, "Bold."

"Do you doubt the need for the change or my ability to get it done?"

"Never. For either of those." He answered instantly and I watched him closely for a hint of deception. "But I am curious as to why you waited for your young wife to leave the room, or better yet, instructed her to leave before you brought it up. Do you not trust her loyalty to you after all?"

I scoffed and took a sip of liquor from my glass that Manny refilled before the conversation started. "We've been married for less than a week." I poured back a heavy amount, "While I would like to believe that my charm and good looks are enough to hide my poor manners and brute insensitivity with women somedays," the room chuckled and I glared good-heartedly, "I'm not naïve to the fact that it is new, and she owes me no loyalty. To be frank with you all, Emilio beat and tortured Arianna for most of her life to mold her into the perfect little doll that fit his needs. He starved her, drugged her, and isolated her to keep her compliant and ready to perform for him at will. So believe me when I say her distaste for him runs deep. But," I leaned my elbow onto the mantle and looked down into the flames, "My wife's adoration for her siblings, Carmine especially, runs far deeper than any fondness she's developed for me thus far. She won't trust me to not harm the Rosetti heir in my move for Emilio. And I don't blame her, because she is right to worry."

"So, how does West Shores play into it?" Harris, a man from my father's day of rule questioned as his young son watched on, soaking up all the knowledge he could from his first meal with the Don.

"West Shores geographically is closest to the Rosetti home estate, and where most of Emilio's resources are housed. His money, his men, his women, and most recently-," I let my voice die off and looked at Luca.

"His weapons," He hissed. "Fucking prick, I knew those fucking crates weren't being traded out of the district. Fucking drug smuggling cartels." He spit with malice.

Weeks ago I'd been informed of movement within my districts. Movement of weapons and money too large to belong to anyone besides myself or someone like Rosetti. It took far longer than it should have, but I was able to trace them back to my new father-in-law and sat on the information until the opportunity presented itself to formulate a plan, given that my wedding was nearing.

I got the opportunity that I needed, when I met with Carmine.

"Emilio is planning something. Something big." I addressed the crowd, "I'd be a total worthless fuck not to notice the way he schemed and relied on his daughter's marriage to me to come to fruition for me to believe it doesn't affect me somehow."

"So, what's the plan?" Harris leaned forward staring directly at me.

Out of everyone in the room, he was the most bloodthirsty, always ready for the marching order to make someone hurt and I could see the same excitement burning in his son's eyes as he looked from his father to me.

"I plan to use Carmine to get those weapons and any more smuggled in as well as the money being paid to the cartel to bring them into my territory without my approval. Then I'm going to destroy him, exposing him to our allies as the traitorous rat he's turned out to be. Lastly, I'll dethrone him. In his place, Carmine will take the lead of the Rosetti family businesses, who has already proven to be far more like-minded to me than his father."

"And your wife?" Harris's son questioned boldly, stepping far enough out of place that my father would have had him beaten for it, but I didn't need to use my fists to align my soldiers.

I used my cunningness, "My wife is essentially only here to serve one purpose. Give me sons. Above that, her happiness or loyalty does not interest me. If she has a problem with me killing her father, too bad. But I don't anticipate her being a problem."

"How are you planning on ensuring that?" Leo questioned, "Women like your wife are the ones to watch the closest in my personal opinion. She's the type of woman who would gladly run a knife along your throat in your sleep for the pure joy of saying she bested someone that got the up on her first. And if I know you at all, you've gotten the better of her at least a few times already. Do you not fear having her so close without having her loyalty first?"

"My need for sons, children of any gender," I corrected, "far outweighs most of my other problems currently. And I've already seen to starting that process, and once she is pregnant and attached to the baby, she won't jeopardize their safety or happiness. Not even for her brother."

"You plan to use your own child against their mother to keep her in line?" Harris asked surprised, with a hint of approval in his eyes.

"You act like that hasn't been the way of every Don in the history of the Cosa Nostra. I'll do whatever is necessary to get what I want, and what I want most is to eradicate Emilio Rosetti and as much of his tainted bloodline from this earth as possible. Using my wife or our unborn child that she will soon carry in her womb against him is just one of the ways I will do that."

I stared the old-time *button man* down, showing him that I didn't care if he made his name for himself through hits and bloodshed ordered by my father or not.

I was the fucking Don.

I fucking dared him to question me again after tonight.

He stood up and nodded to me with respect, "I'm so looking forward to seeing your rule flourish, Capa." He bowed his head and gave me his hand, allowing me the respect due to me.

"Very well." I looked to the other captains in the room and watched as each and every one gave their allegiance until the entire room stood and pledged their newly vowed loyalty to me and my way of ruling.

CHAPTER 9 – ARIANNA

Nico's fetish to dress me was quickly becoming a huge turn-on for me. Which was scary.

After being told what to wear and how to act my entire life, I would have thought that the idea of letting someone dictate things like my wardrobe even as a married woman would irritate me. Yet, with him, the way he did it, left me feeling... excited.

Filled with anticipation, if you will.

I ran my fingers over the red satin laid out on the island in the master closet and smiled to myself knowing it wasn't just a turn-on for me. It was an aphrodisiac to my husband as well. Which made no sense if he was resolved to hating me. Yet sometimes, when it was just the two of us, I could almost pretend he didn't actually hate me like he said.

Therefore, I'd have to acknowledge that maybe I didn't actually hate him either, which I wasn't ready to do.

I slid the lace dress off my body that he picked out for me, and began putting the cool ruby-red fabric of the lingerie over my heated skin.

I looked in the floor-length mirror and turned to admire the piece. A halter neck tied the piece with black lace before smooth satin draped down over my breasts in a v-cut that went straight to my waistline where it split and wrapped around my legs and ass leaving the crotch completely bare and exposed. Of course, there were no other panties laid out for me to wear.

Dirty, old man.

The diamond choker he laid out with my dress earlier in the evening sparkled brightly in the warm light of the mirror and compared to the red and black fabric it nearly glowed.

I slid the matching red satin floor-length robe over the ensemble and tightened the sash as a knock sounded at the bedroom door. "Ari?" Molly called and I walked out to her.

"Do you ever sleep, Molly?" I smiled at her and looked at the ornate clock on the wall. It was nearly ten at night and she had been up and attending me first thing that same morning, as she would be tomorrow as well. "Do you live here?"

She chuckled and stepped aside so Dr. Travis could come into the room with her sleek black medical bag before answering. "I do live on the estate grounds. Most of the staff does. And I sleep more than enough, thank you."

"Hmm." I hummed, fingering my smooth hair before addressing the doctor, "Hello, Dr. Travis."

"Mrs. Capasso," She nodded politely, "How are you feeling this evening? How's your hand?"

"It's better," I lifted my hand and slowly clenched it into a fist feeling only a slight twinge of pain still. "I'm managing."

"Good to hear." She smiled and set her bag down, holding her hand out for mine and gently probing the knuckles that she had replaced a few days ago. "It looks to have healed perfectly; I'd expect the last of the tenderness to resolve in the next few days. You may have some long-term effects from the injury, like occasional stiffness or throbbing when the weather changes," She smiled sweetly, "Things like that. But I wouldn't expect too much of a hindrance on your life from it."

"Thank you." I took my hand back and looked to where Molly stood waiting for the doctor. "Is that it?"

"Actually," Dr. Travis drew my attention back to her, "I need a urine sample from you." She turned to her bag and withdrew a specimen cup and a tray of test strips. "And a blood sample."

"For what?" I took a step back from her as she laid a blood draw kit out on the table. "What does that have to do with my hand?"

"Nothing, Ma'am." She continued setting out her things, "Mr. Capasso requested it."

"For what though?" I snapped, hating how she avoided my gaze.

"Your physical." She finally faced me, "And your reproductive analysis."

My ears burned red with embarrassment and a ringing pulsed inside of my head as her words penetrated my brain.

Reproductive analysis.

Broodmare.

I was only here to give him sons.

Anger flared inside of my chest as his words from our wedding night repeated on a loop.

"Reproductive analysis," I repeated and even if I tried, the sneer behind my words was obvious, catching the doctor off guard.

"Yes," she faltered, "To make sure your hormones are all level and to make sure they match up with where you are in your cycle." Her eyebrows knitted in the center of her kind face. "Mr. Capasso said you two were hoping to get pregnant soon."

"Ha," I scoffed bitterly, "I assure you, only one of us has made that our plan." I crossed my arms over my chest defiantly and paced in front of the fire. "What are my options for contraceptives?"

I felt bad for the doctor as she stared at me, completely unprepared for the conversation. Even Molly looked uncomfortable, though if I bothered to look hard enough, I could almost see a bit of outrage in her gentle eyes as well.

"I wasn't permitted to give you any contraceptive," Dr. Travis finally said, stiffening her spine. "I don't think Mr. Capasso would approve given his previous statements to me."

"I don't care what *Mr. Capasso* wants." I hissed, "Doesn't what I want matter?"

She sighed almost sadly and looked at me like an errant child.

Like my parents used to when I dared to balk at their rules.

"Even if I did give you some sort of contraceptive Arianna," She said kindly, "He'd fire me and bring in another doctor, probably a male who would care very little for your comfort or well-being, and he'd have them counteracted."

"So I have no choice but to be bred?" I snapped and then looked away, hating how my fight wasn't even with her but instead with Nicolas. Who conveniently wasn't here to receive my anger. "Whatever." I picked the cup up off the table and stomped my way to the ensuite. "Maybe I'll be infertile, so he can off me and find another wife better suited for his *needs*."

I slammed the door shut behind me and leaned my head against it as a sudden feeling of despondence fell onto my shoulders.

I was once again, just a piece in someone else's sick and twisted game. My feelings, wants, and needs didn't matter.

I didn't matter.

My whole life my parents had beaten into me that everything they did to me was for the bettering chance to one day be important to them.

To someone else.

But I wasn't important. I wasn't consequential. I wasn't loved.

Never loved.

Never wanted.

Only used.

As the hardwood of the door bit into my forehead I felt a hardness growing around my heart and through my spine.

If he thought I'd just be a good little wife and play the part he wanted me to, he was wrong.

I wasn't going to just lie down and let him use me to serve his needs.

I may be a Capasso now, but I was still Arianna.

It was time I started acting like my own savior since I was starting to realize I was never going to have a knight in shining armor come and rescue me from this tower I was locked in.

I'd traded my parents' cruelty for captivity and sexual exploitation.

I wasn't sure if I'd rather go back to being drugged, starved, and beaten than be manipulated by a man who was so good at playing with my mind that I let him play with my body without even realizing how uneven the scoreboard was.

Not anymore though.

I took the cup to the toilet and angrily stripped out of the offensive red satin and gave my sample, simply because I knew there was no way around it. When I was done, I washed my hands and wrapped a fresh white towel around my body staring at myself in the large mirror and I hardly recognized the anger burning in my eyes.

I opened the drawers of the vanity until I found the dainty pair of scissors, I'd seen there the other day and held them in my hands, contemplating how effective they'd be to stab my husband with, in his sleep. However, I knew that was ridiculous because the blades were barely an inch long. Was I even the kind of woman who had it in her to harm another person, even a man so deserving of it as Nicolas Capasso.

The blades *were* long enough to shred satin though.

I picked up the robe and body suit and sliced them both to tattered shreds with shaking hands until I was left with a pile of fabric completely unrecognizable from what they had resembled moments ago.

A feral smile pulled up one side of my lips when I looked back in the mirror. I may not be able to best my husband at his own game. But I could sure as hell make him as miserable as I was along the way.

I tore the beautiful diamond choker from my neck that he had told me to leave on and flung it against the opposite wall, reveling in the way it clattered to the marble floor in a heap.

Fuck him.

Fuck his commands.

Fuck it all.

Adrenalin and anger pulsed inside of me like a living thing, and I needed a new outlet for it, or I'd go insane. I left the bathroom, ignoring the doctor and my maid completely, and walked to the master closet. I found the thickest and most drab clothing I owned, a black hooded sweater and a pair of grey leggings, and pulled them on over my body, shielding it from anyone who dared to look at me.

Next, I turned my attention to the drawers full of expensive lingerie that my husband was so fond of instructing me to wear.

Well, like I said before, fuck him.

I pulled piece after piece out, shredding them each with the scissors and throwing them in a pile on the floor like I was preparing for a large fire. Molly cautiously walked into the closet and stood at the doorway, watching me destroy the clothing like it had personally offended me and while I felt powerful for doing it, I also felt childish.

Used.

"I actually felt pretty in them," I whispered after a long stretch of silence between us, with only the noise of me shredding the clothing to fill the space. "Stupid, huh?"

"No," Molly replied gently, walking into the room to stand on the other side of the counter where I mutilated thousands of dollars of apparel that she had painstakingly folded and arranged by color for me. "I think you're justified in your anger right now."

"Hmm," I huffed and then paused when she handed me a new pair of lace panties to shred. "Doesn't this piss you off?" I nodded to the pile of chaos before me. "The mess of it all?"

She smiled and shrugged her shoulders, "If I know Mr. Capasso at all, he'll simply buy you more. And I'll arrange those pieces the same as these. If it makes you feel better to take your anger out on something, then I'll help." She sighed, "Because I'm unable to help you in a way that matters."

I dropped my hands to the counter and looked at her across the marble top and felt my shoulders deflate. "I don't want to be a mom," I whispered, voicing my feelings out loud for the first time in my life.

"For what it matters, I think you'd be a great one." She smiled gently at me.

That only made me sadder. "I have no idea how to be a good mom to someone." I put the scissors down on the counter and pushed the lace away. "I've never even seen what a good one looks like."

She pursed her lips and picked up the scissors, sliding them into the pocket of her dress like she was afraid I'd pick them back up and hurt someone with them.

Or maybe she was afraid I'd hurt myself.

It was anyone's guess.

"There's a centuries-long debate about motherhood and human nature." She said, busying herself with piling up the destroyed lingerie. "Some people, like yourself, think that you need to be taught how to be a mother. That the lessons need to be learned before you know what to do in situations."

"But you don't think that." I twisted the drawstrings from my sweater around my fingers as she simply shrugged her shoulders.

"I don't. I'm from the side of the debate that thinks knowing how to be a mother is merely engrained in our DNA through biology. I believe that creatures, human and animal alike, were put on this earth to create life." She looked up at me, "I think that nature will take hold of someone when they're faced with the challenges that creating life will bring up. Then our bodies will simply know what to do, or at the very least, be equipped with the problem-solving techniques to figure it out. Sure there's going to be a lot of free will encompassed in the equation, but you don't strike me as the kind of person to let an innocent child suffer because of circumstances they didn't have a say in."

I chewed on my bottom lip and looked out of the closet door to where Dr. Travis walked out of the bathroom with my urine sample and a bunch of used test strips.

"You have a good mom, don't you, Molly?" I looked back over at her.

A knowing smile graced her sweet face. "I do." She nodded and chuckled gently, "She's the sweetest person I've ever met before." She stepped around the island and stood close, "And you'd never know by looking at her or watching her parent, that she was the product of a broken and abusive household. She's kind, gentle, and patient. She loves everyone first and gives them chance after chance to get things right."

I chuckled sadly and looked away from her penetrating blue eyes. "I wonder how different my life would have turned out if I had a mother like yours."

"Well, I'll tell you what," She took my hand and patted it gently, "I'll ask her if she'll adopt you. We do Sunday dinners every week and you're always welcome to come get a taste of her kindness, whenever you want."

I laughed and smiled at her absurd offer. "I'll see you there someday."

"Good." She smiled back, proud of herself for pulling me out of my manic rage. "Now." She grimaced. "I should probably pick this mess up before Mr. Capasso retires for the evening."

"Ach," I tossed my shoulder carelessly, "Leave it. And go home for the night."

"I don't mind," She started to argue but I held my hand up.

"I don't think you'll want to be around when he retires, Molly." I said firmly, "Take your out when I give you one. Because while you came from a loving and sweet home, I came from one that really knows how to throw a temper tantrum. And that's exactly what I plan on doing." I winked at her. "And I don't want you to witness another one of my falls from grace." I eyed the pile of lingerie still thrown around the room. "One a day is plenty."

She chuckled and nodded her head, "As you wish."

"Have a good night." I walked with her out of the closet and then gave my attention to the doctor who was doing a whole ass science experiment on our coffee table. "Let's finish this exam, shall we."

She nodded dutifully and motioned for me to sit in the chair as she pulled on a fresh pair of gloves.

Molly left silently and the doctor carefully wrapped the tourniquet around my upper arm after sliding my baggy sweater sleeve up. "When was your last period?" She asked as she worked.

"Three weeks ago," I answered, having already done the math while I was having a breakdown in the bathroom. "Which means it's too late for me already isn't it?" I eyed the different colored test strips on the sterile barrier she laid on the table.

She swallowed and tapped my arm, looking for my vein, "Judging off your urine tests alone it looks like you've recently ovulated." She grabbed the needle and I looked away, "Little pinch." She placed the test tubes one by one, collecting my blood. "When was the first time you were intimate with Mr. Capasso?"

"Almost a week ago," I whispered.

She finished pulling the tubes and then set them down next to her. "Then yes, my medical opinion is if it was going to happen this month it would already have occurred."

"Spectacular." I sighed and leaned back into the chair, holding the cotton ball over the spot she took the needle out of.

"I wish there was something I could do to help you-."

"Don't," I shook my head, "It's not your battle."

"There are ways-." She shrugged, not meeting my eyes, "To make it less likely to conceive if it didn't already occur this cycle."

"What do you mean? I thought you said you couldn't give me contraceptives."

"I can't." She sighed and then sat up and looked at me. "But certain positions can give a shallower angle of penetration, therefore making it harder for the sperm to make it to the womb. Or tricks like using the restroom immediately after intercourse and bearing down, pushing out the sperm as much as possible. Or ways you can perhaps entice your husband to ejaculate in other places."

My face bloomed red again at what she was insinuating, and I nodded my understanding.

"Cowgirl." She said gently, keeping her hands busy, "The position with you on top, can be one of the shallowest positions. It also leaves you in control to remove yourself before he is completely done, though that may alert him to your attempts."

"Got it." I sighed, facing this headfirst, "Any other tips."

"Spermicidal lubricant." She added, "Though that may be hard for you to get your hands on without him seeing the label." She loaded the test tubes into her bag and removed her gloves. "I wish there was more I could offer you, Mrs. Capasso."

"I know." I stood up from the chair and wrapped my arms around my waist, "I'm sorry for taking it out on you before. I just let myself forget my reality for a moment and that was a cold splash of water on my fantasy."

"What is your fantasy, exactly, Mrs. Capasso?" She asked freely, "If you could choose your path, what would you want out of life?"

I chuckled lifelessly and turned to look down into the flames of the fireplace as I answered her. "I'd choose love." I smiled sadly, "I'd choose someone who didn't want me just for my uterus, or my family, or anything else. Just me." Tears burned behind my eyes as I let the sadness bloom inside of me again. "The worst part of it all is I could have been happy here," I admitted. "I could have built a life here and that life could have included kids and us all being a family. But I'll never have that if I'm just the means to an end for the man that should be the center of my world. That's not a game I get to win." I sighed again, "Which seems to be the trend of my life so far."

"Mr. Capasso." Dr. Travis said with surprise. "We were just-." I looked over my shoulder and found my husband staring at me from the doorway with what looked like anger glowing in his perfect green eyes. "Did you get what you needed Doctor?" He snapped in his authoritative tone.

"Yes, Sir." She replied demurely and grabbed the last of her things. "I'll have the results to you in the morning."

"Very well." He moved to the side, indicating her exit, all the while keeping his eyes locked on me.

I turned away, giving him my back as I stared back down into the flames. I fought against the anger that burned inside of my gut and focused more on the hurt. Because I knew from past experiences that Nico could take my anger and turn it into passion. However he couldn't morph my pain into anything but what it was, so I used it to protect myself from him.

I listened to him slowly prowl across the room toward me and heard him pause at the door to the closet where the mess of lingerie still lay in a heap across the room.

I didn't even feel shame at him finding the pile. I still only felt defeated.

"Do you not like my gifts anymore?" He finally asked from a few feet behind me.

"I don't see the purpose of them." I replied cooly, "Lingerie is a form of seduction and foreplay. My willingness to sleep with you has never stopped you before, so there's no point in disguises."

"You're angry with me." He stated plainly.

"I'm frustrated." I corrected him, finally turning from the fire. "But it doesn't matter what I am, does it?"

"No." He replied, scowling down at me. "It doesn't."

"Glad we have that covered. The doctor said I ovulated already, so your chance to get me pregnant is over for this month."

He chuckled but didn't smile. "That's what has you so angry is it?"

"Does it matter?"

"Surprisingly yes, Little One, it does."

I walked away from him, angry with myself for opening my mouth at all, and went into the bathroom to wash my face for bed.

He leaned his shoulder against the doorframe and crossed his arms over his massive chest as I went about my nightly routine. "This isn't anger," He said after a while. "I've seen your anger, and this isn't it."

"Well, the designer clothes in the closet disagree." I snarked back before drowning my face under the faucet and scrubbing the makeup off that I painstakingly applied hours ago to look good for him. Like a stupid foolish girl.

I washed my face until it was raw, and I had no choice but to come up for air and face him again. When I patted the skin dry I caught his reflection in the mirror, still standing exactly as he had been, and for some reason that frustrated me further. "What do you want?" I snapped.

"To understand you."

"Why?" I turned and put my hand on my hip, "Why do my emotions or feelings matter? You've made your intentions clear. I understand exactly where I stand, and I'll be sure not to forget it again." I flicked my hand, "So go on. Go back to your important boy's club downstairs and just leave me alone."

He moved quickly for such a large man, crossing the space in a few effortless steps leaving me no exit from the room that didn't involve getting past him. I stood my ground leaning up off the counter and faced him head-on.

He wrapped his hand around my neck and pushed me until my back pressed flat against the wall. His nostrils flared and his chest rose and fell quickly as he silently stared down at me.

But I wasn't afraid. My life was already in his hands before he physically wrapped his hand around my neck in domination.

"Should I start calling you Daddy?" I asked defiantly, "I feel like I'm right back inside of the Rosetti familial residence."

His hand tightened around my throat until I could feel the blood beginning to pool in my face as he restricted its flow. "I never wanted your anger, Little One."

"No, we both know you just wanted my body." I hissed, "Would you prefer me to just lay on my back in the center of your bed and remain silent and still while you fuck me? Or perhaps bent over so you don't have to see the disgust I feel for you in my eyes while you rut into me. Would that be easier for you? It must be such hard work being a rapist."

"Fuck you." He growled, shaking me slightly and bouncing my skull off the wall. It didn't hurt, and I knew he was restraining his true anger. "You're just like your father, yet you spit your accusations at me." He leaned down until his face was right in front of mine so I could feel the heat of his breath on my face. "That Rosetti blood is just as toxic as I knew it was. Even if I was a sweet and doting husband, your shrewdness and manipulative streak would still cut me."

"Get off of me." I shoved at him, trying to dislodge him as his hand tightened even more around my neck. He restricted not only the blood to my brain, but now my breath. "Do it." I whispered, "End it all. Prove you're the big man here."

"I don't have to kill you to prove I'm the bigger monster here, Ari." He hissed, against my lips, "But I will kill your darling brother for the fun of it. And then you'll never doubt it again."

I reacted violently, shoving, scratching, clawing, and kicking at him as his hand cut off my breath completely. I hit him in his face over and over, but my hands bounced off and he never flinched as my vision darkened and my lungs screamed for air.

His green eyes were the last thing I saw before darkness took me completely.

CHAPTER 10 – NICO

"You can't do this!" The bitch in front of me screamed, hurling anything she could get her hands on my way.

Nothing hit its mark, and Matteo quickly had her subdued. Ropes tied her wrists behind her back and her ankles together, and a rag from her shitty kitchen was shoved into her mouth to silence her protests.

"Finally." I sighed, "Silence."

Her husband lay in a heap at my feet, barely conscious and bleeding from a deep gut wound that he got for trying to run when we broke in.

Coward.

"Now," I turned to where the three sons of the bastard coward sat along the wall, watching their father bleed out and their mother fight her bindings with more fire than all three of them had in their guts put together. "Which one of you is the oldest?"

The three of them remained silent before finally, one raised his hand, "I am, Mr. Capasso."

"Your name?" I motioned for him to stand up.

"Anthony."

"How old are you, Anthony?"

"Twenty-three."

"Good," I responded and put my hand on his shoulder. "Old enough to do what is necessary of you, but young enough to still learn how to do things the right way." I looked down at my feet, "Unlike your father here."

The kid swallowed but kept his eyes on me, "Yes, Sir."

"Do you know what your father used to do for me?"

He nodded, "Yes, Sir."

"And did you know that he was stealing from me while he did it?"

I watched the young man's face and could see instantly that he didn't. "No, Sir."

"Good." I put my hand around the back of his neck and forced his head down, so he stared at his father who had a peculiar gurgle coming from his lips with each breath. "Let this be the only time I have to show you what happens to men who steal from me. Because if I have to show you again, you'll be the one bleeding out on the floor while your family watches. Understood?"

"Yes, Mr. Capasso." He nodded eagerly.

"Good," I repeated and let him go, shoving him back toward the wall. "You'll take over pickups in your father's place. Three times a week you'll travel to the meat district and pick up packages of fish for me. You'll then deliver them to my warehouse along the East River, and finally you'll go about your merry business the other four days of the week, and you'll be paid well for it. It's a simple job, far easier than going to work in a boring factory to make a third of the pay for seven days straight of labor wouldn't you say?"

"Yes, Mr. Capasso." He nodded quickly.

"You'll have a man watching you for a while, so don't fuck it up." I pressed the toe of my shoe into the seeping wound on his father's stomach causing him to cough and cry out for mercy. "Worthless." I turned my attention nodding to where the woman seethed at me with daggers flying from her eyes. "Would you be so angry at me for killing him if I told you he has another family near the warehouse that he visits on his delivery days?" She stilled, looking at her husband and then back to me. "A woman half your age with two sons of her own made directly from his loins, ages six and four." I kicked her worthless husband again. "She gets more than half of the money he makes from me each week while you've been what I'm assuming is a loyal wife to the man for more than two decades; living in poverty." I tsked my teeth and shook my head, looking back to Anthony and his brothers. "Something tells me you three will make quite the names for yourselves without your father's despicable shadow keeping you here inside while he plays both sides of the game. Just remember who is giving you the chance to do that."

They nodded their heads, no doubt out of fear alone. Matteo, waiting for me to conclude, opened the front door and we walked out of the rundown apartment onto the pavement outside. "Where to now?" Matteo asked.

"Back to the penthouse." I slid into the back seat of the car while he got in on the other side before my driver pulled off.

"Thought you'd be chomping at the bit to get back to Armarow." He taunted me as I scrolled through my emails, trying my best to ignore him. "You've avoided it for three days now."

"So what."

"You've avoided her for three days straight. I'll be honest, I didn't think you had it in you."

"Fuck off." I snapped, closing my email and putting my phone back in my pocket. "Before I break your teeth."

"Eh," He shrugged and ran his hand over his jaw, "They're all fake at this point anyway. If you want to take a couple shots at them to avoid acknowledging your own fuck ups, go ahead."

"Asshole," I grunted.

"So what did you do?"

"Who said I did anything?" I argued, hating that he knew me so well. In truth, it was me who did something. I had choked her out, cutting the blood and air off to her brain long enough for her to faint and then I carried her limp body to our bed and laid her down in the center of it.

I stood over her body and watched her chest rise and fall as her neck bloomed red with my mark until I couldn't stand to look at her for a moment longer.

And then I packed a bag and left.

For her safety.

She turned me into a monster that even I didn't recognize. I never intended to render her unconscious or leave her as long as I have. I had envisioned my evening with her turning out completely different. She had been a perfect angel on my arm at dinner and then after, charming my men and following the cues I gave her. I planned to retire for the evening and spend it buried between her thighs, giving her everything she deserved for being my good girl all evening.

But instead, I walked into my bedroom and overheard her telling the doctor of all the things she fantasized about for her life and how everything she'd experienced with me had fallen flat and I... lost myself to the monster inside.

She was the last person I wanted to lose my composure with, yet I had done it twice. First on our wedding night when I bent her over the chair to show her who was in charge, and then again after the dinner.

I showed her the monster everyone else knew I was, and it left me feeling unsettled.

So I ran.

"Our thirty-year-long history did." He scoffed.

I grumbled and adjusted myself in the seat, trying to ignore him and watch the city pass by the tinted windows of my car, but I gave in to his bait. "I didn't do anything I didn't plan to do." I finally said after a while, when I could feel his eyes still on me.

"Then why does it bother you?" He questioned and I glared at him, "And don't say it doesn't bother you, because if it didn't, you wouldn't be hiding out at the penthouse. Avoiding your blushing new bride."

"Blushing bride my ass." I grunted, "The woman has more claws than a lioness. Teeth too." I rubbed the spot on my chest that she bit the first time I took her the night before our wedding. The mark had faded, but her brand remained, deep inside of me.

"Does that really surprise you? She is a Rosetti after all."

"Don't remind me." I fisted my hands on my lap, to stem off the desire to pull up the security footage of her in my home for the hundredth time today alone. Dr. Travis called me the morning after Arianna's exam with her results. Turns out my wife wasn't only fertile, but she was medically in perfect shape to create and carry my baby.

Babies if I had any say in it. Now we just had to wait a week longer to find out if I'd managed to get her pregnant or not. Part of me was hoping she was, so the troublesome part was done, given her renewed dislike of me. The other part of me hoped she wasn't so that perhaps I could return to Armarow and do it right.

Woo her.

Treat her the way she obviously desired to be treated.

But I wasn't a man of romance, I didn't know how to give her the things she wished for. Mostly because I only overheard her telling Dr. Travis what she wanted, and I had no idea how to give it to her. And hell if I was going to lower myself to ask her either.

"So," Matteo continued ignoring my anger like only an old friend could do. "Spill it."

"Would you drop it already?" I snapped, "Bother someone else with your meddling and curiosity, I don't have the energy for it."

"Weird." He mused, "Because you were full of energy and more on top of your game the entire week we were at Armarow. Yet now that you're away from the problematic wife of yours, you're back to the miserable son of a bitch that you've been for years."

"Fuck off." I hissed, turning on him. "You think sitting there and insulting me is going to get you what you want?"

"Me?" He raised his eyebrows in surprise, "What is it that I want exactly?"

"My guess," I challenged, "is into the panties of that blonde maid you can't keep your eyes off of when we're at Armarow." I argued and his jaw ticked, "Perhaps that's why you're so overly eager to get me back there. So you can get a piece of ass from the sexy little thing?"

"Wrong." He countered.

"Fine." I shrugged, looking back out the window, "Then we'll return to Armarow tonight, simply so I can fuck the maid in the middle of the dining room table at dinner time. You wouldn't mind, would you?" I looked back over at him and his face was murderous, "God knows my wife isn't going to let me near her without a fight right now, so maybe I'll just tell sweet little innocent Molly to get on her knees for me to take the edge off." I shrugged, "Thanks for the idea."

He shook his head and cracked his neck, "You're a real piece of shit somedays Nico, you know that right?"

"Well aware." I agreed, "Don't ever try to manipulate me for your own interests again Matteo. I know you too well, just as you know me."

"I wasn't trying to manipulate you."

"Call it what you want, but it wasn't genuine." The car pulled up out front of the penthouse and I got out and walked through the crowded lobby, feeling the stares of the other patrons and guests watching my every move. I also spied the paparazzi camped out front, pointing their cameras in through the front glass, desperately trying to get a photo of me doing something exciting to sell to the highest bidder.

Halfway across the space, a woman stepped out in front of me, and I stopped, simply so I didn't mow her over. She wore a blood-red dress that hugged her average curves and sky-high stilettos like she was trying to mix business and pleasure, but she missed her mark. "Mr. Capasso." She purred as she flicked her brown hair over her shoulder, exposing the deep cut of her dress's bust line to my eyes. Purposely, I'm sure. "Anna Devon," She held her hand out and I took it, entertaining her. "I was wondering if we could chat about your recent acquisition of the Milton Logging company."

"Ms. Devon," I raised an eyebrow at her, "What interest do you have in my acquisitions?"

She smiled seductively as I let my eyes fall on the assets, she was trying to display for me. "I think I have something that may interest you, Mr. Capasso. Something that may lead to be mutually beneficial."

"What's that?" I fought the urge to shudder from the sexual prowess she was trying to drown me with and dropped her hand. "And don't be vague." I nodded to the crowded room. "I have no time for smoke and mirrors."

I took a step forward, causing her to move back one so that she stayed in front of me, keeping my attention. "Information." She hurried, "On Milton's biggest competition in the district."

"Who?"

"Devon and Sons." She said, once again taking another step as I tried to continue my way to the elevator.

I paused, raising an eyebrow at her, finally interested in what she was trying to sell. "Familial connections?" Flashes from the photographers lit up the dimly lit lobby as I stood with the woman. She was giving them what they hoped to get when they camped out waiting for me, and that pissed me off.

"My husband's family." She raised her chin and fluttered her eyelashes in what I'm sure she hoped was a seductive manner. "A family I'm interested in making very uncomfortable for a time."

I eyed her, seeing her for what she was. "Leave your info with the desk," I nodded and then slid my hand around her hip to pull her in close and leaned down to her ear. She gasped and leaned in flush like she was melting into my touch. Which positively repulsed me. "And if you ever approach me in public like this again, I'll strip you bare and chain you to the front window. Used and worthless to be photographed by the media when my men get done with you." I kissed her cheek like I was saying goodbye to an acquaintance and smiled down at her as I pulled back. "Now get the fuck out of my way."

I kept my face impassive, knowing the media had no idea what I actually said to her, but knew what it looked like occurred between us.

It looked like I chatted with a woman of mine in broad daylight. A newly married man, and the most feared Don in decades.

Cunt.

But I'd use it to my benefit one way or another.

I got to the elevator and hit the button as Matteo slid next to me with a questioning glance. "Make sure the pictures they took end up all over the front of every paper. Make it sound like I entertained her inside. Use her name."

"Why?" He asked, looking over his shoulder as the woman stood at the front desk, leaving her information for me. When the elevator door opened and he looked back at me, he already knew the answer though. "Let me guess, you then want those papers delivered to Armarow?"

"And West Shores," I smirked. "Let my wife and her father both see it."

"And do you plan on actually entertaining the jaded housewife?" He raised a brow.

"Fuck no." I grimaced, "That woman smells of desperation. And I like a challenge."

He chuckled and shook his head, stepping back towards the lobby to do my bidding. "Twisted motherfucker."

"Just like you, old friend," I smirked back as the elevator door closed, silencing the noise of the lobby.

D ays later, I was still hiding out at the penthouse.

At least that's what Matteo kept calling it, and I stopped correcting him.

He was right after all, though I wouldn't tell him that.

It was the end of a long day, and I was nursing a drink and contemplating a business deal that should have been a no-brainer, yet I couldn't focus on the fine details.

"Capa." Matteo barked, rushing into the room. "They've lost her."

"Who?" I turned on him as he gripped his phone to his ear.

"Arianna." He held his phone out and I took it from it, seeing Saul's name on the screen.

"Talk to me."

"She gave us the slip." Saul cursed and I could hear air rushing around him like he was running. "Dio's reviewing footage to see when she left and how. Neither of us has any fucking clue how she got away."

"Fucking bastards." I cursed, running to my computer and pulling up the footage of the house. "Where was she last?"

"Your bedroom. She retired at four, said she had a headache, and that she wasn't coming down for dinner. Molly is the only one that went up there after that, just like you instructed."

"What does Molly say?" I rolled the footage back to four pm and watched it in double time until my wife's beautiful body walked through the door to our bedroom. She wore a blue sweater dress that hugged her curves and showed off the silky-smooth skin of her upper thighs above her knee-high lace-topped socks. They made her look young and girly and somehow the combination of sex appeal and innocence made my cock stir in my pants.

"She's off Sunday afternoons. She left a little after four, right after she checked on Arianna one last time."

"Tricky woman." I cursed, figuring out where my wife was even before I saw proof. "She's with Molly." Saul paused as I stood up and grabbed the important things I needed from the penthouse with Matteo on my heel. "Molly dines at her parent's every Sunday evening; my guess is that's where my wife is. Go there, and wait outside, but don't let anyone know you're there unless you need to. I'll be there in an hour."

"Yes, Boss."

"Molly's, huh?" Matteo asked as we stood in the elevator moments later, ready to return to Armarow far before I was prepared.

"Meddling woman that she is." I glared at him, and he smirked. "I've killed servants for far less."

"Yes," he nodded and walked out in front of me as we got to the private garage entrance where my cars were parked. "But, Molly's parents have worked for the Capasso family longer than either of us has been alive. Arianna could have picked a worse place to spend her evening, and I think she knows that."

It was true. Molly's father was the head gardener at Armarow, and her mother had been my nanny before she left Armarow to start having her own children. They lived in the center of the village next to Armarow and while not ideal, if Arianna was truly there with them, she was relatively safe.

Defiant.

But safe.

However, that wouldn't save Arianna from the discipline lesson I'd give to her when I got to her. Regardless of who was around.

I needed to send a message, even to loyal employees of mine, that my wife wasn't theirs to help. She belonged to me, and so did they. There were rules to follow, even for them.

When we were on our way, I finished watching the footage of my wife's escape. Molly left the property a few minutes after checking on her and my wife changed into a pair of blue jeans and a grey wrap-style cardigan and then... disappeared.

I wasn't sure how she did it, but she went into the bathroom and never returned.

I scanned footage from outside of the bedroom and then from the exterior of the house and four minutes after she walked into the bathroom, she walked out the butler's entrance on the lower level and walked straight down the driveway. She wore a thick black coat that one of the maids wore when walking the grounds and kept her head down as she left through the servant's gate.

Gone.

My gut burned, trying to tell me that I was wrong about where she went. Perhaps she didn't go to Molly's, and she was well and truly gone.

But I couldn't stand to think about that. She never would have gotten so far away, or at least had her absence unnoticed if I had been in residence.

If I hadn't been hiding.

I knew people, I studied them and could read them easily. Except for Arianna. Like I told her, I couldn't read her. I didn't know what she was thinking or what she was going to do as I could with everyone else.

"Do you think Molly helped her?" Matteo asked a while into the ride, having watched the footage himself.

"I think Molly is aware that my wife is not at home in our bedroom where she is supposed to be." I replied, "But I also don't believe that Arianna would have allowed Molly to actually help her and jeopardize her safety and position at Armarow."

"Why is that?"

"My wife is many things, Matteo. Proud. Strong-willed. Stubborn as the day is long." He snorted and I kept going. "But she is kind above all else. And she cares for Molly, so I don't think she'd risk my wrath being aimed at your maid."

"She isn't my maid." He rolled his eyes, rubbing his jaw absently.

"Whatever you say."

"What do you plan to do when we get there exactly?"

I cocked my head to the side and took a deep breath. "What I do will depend on what she does when I arrive. So I plan to play her game however she sees fit to play it."

"I can't wait to see this." He smirked and leaned his head back against the seat. "I've never known Nico Capasso to take ques from someone else, much less a woman." He winked at me when I glared at him. "I like the change."

CHAPTER 11 – ARIANNA

"This all smells amazing," I said inside the Bussa home kitchen as Molly's parents and siblings worked in sync, preparing their Sunday family dinner. "Are you sure there's nothing I can do to help?" I asked for the third time since I arrived.

"Please, Ari," Molly's mother Isabella smiled brightly, "just relax and let us show off our language of love." She said sweetly.

Isabella was by far the sweetest person in the world, just like Molly said she was. When I had shown up at her home, unexpectedly and empty-handed, she hardly missed a beat as Molly pulled me inside and told them all that she had invited me. Sure, Molly didn't think that I was going to get off of the grounds of Armarow Estate undetected but was happy about my arrival nonetheless. Even if she knew eventually my absence would be noticed and my outing would be no doubt cut short.

When Nico left the estate last week, I was happy to see him go.

Or at least relieved to have some space to get my feelings and emotions in check.

I took my first deep breath in days when I realized he was gone with no expectation to return quickly.

As the days rolled on without him in the magnificent home, the loneliness crept in. Which was absurd, given that the last time I saw him he literally choked me unconscious after telling me he was going to murder my brother.

I was so fucked in the head to feel more outraged that he left without a word, waking up alone in our bed when I had been standing in the bathroom with his hand wrapped around my neck what felt like only moments before. Alas, I had missed him and our verbal sparing as the days dragged on.

I missed his touch.

I missed what I wanted our marriage to be.

I missed the chance to make it that.

Molly had reminded me yesterday that she was seeing her parents for Sunday family dinner and I knew I had maybe my only opportunity to experience the kind love of a giving family firsthand.

So I hatched a hair-brained plan, with Molly, thanks to her knowledge of the secretive tunnel system in the walls of Armarow and my ability to blend in as a nobody.

Molly's father, Davide, had been wearier of my sudden appearance. Molly told me he was the head gardener at Armarow and he no doubt knew the trouble I was bringing to his doorstep. Though he chose to remain quiet about it, placing a smile on his kind face and allowing me to fold in with his wife and four daughters.

"Tell me, Ari," Isabella asked as she stirred a pot of sauce on the stovetop in their simple yet efficient kitchen. "How have you found your time at Armarow so far?"

"It's been-," I bit my bottom lip as Molly looked up from her task of tossing a salad. "Different." I tried to find a gentle way of expressing my feelings towards the estate that both of Molly's parents fondly worked at most of their lives. "My home in West Shores was inside of the city, so I didn't grow up with the beautiful scenery that surrounds your town."

"It is quite beautiful this time of year, isn't it?" Isabella winked.

"I enjoy the serenity that it offers. The noise of the city could be deafening if you let it."

"The shopping is much better though," Molly smirked and added toppings to the salad.

I chuckled and nodded, "How far is the nearest city from here?"

"About two hours." Davide answered, "If you go, make sure you visit the Café Rosa in the city square." He groaned and kissed his fingertips in a traditional Italian way and I giggled, "It's the best."

"It's where we met," Isabella added, smiling at her husband affectionately.

"Not this story again Mama." Molly's younger sister Rosa groaned and rolled her eyes.

"Is that where you got your name?" I questioned.

"I think I was conceived there." She grimaced and shuddered as I hid a laugh at her expense behind my hand.

"Oh, hush." Isabella swatted at her daughter playfully, "You're embarrassing our guest."

"She's fine, honestly. I enjoy the banter. It's refreshing to see from a family."

Davide nodded from his seat at the island with his cup of coffee. "Molly tells us your family dynamic is-" He paused, "strained."

I chuckled and raised my brows at him, "Strained is putting it gently. My parent's marriage was one of business. There was no love between them, and I don't think any ever grew between them over the years either. Therefore there was no love for them to share with us growing up."

"That's a shame." Isabella looked sad as she wiped her hands on the dishcloth.

"At least I'm free of it now." I tried to sound reassuring, "It's my siblings I feel poorly for, they're still there inside of a loveless home with one less person for my parents to disperse their anger onto."

"Yeah, but you married Nicolas Capasso," Rosa said like it was as clear as day. "You could have done far worse."

"Rosa." Molly snapped. It was the first time I'd seen any real outwardly display of anger from her before and I raised my brow at her quizzically. "She doesn't know what goes on between a husband and wife, and she shouldn't comment on it."

"Thank you," I nodded but turned to her younger sister who reminded me so much of my sister Anita. "You're right, there were far worse men my father entertained when taking bids for my hand in marriage," I said calmly and her eyes widened in shock. "My life at Armarow is much better than the one I had before with my parents."

"But is there love?" Isabella asked quietly with a knowing look.

"Mama." Molly hissed. "Not appropriate."

"It's fine." I grinned at her and took a deep breath before answering her mother. "There could be, maybe someday," I said truthfully. "I think Nico is a complex man who carries many burdens on his shoulders as the Don. And being a husband is unchartered territory for him, but I do think he wants to be a good one, even if he tries to hide it."

She smiled and nodded, "I was there the day he was born," She shook her head in memory, "It was the first birth I ever attended."

"You worked at Armarow?" I asked in surprise; Molly hadn't told me that.

"I was his nanny. His and his brothers. Until I got pregnant with Molly and decided to raise my own babies instead of the Capasso babies. He was such a loving child when he was small. He was affectionate and kind and absolutely the smartest kid I've ever met."

"Gee, thanks." Molly rolled her eyes with a smirk.

Isabella patted her shoulder as she passed her daughter on her way to me, "I will always hold a special spot in my heart for Nico." She smiled and put her hand on my arm squeezing it lightly, "Deep down I know, he's a good man, Ari. I also know sometimes he prefers to let everyone think he's some scary monster, but deep down," she smiled, "he's good."

"I believe you." I admitted, "I saw small moments of that man before he left for the city."

"Well," she patted my arm and nodded like the matter was settled, "I hope he returns to Armarow soon so you both can continue to get to know each other and build something more than what your parents had." She looked over her shoulder at her husband, "Something like what Davide and I have."

"I honestly would like nothing more. Like it or not, this is my life now. And I'd like to make the most of it instead of spending my time stuck in denial and self-pity."

"Good girl." Isabella smirked, "You're smart too, a match made perfectly for Nico. Though if I had to guess, one that will challenge him and make him change who he is as a man too."

"One could hope." I winked at her, and she tipped her head back and laughed.

"God help him." Davide shook his head and smiled into his coffee cup.

"You all have outdone yourselves," I said in awe an hour later as the giant feast the Bussa family had prepared was set out on the large table, served family style. "Is it always this lavish?" I whispered to Molly who sat next to me.

She smirked, "Well the food is usually this nice, but I won't lie and tell you that we eat on this nice china every week. That's all for you."

"This is more than I could have imagined, and I'm honored to be included."

"Good, now eat," Isabella instructed, passing a platter to me. "Once Davide gets ahold of a dish, there's no guarantee that you'll get any."

Davide had walked outside on a phone call a few minutes before we sat down, and I would be lying if I said I hadn't watched the front door the entire time he was gone, feeling an impending doom settling over my bones the longer he was missing.

I took the offered platters, scooping at least a small amount of every dish onto my plate, eager to try it all when the door opened and Davide walked back into the happy home.

And the doom I'd been feeling settled onto me fully when my brooding husband walked in behind him, instantly locking his piercing green eyes onto me across the room. He wore a pair of dark blue jeans that hugged his muscular thighs and a light grey sweater that matched the streaks of grey that started to color the hair around his temple.

He was a masterpiece, and even on his worst days, I was unable to deny how breathtaking he was to look at.

"Nico!" Isabella cheered excitedly, standing from her seat and hurrying towards him. "What a pleasant surprise!"

"Isabella," He said warmly, leaning down to kiss her cheeks without ever taking his eyes off mine. "I'm sorry to interrupt your meal."

The food I'd managed to taste turned to sawdust in my mouth as my peaceful outing came to a screeching halt.

"Nonsense!" Isabella patted his arm, turning them both towards the table, "Join us? We have plenty."

"I couldn't infringe on your family time." He answered politely, finally looking away from me as I took a sip of wine to push the clump of food down my throat.

I expected his anger when I imagined how it would play out if he found me after my escape.

What I wasn't expecting, was politeness to his former nanny. He was almost affectionate to the woman, something I hadn't seen from him aimed at anyone.

Anyone but me anyway. I didn't have any false expectations that his anger wouldn't surface the moment we were alone though.

"Please," She said emphatically, "We're so enjoying our time with Ari. I'm assuming that's why you're here?" She questioned, "She managed to slip the estate and you're here to bring her back aren't you?"

My eyes rounded and I looked at Molly curiously, but she whispered, "She knows everything. I've never gotten away with a single thing in my life."

I watched in horror as Davide pulled a chair up to the table and ushered Molly down the side of the table to it, opening up the chair next to me. "Please join us."

Nico bowed his head and slid his jacket off his wide shoulders. "I will admit it all smells mouthwatering." As he said the last word he looked up and stared right at me, causing my body to overheat under his intense gaze. He walked around the table and pulled out the chair that Molly had vacated. Before he sat down, he ran his fingertips along my jaw and pushed my hair over my shoulder, exposing my face and neck. I tipped my head back to look up at him in confusion, finding his mesmerizing eyes staring directly into mine. "Wife." He said gently as he leaned down and kissed me.

The touch of his lips against mine was electric and I found myself disappointed when he pulled back all too quickly, taking his seat next to me.

He licked his lips like he was savoring the taste of me on them, and I took a shuddering breath to calm my body's visceral reaction to it. "Hi," I whispered back as the Bussa family resumed passing food around, chatting amongst themselves while we were lost to ourselves.

"You look breathtaking." He still had his hand on the back of my neck and he stroked his fingers along the sensitive skin there a few times before withdrawing them and placing his napkin in his lap.

The man had managed to soak my panties with a simple peck and only the touch of his fingertips on my neck yet was sitting there being polite like he was completely unaffected by me.

"Ari tells us that you've been out of town," Isabella chatted. "Are you back for a while, or will your business take you back to the city?"

"I left the city early, unexpectedly," He looked over at me and I shrunk in my seat under the scrutiny of it, "But I was overdue to return home anyway. So I'll probably stay for a while if I can manage."

"Good to hear." His old nanny beamed at him, "New marriages take nurturing and care to grow. You can't do that from the city with sweet Ari here alone."

"Sweet Ari," He raised an eyebrow, once again glancing at me, "Will be lonely no longer." He spoke about me like I wasn't there and it just fueled the errant child feeling I was experiencing from the guilt of bringing drama to the Bussa doorstep.

Thankfully, my husband remained on his best behavior and didn't embarrass me even further.

"Davide tells me that the expansion of the north lawns will be the biggest renovation Armarow has seen." The matriarch changed topics and I picked up my fork, once again trying to enjoy the way the food tasted.

Nicholas answered her, telling her of plans I didn't know a thing about and I silently ate my meal. I was beginning to relax and allowed the conversation to draw me back in, chatting easily with the family when my husband switched his fork into his left hand and then reached over and put his warm palm on my thigh. I forced the bite of food down and licked my lips, risking a glance at him from under my eyelashes, and found him completely ignoring my reaction to his touch.

He chatted on, charming the entire Bussa family, Molly included, with his attentive conversation and easy-going nature.

Meanwhile, I felt perspiration collecting on the back of my neck, slowly running down my spine as he slid his hand further between my thighs, forcing me to uncross my legs so he could fit.

My face bloomed bright red from the effect he was having on my body and I took a calming breath to relax my tense body.

"Ari," Isabella asked, drawing my attention from where I sat staring down at my fork unmoving. "Are you okay?"

"Hmm." I nodded, grasping my wine glass with a shaking hand and taking a sip, "I'm quite well, thank you. Just lost in thought."

"You look flushed," Her brows pinched in the center. "Is it the wine? The vintage is quite heavy."

"That's probably it," Nico answered for me, taking the glass from my hand before setting it down in front of his plate. "Drink some water, Little One." He switched the red wine for my glass of water, and I fought the urge to glare at him.

I brought the glass to my lips and let the cold refreshing liquid slide over my tongue as everyone watched me questioningly. My darling husband, however, took their distraction to slide his hand even higher, pressing the knuckle of his pinky firmly against my hot center and rubbing a fast circle around it.

I coughed and choked on the water, barely covering my mouth to stem the flow of water before I made a true fool of myself.

"I'm sorry." I gasped, covering my face with my hand as my blush built even more. "I don't know what's come over me."

"Perhaps we should get home," Nico said, pulling my napkin from his lap and scooting his chair back. "I apologize." He said to the hosts.

"No worries," Isabella and Davide both stood, reassuring us as they watched on in concern.

I grimaced at Molly who nodded knowingly and I ran from the house, positively mortified.

I angrily walked down the road away from the house and glared at where my guards Saul and Dio leaned against the hood of a sleek SUV parked next to Nico's with his second Matteo watching me closely from the front seat. "Just couldn't give me a few hours, could you?" I yelled at them, not expecting a reply, which of course they didn't give me.

"Where are you going?" Nico caught up behind me and pulled my arm back, forcing me to face him. "The cars are back there."

"What is wrong with you!" I snapped, shoving his chest angrily but he simply smirked down at me.

"I missed you too, Wife."

"Ugh!" I groaned loudly and turned away from him before I gave in to the urge to strike him in the middle of the dark street.

It was late, and the street was empty, but it was still *his* street. This was his town and I wasn't dumb enough to poke the monster in him in front of his people.

I learned that lesson hard enough as a kid with my father.

I heard him call back to my guards, and moments later both SUVs drove past me towards Armarow.

I could see the glow of the elaborate estate through the trees but I knew from my walk to the Village, it wasn't as close as it looked. "Just leave me alone." I huffed, swinging my arms and walking on the uneven brick walkway.

"Why?" He asked, walking a few feet behind me. "You wanted me here tonight. So why pretend like you didn't?"

"I didn't want you here!" I turned on him and poked my finger into his chest.

"Liar." He grabbed my hand and pinned it behind my back so fast I didn't have time to prepare for him to be in my personal space. "You defiantly left Armarow and snuck off so I'd come home and bring you back." His nostrils flared as I fought his hold on me, pushing against him with my free hand. "You're a brat. You were pissed because I wasn't giving you the attention you crave, so you acted out."

We were under the last streetlamp before the road turned nearly pitch black and I could barely make out the details of his face thanks to the shadows. It didn't matter though, I had them memorized. "Fuck off." I seethed, "Just go back to doing God knows what with God knows who in your dirty little city and leave me alone!"

His eyebrow rose and a smirk pulled his lip back. "Is that what has you riled? Does the idea of me fucking my mistress in my penthouse bother you, Little One?"

"Ugh!" I yelled, bucking against him and twisting until he let go of my arm a millisecond before it broke. Shock darkened his face at my recklessness. "I don't care what you do as long as you leave me alone!"

I turned and started to walk away again but he grabbed a handful of my hair and pulled me around, backing me up until my back pressed against a tree just out of the lamppost light. "Liar." He breathed against my lips, pressing his body against mine and the fight I had in me dissipated as I sagged against him. His hold on my hair loosened but he didn't let go, "I didn't come here to fight with you."

"You just came to boss me around then, is that it?" I questioned, looking at his chin and letting my eyes adjust to the darkness until I could make out the features of his perfect face at such a close distance.

"I came-" He paused, "Because you scared me."

I swallowed and looked up further until I met his eyes, "What do you mean?"

"When I got the call that you were gone," He slid his thigh between mine and lifted me by it until my toes hardly touched the ground. The rough bark of the tree dug into my back, and I gripped the soft fabric of his sweater in my fingers. "I was scared that you were *really* gone."

I sighed and watched his eyes dip to the cleavage showing above the neckline of my sweater. "Would that even bother you? If I disappeared?"

"Yes." He answered instantly.

"Why?" I prodded. "Because I'm your property?"

"No, Little One." He sighed, leaning down until his lips were barely touching mine, "Because I'm obsessed with you." He licked my lips and I melted further. "Even if you hate me."

"I don't want to hate you," I whispered, admitting something I didn't even realize myself until I uttered the words.

He smiled and I could feel it, "We don't exactly make it easy on each other, do we?"

I shook my head.

He removed his thigh from between mine, letting my feet fall flat on the ground, and pulled me off the tree. "A truce then?" He slid his fingers free of my hair and then gently smoothed it out. "Because I don't want to hate you anymore either, Arianna."

"But you do."

He didn't answer right away and backed up, letting go of me completely until he stood under the light again, "I don't know." He ran his palm over his jaw, "I don't think so though."

"I think that's the nicest thing you've ever said to me." I offered with a small smile, and he gave me one back, drawing me out of the darkness.

"Wrong." He grunted, turning back toward Armarow and nodding for me to walk with him. "Telling you that you have a very pretty pussy was probably the nicest."

"Good lord." I groaned, cringing. He tipped his head back and laughed into the moonlight. For a second I just watched him as we walked down the path towards his house. "You should do that more often," I said, as he glared at me, "Makes you look less like a wildebeest."

"A wildebeest?" His eyes rounded and he scoffed, shaking his head and sliding his hand against the small of my back as I stumbled on the uneven ground in the dark. I let myself lean into his side as he steered me and told myself the butterflies swimming in my stomach were from the wine, he blamed my earlier outburst on when we both knew I was stone-cold sober.

"Okay, maybe more of an ox."

"Watch it, Wife." He swatted my ass and pulled me closer when I gasped and jumped. "Or I'll give you a real spanking."

CHAPTER 12 – NICO

Ari walked into the house ahead of me and I watched her supple hips sway with each step. I couldn't remember the last time I walked home from the village but having the alone time with her in the darkness with only nature around us had cleared my head.

And I think it cleared hers too.

She had been fighting mad at me when we left Davide and Isabella's home for embarrassing her by playing with her body right in front of them. To be honest, I simply couldn't keep my hands away from her, and that's why I had done it.

When I walked in, I expected outrage from her. Instead, what I got was silent wonder from her beautiful brown eyes as she stared at me across the room.

Wonder and fear.

Considering the last time I'd seen her I'd choked her unconscious, that was warranted.

She was waiting for me to cause a scene, maybe even drag her from the house kicking and screaming. I wasn't an animal though.

Well, all of the time.

Instead I greeted long-time friends of mine and tried to exude the picture of perfection and act like a doting husband which only served to shock my young wife even more.

Something I was finding I quite enjoyed doing.

Now we were home and I felt her steeling herself to me more and more with each step inside of our home.

Matteo and Dio waited for me in the foyer when we walked in, but I waved them off before either of them could open their mouths. "Whatever it is, figure it out and handle it. Don't bother me for the rest of the night."

Matteo smirked and winked at Arianna as she whipped her head around to look at me, "Whatever you say, Capa." Then he nudged the silent Dio from the room towards the wing my men spent most of their time in.

"What are you doing?" Ari asked, eyeing me as I walked toward the stairs.

"Going to bed." I bumped her along ahead of me, "Same as you."

She opened her mouth to say something but then snapped it shut and turned away, hurrying up the stairs as I smirked after her.

When we got to our room she eyed me once again as I walked toward the closet, pulling my sweater off over my head.

I could feel her eyes on me as I stood inside, toeing off my shoes and then undoing my belt and jeans.

Good girl.

I hadn't spent a single night in this room with her since marrying her. Not once had I fallen asleep next to her even though we had been married for weeks now.

I intended to change that tonight.

When I stood in my black boxer briefs I walked back out, catching her snapping her jaw shut before scurrying away into the privacy of the bathroom. She shut the door behind her, but I didn't care.

I followed after her, opening the door and catching her standing at the vanity staring at herself in the mirror. "Do you mind?" She asked in shock.

"Not one bit." I walked over to the toilet and lifted the seat, took my dick out, and started to piss.

She scoffed and I looked over at her, finding her eyes zeroed in on my dick as I urinated. "Do you have a pissing fetish, Wife?" I challenged and she clenched her jaw once again and then turned the water on, facing the faucet and actively trying to ignore me. I chuckled at her, shaking myself dry before flushing and walking over to her. "Tell me, why the sudden silence?"

"I'm utterly speechless," She said before dropping her face down and splashing water onto it, scrubbing herself free of the light makeup she wore to dinner.

When she came back up, I took the towel she blindly felt for and held it out of her reach until she cracked one eye open and glared at me until I handed it to her. "Why are you speechless?"

"Does it bother you that I'm not yelling my feelings out to you?" she countered from behind the towel and then stood up straight, revealing her smooth face.

"Yes, it does. I've already told you I can't read you. You usually at least have the decency to scream at me, so I know what you're thinking," I admitted honestly and she smirked.

"I do not scream at you."

I scoffed and grabbed my toothbrush and squeezed toothpaste onto it. When it was centimeters from my mouth I realized she had frozen stiff next to me, watching me. I slowly pulled it away, eyeing it, "What did you do to my toothbrush?"

Her lips twitched and then she grabbed her own and put paste on it and started brushing her teeth. "Scrubbed the toilet with it." She shrugged her shoulders, and I grunted in revulsion, making her giggle.

I tossed it in the garbage as she rinsed her mouth and put hers back in the drawer. I grabbed hers and reapplied paste to it and started brushing my teeth while smirking at her, besting her at her own game. Glaring at me before rolling her eyes, she walked out to the bedroom, muttering under her breath what sounded a lot like 'Neanderthal'.

I finished and followed her back out into the bedroom, giving chase to the siren on the shore even though I knew she'd draw blood if I got too close to her. She stood in the closet with her back to me, unclasping her bra and taking it off while shyly looking over her shoulder before sliding a shirt of mine over her slender body.

Troublemaker.

"Have you been sleeping in my shirts while I've been away?" I teased her as she undid her jeans and shimmied out of them. The shirt was so long on her I didn't see anything good before she kicked off the jeans and tossed them into the hamper. "Pining away for me, were you?"

I pulled the blankets back on the bed and climbed in, resting my back against the headboard so I could watch her.

"You wish I was, big guy," She challenged bravely, but I could see the trepidation in her eyes as she neared the bed. "Where am I supposed to sleep?"

I raised an eyebrow at her before pulling back the covers on the other side, "Right here."

"We haven't-" She stopped, biting her lip.

"I know." I took pity on her and patted the mattress next to me. "Truce, remember?"

She squinted her eyes and played with the hem of the shirt before sighing and walking to her side, climbing up into the bed. "You strangled me the last time we shared space for any length of time." Her voice wasn't angry, and if I didn't know better, there was almost a hint of hurt to it.

"I rendered you unconscious in the middle of your manic rage."

"I wasn't raging." She stared down at her fingers on the hem of the blankets. "I was actually pretty calm by that point."

I sighed and leaned back into the pillows more, feeling the fatigue of burning the candles at both ends for the last few weeks catching up. "Would it make you feel better if I told you it wasn't one of my prouder moments?"

She looked up at me with her big brown eyes and chewed on her bottom lip like she was contemplating it. "Maybe."

Silence fell over us as we waded into uncharted territory. I didn't know the first thing about tending to a woman's feelings, worse yet, a young woman who had never been in a relationship before.

And I doubted she knew how to deal with a man that was so used to getting what he wanted whenever he wanted it, that he didn't even know how to ask anymore.

Neither of us really had a clue what we were supposed to do.

"Would you like an apology for it?" I questioned.

"Only if you were actually sorry for it." She countered, turning her body to face me.

"I'm not," I replied and then took a deep breath before continuing. "I'm not sorry for it because I don't remember a time in my life that I've ever dealt with a woman in any way other than how I did at that moment. I don't know any difference. But I do acknowledge that I shouldn't have acted that way towards *you*."

She watched me like she was trying to decide if I was telling the truth or not before rolling her eyes and twisting back around in the bed to face forward, "Well, I'll tell you this." She smoothed out the blankets on her lap with prim grace, "If you ever do that to me again, I'll stab you in your sleep."

I smirked at her and she looked out of the corner of her eye at me and then glared at my amusement. "I think I'd like to see you try, Little One."

"Hmm." She leaned over the side of the bed to the end table and clicked off her lamp. With my lamp still on I caught a glimpse of her naked bottom as the hem of the shirt rose and I licked my lips. She had no idea, but she was baiting a very needy bear. "Good night."

"No kiss goodnight?" I asked as she lay on her side facing away from me, covering herself up with the blankets.

"Nope," she popped the 'p' on the end, and I grinned at her back.

I turned my lamp off and then kicked my boxers off and tossed them onto the floor before turning to face her in the darkness. I slid up against her back and lifted the shirt that she'd pulled down until my bare cock nestled right against her ass and pulled her tight to my chest.

"Nico!" She gasped.

"Shh," I crooned, sliding my arm under her pillow, essentially molding us together from head to toe, "If you won't kiss me goodnight, the least you can do is let me cuddle."

She scoffed and then huffed before finally adjusting the blankets again and relaxing into my embrace. "Big bad Nicolas Capasso likes to spoon. Who would have guessed it?"

"Wrong." I took a deep breath, inhaling the perfect sweet fragrance from her hair, and clenched my muscles to make my cock twitch between us. "I've never slept next to a woman before in my life, let alone bothered to cuddle. Turns out, I don't hate it so far."

She was silent for a long time and I started to think she fell asleep until she whispered, "Goodnight, Nico."

"Goodnight, Little One." I kissed the back of her head and pulled her even tighter.

It took her a long time to fall asleep, but when she did, her body relaxed even further, melting into my arms as she made sweet soothing noises as she dreamed.

I told her the truth about never sleeping in the same bed as a woman before, as well as how I wasn't hating it yet either. To be honest, I quite enjoyed the way she felt in my arms, tucked in tight against me and before long I felt my slumber starting to pull me under.

I felt like I was on a boat, drifting in and out on the waves, grasping for reality yet beckoning for dreamland to take me back under. I couldn't remember the last time I woke up in the in-between place of consciousness because usually, I didn't sleep long or hard enough to ever get there.

Something had woken me up.

"Mmh," a sweet angelic voice whispered, and I opened my eyes to get my bearings as it all came back to me.

Arianna.

My wife.

I laid on my back and my wife was sprawled out half on top of me with her head on my chest and her legs wrapped around one of mine.

She was grinding against my thigh. The clock on the bedside table read two AM and the room was dark except for the glow of the numbers, but it was enough light for me to look down and see her eyes were closed as her hips moved up and down.

Wetness coated my thigh underneath her and I smiled to myself in the darkness as I realized what was happening.

My wife was having a wet dream and was using me to pleasure herself.

I looked up at the ceiling as the war began carrying on inside my head and my body. I could let her be, allowing her to rub her wet little pussy against my leg until she climaxed and never tell her I knew the truth of what she did in her sleep. Or I could assist her in her chase of pleasure until we were both a little less frustrated.

It had been a week since I had her last, and no amount of jacking off had managed to soothe the ache inside of my balls that wanted to fill her up again. And I had fucking tried, over and over again.

My cock was hard, laying against my stomach and leaking pre-cum from the way she rocked against it, and I was struggling to resist sinking into her.

"Nico," she moaned, turning her face and pressing her lips against my chest as she slid onto my body more, essentially riding my thigh like a horse. Judging by the way her eyes stayed closed, she was still asleep. Or at least somewhere in between like I had been.

"What do you want, Wife?" I whispered, bending my knee on the leg that she was straddling and lifting it into her dainty body, drawing a long moan from her lips.

"Please," she begged sweetly in her dreams and any restraint I had, was gone.

I rolled us both until she was on her back, and then I slid the length of my cock up through her folds. Her knees fell wide, begging me to give her what she wanted as her head tossed back and forth.

"Such a good girl," I praised her, pushing the shirt she wore up to expose her large breasts. How good they would look feeding my child someday soon, I imagined as I leaned down and sucked one of her nipples into my mouth.

Her nails dug into my neck as she arched her back, pushing her breast into my mouth more. "Please," She repeated, lifting her hips seeking the friction I gave her before.

I leaned down and bit her earlobe, eliciting a gasp from her as her nails dug in deeper, "Wake up, Little One, you don't get to beg for my cock and claim you weren't in your right mind later."

When I pulled back, her eyes were open, and she was blinking rapidly in confusion. I dropped my hips back down, sliding my cock through her wetness again. "What are you doing?" she groaned.

"There you are, you woke me up humping my leg like a needy little sex kitten." I rocked through her again, "Begging me to fuck you and give you what you needed." Her mouth opened and closed before she bit down on her bottom lip, no doubt to silence the moan I was trying to draw out of her.

"I was asleep!" she argued like it could weaken her embarrassment.

I took her hand from my neck and slid it between our bodies, "Feel how wet you are, Little One," I pushed her fingers against her clit and rubbed a circle over it before dropping my fingers to her entrance and pushing two inside of her.

"Fuck!" She gasped, arching away from the invasion, "Stop, Nico."

"No," I countered her half-hearted plea, "You woke me up with this wet pussy, making my cock pulse and leak for you. You're going to take everything I give you in return."

Her eyes shifted all around as she tried to come up with an argument, I could tell. So I pushed her over the edge to ensure she wouldn't tell me no. I lifted our fingers from her dripping pussy and brought them to my mouth, sucking both of hers and mine into my mouth and groaning. "So sweet, baby."

"God," she moaned and one leg wrapped around my hips, drawing me down against her again, "You're driving me crazy."

I chuckled and lined the tip of my cock up with her entrance as she stilled and held her breath under me. "You're one to talk, Ari." I pushed forward and gave her three inches before pulling back out and doing it again, adding another to the end. "I've been crazy since the first moment I saw you."

"No, you're not," she groaned, giving into me and wrapping her other leg around my waist. "You're the most unaffected person in the world. Nothing seems to draw your attention. I could run through this house with my hair on fire screaming bloody murder and you wouldn't bat an eye at me." There was anger in her voice, and I smirked as I pushed deep again, giving her more, loving the way her eyelids fluttered closed.

"Do you want me to tell you I can't think of anything else when I'm not with you, dear Wife?" I asked and pushed into her body, past the resistance of her tight body until my balls hit her ass. "That, unless I'm just like this, buried deep inside of you, touching you from head to toe, that I can't breathe?" I rolled my hips, and she arched her back, pressing her clit against me harder. I leaned down and bit her ear and then sucked on it until she moaned and hugged me to her chest, "What would you rather have, Little One? My hate, or my obsession?"

"Obsession," she cried out and panted, "I want you as crazy for me as I am for you. Fuck, I'm coming."

"Good girl," I slammed into her and rolled my hips, "That's my good girl, coming on my cock."

"Yes," she cried, digging her nails into my back, "Fuck me, Nico, please."

I smirked and lifted her legs over my shoulders, loving the way her eyes widened in fear before they fell closed in pleasure as I bottomed out inside of her tight little body again, "As you wish dear. I aim to please."

"Jackass," she hissed, and then I fucked her so good, only incoherent moans and pleas fell from her lips for hours.

CHAPTER 13 – ARIANNA

I didn't understand my husband.

As I walked through his large home I tried to calm the erratic heartbeat in my chest, knowing that I could run into him any moment.

It was weird having him back in residence even though I'd never admit I liked having him close again.

After the way he spent the entire night wrapped around me and holding me— God. I needed to get a grip, or he'd smell my arousal the second we inadvertently ran into each other.

He was primal like that, using his animalistic tendencies to give me shivers.

So instead of allowing the thought of him to arouse me, I followed the scent of savory food cooking and went into the kitchen, finding Mariella, Nico's housekeeper, chatting with Chef Alec as he prepared lunch.

"Mrs. Capasso," they both said, bowing their heads as I walked in, "Are you ready for lunch?" Chef Alec asked with a bright smile.

"I am," I smiled back, eyeing the spread on the stove, "I'm starving actually." I rubbed my stomach, realizing just how famished I was. Breakfast didn't hold me over today and I was ready to taste whatever delicious concoction that Alec had created.

"Where would you like to sit today?" Mariella asked. When I first arrived, she set a place for me at the table for my meals, but after the third or fourth time dining alone, I picked up my plate and carried it to the kitchen island preferring their company over the silence of the dining room.

"Here is fine, if you don't mind having me."

"Of course not," she smiled, grabbing a table setting and placing it for me. "What would you like to drink today?"

"Prosecco would be great please." I took my seat as she lifted my glass to go fill it for me.

"No wine," a deep voice called from the entrance of the kitchen. We all turned and found Nico walking in. My eyes assessed him, starting at the dark rumpled hair on his head that looked intentional and haphazard all at the same time, and down to his light blue button-up that was undone at the throat and rolled up over his forearms showing off his tattoos. Finally, I let my eyes travel down to his navy-blue slacks that hugged his legs perfectly before his words sunk into my brain muddled with arousal.

"What did you say?" I asked, scrunching up my face as his words echoed through my head.

He looked away from me and straight at Mariella and Alec, "No alcohol for my wife until I tell you differently." He walked to my side like he hadn't just spoken about me to his staff like I wasn't even in the room and laid a gentle kiss on my temple, sliding his warm hand over my back.

His touches were gentle and it confused the anger trying to build inside of my gut from being treated like a child.

I turned to look at where he stood at my side, "I'm old enough to drink. Or have you started going senile already?"

He smirked down at me and Mariella backed out of the room as he took a seat next to me, leaving the poor chef chained to his stove with our embarrassing exchange going on ten feet away.

"I know you're old enough to drink, Ari," he replied, not rising to my level of snark. Which just flamed that fire in my stomach. "But you aren't drinking anymore. Not right now anyway."

"Why?" I snapped, glaring at him.

He turned and parted his legs around me, one along my back and the other against my knees, caging me in as he leaned forward until his face was right by mine. "Are you trying to break our truce already, Little One?" Leaning forward to lay a kiss on my parted lips. "I'll admit, I'm kind of enjoying the perks of the truce and I'm not overly ready to have you angry with me again."

"Then don't try to tell me what to do like a child."

"I'm not treating you like a child, Arianna; I'm trying to think of our unborn child," he looked down at my stomach and then raised his eyebrow at me.

My mouth opened and closed like a fish out of water as I processed his words.

Then I started doing math in my head and realized with his sudden return to Armarow, I'd forgotten I was due for my period.

Today.

Yet I had no sign of it coming like I usually did.

"You're panicking," he said, sliding his hand down my back, "Tell me why."

"You-" I shut my mouth and swallowed, "I'm not-" Shaking my head I looked away from him, unable to finish the statement, because I didn't know anything for a fact.

"You don't have your period. Yet according to Dr. Travis' report, you're due."

"How do you know?" I snapped, letting my fear overwhelm me.

Along with the urge to smack the gentle and amused look off his face.

"Because when I slid my cock out of your body," he lifted his wrist and looked at his watch, "no more than six hours ago, there was no evidence of it coating me."

I blushed, sneaking a glance at Alec and then glaring at my husband. "Stop it," I whispered.

"I will not," Nicolas sat up straight, pulling away from my body, "I'm in my home, and my staff is paid well to ignore my conversations or at least be professional enough to keep their opinions to themselves about them."

"Nico," I sighed, looking at him, "I'm not pregnant."

"How do you know?"

"I don't feel pregnant," I answered honestly, "Wouldn't I feel... *different*?"

"I don't know," he said with an unlike-him shrug, "I've never been pregnant before."

I rolled my eyes at his attempt at a joke and picked up the glass of water that his housekeeper had laid down with my place setting.

He turned his attention to the plate and then back to me, "Why are you sitting here for lunch?"

"Where else should I sit?"

"A table." His eyebrows pinched over his green eyes like it was a dumb question. "One of the six available inside of this house."

"All alone, with no one but the obnoxious wallpaper to keep me company?" I scoffed, "No thank you. I've spent enough of my life alone." I nodded to the kitchen around us, "I quite enjoy Alec and Mariella's conversation. They're teaching me things."

He scowled but leaned back, "Mariella," He yelled, "A plate for me as well please." Moments later the woman walked out of the butler's pantry with another place setting. "What kind of things are you learning?" He asked me as she arranged his utensils and then backed away.

"Household things," I said and then shook my head, "Why are you sitting with me?"

He scoffed, lifting his glass of water and taking a sip. My eyes watched the strong muscles in his neck work the liquid down and I caught the edge of a red scratch on the back of his neck, causing goosebumps to break out over my body.

I did that.

While he did so many delicious things to my body all night long.

Fuck, Ari, get your head together. I chastised myself silently.

"Am I supposed to sit at the table alone with only the wallpaper that my sweet, dead mother painstakingly picked out and loved, to keep me company?" He raised an eyebrow at me and looked out the corner of his eye as I shrunk in my seat at my blunder. "I'll take your company today instead," he finished, letting me off the hook.

"Hmm," I hummed but was saved from needing to reply as Alec brought over our plates with our lunch on them. "Alec," I groaned, leaning forward to take a sniff, "You're spoiling me."

On each of our plates were the most beautifully crafted slices of pizza with fresh basil and mozzarella chunks melted to perfection, paired with a beautiful green salad filled with fresh vegetables and vibrant fruits.

"My pleasure, Ma'am," Alec said, bowing his head once as he wiped his hands on his apron. "I spritzed the pizza with lemon since you so enjoyed it last time. Be sure to let me know how you find it today."

"Oh, I will." I swallowed, eager to dive in. My mouth watered as I eyed the gooey cheese. "Thank you so much."

"Enjoy," he replied and backed out of the kitchen to leave us in privacy.

I ate in the kitchen to enjoy their company, but with Nicolas' presence at my side, both Alec and Mariella had abandoned me.

Traitors.

I covered my lap with my napkin and realized that Nicolas was silent at my side, so I looked over at him.

Finding him scowling down at me.

"What now?" I groaned. "That face alone is trying to ruin this meal for me and I'm going to get angry if you succeed."

"Are you fond of my chef?" he asked firmly, "You're both overly comfortable with each other."

"Oh, knock it off." I rolled my eyes dismissively and reached to pick up my pizza, realizing my mistake too late.

Suddenly, I was pulled off my stool and sat directly on the counter in front of Nicolas who narrowly moved his plate and utensils before I swallowed them with my ass. "Nico!" I gasped in shock, "What is wrong with you?"

"Are you fucking my chef?" he snapped, staring directly into my eyes, thanks to his height.

"Do you honestly think I'm fucking your chef?" I snapped back, "Simply because he is nice to me? You've never been nice to me, yet I still fuck you. Clearly niceties aren't what gets me off."

He stood up and pushed my legs apart, stepping between them as I leaned backward to keep space between us as fear and excitement pulsed through my spine.

No, niceties weren't what got me motivated at all.

"Nobody touches what's mine," he snarled, resting his hands on the marble countertop underneath my ass. "I thought I made that explicitly clear when I took your virginity."

"I'm not a whore, Nico," I argued back, "I'm not like you."

He raised his eyebrows and his upper lip pulled up in a sinister smirk. "Are you calling me a whore, Wife?"

"I think the tabloids did that for me recently." I hissed and instantly regretted it.

Last week, when he was gallivanting around the city, paparazzi photographed him in the lobby of his penthouse with a woman. She was dressed to the nines and dripping with sex appeal, as she stared up into his eyes like he was the sexiest man on earth.

Which he very well may be.

The story said:

Notorious businessman Nicolas Capasso was seen entertaining the wife of one of his rivals in the lobby of his building. Sources close to the businessman confirmed the woman had spent the evening in the penthouse suite multiple times recently.

I'd been so enraged when I read the newspaper that had been laid out on the floor outside of my bedroom door one morning, I tore it to shreds and then flushed it down the toilet.

Comic section and all.

Hours later when Molly had finally gotten out of me what was wrong, she smiled to herself and pulled her phone out of her pocket.

"I could get into really big trouble for this," She told me as she pulled up a message from a contact listed simply as 'T-r-o-u-b-l-e'.

If it gets out of hand, assure your mistress that the wolf is simply trying to rattle her cage. Nothing else.

"I didn't understand what on earth he was talking about at first, but I think I get it better now," She said, confirming my intuition that the story was fabricated.

The woman in the newspaper looked dressed to the nines, not like she was doing the walk of shame, and something else made me think she wasn't Nico's type at all.

When I asked Molly who her source was, her cheeks reddened, and she chewed on her lip. "No one I have any business talking to." Had been her reply, so I dropped it after thanking her for the information.

Nicolas had tried to set me up, simply to piss me off and make me jealous.

It had worked until logic made its way through the haze of anger because I knew better.

But that didn't mean I wasn't going to throw it in his face when he tried to bait me into it now.

He smirked like he won a prize, which pissed me off. I hated when men tried to manipulate me into giving them what they wanted.

It was something my father had done for decades.

Instead, I leaned forward and slid my hand over the bulge in his pants that I knew our argument would have given him, and squeezed, stroking him as I brought my lips to the rim of his ear.

"Except we both know my pussy is the best you've ever had and no one, especially not some used-up boring woman like her will ever hold your attention again. That's why you came running the second I wanted you to; you just couldn't get enough. You needed more of *me*. You craved *me*." I pushed him backward, using the shock I no doubt left him in to aid me. I slid off the counter and onto my own stool, crossing my legs seductively and replacing my napkin. "Now sit down and eat the meal your nice chef prepared for you before it goes to waste," I added for an extra kick to his manly balls as I picked up my pizza and took a bite, moaning at the deliciousness.

I kept the mask of dominance in place until he sat back down on his stool and turned to face me. "Do you feel like a big dog right now, Arianna? Like a king amongst peasants," he asked in a voice meant for men to hear right before he ended their lives. I looked over at him and raised an eyebrow, but he leaned forward, wrapping his hand around my neck, and pulled me until our faces were almost touching. "Make no mistake, Wife, when you were a Rosetti, you wouldn't have dreamed of speaking like that to someone as dangerous as me." He licked my lips and tightened his hand around my throat. "But I've filled your pussy so full of Capasso DNA that you're finally beginning to act like one." He licked my lips again, biting my bottom one and sucking it into his mouth as I opened for him, giving him what he wanted. "You'll be a good wife yet, Little One."

I hung on to his every word like a carnivore desperate for another morsel of meat. I wanted more.

More praise.

More roughness.

More touches.

But he pulled away, dropping his hand from my throat, and turned back to the counter like he hadn't just rocked my world. I sat there panting and aching for more of him as he dismissively picked up his pizza and took a bite.

Fucker pulled a checkmate on me while I was trying to set up a game of checkers.

Quickly reminding me he didn't play by anyone's rules but his own and I needed to quickly get on the same page as him.

"**M**rs. Capasso," Dr. Travis called as she walked into my bedroom.

"Doctor," I replied cooly, "No offense, but I'm really starting to dread your visits."

She nodded her head knowingly, setting her bag down on the coffee table. "That's fair. I'm here to collect a urine sample."

"To see if I'm pregnant, correct?"

"Correct."

I took a deep breath and held my hand out for the sample cup I'd gotten used to filling for her. "Let's get this over with then."

She gave me the cup and I went into the bathroom, shutting the door behind me, and avoided looking at my reflection in the mirrored vanity. I set the cup down on the back of the toilet and started to unbutton my jeans when I heard a faint tapping on the panel in the wall at the end of the shower.

The panel to the secret passageway that Molly had told me about before I escaped to her parents' house for dinner. I quickly buttoned my jeans and silently ran over to it, feeling for the nearly invisible latch behind the tiled wall, and opened the panel.

"Molly?" I whispered as she came through the opening and held her finger to her lips.

"Shh," she hissed, "Did you take the test yet?"

"No." I nodded to the cup on the back of the toilet. "Why?"

"Good!" She ran across the room, pulling a specimen cup from her apron and switching it out for the empty one.

"Is that pee?" I cringed as she turned back to me and rolled her eyes. "What are you doing?"

"I thought maybe you'd want to find out in private. Then you could decide what to do with that information and when." She pulled a plastic container from the other pocket of her apron and handed it to me.

A pregnancy test.

"I'm confused."

"That's my pee," She nodded behind her to the cup as she handed me back the empty cup. "I assure you, I'm not pregnant." She smirked, "But you probably are, and the second that Dr. Travis tests your pee, she's going to tell Mr. Capasso and then your already tense relationship will get worse. So give her my pee, get the negative test from her, and buy yourself some time. Take the other test in private after she leaves to know for sure. But at least then you'll be in charge of the outcome for a little while."

I grabbed her shoulders and pulled her into a tight hug, trying to express how much her act of defiance meant to me. "You must really hate your job to keep putting it on the line for me." I said after a while, "But thank you."

She hugged me back, squeezing me tight before pulling back, "I love my job way more since you arrived, to be honest. But I have morals and you deserve to have someone unapologetically in your corner."

A light knock sounded from the door, "Mrs. Capasso, is everything okay in there?" Dr. Travis asked and Molly's eyes rounded wide.

"Hurry, hide the test and the empty cup, and get back out there. Mr. Capasso was on his way back inside when I ran up here."

"Okay." I tucked the stick and cup in the back of my makeup drawer as she opened the false panel of tile in the wall. "Thank you," I whispered.

She winked and disappeared into the darkness.

"I'm coming!" I called, picking up the filled cup and taking a calming breath before walking out to the bedroom where the doctor waited.

With my husband.

"I'll take that, Mrs. Capasso," Dr. Travis said as I stood frozen in the doorway, hesitant to betray Nico.

I bit my lip to keep my mouth shut as she took it over to her test station and got busy dipping strips into the urine. I avoided Nico's stare and walked to the window to distract myself.

I didn't want to lie to him. But I wasn't ready to be completely bombarded by him either. A part of me knew, if I was pregnant, the second he found out, he'd tighten up the already tight restraints he had put on my life. Because he was a protector first, that was easy to tell. He'd protect me to protect his unborn child, to a fault.

I just wasn't ready to give up what little freedom I'd gained in my time at Armarow.

I would take the test later and find out the truth, and if I was pregnant. I'd tell him the truth eventually.

Just not yet.

I just wanted a little bit longer to be... me.

Before I was simply the vessel carrying the future Don.

"What is it?" Nico startled me when he spoke directly behind me, setting his hand on my shoulder, "You seem nervous."

I shrugged, refusing to face him. "Just waiting for the news."

"Does the idea of being the mother to my children still repulse you so much?" he asked and I couldn't fight the urge to look at him any longer.

I turned and looked up at him, feeling the anger and rejection radiating off of him. "The idea of having kids with you has never repulsed me, Nico," I said gently.

"Then tell me what it is that has you so upset."

I dropped his gaze and stared at a button on his shirt, letting my finger drift up to feel the cool metal under my fingertips. "I never fantasized about being someone's broodmare." His hand slid over mine, pressing it flat against his stomach. "I wanted to mean more to someone." I looked up, "Is that so hard to imagine?"

"The tests are done," Dr. Travis interrupted before he could reply and I pulled my hand from his stomach and took a deep breath.

Nico's jaw clenched but he remained silent, turning to give his attention to the doctor as I looked back out the window already knowing what she was about to say.

"It's negative."

"Thank you," Nico replied coolly like the news had been something as simple as the chef declaring the menu for dinner instead of something he had been so passionate about.

"We can start hormones to better time ovulation for a higher chance of impregnation in two weeks-." She said but Nicolas cut her off.

"No." He said firmly, "Thank you for your time tonight, Doctor, that will be all."

"Very well." She said, packing her things all the while I stared out the window, feeling like the world had started spinning faster and tilting to the side as the deception burned in my gut.

She left the room, and a wave of nausea overcame me as the guilt became too much to bear. I wasn't a liar. It wasn't in my nature and doing it to Nico felt wrong. I opened my mouth to tell him the truth when his emotionless voice cut me off.

"I'll send Molly up to help you pack your bags."

I whipped around to face him so fast my world spun as disbelief rolled through me. "What?" He was casting me out. Because I didn't get knocked up in the first month. Was he fucking serious?

"We leave in two hours. So be quick about it."

"I don't understand," I stammered as a cold sweat broke out over my skin. "You're making me leave?"

Wait, we? Did he say we?

He took a deep breath and I watched as his shoulders visibly lowered like he was forcing himself to relax. "Yes, Arianna," He replied, closing the distance between us and lifting his hand to my jaw. I flinched when he touched me, even though his touch was gentle and lacked any anger I expected. His brow cinched and his nostrils flared even as his thumb lightly swept over my cheek. The touch was belying of the emotion I could see burning behind his green eyes and it made me even more uncertain. "It's hard to take you on a honeymoon, without leaving our home."

"Honeymoon?" I whispered in complete shock, gently shaking my head as I tried to comprehend what had happened in the last few minutes.

"Yes, Wife," He slid his hand around the back of my neck and pulled me in against his chest. "Three weeks, yachting around the Mediterranean, from Ibiza to Athens. Would that please you?"

"I thought-." I swallowed and took a deep breath. "I thought you were kicking me out."

"I know," He sighed, tightening his hold on my neck. "By the end of our trip, you'll probably wish I had. Make no mistake about it, Little One," He slid his thumb under my chin and tipped my head back even further, putting pressure on the exposed windpipe in my throat, asserting his dominance over me in a way that made my knees weak and my panties wet. "I have no plans for the next three weeks aside from filling your womb with my child," he growled and I grabbed onto the shirt covering his hard abs for support as his words turned me to mush. "But I'm going to do it the right way. So don't plan to be doing much besides taking my cock on repeat while I wine and dine you from island to island. Understood?"

"Yes," I whispered, too shocked to say anything else.

"Good," He leaned down and pressed his lips to mine, giving me a warm and expectant kiss, that I returned eagerly. "Make sure all of your new lingerie makes it into your suitcase. You won't need much else."

I bit my lip and sagged into him further, unable to even pretend that everything he said wasn't turning me into mush for him.

He was trying.

In his own domineering and controlling way.

"Yes, Sir," I said and fought a smirk when his eyes darkened before he leaned down to kiss me again.

"Hurry along now, Little One."

With that, he left the room and moments later Molly rushed in, with wide eyes. "What the heck did I miss? A honeymoon?" she gasped as confused as I was.

"More like a baby-making mission, but I'll take the views of the seas while the inevitable happens."

"If it hasn't already," She smirked and nodded to my stomach before shaking her head and taking a deep breath, "Alright, let's get you packed to go get knocked up."

"Jesus Christ," I groaned, but smiled to myself, nonetheless.

CHAPTER 14 – NICO

I watched Arianna's face as we walked up the dock to where my yacht was waiting for us, anticipating what her reaction would be.

I had made plans to take her away for a makeup honeymoon a few days ago, deciding that regardless of what her test said, we'd get away for a while.

I'd be lying if I said I wasn't both relieved and disappointed that my wife wasn't pregnant yet. Part of me wanted to start building my family, sooner rather than later. While the other part of me wanted to do it the right way. In a way that didn't involve lies and force.

Even if I didn't know any other way to do anything.

I was willing to try.

"Wow," She whispered, taking in the sight of the vessel all lit up in the night sky.

"Like it?" I asked, anxious for her response.

"It's incredible."

"It's bigger than your father's," I said, hating the way I was trying to impress her with my possessions.

She shrugged, sliding her hand into mine when I offered it to her to help her up onto the walkway. "I wouldn't know, I didn't even know he had one."

I followed her onto the ship where the captain, boson, and chief stew waited for us. "Good evening, Mr. Capasso," my captain said before taking my wife's hand and shaking it, "Mrs. Capasso, my name is Reck and I'll your captain for the duration of the trip. He turned and introduced Martin, the boson, and Cher, the chief stew.

There were others on board, but only the most elite from each department would have much to do with us. That was the only way to make sure the standard of service I expected was met, time in and time out on board.

I watched as Arianna charmed them all, accepting their greetings and giving her own like the perfect wife of the Don and pride swelled in my chest.

"When do we depart?" I asked, drawing everyone's attention away from my charming wife.

"In the morning," Rex confirmed, "At first light, we'll disembark and start your journey through the sea."

"Perfect," I turned to Cher, "We'll take our meal in the sky lounge tonight." I slid my hands over Arianna's shoulder and led her deeper into the elegant saloon, "It's getting cold out."

"Very well, Mr. Capasso," Cher bowed, "I'll have the chef prepare your meals now. Your rooms are ready."

"Thank you," Arianna called as I ushered her toward the stairwell to my private quarters. "Is this all ours?" She asked, walking down the hallway to the main bedroom door.

"Yes, there are only three other bedrooms on board besides the crew cabins."

"That seems less than I would expect on a boat this size," She mused.

"It is," I affirmed, "I don't often invite others with me to the sea. If I don't have empty bedrooms, it makes it easy to leave them all behind."

"And what do you do when you are at sea?"

"Work, mostly," I admitted as we walked into our bedroom. "I rarely take time off."

"Do you plan to work these three weeks?" She asked tentatively, and I saw the way uncertainty filled her gaze as she tried to pretend to take in the furnishings.

"There will be times I am attending to business."

"What will I be doing while you work?"

"Whatever pleases you. You may sunbathe, read, sleep, relax." I shrugged, "I have pampering planned at each dock for you, both onshore and on board. There's shopping and dining available at each stop as well."

"What if I wanted to just stay out in open water and ignore the existence of the rest of the world?" She faced me and wrapped her arms around her abdomen like she was comforting herself in a way.

"Is that what you want, Little One?" I lowered myself down into an armchair in the seating area across from the bed and spread my legs wide before holding my hand out to her, beckoning her near.

She hesitated, swallowing as her eyes flicked from my hand to my face and back.

I dropped my hand to my knee and sighed, "That's it, is it?" I questioned, "Our truce ending as we begin our vacation?"

"You said you were working on our trip," she countered, "so don't claim it to be a vacation."

"Does that bother you?"

"No," she replied instantly and chewed on her bottom lip as I left the space after her empty answer. "Maybe," she finally admitted and sighed. "Yes."

"Why?"

"I couldn't begin to tell you," She answered, and I could tell it was honest.

"Then why don't you tell me what you envisioned our trip to look like before we arrived?" I ran the pad of my thumb over my bottom lip as she mulled her answer over before giving it.

"What does a honeymoon look like?" she shrugged, "Because I wouldn't have a clue."

"Romance," I replied, tilting my head as she watched me closely like she didn't expect that answer. "Intimacy," I added, "Connection."

Her shoulders deflated marginally and she looked away. "Right, which is why this is going to be a work trip then. Got it." She ran her fingers over her forehead and busied herself with opening drawers and cupboards in the closet as I watched her.

"Do you think I can't give you those things while working?"

"I don't think you can give me those things, period," she replied effortlessly, but I saw the way she tensed after the words left her mouth.

My wife was an enigma to me.

Completely unknown and unstudied before, leaving me second-guessing every instinct I had where she was concerned and constantly questioning what it was that she wanted or needed.

But I realized I didn't have to guess too awful much if I bothered to just ask her.

Because while my wife was a mystery to me, she was an open book to herself. When she was open and honest with herself, I could tap into that connection and read her better than any other time thus far.

"Come here," I commanded her, causing her back to stiffen as she tried to ignore my directive and her body's natural desire to comply. "Now, Arianna."

She looked at me over her shoulder before turning around, "Why?" She continued chewing on her lip. "Dinner will be ready soon," She back peddled.

"Our meal will be ready, only when we are ready to eat."

"That's rude to the staff that works so tirelessly to serve you," She huffed, deflecting the conversation.

"Arianna." I held my hand up again, "Come here, I won't ask you again."

"You didn't ask me the first time." She whispered.

"Wife," I growled and her foot tentatively took a step forward, bringing her closer to me. "Better."

She flicked her eyes toward the cabin door and then back to my hand as she crossed the room. "What do you want from me?"

"For you to come here." Sliding my hand around her hip as she finally got within reach, I pulled her down into my lap. I lifted her feet over the arm of the chair and settled her, so she had no choice but to lean against my chest and look at me, which was what I wanted.

"What do you really want?" she whispered, playing with the hem of her flowy pastel-colored dress where it fell at her knee. It was the perfect dress for a warm summer evening onboard, but it was fall and we weren't south enough yet to enjoy the warmth of the season. It would be a few days before we made it that far and her skin pebbled as I stared down at her bare legs laid out over my lap.

"To tell you how exquisite you are," I said plainly, sliding my palm down her bare calf to slip her shoe off her dainty foot. "To tell you how painful it is for me to stare at your beauty and know you don't see even a fraction of it in the mirror when you glance at it on your way by." I pushed her other shoe off and then took her foot in my hand, squeezing it and running the pad of my thumb over the arch until she moaned softly.

Then I did it again.

"You tell pretty tales," she whispered, absently playing with a button on my shirt before chewing on her lip again to hide another moan when I squeezed.

"Said with the lips of a goddess."

"Looks are curses," she countered. "You said it yourself; my appearance was what made you decide to go through with the marriage to me."

"Do you still believe that marrying me was the losing bet?" I asked, holding her gaze as I switched to her other foot. "I thought we were past that false-hood."

"I didn't say it was the worst option," She challenged and I smirked, gliding my hand up her ankle and calf, smoothing the cool skin as I went.

"You told the doctor you could have been happily married to me." I trailed my fingers over her knee. "You made it sound like you didn't believe in that anymore."

"I don't."

"Then why would you be upset with me working on our honeymoon?" I implored.

Her nostrils flared and she clenched her jaw, having been caught in the lie, and looked away from me.

I tilted her head back with my finger under her chin until her warm eyes met mine. "I'll tell you my theory on it if you'd like." She didn't respond but I continued anyway, "I think you still believe you could be happy with me. I think when you tell your brain to fuck off and let your body take control, right here," I let my fingers glide down her chest until they rested above the cleavage that teased me at her neckline and tapped her sternum, "with your heart, that you know you're happy with me." I tilted my head to the side and kissed her cheek, letting my lips linger there. "I think you want to let yourself have everything I offer you, but you feel like you need to protest it out of some obligation to your feminine independence." I lowered my lips to her ear, and she turned her head, giving me better access. "I think you need to admit that the pleasure I give you is worth letting go of the fight."

She chuckled and quickly shifted in my arms until she straddled my lap and ran her nails up the back of my neck. "What are you giving up, being with me?" I slid my hands under her dress and grabbed both of her ass cheeks, pulling her against my crotch. "Because we both know I'm not going to just give, give, give, without a little take."

"I'm giving up a whole lot more than you realize, Little One." I rocked her against me, and she tilted her head back and rolled her hips, rubbing herself against my body.

"Tell me," She whispered with her eyes closed. "Give me the words."

"I will." I weaved my fingers through her long hair and forced her face back towards mine, "Someday. When I can trust you."

"Lies," She hissed and licked her lips. "If you're going to lie to me, the least you could do is fuck me while you do it so I won't notice."

I gripped the elastic of her panties and ripped them off her body, tossing them onto the floor before scooting her backward in my lap. "Be a good girl and take my cock out if you want it so bad."

Her eyes darkened as she squinted at me. "Don't act like you don't want me." She stilled in my hands. "That's twice today you've feigned like you could get this somewhere else from somebody less bothersome." Her body vibrated with anger. "You want to possess my body with little care for my comfort, fine. You want to come and go as you please and expect me to be dutiful and waiting for your return, fine. You want me to be a good little wife and beg you to give me babies, fine. But don't you dare try to pretend like you aren't as fucked in the head over me as I am for you."

There she was.

My goddess, revealing herself and her feelings for me to read.

I took her hand from where she had her nails dug into my neck and lowered it to my zipper, gripping my rock-hard cock through my pants. "Does this feel like I'm unaffected by you, Wife?" Her fingers squeezed me, and I groaned. "You were right earlier in the kitchen when you called my bluff." I wrapped my free hand around her throat and pulled her forward until her lips brushed mine. "No other pussy has ever felt as good wrapped around my cock as yours does. No other set of lips has ever tasted as good as yours do. No other moans have ever weaved a siren's song in my head like yours do." I kissed her and she instantly opened her lips and let my tongue in. "I'm fucked in the head over you too, Arianna. If that's what you want me to say, then you need to tell me that."

"I want that," She moaned, "I can't stand when you act like I'm not enough." She pulled my belt free and undid my pants, freeing my erection and stroking it in her hand. It was the first time she had freely touched me and my eyes crossed with pleasure. "I can be enough for you, Nico."

"You are," I affirmed sliding her straps down off her shoulders to expose her perfect breasts to my eyes. "Just like this." I lifted her hips and lined my cock up with her wet entrance. "Open and honest with me, Ari, you are more than enough."

"Yes," She hissed as she lowered herself onto the head of my cock, stretching herself open.

"Good girl, Little One," I praised, tightening my hands on her ass and leaning forward to suck on one of her pink nipples. "Take my cock like such a good girl."

"I don't know what the fuck I'm doing," She moaned, even as she pushed herself down further. "I don't know how to do this."

"I got you." I lifted her and let her wetness recoat my cock before thrusting into her body, going further than the time before. "Your body knows what to do. It knows what it needs if you just give into it."

"You." She licked her lips and looked at me as her pussy tightened around my cock even more. "My body needs you," she groaned and threw her head back like she was frustrated, "You've turned me into a whore for you."

I smirked at my sexy wife, topless and riding my cock even though she swore she didn't know how with her head thrown back in self-loathing as her pussy slickened around me more. "Then be my good little whore, Ari, and take what you want from me."

I dropped my hands from her body and linked them behind my head, tilting my hips up for her as she slid down the rest of the way until her ass cupped my balls.

"God, you're so big, Nico," She groaned, putting her hands flat on my pecs and leaning forward to slide up the length of me and back down.

She was a goddess.

And she was mine.

"You're perfect." I dropped my hands, unable to keep them off of her as she tentatively rode me. "Riding my cock like a good girl. So fucking sexy Ari, you're absolutely breathtaking like this."

"Crazed?" She smirked, opening her eyes to look at me before they fluttered closed when she rocked forward, grinding herself against my pubic bone, "Holy fuck," she gasped.

"That's it, baby." I rocked her forward and back with my cock buried deep inside of her, rubbing her clit and her G-spot at the same time.

"Oh, my God." She rocked faster, tilting forward and giving me the access to her nipples I needed. I sucked on them, alternating back and forth with deep suction and intense bites until she was shaking in my arms, desperate for her orgasm. "Don't stop, please, please, please," she begged, "Please don't stop."

I didn't fucking stop.

I kept up the same motion and stimulation until she froze altogether in my lap, arching her back and screaming to the ceiling as she came.

Then I fucked her like a madman.

I slammed up into her body as she convulsed around me and watched her tits shake with each punishing thrust as she dug her nails into my chest through my shirt. I regretted not stripping us both down when I couldn't feel her skin against mine, but I hadn't expected our conversation to invoke such a primal reaction.

I'd be damned if I was going to stop now just to get naked.

"Harder," she gasped, opening her eyes and staring at me as I fucked up into her tight pussy. I could feel the wetness of her orgasm coating my balls and they tightened as I neared my orgasm.

"Careful, baby," I grunted, "Or I'll fuck you raw and leave you sore for days."

"Yes," she moaned, bending her elbows and leaning over me further. "That's how it felt after the first time you took me," she whispered, "When you snuck into my bedroom and spread me wide, branding my body as yours." Her jaw hung lax and her eyes rolled, "I felt you inside of me the entire time I got ready for our wedding the next day like you were still buried deep, and I didn't even know who you were. I thought I was lusting after a holy man who gave me my first-ever real orgasm."

"Fuck," I grunted and roared as I felt her tighten around me again, milking my orgasm from my body with her own.

She collapsed onto my chest as I continued to fuck her, so I wrapped my arms around her as she buried her face in my neck and moaned dreamily until I finished.

"Oh, my God," she sighed, laying limply in my arms as I loosened my hold on her and sucked air.

"I told you that night, that I was your god now."

I slid my hand over the back of her head, smoothing down her hair and she chuckled lightly into my neck.

"What a conceded thing to say," She chided and I smacked her ass, causing her to jerk and then moan.

She lifted off of my cock and I held her dress out of the way to watch as our mutual orgasms dripped onto my cock when she was free of me.

A knock sounded at the cabin door and Cher cleared her throat professionally before softly announcing, "Chef is ready to serve dinner whenever you are, Mr. Capasso."

Ari's eyes widened as she covered her lips with her fingertips in embarrassment.

I winked at her and called out, "We'll be up in fifteen minutes."

"Yes, Sir," Cher called back, retreating to the service quarters.

"Fifteen minutes?" Ari questioned, "That's rude if dinner is ready." A flush colored her breasts that were still bare and burned up her neck to the sweet apple of her cheeks.

I scoffed and picked her up, turning, and then set her back down in the chair with her ass on the edge of the seat. "No, it would be rude if I made you go sit through an entire meal with such a mess between your thighs." I tucked my cock away and righted my clothes as she tilted her head in confusion. I knelt at her feet and pushed her shoulders back until she reclined in the chair before lifting her legs from behind her knees and spreading them wide, revealing her dripping pink pussy to my hungry eyes. "Now, be a good wife and let me clean you up so we can go eat our meal without me having to worry about you staining the dining room chairs."

I leaned forward and flicked my tongue across the tight bud of her clit as her eyes rounded wide. "Nicolas!" She gasped before moaning when I sucked it into my mouth and pushed my tongue into her pussy, tasting us both there. "Holy fucking hell." She collapsed back into the chair and widened her legs for me as I ate the best-tasting meal I could ask for.

Good girl.

CHAPTER 15 – ARIANNA

T he waves rolled on around us as we cruised through the open water. The land disappeared days ago, and we rarely saw any other boats in our travels.

I loved every single second of it.

Living simply because you chose to, but not for anyone else in the world, was so invigorating. No one aside from those onboard mattered. They merely didn't exist.

I laid out on the sun deck on the bow of the yacht and let the wind cool my sun-kissed skin as I fantasized about my sexy as-sin husband. He mattered, there was no way to deny that now.

Nico had been the picture of marital perfection since we stepped on board, and I fought the urge to start anticipating the fallout of all the happiness I was feeling. I hadn't been afforded such pleasant things in life before, so I continuously feared it would all come to a screeching halt at any point.

"Arianna," Cher called from the edge of the lounge cushions that covered the large deck and I opened my eyes and sat up to give her my attention. "We're going to be docking in Ibiza in an hour or so."

I looked out over the port side of the boat and sure enough, land decorated the horizon.

"Already?" I let the word slip before I offered her an apologetic smile and nodded, "Thank you. Are there any plans for when we dock?"

"Mr. Capasso has arranged for the two of you to depart the ship for the afternoon. He has dinner and an evening out planned."

I nodded, accepting the news with both trepidation and excitement, "Thank you, Cher. I suppose I shall go find my husband and ask him for more details."

"He was in the office the last time I saw him." She left and I laid back on the lounger, eyeing the impending port getting nearer with each minute that passed.

I'd never traveled much outside of a few trips around Italy or the UK with my parents when it suited them, and I admit the idea of exploring Ibiza excited me. Doing it with Nico excited me even more.

I just wasn't ready to let anyone else into our small bubble of quiet and peacefulness.

But it seemed I wasn't given a choice, so I forced my feet over the edge of the seat, wrapping my sarong around my waist before heading down to the stupidly large office Nicolas had outfitted for himself on board. One of his added ways to avoid having room for extra cabins.

Which was fine with me.

Molly, Saul, and Dio were on board with us, along with the other staff that worked the ship exclusively. I was more than happy to have their company, I didn't need anyone else's.

I shook the gloom from my shoulders as I got to the office door, knocking gently before opening the door.

Nicolas looked up from his computer screen and leaned back in his chair as I walked in. Even with all of the time we spent together the last few days, I was nervous about entering his space and interrupting him. I knew as his wife I was allowed near him, yet he was still such a paradox to me.

"The sun is being kind to your young skin," He said in place of a greeting, and I cocked my head as I neared him. When he made comments like that or called me Little One, I remembered the large age gap between us. Short of the smattering of grey hairs on his temples, he didn't act like a man in his late thirties. Nor did he act young though, he defied labels completely.

"I have no idea what that's supposed to mean."

"It means the bronze color covering your body makes me ache to see where the lighter-colored skin lies underneath your small bikini."

"Who said I had any tan lines?" I challenged and his eyes darkened.

"Are you trying to bait me into thinking you've been lying aboard the bow of my ship naked?"

"Does the idea of that do something to you?"

"It does." He reached forward and pulled me into him, placing me on the desk in front of him and setting my feet on the seat of his chair. "It does bad things to me."

"Elaborate."

"If you were naked for the twenty-seven crew members on board to see, I'd have to kill every single one of them. No questions asked. And then our honeymoon would be over."

"What if I told you that I wanted to be naked in front of them?" I bit my bottom lip to sell it, and his eyes dropped to it expectantly. "Or at least a few of them."

"Why would you want that?"

I leaned forward until we were face to face. "Because the idea of you fucking me with an audience, *excites* me."

His nostrils flared and he pressed his palm against the front of my throat as he stood to his full height, dominating me with his strength and power. "You want someone to watch you get fucked?"

I shrugged my shoulders, feigning indifference. "Maybe."

"Liar," He challenged, tightening his hand around my throat.

"You're right," I gave in, smiling at him as I ran my hands up the front of his chest which was bare through the opening of his linen button-down shirt. "I don't want anyone to see me but you."

"Troublemaker."

"More like a bored housewife that resorted to baiting her husband for his attention."

"More lies," He said expertly. "You're thriving in the peace we've been afforded on board. And I've only been working for two hours."

I shrugged, sliding my fingers into the band of his shorts, "Okay fine. Horny housewife that aches to come again. It's been hours since the last time you made me orgasm."

"Now that, I actually believe." He smirked, loosening his hand around my neck and kissing me. "But your hungry cunt will have to wait because we have appointments to keep."

He grinned, causing my glare as he pulled me off of his desk and from the office with his hand in mine. "Do we have to leave?" I stuck out my lower lip.

I never pouted. But I was feeling particularly moody and not at all interested in mingling with others when for the last forty-eight hours I had been blissfully naked and content to allow the truce between my new husband and me to benefit me.

"Do you want a ring for your finger?" he questioned with a cursory look over his shoulder, "Because if not, then by all means, we can skip the first appointment. But the second and third are nonnegotiable."

"Ring?" I froze mid-step, causing him to stop and turn back to look at me.

"The wife of the Don can't walk around without a visible representation of our marriage."

"Right," I whispered, mentally kicking myself for thinking anything else of it. I had looked down at my bare left-hand numerous times since saying, 'I do' and wondered what my perfect wedding ring would look like in an alternate universe where I married the man I loved. But I never thought about one in this life. "Got it." I started walking again, until he stopped me with a hand on my hip, making me face him as he tried to read my face.

That was something I had picked up on lately. When Nico was trying to understand me, he studied me intently, like he was trying to solve a puzzle.

"You didn't like that answer," He stated.

"It wasn't what I was expecting is all." I steeled my spine and tried for indifference. "It makes sense now that I think about it. There are images to protect."

"Wrong." He shook his head and crouched slightly until I looked him in the eye. "I could have had any ring delivered to Armarow before or after our wedding, Ari, if it was simply just the physical metal on your finger I was worried about. But that's not why we're going to get you one now."

"Then explain it to me so I understand it."

"Rasul Diamonds here in Ibiza are some of the best quality jewels in the world. The class of stone is unmatched and I wouldn't even consider picking out the ring you wear from anyone else. Do you want to know why?"

"Why?" I humored him, giving him what he wanted, simply because I was needy for the answers he was freely offering.

"Because I've grown quite fond of you since we decided to get along and enjoy each other's presence." He stepped forward and ran the pad of his thumb over my cheek. "Despite what you think of me as a man or a Don, I am trying to figure out how to be a good husband. So I want to give you the very best in this, as a sign of the beginning of something true."

"Nico," I whispered, overwhelmed by the sincerity of what he was telling me.

"Let's go pick out a ring that will mean something to the both of us, together."

"Okay," I agreed because never before in my life had someone made me feel like I was the center of their world like Nico did when he gentled himself to me like that. "Okay," I said again, with more conviction.

"Okay." He leaned down and kissed me, and I eagerly deepened it, trying to express the depth of what I was feeling with touch.

Words and honesty hadn't always been our strong suit, but the touch was undeniable between us.

Our bodies said everything we didn't know how or were unwilling to vocalize. From the first night he touched me, the lies and deceptions of our relationship couldn't hide the truths of what we felt physically. So, I was going to trust in that part of our relationship and allow his words to feel as honest as his touch did.

"Nicolas, my most loyal customer." A man in a flashy cream-colored suit walked into the private room with three women in pristine white dresses carrying large cases in their hands that were easily half the size of them.

Didn't hurt that each of them was the size of twigs with professionally enhanced figures either.

I tried to ignore them altogether in my seat with Nicolas at my side, instead of nitpicking my appearance compared to theirs. He picked out a sage green sundress and a pair of cream-colored wedges for me to wear when we got ready and because he had soothed the fire inside of me with his sweet words right before that, I allowed him to dress me without a complaint.

Sitting at his side, where he casually leaned back on the suede couch wearing cream-colored slacks and a black linen shirt undone to the bottom of his sternum with the sleeves rolled up on his arms, looking downright devilish and delicious all wrapped into one, I was glad I was dressed how he wanted.

"Roberto," Nico said, standing and embracing the man before sliding his hand over my shoulder and looking down at me, "Meet my beautiful wife, Arianna."

"Ah," Roberto embraced my hand in both of his, "What a beautiful woman you are indeed, my dear." He smiled brightly before walking back around the table in front of us and signaling to the woman to lay the cases down. "So," he clapped his hands excitedly, "I've brought you only the best of the best and my jewelers are all waiting anxiously to create the masterpiece you build today so you can have it ready before you depart Ibiza in two days."

"Perfect," Nico replied, sitting back down next to me and sliding his large palm between my crossed legs above the knee, and smiling at me. "I don't want any more time to pass with you looking available."

I smirked at him and leaned into him, keeping my snarky retort inside because of the audience we had.

The women worked silently, opening the cases and taking out tray after tray of beautiful sparkling diamonds and endless bands and example rings to look at. I finally ignored the way the women looked Nico up and down appreciatively thanks to the distracting diamonds laid before me.

Which was probably good for the women because the urge to tell them to get their eyes back into their heads was growing with each fluttered eyelash. They would smile and flirt with Nico, and then glare at me in the very next second, in a way that only a true conniving woman could master. And all three had mastered it if the way my shoulders shrunk with each minute spent in their presence, indicated anything.

The green monster on my shoulder was growing larger along with the moodiness I had felt earlier.

"Do we have any requirements or restrictions?" Roberto asked Nicolas.

"Five carats or bigger. Platinum only. And something that will pair well with matching jewels to be purchased in the future. Cut and shape are up to Ari."

Roberto excitedly pushed away trays that held smaller stones as he placed the three trays with the biggest diamonds directly in front of me. Behind them he placed the example rings and bands that would hold such large stones, explaining things about weight and sturdiness that meant nothing to me.

I looked away from the beauty of them and glanced up at my husband who watched me closely as uncertainty rolled through me.

I'd never picked out a piece of jewelry before in my life, but I didn't want to admit that in front of women who were already looking down at me like I wasn't worthy of the seat at Nico's side.

"Send your women away Roberto, this room is far too crowded," Nico said firmly, like he could read my very thoughts.

"Of course," Roberto waved his hands at his assistants, "Shoo, shoo."

"Take a deep breath," Nico said against my temple as I looked back down at the trays. "Just tell me what ones jump out at you and what you like about them."

"They're all so, *large*."

Nico smirked and ran his hand over my back, "To match me."

I rolled my eyes but let his uncharacteristic playfulness relax me. He was trying to make this easy on me, I could tell. So I didn't want to make this hard on him either.

I took a deep breath and leaned over the table to look at them closer, letting my eyes tell me which style at least I liked the most.

"Round," I said, looking up at Nico, "I like the round ones."

Roberto moved a bunch around until only the round ones remained on the trays.

"What kind of setting is attractive to you?" He pointed to the different options, naming them off until he got to the one I couldn't look away from.

"That one," I smiled at him, "It's perfect."

"Very timeless," The flashy man said with a wink. He picked up a platinum band with prongs set for a solitaire diamond and then looked to Nico. "Which stone?"

Nico looked at me, but I simply shrugged, "They all look positively identical to me. You pick."

"A Royal Asscher with the largest table," Nico replied effortlessly. He could have been speaking Greek and I wouldn't have known the difference, which was why I wanted him to pick. He clearly knew more about this than I did. "That one," He pointed out when Roberto thinned out the selection once again.

"Wow." The diamond left before me, after its opponents were eliminated like in a game of Guess Who was breathtaking.

"Perfect selection," Roberto said, picking up the diamond and the band we had selected and holding them together with his tools to show what it would like once completed. "This diamond is one of the rarest we carry, it's almost seven and three-quarters carat, with ideal cut and clarity. I can assure you that you will never run into someone else with this exact ring."

"Perfect," Nico mused, kissing my temple once more. "What do you think?"

"It's fit for a queen." I mused, suddenly feeling inadequate again.

"No," Nico tilted my head back with his finger under my chin, "a goddess, Arianna. It's a perfect match for you. A goddess has powers and immortality whereas a queen simply sits atop a throne until she is often beheaded by mere men. A goddess reigns with her own strength."

"Nico," I whispered, having absolutely no other words to do justice to what he just uttered himself.

"Let's get this finished so that we can get to our next stop, Little One." He turned his attention back to Roberto like he hadn't just gifted me with the nicest thing anyone had ever said to me before and moved on.

While I sat there trying to name and control the emotions rolling through me.

Disbelief.

Excitement.

Fear.

Hope.

Worry.

Adoration.

The biggest of all, doubt. But I had to let that settle somewhere deep inside of me so I could bury it and thrive in the feelings I was experiencing. I deserved this.

I deserved happiness and fulfillment, regardless of what doubts had been planted and grown inside of me as a child.

"I'll have it delivered to your ship tomorrow evening at the latest," Roberto said when business was concluded between the men.

"Perfect," Nicolas replied, shaking the man's hand before leading me from the room. "Let's get to our next stop."

We rode in a hired car through the city in peaceful silence as I watched the sights out of the car window, before long we stopped at another storefront with elaborate decorations lining the windows.

"What is this place?"

"Wait and see, Wife," He said, helping me from the car with the calm smoothness that had inhibited him since our truce.

When we walked inside the store, employees rushed over to us and greeted my husband.

"Mr. Capasso!" One woman said, of course, the store only employed women, as she eagerly shook his hand. "My name is Elina, thank you so much for choosing us for your decorating needs. We're so excited to work with you on your renovating project."

"I'm anxious to see if you have what we're looking for," he replied, keeping his arm tight around my waist. "My wife, Arianna will be in charge of everything though. All decisions will need to go through her."

"Of course!" Elina gushed, finally turning her attention to me and holding her hand out for me to shake. "I'm eager to see your visions and take them from paper to reality for you."

"Me too," I answered coolly, feigning like I knew what the hell she was talking about before raising an eyebrow at my husband.

"Give us a moment to look around, and then we can get started," Nico said with a curt nod.

"What are we doing here?" I asked in a hushed tone. "And why do you insist on keeping me in the dark about everything?"

He rolled his eyes and smirked as we walked towards a wall that was covered floor to ceiling in tile backsplashes. "You're a hard woman to impress, did you know that?" He mused.

"Nicolas," I warned, leveling him with my best glare.

"You're renovating Armarow, Wife." He nodded to the wall and then the others around us. "Elina will be the lead designer who will work with architects and engineers and then come directly to you for approval on everything."

My mouth hung open as his words swarmed inside of my head, "Renovating Armarow?" I shook my head and tried to grasp what he was telling me. "What's wrong with it how it is currently?"

He cocked his eyebrow at me and smirked yet again, "You mean besides the offensive wallpaper in the dining room that burns your eyes so badly you can't

stand to eat in there?" I rolled my eyes at him and then glared. "It needs a fresh
touch to it, and I want that touch to be yours."

"Why?" I questioned, "You barely even like me, why on earth would you
want me to change your home? I don't know if you've noticed or not, but I'm
fucking useless when it comes to deciding things. I couldn't even pick out a
ring because I've never been given choices before."

He stepped forward quickly, backing me into the wall of tile behind me
before sliding his hand around the side of my face. To those around us, it
probably looked romantic and passionate, but what they couldn't see was how
his thumb dug into the pulse at the base of my jaw as he tilted my head back,
dominating me until I submitted to him. "Do not disrespect yourself like that
ever again, Arianna," he commanded with a scowl, "Just because something is
new to you, does not mean you will fail at it. You are exceedingly resourceful
and when you decide to do something, you find no hurdles you cannot cross.
Don't ever say something so demeaning about yourself again." He lowered his
face to mine and kissed my parted lips, lingering there. "Or I'll take you over
my knee, regardless of where we are, and teach you the lesson you desperately
need to learn. There is no woman more powerful than you, Little One. By
right as my wife, you are untouchable. But you didn't need my last name to
earn your title, for you were born for this." He kissed me again, "Even if it was
to the wrong parents who did you such a disservice for the first twenty years
of your life. Mark my words here and now, I intend to nurture that natural
born power that lives inside of you until you believe it too."

"And what happens if I take that power and turn it against you?" I challenged stupidly, "You've said it yourself, the Rosetti runs deep inside of me."

He smirked, kissing me once more before tilting his head to kiss the mark
on my neck after releasing his thumb from my jugular, standing back up
to his full height, "I'll die smiling if you best me, for if you ever do, it will
mean you've earned it." He stepped back and reached down, adjusting his
erection that grew down his pant leg obscenely like he didn't care that the store
was crowded with nosey onlookers as he gripped himself. "Now let's get this
project started before I take you out to the car and fuck you to relieve the ache
you've caused in my balls."

"Me?" I asked innocently, fluttering my eyelashes up at him.

"Yes, you," he quirked one brow, "You know sparing with you, gets me
hard. It's why you insist on being a pain in my ass daily."

"Ha," I tilted my head back and mocked him with a maniacal laugh until he spanked my ass as I walked away, turning that laugh into a yelp and a moan. "That's not fighting fair."

"I wasn't fighting," He whispered in my ear from behind me, pressing his erection into my ass. "I'll save that energy for tonight."

CHAPTER 16 – ARIANNA

"Shopping should be fun, not daunting," I huffed, walking out of a boutique that smelled like a whore house.

Molly chuckled as she walked beside me towards the next store we were going to. "You just have a sour attitude today, that's all."

"I do, don't I?" I huffed, blowing my bangs off my face dramatically. It was hot as balls out, and we'd been in and out of shops all morning, but the sun was high up in the sky and I was tired.

"It's to be expected when you're getting so little sleep, thanks to your delicious husband." She smirked with a side-eye glance as I nudged her.

"I don't know what you're talking about." I rolled my eyes back and winked at her.

She wore a black skirt and maroon collared shirt to match the colors of the ship we were sailing around the Mediterranean on, but I knew she must be far warmer than I was in my light sundress.

"Are you purposely trying to look like the crew on the ship?" I asked, nodding to her wardrobe.

She shrugged and adjusted her purse on her shoulder, "It would look odd if I wore my maid's dress from Armarow on the streets of Ibiza. Mr. Capasso expects that there be a sort of uniform appearance wherever his staff is."

"It looks odd to have you wearing long sleeves and a skirt down past your knees in this god-awful heat," I said and then an idea crossed my mind. "Let's fix that."

She stopped walking and squinted her eyes at me. "I don't like the sounds of that."

I grinned at her and took her hand, dragging her along as she gave Saul and Dio a questioning glance, who just shrugged and followed after us. "This is going to be so much fun."

"No. No way, absolutely not," Molly said from inside her changing room an hour later.

"Show me," I demanded excitedly from the velvet chair I took over while she tried on all the clothes, I instructed the shopkeepers to get for her.

"No."

"Yes."

"It's not in my job description."

"Pleasing me is in your job description, and this pleases me so damn much it's alarming." I giggled.

"Ari," she groaned. "I can't wear this!"

"Show me!"

"Ugh!" She ripped the curtain back and stormed out into the private room we commandeered. The keepers were more than happy to assist Mr. Capasso's wife with whatever I wanted after Saul made introductions. It should have revolted me that they were less than helpful before they knew my last name, but I decided to utilize their shallowness to Molly's benefit.

Didn't hurt that I had no spending limit on the black card that Saul carried in his wallet with Nico's name on it either.

Wifely perks I suppose.

"Oh, my goodness." I whistled and covered my cheshire grin with my hand.

"I know, it's terrible." Molly groaned, turning around to go back in.

"It's perfect!" I screeched, standing up to chase after her, "Absolutely perfect."

Her face contorted as she looked back at me. "For what? I have nowhere to wear this."

"Uh hello!" I sang, "We have two and half weeks left on board."

"And?"

"And you have your new uniform," I said plainly. The teal tennis dress she was wearing was far more serviceable than what I would have loved to see her in, but I was trying to warm her up to the idea of feeling more comfortable in clothes better suited for her age and beauty. The dress was sleeveless with a fitted skirt that landed mid-thigh with a pair of shorts underneath for modesty and activity. It was cute, fun, and flirty, and she looked like a twenty-some-thing-year-old wearing it. There was no reason for her to hide behind more clothes than a nun, especially when we were on vacation for Christ's sake.

I wanted it to look like I was out sightseeing with a friend, not a staff member. Because I didn't have any friends besides Molly, I needed her to be my equal when we were out alone and free to be just us.

I needed it.

"You're getting it," I insisted, "One in every color for on board the ship, and then we'll find sundresses for days we're out doing things like this, and-" I paused and then grabbed onto her with even more excitement, "bathing suits!"

"No!" Her pretty blue eyes rounded in fear as I giggled enthusiastically. "No way!"

I paused and bit my bottom lip, "You can sunbathe with me Molly, it is allowed."

"No, it's not. It's the exact opposite, I could lose my job!" she hissed.

"Molly!" I grabbed onto her arms to stop her from unraveling down a road of hysterics. "You helped sneak me out of Armarow using secret passageways and then helped me cheat on a pregnancy test using the same secrets." I deadpanned as she paled even a bit more, "Where did that brave girl go?"

"There are limits to what I can get away with in my position."

"I agree," I said evenly, "But those limitations don't even begin to cover what I can get away with in my position. Nico knows I adore you, there isn't anything you could do to jeopardize your position or employment if it is done to make me happy." I gave her a look, "And you know it."

She chewed on her lip in contemplation and then relaxed her tight shoulders as she realized I was right. "Tennis dresses, yes. Bathing suits, no."

"Fine," I shrugged, turning away to sit back down in my seat, "But sundresses are a yes then." She opened her mouth to argue, but I held my finger up, stopping her. "Did I tell you that I saw Matteo on board before we left this morning?" I asked, watching her closely for the reaction I expected that news to have on her.

Her eyes fell to the floor as a blush crept up her cheeks while she played with the hem of the skirt. "Really?"

"Yep." I popped the 'p' and tilted my head. "Nico said he was joining us for a while. Something to do with business in Sicily." She watched me as I simply smiled at her. "Sounds like *trouble* to me, huh?" I used the name of the informant in her phone that told her Nico was just trying to rile me up with the woman in his penthouse when he left Armarow. The same person she claimed she had no business talking to but couldn't seem to meet the eyes of whenever he was around at the estate.

"How did you figure it out?" She asked quietly like she felt ashamed.

I walked back to her and put my hands on her shoulders, giving her a squeeze and a gentle smile. "I may be new to marriage, but I'm not new to affection and the way men look at women that they're completely engrossed with."

"No, he doesn't-" She started but I shook my head, silencing her again.

"It's okay to let someone have a crush on you, Molly."

"He's way out of my league."

I scowled and dropped my hands. "He's good-looking, sure." I shrugged, "But not anywhere near how good-looking you are."

"No, I mean rank." She sighed, "I'm just a maid. And he's-" She paused, "He's the second in command to the Cosa Nostra."

"And?" I deadpanned.

She rolled her eyes and deflated even more. "And he could have any woman he wants."

"He wants you. I don't understand what's stopping you from exploring that. You obviously want to."

"I just don't see the point," She huffed, "Even if he is interested, he'll get bored and become *uninterested*. Quickly."

"Listen to me," I said plainly and pulled her over to the large couch I had sat on while she refused to come out of the dressing room. "I won't lie and pretend to know anything about Matteo other than that Nico trusts him and that he seems like a very intense man."

She chuckled, "That's putting it lightly."

"But I do know you." I held her hand in mine, "And I think that you're phenomenal. You're beautiful and kind and selfless and so incredibly humble and I love that. It's what drew me to you that very first morning that I met you. But do you want to know what else drew me in?"

"I don't think so," she joked with a small smile.

"Your strength. You stared my mother down. A woman I literally cowered away from my entire life. And you did it without a second thought. Then you helped me in my times of need, twice now. That's stuff you can't find in just anyone, and I think Matteo can see that. I think it's probably what draws him to you as well. I think you deserve to give it a shot to at least see if there's something there worth entertaining."

She took a deep breath and slowly let it out. I had her, I knew I did.

"Maybe."

"Well until you decide, one way or another, we're padding your wardrobe to be more comfortable in this heat regardless." I shooed her back towards the dressing room with a smirk and she chuckled as she rose and headed back. "Excuse me!" I called out and seconds later two shopkeepers hurried into the room, eager to do my bidding. "We're going to need one of every color of that dress and a dozen more different styles like it. And at least two dozen casual dresses as well."

Molly rolled her eyes and pulled the curtain shut behind her, closing herself out of the conversation as the keepers nodded and turned to leave.

"And bikinis too!" I yelled out after them. "In every single color!"

"Ari!" Molly hissed and the keepers ran to grab the items as I sat back on the couch with a smirk.

I was going to use my new 'power' as my husband called it, to benefit those important to me.

Maybe then I'd feel comfortable doing it for myself.

"Gosh it is hot." I placed the condensation-covered glass of water against my forehead and longed to pour it over my head to cool down, but refrained considering we were in the middle of a crowded upscale restaurant.

"Are you okay?" Molly asked, leaning over the table to look at me closer, "You're awfully pale."

"Am I?" I asked, "I would have assumed I was red from how boiling hot I am inside."

"Maybe we should go back to the boat," Molly said, signaling to our waiter for the check. "I think you need to go lay down and relax."

"I think that's the best thing you've said all day," I agreed, already envisioning how good the cool sheets inside the master cabin would feel. We'd been out all day, giving Nico time to conduct business with associates in the city, but I was done.

"Let's go," Molly said, standing up and adjusting her new baby pink sundress. She looked magnificent in it with her pretty blonde hair pinned up in a neat twist.

But as I stood up to go with her, the pink of her dress darkened to a mauve color as the edges of my vision blackened and a lightheaded sensation overtook me. "Whoa," I said, but it felt like my voice was in slow motion as I tilted to the side.

"Ari!" Molly cried, jumping forward as I toppled back into my chair, and catching me before I tipped it backward with me in it. "Oh, my God." I couldn't see her at all, and her voice felt far away even as I felt her cool hands grip the back of my neck and steady me. "Dio, get in here."

I assumed she was on the phone but couldn't tell. A cool cloth took the place of her hands, and someone tucked me forward to put my head down toward my knees as my vision started coming back.

"Mrs. Capasso," Dio said from beside me, crouching down, "Look at me, what happened." I turned and tried to focus on his face, but it was still blurry.

"I just got lightheaded I think." I sat up a little straighter and caught nearly every pair of eyes in the crowded restaurant staring at me. "Get me out of here," I whispered to Dio in absolute horror.

"Let's go." He stood up, tucking me in his arms and lifting me effortlessly against his chest, walking straight out the side patio door to the sweltering heat of the city. But I was glad about it because I was away from the crowd. "Open the door," He barked to Saul who had the car idling at the curb and the next instant I was inside the back seat, shrouded in privacy thanks to the dark tinted windows.

"Air. I need to cool down," I begged, reaching for the vent on the ceiling as Molly jumped in next to me.

They worked quickly, pointing every fan in the car my way and cranking the air conditioner full blast.

"What happened?" Saul asked and Molly answered after passing me an ice-cold bottle of water.

"She's been overheated all day and then after we ate she started getting paler and paler and then she stood up and fainted. I barely caught her before she hit her head off the table."

"Let's get her back to the boat. Call Reck and have him get a doctor on board now."

I listened as they all worked around me but stayed silent. I was incredibly embarrassed by the weakness I just showed the entire restaurant and wanted nothing but the privacy of my bedroom on board where I could rest and cool down.

"I just overdid it," I finally said as we neared the dock. "I shouldn't have stayed out so long, and I think I didn't drink enough water."

"We'll get you looked at to make sure," Molly said pointedly, and I knew what she was thinking without her having to say anything.

We didn't know if I was pregnant or not yet. Because I hadn't started my period or taken the spare test after Nicolas interrupted us with the impromptu getaway. I had the single test stick buried in the bottom of my makeup kit in the bathroom on board but hadn't taken it.

Simply because I was afraid of the results.

Could that be why I got so lightheaded though?

Was I pregnant?

"Here we are," Molly said as the car stopped directly behind the lavish yacht. "Let's get you on board."

"Is Nico on?"

Saul helped me out of the car and steadied me as I tilted a bit again when my feet were on solid ground. "I'm not sure yet," he said, "He's been on and off all day in meetings."

"Don't bother him if he's not here. I'm fine now, I feel much better. I'm just tired."

He didn't agree but nodded dutifully.

Molly hovered close with her hand on my elbow as we walked through the living space on board. When we neared the saloon, voices carried through the open door onto the sky deck and I cringed but forged on, shrugging Molly off.

I had to go through the saloon to get to the private staircase down to the master cabin unless I wanted to walk all the way around to the service staircase from the crew quarters, and it sounded like Nico was entertaining in there.

When I crossed the threshold a cloud of cigar smoke assaulted me, causing me to cringe and cough.

"Arianna." Nico stood from where he sat on a lounge chair surrounded by men in expensive suits all drinking liquor and smoking on cigars. "I didn't expect you back so soon."

"Hmm." I smiled weakly, trying to avoid breathing all of the smoke in. My eyes watered from it as I tried to seem unbothered. "I won't bother you; I'm just going downstairs for a while." He walked over and kissed my temple with a crease in his brows.

"Everything okay?" He asked quietly and I nodded, unwilling to lie directly.

"I'm just tired, I'm going to go rest for a while."

"Are you well?" He tilted my head back to look down into my eyes.

"Get back to your," I paused, looking over his shoulder to the men who looked quite merry and not at all businesslike, "meeting. I'll be fine."

"I'll be down when I'm done," He said as I disentangled from his hold. It was his way of saying he didn't buy it, but I had to get away from him and the peering eyes.

"Excuse me," I smiled politely to the men who nodded back in greeting and made it to the staircase before taking a deep breath of fresh air. "Jesus," I groaned, running down the steps with Molly at my heel.

"He won't wait long before coming down," She said quietly.

"I know. I just need to shower and get into bed."

"Okay." She opened the door and held it open for me and I rushed in.

And then froze still in my tracks as I took in the sight before me, causing Molly to crash into my back.

A woman laid out in the center of my bed, naked, with her head propped up on her elbow smiling seductively towards the door, like she was waiting for someone. When she saw me she simply raised an eyebrow and sat up, not even bothering to cover up her body. "Hello."

"Who are you?" I snapped angrily.

She smirked, standing up from the bed and walking over to the end table where she picked up a silver metal case and pulled a thin cigarette out of it, tapping the end on it casually. "Do you have a light?" She purred, "I seem to have lost mine."

"Who the fuck are you?" I demanded again. Molly gripped my arm tight as I took a step forward without even realizing it.

The woman rolled her eyes and flicked her wrist at me dismissively, "No one you know."

"Then get the fuck out of my bedroom." Anger bloomed through my body replacing any bit of weakness or fatigue that had been plaguing me beforehand. She was beautiful. Downright breathtaking with a tall lean body that looked like she spent every day in the gym to keep it perfect. Her platinum blonde hair was long flowing around her shoulders in perfect waves.

And even though I tried not to notice, her breasts were the size of my head and perfectly sculpted by a surgeon to defy physics and look weightless.

She was a walking, talking Barbie and I hated every single thing about her.

The woman finally let the cool mask on her face slip as she rolled her eyes and picked up a silk robe off the end of the bed, tsking at me. "Now, now love," she purred again in her thick exotic accent, "Don't lower yourself to lies by claiming anything on board here. We both know it's Nicolas' bed and I was warming for him." She slid her arms into the robe but didn't bother to tie it. "Though I'm surprised to see he'd invite you along as well, you're not his type at all."

"Get out!" I hissed, shaking Molly off. "Get out of this bedroom right this instant or so help me God, I'll drag you out by your fake ass hair!" I screamed.

The stress of the day and my insecurities turned me into a violent person I didn't recognize. Or maybe it was my jealousy from finding out that Nicolas had this woman waiting for him in our bed when he expected me to be gone for hours more.

Everything had been so fucking perfect between us.

Or at least I had thought it was.

"No." The woman stepped forward menacingly. "I've been with Nicolas for years. You aren't going to get rid of me that easily. I don't care if he's dating you or not, I'm not going anywhere. You won't be the first little socialite that's tried to tie him down unsuccessfully while he's still kept me on his arm."

"You need to leave," Molly said firmly, "Mr. Capasso will be angry to find you upsetting his wife." She opened the cabin door that had closed behind us and moved to the side, indicating for the woman to leave.

"Wife?" she sneered, not taking Molly up on her offer, "Not possible." She looked down her nose at me. "You're the last person Nicolas would marry. The very fucking last, I assure you."

I snapped.

That's the only word I could find to describe it. One second, I was standing by the door with my hands on my hips, demanding the infuriating woman standing naked in my bedroom leave, and the next, I was flying towards her with my fists clenched.

I connected both of my fists to her face in quick succession before I realized I had moved at all, and then I simply didn't care that I was being physically violent with someone for the first time in my life.

The bitch had it coming.

The woman screamed, scrambling to cover her face as blood coated my knuckles as I buried them in her perfect hair and yanked her off her feet and onto her knees.

She might have had a full foot of height on me, but on her knees, I towered over her.

"You listen to me you cunt, and you listen well." I snapped her head backward as Molly screamed for help from the doorway. I knew Saul and Dio would be breaking this up any second, but I wasn't done. The whore's hair pulled away from her skull as the extensions ripped out, but I grabbed onto her real hair tighter and tilted her head back further to make sure she was looking right at me. "If you ever so much as look at my husband ever again, I'll tear your face off your fucking skull and feed it to the dogs." I shook her, wrapping one hand around her throat for emphasis. Her eyes rounded in fear. "Do you understand me?" I screamed.

"Arianna!" Strong hands gripped my wrists as a body pressed flat against my back and pulled me away.

Nico. His familiar scent which used to warm me, revolted me now.

"Don't touch me," I sneered, letting go of the cunt's hair and throat and shoving her backward onto her ass, and fighting my way out of my husband's hold. I turned on him and glared at him with wild eyes. "Get your whore out of my room."

His chest rose and fell with barely restrained anger, his green eyes were pure liquid fire as they flicked to the woman on the ground finally gripping her robe closed. "Get up." He grabbed her under her elbow and hefted her to her feet.

"Nicolas," the woman gasped and threw herself against his chest, "she attacked me! Completely unprovoked, she's unhinged."

"I'll show you unhinged!" I yelled, lunging forward for the cunt again as she screamed and tried to hide behind Nico, who effectively shoved her out of his arms and into Dio's, catching me and pulling me toward the bathroom.

"Get her off this fucking boat!" He bellowed to his men, as I fought him off. He was far stronger than me though and managed to manhandle me into the bathroom, slamming the door shut behind us and putting his back against it. Locking me inside to keep his whore safe.

"Stay away from me," I pointed my finger at him with menace, "You son of a bitch."

"What happened?" He straightened his shirt out and crossed his arms over his large chest as I started pacing the large bathroom angrily.

"Your wife interrupted your afternoon affair with your whore, that's what!"

"I didn't know she was here. I didn't invite her here."

"Bullshit!" I snapped at him with a glare on one of my laps back and forth, "She was naked in your bed waiting for you!"

"I didn't know she was here," He repeated with far more calmness than I had but I wasn't dumb enough to think he was anywhere near relaxed. He was a caged animal, waiting to pounce at the first opportunity, I could see it in his eyes. He was riled.

Yeah, me too buddy.

"I don't care!" I screamed, throwing my hands up in the air. "I don't care if you invited her over or not. I care that she was here at all!"

"I'm sorry, Little One."

"Whatever." I huffed, crossing my arms over my chest as I stopped pacing and turned away from him to look out the window over the tub. The adrenaline was wearing off and the fatigue was setting back in.

"Did you do that to her face?" He asked and I looked over my shoulder at him and rolled my eyes.

"It sure as fuck wasn't Molly." He smirked and I flipped him off. "Did you fuck her?"

"Not in months." He uncrossed his arms and leaned up off the door.

I held my hand out and cocked my head, warning him, "Don't touch me."

He took a few slow steps toward me, "Will you punch me like you did Edna?"

"Edna?" I snorted, "What an ugly name for such a beautiful woman." He rolled his eyes and I turned to face him, squaring off. "I mean it Nico, don't touch me right now."

"Why?"

"Because I'm disgusted.""With me?" He stopped right in front of me. "Because you met a woman I used to fuck?"

"Watch yourself," I snapped, "I'm disgusted because she was naked in your bed where you fucked me just this morning."

"Our bed," He corrected me and clenched his jaw like he was trying to control his anger. "Our bed, Arianna."

"No," I shook my head, "I realized just now that everything is yours, and I'm just a guest."

"Fuck that." He slid his hand through my hair at the nape of my neck and tightened it in his fist, forcing my head back. "You are my wife. I haven't spoken to her in months, I don't know how she got on board or even knew I was here. I promise you I didn't touch her. Her unwelcome visit changes nothing."

"It changed everything."

He opened his mouth to say something, but a soft knock came from the door behind him as Molly's voice interrupted the space. "Ari, the doctor is here."

My eyes snapped to Nico's as his brow furrowed and his jaw clenched. "Why is there a doctor here?"

"Doesn't matter," I said, trying to shake him off but he tightened his hand in my hair holding me hostage. "Let go."

"Molly, come in," he barked and a second later, the door opened, and my maid and friend stood in the doorway. "Why is a doctor here?"

I could see a flurry of people behind her, Cher's crew of stewardesses stripping the bed of the sheets and cleaning everything in sight.

Molly's eyes flicked to mine for a fraction of a second before going back to Nico's where he looked over his shoulder at her. "Arianna fainted at a restaurant an hour ago, Dio had to carry her to the car she was so weak. We called the doctor to have her checked out."

Nico's hand tightened painfully before loosening and wrapping around the back of my neck as his other arm wrapped around my waist, pulling me flush to his front and supporting my weight. "Fainted? Why wasn't I informed?" He asked her but I beat her to the punch.

"Probably because you were busy entertaining your whore."

"Wife," He snapped and then sighed, dropping his forehead to mine. "Truce, remember?"

I clenched my jaw to keep myself from telling him that the truce was over, because the truth was, I didn't want our progress to go backward.

But I was angry.

So, I sighed and forced my body to relax in his arms and he kissed my temple in response.

"We'll be up to my office in a moment to see the doctor," Nico replied to Molly who gave a curt nod and backed out of the room, closing the door behind her. "What happened to make you faint?"

"I don't know," I groaned, pulling back for space. "I think it was the heat, I don't know."

His brow creased again but he kept the retort of disagreement to himself. "I shouldn't have let you go out all day long. I should have been there with you."

I waved it off and leaned back against the counter, as emotions bubbled up in my chest. But then I felt something tighten lower in my abdomen and I turned away from him as realization dawned on me.

"What is it?" He asked, watching me in the mirror, "Ari, what's wrong?"

I shook my head as my nose burned with stupid useless tears. "Nothing."

"Tell me," he demanded, standing next to me as I dropped my head and gave in to the urge to cry. "Hey," he rubbed his hand up my back soothingly as tears hit the marble countertop, "talk to me."

"I have cramps," I said, feeling stupid and pathetic that I was crying over it. "It means my period is going to start soon."

He took a deep breath and wrapped his arms around me, pulling me into his chest and I went willingly frankly because I was too worn down to fight his comfort. "Getting your period is upsetting you? I thought the idea of being pregnant upset you."

I shrugged my shoulders as I begged the tears to stop. "Hormones are a fucking cunt sometimes."

"Could you possibly be a little upset that you aren't pregnant after all? Even though the test already told us you weren't."

"No, that's stupid," I snapped and then groaned, "Stop talking to me."

He chuckled and ran his hands up and down my back, "Let's go get you checked out and we will go from there."

"Whatever," I sighed, feeling a bit better for being rude to him when he didn't deserve it. As I said, hormones were weird.

CHAPTER 17 – NICO

I sat in the armchair at the side of the bed and watched Arianna sleep. It was almost four am and I just let her go to sleep a few hours ago, so she was positively comatose. She lay flat on her stomach with her arms stretched out at each side, naked and covered with the cool white sheet to keep her from getting overheated again.

Her new wedding ring set sparkled on her ring finger and the sight of it made my cock hard, regardless of how spent it was from the last few days. After tonight alone, I would be raw for days. I knew it wasn't right to use her body to ease the fear inside of me, but I didn't have any other option.

When I heard Molly scream for help after she and Ari went down to our bedroom earlier in the afternoon, my heart seized in my chest. It didn't matter who I was in the middle of meeting with, I jumped up and ran towards her. It wasn't until I laid eyes on Ari myself, alive and well, that I took a breath.

I was afraid something had happened to her.

I didn't expect to find her with bloodied knuckles from the nose of a woman I had a casual affair with before we met, that was for sure. Nonetheless, I had to pry Arianna's hand from Edna's throat to get her to let go.

I think it was at that moment that I realized I was falling in love with her.

My wife.

My once-upon-a-time enemy.

And now my ally.

Or at least I considered her my ally, but she had been ready to cut ties completely when she thought I had invited Edna on board when she was gone.

I smirked to myself remembering the fire burning inside of her when I discovered what riled her up so much.

She was jealous.

The first glimpse of affection towards me outside of the physical relationship we had fallen into. The first indication that she felt something for me more than just her inclination to let me give her orgasms.

She cared for me as well.

But that discovery had been enjoyed so shortly after finding out that Arianna had only returned to the boat early because she fainted at lunch. Then I felt nothing but worry.

Which was so foreign to me, I didn't even recognize myself.

The doctor checked her out, diagnosing her with heat exhaustion and dehydration. She said her period had started with cramps earlier and perhaps that had added to the stress of the day, though I wasn't convinced. He gave her an IV and a bag of electrolytes and instructed her to stay out of the sun for a few days.

But it didn't ease the worry inside of me. Add on the fact that I was heading ashore for three days while Arianna continued sailing on to our next stop where I would meet her again, I was restless and uneasy.

Which led me to sit in the chair watching her lying in bed asleep when I should be wrapped around her still, letting her calmness ease me.

"No," Ari's melodic voice cut through the dim light of the bedroom as her face creased above the brow. "Please, don't."

Nightmare.

I unfolded myself from the chair as her fingers gripped the sheet underneath her and her body tensed.

"Little One." I ran my fingers through her hair and slid back into bed beside her, pulling her body against mine. "Shh, I've got you." She buried her face in my neck and crawled up my body until she lay across my chest with her legs wrapped around mine. I grinned to myself in the darkness at how easily she gave herself to me in the night when she didn't fight her body's desire to be close to me.

"What time is it?" She whispered, waking up enough to get out of her nightmare.

"Almost dawn. You were having a nightmare. What was it about?"

She groaned and tightened her hold on my leg with hers, "I have no idea," She responded before stretching. "I'm not ready to get up. You kept me up too late."

I didn't believe that she didn't remember, but let it slide for the time being. "You're going to stay in bed all day long. I don't want you getting up for anything other than food and then back to bed to rest." I traced the length of her spine with my fingers, and she rocked her hips, rubbing herself against my thigh like she had one night in her sleep, making me grin again.

"I could probably be persuaded to stay in bed all day if you stay with me."

"I can't," I sighed, "I'm flying to Milan in a few hours. I'll be gone three days." She stiffened but remained silent. "Does that upset you?"

"I thought this was a honeymoon." She finally said quietly.

"It is. But something has come up and I can't leave it unattended for the rest of our trip. I'll be back in just a few days, then I'm yours."

"Take me with you."

"You'd be sitting alone in my penthouse while I conducted business, Ari, wouldn't you rather be here on board relaxing?"

"No," she said and then took a deep breath, "Maybe."

I rolled over and slid down until our faces were even before sliding my hand around the back of her neck to anchor her where she was. "Will you miss me?"

"Yes," she said without hesitation, and I rewarded her with a kiss. "You've made me an addict for you."

"Hmm," I smirked and kissed her again, sliding my tongue over her lips. "I kind of like the idea of that."

"Because that's not conceited or anything," she smirked in the darkness, and I spanked her ass cheek, rocking her forward against my groin. "Mmh, again." She dug her nails into my shoulder as she threw her leg over my hip and propped her ass up higher for a clearer shot.

"You want me to spank you, Little One?" I rubbed my palm over her warm cheek.

"I'm not too proud to beg you for it, Nico."

"Good." I landed another sharp spank on her ass for her honesty. She moaned and pressed her lips to my neck as I slid my thigh firmer between hers. "You're supposed to be sleeping."

"You just told me I have to go without you for three days. You've been gentle with me all night, but I want more. I don't want your niceties, remember." She ran her tongue over the pulse in my neck and then tentatively bit the skin there. She was getting bolder sexually and I fucking loved that I brought that out of her. "I'll be a good girl and sleep for those three days."

"Hmm," I hummed again and rolled over her body until she laid flat on her stomach with me on her back. I took both of her wrists and pinned them above her head, "Don't move them."

"Yes, Sirs" she whimpered and bit her bottom lip as she tried to look at me over her shoulder. I ran my bare cock between her lush ass cheeks and spanked her again, watching the supple flesh ripple and redden. "Yes." She hissed and sighed like it released something inside of her.

I sat up off her back and pulled her hips up into the air, "Keep your chest flat on the bed and spread your legs." She shifted herself and spread her legs a couple of inches but kept her back bowed in uncertainty. "Wider." I spanked her cheek again and pressed my hand flat to the small of her back. "Arch it down towards the bed, pop this luscious ass into the air for me, baby."

She spread her knees wide and lowered her ribs to the bed, giving me exactly what I wanted from her. "Like this?" she purred, looking back at me seductively.

"Perfect." I praised, shaking her cheeks in my hands before spanking them both and then spreading them wide to see her pretty pink pussy. "You're perfect." I dropped down onto my elbows and ran my tongue up the length of her slit, surprising her. She bucked forward before I pulled her back onto my face and sucked her clit into my mouth.

"Fuck!" she gasped and then pressed back further, opening her legs even wider and arching further for me. "Yes, God yes."

"You taste divine." I tongued her pussy and spanked her ass until she came on my face, gasping and pleading with me for more.

"Please, Nico."

"I got you," I said, rising to my knees behind her and running the head of my cock through her folds, coating it before sliding it into her tight hole. "God," I groaned, tipping my head back as I buried myself inside of her, "You take me so good, Little One."

"Fuck me. Please stop talking and fuck me," she begged and I spanked her again before pulling out and slamming back in, making us both groan.

"I'll fuck you so good, baby. You're going to be sore for the next three days remembering how fucking good I gave it to you."

"Yes," she hissed and pushed back against me, "It feels so good like this."

I wrapped my fingers around her slim waist and started thrusting hard, giving her exactly what she asked for even as my own orgasm started building faster than normal. Every single time I was with Arianna I fought off the urge to blow early like some chump in ways I hadn't since I was a young kid getting my dick wet for the first time.

"Be a good girl and come on my cock. I know you want to," I grunted, feeling her body tighten more with each stroke. I spanked her ass and wrapped her long dark hair around my fist for leverage and slammed into her so hard the bed shook against the wall.

"I'm coming!" she screamed into the pillows, "Fuck I'm coming, so hard."

"Good girl," I praised her and felt her pussy clamp down hard around me, squeezing the life out of my dick and accentuating every inch of friction. "Fuck." I tilted my head back and roared to the skies as I filled her up with every drop left inside of me. I already fucked her three times since the doctor left, but I wasn't able to contain my need for her when she was open and asking for it like she did tonight. "My fucking good girl."

"Yes," she sighed, rolling her hips after I stopped thrusting, extending her pleasure until she collapsed onto her belly with a grunt and a smirk on her pretty lips. "Not bad for such an old man," She joked and I spanked her once playfully before falling to my back next to her.

"Be careful, or this old man will let you go dry for far longer than just the three days I'm gone."

"Hmm." She rolled over onto her side, cocking her hip up and exposing her perfect breasts to my eyes, "Yeah, okay," she said as I stared at her beauty longingly, "Whatever you say, big guy."

"Are you sure about this?" Luca asked as we drove through the city of West Shores.

"Absolutely," I responded, checking my phone again for the time. We had to calculate the hit perfectly or none of us would be sure about anything.

Because we'd be dead.

"Good news," Harris radioed through the speaker, "Target's been located. We're good to go."

I picked up the radio and responded, "Great, wait for my arrival and follow as planned."

I looked over at Luca and his wide shit-eating grin, ready to bite into the flesh of the traitors in our circle, and nodded back. It was calming having a good fella riding alongside me, even if I usually preferred to have Matteo at my side.

He was still on board the yacht with Arianna, Molly, Dio, and Saul. It wasn't that I didn't trust Dio and Saul, but having her traveling internationally, I wanted another man on board that I trusted with my own life.

Just in case anything went south here in West Shores.

If everything went right, I'd be back on board tomorrow night with her and everything would be perfect again.

As soon as I stole back the weapons that her father had smuggled into my territory.

"On-site, Capa," My driver said, snapping me back to reality as we drove through the dark alley towards the warehouse that my men already surrounded.

"Let's go." As soon as the car stopped at the front door, armed men flanked every entrance and window to the building, alerted to someone's arrival.

"Who goes there?" A man called out from the second-story window as I got out of the back seat of my car.

"The fucking Don," I sneered openly up at him, "Lower your fucking weapon unless you want your mother's throat slit for your disrespect."

I watched as the men looked between themselves, lowering the barrels of their riffles marginally in uncertainty. I wasn't their boss. But I was their boss's boss.

"Do it now!" Luca bellowed from my side and the men complied. I didn't look like a threat to them, considering it was only Luca and me that arrived, but they knew better than to believe I wasn't packing more soldiers than just what they could see.

The door opened and a man I recognized stepped outside to greet me.

Cristian.

Arianna's older brother, and second in line to the throne.

"Nicolas," He said with a slight nod of his head to his men, who lowered their weapons, "I heard you were abroad."

"Is that what you were counting on, *Brother*?" I elongated the title and watched as his eyes rounded slightly at the menace behind them.

He was my wife's brother, but I didn't know his character in the least. I had never had a conversation with him before this moment to get a read off him like I had Carmine.

With Arianna's oldest brother, I could read his sincerity and character by the way he carried himself.

Cristian was more reserved.

Keeping his cards closer to his chest, and while that was admirable and a good trait to possess as a soldier, it was a bad trait to find in a possible opponent.

And finding him here, with nearly three million dollars of smuggled guns on my turf that I wasn't made aware of, didn't bode well for him.

He cocked his head slightly and held his hands out at the sides of his waist, "Just an observation made through the long grapevine from Armarow to West Shores is all." He adjusted his suit jacket. "What brings you this far away from my lovely sister this evening?" He nodded to the car behind me, "Unless of course, you've dragged her along on this visit?"

"My wife couldn't make it this evening, though she sends her best." I raised an eyebrow at him. "Are you planning on explaining the weapons hidden inside, or is your father around to do that?"

I cut straight to the chase, finding the urge to get this over with sooner rather than later.

His face blanched a bit, but he gave no other outward sign of distress. Just that one. And most people would have missed it.

But not me.

"I wasn't aware we were hiding anything from you, Nicolas."

"You will call me Don, or Capa." I took three steps forward until he was close enough to reach if I wanted to. "You haven't earned the right to call me by my familial name yet, boy." I spat on the ground next to his shoes. "Now get the fuck out of my way before my patience fades past what even Arianna's desire to keep you safe can control." I walked around him and paused at the open doorway as he turned to watch me with fear in his eyes. "Hopefully by the end of this conversation, we'll be on the same side of this entire thing,"

I shrugged my shoulder, "Because your father will be one child short of a five-pack if we're not."

I didn't explain which one of Emilio's children was at risk, that was the point of the threat.

"After you." He lifted his hand, motioning for me to do what I already was on my way to do.

Luca nodded, looking at the skyline of the buildings around us discretely before following me inside.

The crates of weapons were easy to find in the warehouse, hidden amongst the machinery that hadn't been run in decades and exactly where I would have hidden them if I had been in Cristian's shoes.

But not Emilio's.

He would have hidden them better.

I stopped at one and grabbed a crowbar from a pile of scrap pallets, shoving the end under the locked lid and prying it open. The lock clanged against the cement floor as I looked over to where Cristian stood with his men in arms, watching us closely. "Last chance to come clean."

He swallowed, flicking his eyes from me to the crate and back. "I wasn't made aware that you didn't know the contents."

"I always knew the contents, *Brother*." I shook my head in disappointment. "I was just told by your father that they were being traded out of the district." I pushed the lid off, revealing high-powered military weapons that were only procured by the cartel or the Russians. "And that was months ago."

Cristian didn't reply.

I tsked my teeth and gripped the crowbar in my fist as I looked back down at the crate and then over the others. "You see, when weapons or goods are brought into my districts, and then traded, I get a cut of the deal." I turned to face the younger Rosetti, who, to his credit, remained standing tall and strong, even in the face of danger. "But when they're brought in and kept for other reasons, like perhaps," I tossed the crowbar into the air, flipping it end over end like a baseball bat and catching it again. "for personal gain of the one who smuggled them in, to begin with, I don't get anything out of that deal." I took one step towards him. "Do you see the problem here?"

"Yes, Capa." He nodded his head once, remaining upright and strong.

Honorable quality.

"Where did Emilio get them from?" Cristian opened his mouth to answer but I quickly held my hand up to stop him, "Make no mistake Cristian, this is your one chance to align yourself onto the right side of the conversation. After this, the wheels of fate will already be spun into motion and even I won't stop them once that happens. So answer carefully."

If he admitted that they came from the Cartel, that would mean that Emilio and the Cartel would be on my hit list, as traitors. Two powerful enemies to make for himself. But if he lied and said the Russians, he was admitting to dealing with the only crime organization that could rival my own, our biggest competitors.

And he'd be framing the even more powerful enemy, signing his death certificate.

"I believe the cartel and my father made the deal, but I wasn't here," he answered truthfully, revealing the two traitors.

I smirked and looked back at the crates, signaling to Luca with a single nod of my head. He picked his phone up and made the call.

"These crates are now mine," I announced loudly for his armed guards to hear, "I suggest anyone that wants to stay in my good graces, puts their weapons down and helps my men load them."

At the same time, the overhead bays lining the entire length of the exterior walls opened loudly, revealing my men, armed and ready for a fight.

For a split second, I anticipated a fight.

All it would take was one jackass to let a bullet fly to start a full-out massacre of all involved tonight. For all of our sakes, the guns remained silent.

"Good." I looked my brother-in-law in the eye and nodded to the office off to the side. "We should probably finish this conversation in private." I waited but he didn't walk ahead of me like I indicated. I regarded him, "Unless, of course, you want all of your men to see you getting your spanking?"

His jaw clenched as his men looked between themselves uncertainly before walking away to assist in loading the weapons with my men.

Their men.

We were supposed to be all on the same team after all. Probably ninety percent of them wouldn't choose Emilio over the *Don* in an all-out war. But ten percent of them would.

And that was a fucking problem.

Emilio was a fucking problem that needed to be eradicated.

When I got into the office I pulled the chair out and threw myself down into it, kicking my feet up onto the desk that Emilio and Cristian sat at when they were here.

The younger Rosetti followed in, shutting the door behind him and putting his hands into his pants pockets as he stood in the center of the room.

"Does Emilio want a war with me?"

"Not that I know of," He answered instantly.

"Do you?"

"War with the Don is the last thing I want."

"Do you have any idea how fucking close to war you are right now?" I ran my thumb over my bottom lip as I watched him. "How fucking close you are right this second to no longer existing. Any other man would be gasping as his windpipe filled with blood on the floor right now for this."

"Then why aren't I?" he questioned evenly.

I watched him, holding his stare as I let the space drag out like I was contemplating the answer. "Easy." I took my feet off the desk and leaned forward with my elbows on my knees to stare at him. "Arianna."

"I'm surprised you care for my sister's feelings so soon," he responded, "You've never been rumored to be kind to anyone, let alone a woman."

"Wrong." I stood up and adjusted my suit jacket. "I'm not kind to Arianna. I'm sure if you asked her, she'd tell you that I was the devil reincarnate." His eyes squinted in speculation as he tried to figure out exactly what went on between his sister and me in our home. "But that doesn't mean I wish to punish you for your father's sins. The same way I don't enjoy punishing her for his sins either."

"You punish her?" he snapped, before clenching his jaw like the outburst was unintentional.

Bingo.

I shrugged my shoulders and walked around the desk. "I do what is allowed of me as her husband. What your father allowed me to do when he agreed to marry her to me." I stopped when I stood directly in front of him. "What is allowed of me as the mother fucking Don." Someday I'd give the kid credit for standing tall with me only inches away because he wasn't even flinching as I exerted my power. He was either brave or he was dumb. Either way, he would bleed for it. "When this is all said and done, I want you to remember whose fault this is," I said seconds before slamming my forehead into his, smashing his nose and sending him sprawling backward from the force of it.

"Fuck," He hissed as he landed against the door.

I didn't give him a chance to staunch the bleeding from his nose before I swung and landed another blow to his cheek. Bone cracked under my knuckles, sending a rush of adrenalin through my body, even as I got a sour taste in my mouth from bloodying Arianna's brother.

He glared at me, spitting a mouthful of blood out onto the floor before standing tall and adjusting his suit jacket. "Who's the fucking boss around here?" I sneered.

"You," He answered instantly with his hiss.

I swiped my fist back out through the air, delivering an undercut to his jaw, sending him flying back into the door again before he fell onto his ass, stunned and disoriented.

"Nobody steals from me in my own fucking home." I grabbed him by the collar, pulling him to his feet and slamming him against the door, rattling the hinges and his teeth. "Not even family." I bounced him off the door again, enjoying and hating the dense thud his skull made as it connected with the wood. I leaned forward until my face was pressed against his and spoke directly into his ear. "The next time someone inside your family tries it again, you'll be the first one I come for. And this time I'll strap you down and make you scream for mercy before I disfigure you so badly even your own worthless mother won't be able to recognize you." I slammed my fist into his stomach, doubling him over as all of the air hissed out between his teeth. "And then I'll kill you and the rest of your siblings for the fuck of it. Don't try me again, Cristian." I threw him onto the floor away from the door, in a heap, wiping the blood off my busted knuckle onto my pant leg. "I can't be your ally and your enemy at the same time, Cristian. And from this moment forward, Emilio Rosetti is enemy number one." He panted and looked up at me through the blood pouring from his face with a look of fear. "Only you can choose whose side you stand on in the morning."

I opened the door, taking away his chance to respond, and walked out into the warehouse. His men watched me closely, seeing the blood splattered on my face and hands, but no one moved.

"The line in the sand is now drawn," I announced loudly, causing everyone to stop what they were doing. "There is no chance to go back over that line after you cross it. Choose wisely." I walked out the overhead door to my waiting car and got in with Luca once again at my side.

The car pulled away, and my men finished loading up the crates into our trucks as I headed to the penthouse for the rest of the night.

"Today was a monumental day, Capa," Luca said from beside me as he took out the decanter of bourbon and poured us each a glass.

"Why is that?" I questioned, taking the glass from him, "Because I made enemies with my once biggest ally?"

"No," he shook his head with a smirk on his face, "Because you've fully come into your power and your strength by severing the tie to dead weight and taking on your rule in your way. Generational curses will end under your rule."

"Hmm," I hummed, tossing back the shot in one gulp and holding it out for another, "Something tells me this will get worse before it gets better."

"The biggest rises in power always do, Capa," he mused, tossing back his drink and falling silent beside me.

Chapter 18- Arianna

I lay in bed, refusing to move a single inch for the next twelve hours.

In twelve hours, Nicolas would return to the yacht when we docked in Sicily, and to say I was eager for his return was an understatement.

While the last few days without him were relaxing, they dragged on as I watched the proverbial clock on the wall tick with each passing moment alone without him. I didn't lie when I told him he had turned me into an addict for him.

It wasn't just sexual either, I craved his presence and his energy now too. I was fucked in the head, but so was he. We were both obsessed, two unlikely partners in a union neither of us wanted, yet both of us had accepted it at some point along the way.

I think I accepted it the night he showed up at Molly's parent's home and defied the expectations I had for him, to carry me kicking and screaming from their home. Instead, he charmed them and dined with us like it was the most normal occurrence in the world.

Royalty at the modest dinner table, like a random Tuesday evening.

Unheard of.

Yet, he did it; for me.

That was the turning point in my head, before he called the truce between us even, when I began to think of him as less of an enemy and more of a counterpart.

An ally.

And I missed my ally, my husband.

But he was returning to me tonight, I had already asked Matteo on repeat for the last forty-eight hours straight, to make sure that he was safe and everything was on track to bring him back to me.

The poor man hadn't had a moment's rest on board between my impulsive questioning and Molly's tempted teasing.

Okay, to be fair, Molly wasn't teasing him on purpose.

I, however, was facilitating the teasing as a means of entertainment because Nicolas' second-in-command was hilarious to watch when he was lost observing Molly.

Her new uniforms were a hit, and on top of that, the bikini I finally managed to threaten her into to lay next to me on the sundeck, made the man positively vibrate with need. Even if she was so blind to it all the entire time.

"Morning, Ari," Her sweet angelic voice called from the door to my cabin like my thoughts had beckoned her themselves. "How are you this morning?"

"Eager to get to land," I said, curling onto my side and pulling the blankets up to my shoulders. "I'm not leaving bed until Nico is back on board."

"Are you well?" She paused with her brows knitted worriedly.

"I'm horny," I said plainly, enjoying the way her face reddened as she rolled her eyes. "And tired." I yawned again for the hundredth time since waking up an hour before. "I'm getting all the rest I can today because I doubt I will be getting any tonight."

She grinned and walked to the window, pulling the curtains open and eliciting a groan from me as I dove under the covers a millisecond too late. "Well, while I normally would encourage you to rest. I think you should spend the day above deck."

"Why?" I asked from my cocoon.

"Because we're traveling along the coastline today to our port and it's a beautiful view."

"Hmm," I hummed, unconvinced, "I can't wait to get back on land."

She chuckled and flitted around my cabin, ignoring my comments meant to dissuade her task to get me out of bed. "All the better to get above deck, enjoy an omelet and some yogurt with a nice warm coffee and start the journey to your prince charming."

"Eh," I groaned, hating the way her description of the breakfast foods I loved made my stomach turn. "No breakfast."

"You have to eat breakfast, Arianna," she huffed good-heartedly, "Those were Mr. Capasso's explicit instructions to me before he left. You have to eat every meal without fail and double your water intake so you don't faint again." She pulled my blankets down and I took refuge under my pillow. "If not an omelet, how about a bagel? We have that chive cream cheese you love, or I can ask Chef to whip you up some French toast or something. He only complained a little when you smeared syrup over his strawberry masterpiece last time."

"Stop talking," I commanded pulling my head out from under the pillow and sitting up.

"Ari," she groaned, "Breakfast, lunch, and dinner. Those were the rules."

"Stop," I hissed, but it was too late. Her words had permeated through my ears, into my brain, and directly into my stomach which was souring more and more by the moment. "Move!" I cried, throwing myself out of bed and running for the bathroom, throwing up in the toilet milliseconds after collapsing to my knees in front of it. There wasn't much in my stomach at this hour, but what was left from the night before burned on its way up and out.

"Oh, dear." Molly grabbed my hair and pulled it back off my face as another heave wracked my body, causing agony. "Easy now," She cooed soothingly as the heaves lessened and then stopped completely, leaving me tired and worn out. "Let's get you cleaned up."

I stood up and made it to the sink and buried my face under the cool water, rinsing my mouth out. When I stood back up and patted my skin dry Molly was standing next to me with her hand held out expectantly.

"What?" I looked away from her reflection in the mirror and down to her hand, seeing the plastic-wrapped pregnancy test she had given to me over a week ago when Dr. Travis stopped to check to see if Nicolas had been successful in his task to breed me.

"You still haven't gotten your period, and now you're puking from the mere mention of food. You've slept nearly the entire time that Nicolas has been gone and I think it's time to face the music." She tilted her head as I simply stared at her.

"But I had cramps," I whispered defensively.

"While those *are* a sign of your menstrual cycle, they're also a sign of early pregnancy." She set the test down on the counter and turned me to face her, "And besides, wouldn't you rather know for sure before your husband rejoins you tonight?"

"Ugh," I groaned, throwing my head back in defeat. "I feel like my entire life has revolved around the possibility of a fetus growing inside of me for weeks now."

"Then find out for sure, and you won't have to worry anymore."

"Or worrying is all I'll do ever again," I countered, grabbing the test and taking it to the toilet.

Molly shrugged her shoulders and smirked, "I hear that never ends either."

"Oh fuck off," I complained good-heartedly and she smiled brighter at me, turning to give me a bit of privacy as I took the test.

When I was done, I set it on the counter face down and washed my hands. She watched me with her hip against the marble as I avoided looking at the test altogether. "Do you want me to leave while you look at it?"

"Not a chance," I replied, taking a deep breath and forcing myself to pick it up. I met her eyes over the top of it briefly and she gave me a reassuring smile as I turned it over to read the result.

Pregnant.

"Holy hell," I whispered in complete shock before dropping my hand to my flat stomach like cradling that area in my hand could somehow make it feel real.

"Wow," she agreed, nodding and grabbing my free hand as we both stared at the test. "Okay, sit down before you pass out."

I blindly sank to the floor with her at my side and rested my back against the vanity as my world began to spin. "I don't know how to be a mom," I admitted for the second time to her.

"I know," she agreed again, squeezing my hand in her lap and taking a deep breath like she was calming the both of us. "But we've been over that. You're going to trust your human nature instinct and forget all of the things you were taught about parenthood. You're going to choose to embrace it and allow it to be a good thing because you can't change it now."

"Promise me, you'll help me." I looked over at her as tears pooled in my lash line. "You'll help me figure it all out, right?"

"Right," She nodded her head as her own eyes misted over, "And I think it's time that my mother comes out of retirement since all of her kids are grown and moved out." She smiled brightly. "We will help you, Arianna, I promise. You won't do this alone. We'll be there with you and Nicolas through the whole thing."

"Holy Hell." I sank back into the vanity again as I realized I had to tell my husband. "He's going to be so mad when I tell him I lied to him."

"You don't know that," she assured me. "He'll be happy over the news of it all, and you'll have to just take that high and ride it as long as you can while he processes it all."

"Right," I repeated the word she had used to sound so sure. "He'll be happy."

"Are you happy?" She whispered as I stared off into the distance.

"I think so," I admitted. "Somewhere beneath all of the fear and self-doubt," I shrugged, "Sure. I think I'm a little happy."

"Good," She smiled and took a deep breath, "Because ready or not, your clock has started and there's no stopping it now."

"Gee, thanks." I groaned, nudging her with my shoulder causing her to chuckle.

"Let's get up off the floor and get you to the breakfast table." I grimaced and glared at her but she held her hand up and stopped me from refusing. "I'll make you a fruit smoothie," She said with her eyebrows raised, "My mom swore by fresh fruit during the early stages of pregnancy, to combat morning sickness." She waited for me to decide, and the idea of a strawberry smoothie didn't completely repulse me. "How does that sound?"

"Like you'd better have a bucket ready just in case," I groaned, letting her pull me up off the cold tile floor. "But not the worst idea you've ever had."

She snorted and pulled me into a hug. "I've never had a bad idea in my life."

"Ha!" I chuckled, letting her ease warm me and relax the anxiety trying to pull me under into a full-blown panic attack.

With her by my side, I'd figure it out.

I just hoped I had Nicolas there too.

e're docked," Molly said hours later as she poked her head into my bathroom where I applied the last of my makeup in the mirror and took a calming deep breath.

"Any word on when Nico will be here?" I asked, but she didn't get a chance to answer as my husband himself walked into the bedroom behind her, silencing anything I had to say.

God, he looked magnificent. He wore a pair of light blue jeans and a white t-shirt that hugged his massive biceps and wide chest, revealing the ink down both arms that I'd fallen in love with.

"Right now," Molly winked and backed out of the doorway, giving Nico a small curtsey as she walked past before shutting the bedroom door behind her.

"Hi," I whispered anxiously from where I stood frozen in place at the bathroom counter.

"Are you going to make me come into a restroom to kiss you hello, or will you join me out here?" He asked with a small grin on his perfect face.

I pushed off the counter and walked toward him without a single thought to do so and stopped when my toes met his. "Better?"

"So much better." He brought his hand up to my face and my eyelids fluttered closed as I leaned into it. "Did you miss me, Little One?" His voice was low and thick which screamed sex appeal.

"You know I did," I answered truthfully. "Did you miss me?"

He leaned down and brushed his warm lips over mine, leaning back an inch when I opened them and tried to deepen it. "Every single second that we were apart." He ran the tip of his tongue over my bottom lip, and I clung to his wrist where his hand still held my face for stability as I sagged into him further. "With every single part of my being."

"God," I moaned, melting into a puddle at his feet.

"Yes?" he smirked cheekily before finally giving me what I wanted and kissing me with that hunger that always lay directly beneath his tough exterior.

I opened for him, eager to let his dominance consume me and take away all of the worries that had built inside of me throughout the day, anticipating his return to the boat. Twenty minutes ago I had been a basket case of nerves as the boat started its docking procedures into the Italian port. Worrying myself over telling him our news, and what his reaction would be.

Now, none of it mattered in the least.

"Come here," he purred, pulling me with him as he sat down on the edge of the bed until I straddled his lap. His hands instantly slid under the hem of my short white dress, gripping my ass with their strength. "You smell divine," he growled, lowering his lips to my neck, kissing the sensitive skin beneath my ear, and sucking on it.

"Yes," I moaned, rocking in his lap, desperate to feel him deep inside of me, "I need you. Please."

"How do you want me?" He continued his trail of kisses and nibbles down my neck to the glimpse of cleavage above my dress.

"Like this." I slid my hands between us and pulled at his shirt until he had no choice but to lift his arms and let me tear it off of him. "I want you to pull my panties to the side and fuck me. Right now."

"Ari." He growled as I pulled the button of his jeans open and lowered the zipper, feeling the strain on it from his erection. "Be careful what you ask for. I won't be gentle if you demand it like that."

"I don't want your niceties," I hissed. Biting his jaw as desperation overtook me. "I can't wait. Please, please, please, don't make me wait," I whined anxiously.

"Fuck." He lifted his hips as I pulled his cock out and fisted it before he sprang into action. He gripped my panties and pulled them over, dipping his fingertips into my pussy and growling when he found me wet already. "Were you playing with this sweet little pussy before I got here?"

"Only every single second since you left," I teased, rocking against his fingers as I stroked his cock to steel. "My poor fingers are so tired from rubbing my clit."

"Minx," He hissed, lifting me over his cock and waiting for me to line him up before pulling me down onto his thickness. "Son of a bitch," He growled through clenched teeth, closing his eyes like he was in physical pain. "You're so fucking tight, wrapped around me."

"It's your fault," I gasped, lifting and pushing back down on him until my clit rubbed against his pubic bone. "Your cock is so thick. I've never seen a cock so big before."

He grunted, lifting me and slamming me back down onto him. "How many cocks have you seen, Wife?"

I chuckled and rolled my hips, digging my nails into his neck as I tossed my head back in pure pleasure. "A few."

His hand slid from my waist and slapped my ass cheek before reaching down and rubbing my stretched pussy lips around his cock as I rode him. "Liar."

"No," I panted, "I watched a few pornos before I was a married woman." I rolled my hips again, rubbing my clit on the downward strokes. "I wanted to know what I was getting into."

"Fuck this." He spun us, throwing me down on my back on the bed and spreading my legs wide as he slammed into me, causing a scream to tear from my lips followed by a deep, throaty moan. "No more looking at other cocks. If you want to see a cock, tell me, and I'll show you mine." He was completely feral as he fucked me, and my body soaked his cock even more realizing I did that to him.

"And if I said I wanted to learn how to suck your cock," I purred seductively. I had no idea where I got the bravery or stupidity to poke the already crazed bear, but I was soaring high on sexual excitement and couldn't be stopped. "Would you let me play with yours, testing out what I saw in those videos?"

"I'll teach you." He growled. Wrapping one hand around my ankles and pushing them back so my knees were pressed flat against my chest as he changed angles, thrusting deeper and making my eyes roll back in my head. "I'll hold your head still and push my cock so far down your throat you won't have any choice but to swallow me down. My thighs will wear the marks of your claws for days."

"Yes," I hissed, letting him use my body like a conductor of an orchestra, running the show and making sweet music. "I like marking you. The same way I like seeing your marks on me."

He let go of my ankles and laid down against my body, wrapping one hand around the back of my neck, keeping me anchored in place as he rolled his hips over and over again, pushing me towards bliss. "I need you to come on my cock Little One. Your dirty words and sexual prowess is making it impossible for me to hold back any longer. I'm a breath away from filling you up."

His words and the rocking motion of his hips did the trick, pushing me over the edge of my orgasm as his movements jerked caused by his own pleasure. "Good girl." He groaned, rearing back and clenching his teeth as he started coming. I leaned up and wrapped my teeth around the thick corded muscle of his peck and bit down. Mirroring the way I did the first night we were together that sent him over the edge even harder.

I, of course, had no idea what I was doing that night, only meaning to stifle my screams. But tonight, after a few weeks of being with him, I understood how pain and pleasure mixed in the throes of passion, heightening each feeling.

"Fuck!" he bellowed, "Harder, baby." He slammed deep again as I tightened my teeth on him to the point I was worried I'd taste his blood if I went any harder and he shot off a long line of curse words, exposing his desires before stilling inside of me. I gently released his flesh and traced my tongue over the impression of my teeth before dropping my head back to the bed and staring up at him dreamily, as he came down from his high.

"You've turned me into a lunatic," I whispered with a smirk and an oof when he rolled us both over until I laid on top of his broad chest, his cock still buried inside of me.

"Ditto." He sighed, with a smirk on his lips. "I think I'm going to tattoo your dental impression on my chest so you have somewhere to aim those pretty teeth when I'm on top of you like that."

"Hmm." I mused, tracing the mark with my fingertip. "How romantic."

He snorted and spanked my ass before pulling me off his cock. "Let's get cleaned up and go eat. Cher said you planned the entire meal with Chef for this evening."

I blushed, rolling off of him to stand as he rose. The silky feeling between my thighs made me want to grind against his hard body for the next three days, but I refrained, getting excited for him to see the meal I planned. "I did." I shrugged, feigning indifference. "I figured I'd better start contributing to something around here before you get bored of me and toss me overboard."

"Ha." He smirked, sitting up on the edge of the bed and pulling me forward between his long legs. "You're doing so much more than you know, by simply existing."

"What does that mean?" I whispered, trying to keep my heartbeat steady as my body wanted to run away with his romantic words and let them mean something more than they did.

"Maybe someday I'll tell you." He winked, and I rolled my eyes, hating his usual answer when I asked him to clarify his words.

"Maybe." I groaned, turning and walking to the bathroom to clean up. "Someday."

"This was delicious." Nico sighed, leaning back in his chair with a glass of wine in his fingers as he watched me. We sat at a small table not usually used for dinnertime dining, but the intimacy of it felt right.

He touched me in some way, during the entire meal. Sometimes it was his fingers along my bare knee under the table, or against my neck as he brushed my hair over my shoulder. If he wasn't physically touching me, his eyes would caress me over the candlelight.

"How did your business go while you were away?" I asked, twirling my glass of sparkling water in my fingers like he was.

"It went," he hesitated, dropping my gaze, "as well as it could have."

"That sounded evasive," I raised an eyebrow at him, challenging him for more information.

He smirked at me and took a sip of his wine. "You won't like the full answer if I give it to you."

"Why?"

"Because I did something I'm not proud of, but it was necessary."

Dread filled my stomach as I pondered what he meant. "Did it involve another woman?" I asked quietly, dropping his gaze as I prepared for the answer.

He leaned forward, tipping my chin up with his fingers until I met his stare again. "No, Arianna. It didn't."

I swallowed and forced air into my lungs that I had been unable to until he answered me. "Then tell me what happened."

His mouth opened, but the doors to the room slid open, and he closed his lips turning to the interruption.

"What is it?" Nico asked Matteo as the door closed behind him soundlessly.

Matteo looked over at me with a polite nod, before leaning down to Nico's side and whispering to him. Nico's eyes found mine as his second stood back up, before he nodded, taking a sip of his wine.

"I'll be right there," Nico told him and Matteo backed up, giving me a slight smile before walking back out of the room.

"What's going on?" I questioned, hating that they had some sort of conversation right in front of me, without including me in it.

"I don't know yet," he said, standing up and leaning down over me, making me tilt my head way back to look at him. He lowered his lips to mine chastely. "Go to the aft salon, I'll be there momentarily."

"Why-?" I asked but he shook his head.

"Just do as you're told, Arianna," He took a deep breath and sighed, "Please."

"Fine." I rose from my seat, discarding my napkin on the table, and walked from the room without a backward glance.

Something was wrong, but he still didn't trust me enough to share it with me.

When I got to the salon, Molly walked in with a shawl for my arms. "What's happening?" I asked, knowing she would have more information than I did.

"Someone has come aboard that wasn't expected," she answered quickly, "I don't know who it was, but I know it sent Matteo on edge." She put the shawl over my shoulders, running her hands up and down my arms when she felt the chill on my skin. Moments ago I had been burning from the inside out for my sexy husband, but now I was frozen with dread.

"You were with him?" I questioned as Dio and Saul walked into the room, taking guard at each entrance. "What is going on?" I snapped at them, noticing the way they scanned the room and the exits closely.

"Nothing, Ma'am," Saul answered.

"Bullshit," I snapped again. I would storm out and investigate for myself if I thought I stood even a little bit of a chance of getting past them. But I knew better.

They weren't just there to keep the intruder out; they were there to keep me in.

Minutes turned into ten. Then twenty. I paced the floor, back and forth as I struggled to contain my anger and fear. Even Molly's sweet banter couldn't distract me. When the door opened again, I whipped my head around and my breath caught in my throat when Nico walked in with the 'intruder' beside him.

"Carmine?" I whispered in shock, before rushing forward and flinging myself into his arms. His familiar scent wrapped around me, and I took a deep breath, trying to convince myself he was real.

I hadn't seen any of my family in almost a month, the longest I'd ever gone. And I didn't realize how much I missed him until right that moment. "Easy, Sunshine," He chuckled, using my childhood nickname. "You're going to break my back squeezing me so tight."

"What are you doing here?" I leaned back looking up into his face, trying to read him for any sign of distress. I looked over at my husband who watched us with a scowl on his face but offered nothing else.

"I was in the area and wanted to stop by." Carmine winked at me, and I dropped my arms to my sides.

"Hmm." I sassed at his obvious lie.

He rolled his eyes and nudged my shoulder. "I had business to discuss with, Nicolas."

I turned my attention back to my husband, who still stood over us with a dark expression on his face. "And you couldn't do that with me in the room?"

Nicolas shrugged, not giving away anything else from his demeanor. "I didn't want to ruin the ambiance of the evening with boring business."

"Hmm." I repeated, pursing my lips before looking back at Carmine, "Are you staying with us?"

He chuckled and shook his head. "It would be rude to impose on a honeymoon."

"Glad we agree on that," Nico grunted with no humor, and I cringed at the awkwardness.

"Come, sit." I shook off my husband's presence and pulled Carmine to the sofa as Molly, Dio, and Saul walked out of the room. "Everyone is, okay?" I questioned as soon as his ass hit the couch.

"Everyone is fine," He said, chancing a glance at Nico who stood leaning against the tall bar with his arms crossed over his chest.

"Are you planning on hovering over us the entire time?" I snapped at my husband, and his brows rose fractionally, expressing his dislike for my tone.

Nico worked his jaw back and forth a few times, flicking his gaze from my brother to me, and then stood up off the bar. "I'll give you two some time to visit," he sent a pointed glare at my brother, "But not too much time. It is our honeymoon after all."

"Yes, yes." Carmine nodded, "I won't keep her long."

"Good," Nico said, but instead of turning and walking out of the room, he stalked his way toward us until he stood over me, and leaned down, gently sliding his hand around the front of my throat to tip my head up. "Ten minutes, Little One." He instructed. "Don't make me come looking for you." He kissed me, tilting my head the way he liked and deepening it until I opened my lips for him and gave in to his demands.

The kiss wasn't for me, and I wasn't stupid enough to think it was. It was a show of dominance over me and my brother. He intended to remind Carmine who I belonged to now.

And it worked. Because as he stalked back out of the room, my eyes stayed glued to him as I tried to calm my erratic heartbeat. When he finally was out of sight, I felt my brother's eyes on the side of my face and a blush crawled up my neck.

"Interesting," Carmine mused from next to me and I glared at him. His amused grin slid off his face as quickly as it appeared though as he took my hand in his. "Are you well?"

"What do you mean?" I asked, confused by his question.

"Does he treat you well?" he clarified, "Are you safe?"

"I'm-" I paused, shaking my head, "Yes. I'm fine."

"Just fine?" he pressed on.

"Why?" I shook my head, scowling at him as his hand tightened on mine. He looked around the room before scooting closer and lowering his voice to a mere whisper.

"Do you want out of this marriage?"

I snapped my head back as a violent roll of emotions crashed over me. "What do you mean?"

"If you want out, I'll help you," He affirmed, with the same hushed tone. "There's a way."

"I don't want out," I answered firmly, admitting something I hadn't realized myself yet.

Carmine hissed, pulling me closer, "Lower your voice or you'll get me killed before I have a chance to get off this boat."

"Then tell me what the hell has gotten into you," I hissed back, in a whisper.

He clenched his jaw and looked around again before whispering to me. "I came here to give you a choice. And a warning."

"About what?"

"Nicolas declared war on our family last night," He said plainly, watching me for my reaction. "He didn't tell you, did he?"

I felt my face pale as I pulled back to look at him more easily. "I don't understand."

"After your wedding Nicolas pulled me aside, angry over your treatment by our parents. He made comments suggesting that he was going to take Father's power away."

"What does that mean?" I cried as fear started filling my body. My father was impossibly rich, and great money like that bought great power.

"He alluded to me taking the throne," Carmine answered cautiously. "He said his power and allies could help facilitate the transfer."

"There's no way Father will simply give up his power, Carmine!" I hissed, "You know that."

"I know."

"Then how is Nicolas planning to take it from him? What happened yesterday to cause him to declare war?" I was panicking, sliding down a steep slope of uncertainty the longer we spoke.

Carmine raised his brows and shrugged his shoulders, not voicing his idea out loud. But he didn't have to.

Nicolas was planning to use violence to make the transfer.

"Father smuggled millions of dollars in weapons into West Shores behind The Don's back. Nicolas showed up last night, taking them back and facing off with Cristian over it."

"No," I whispered, already knowing what must have happened to my other brother.

"He ended up in the hospital, Ari."

"No." I cried, squeezing my eyes shut and dropping my head in agony. "No, no, no."

"I don't know how this is going to play out, but my guess is it's going to end in bloodshed," He warned, "But there's more."

"Jesus," I groaned, rubbing my fingers over my forehead as a migraine took place.

"Three days ago, Father met with Matthew Rizzio." The name sounded familiar, but I had trouble placing it with everything else swirling in my brain. "I wasn't invited into the meeting, but Father told me what was discussed afterward." He paused, waiting for me to look back up at him. "Father ended their meeting with a handshake betrothal."

"To whom?" I gasped, seeing my sweet younger sister's faces torment my mind. They were too young to be cast out into this world. It wasn't fair, they weren't ready.

I hadn't been ready, and I was older than them.

"To you, Ari," He whispered.

I recoiled from him as his words physically assaulted me. "Nico won't divorce me, Carmine." I hissed. "He's too proud and possessive." I shook my head, biting my tongue to keep the rest of Nico's attributes to myself.

He was too dependent on the baby I carried in my stomach already, without even knowing of its existence yet.

"Father doesn't plan to marry you off as a divorcee, Sunshine." Carmine reasoned, "He plans to marry you off again as a widow."

"No!" I cried, covering my mouth in shock. "He can't." My world was spinning around me, and I felt lightheaded as I tried to process everything. "He doesn't get to do that!" I yelled, standing up in anger. Carmine grimaced and pulled me back down to the couch next to him.

"Stop yelling!" he hissed. "I didn't tell Nico of Father's plan yet because I wanted you to have a choice in the matter first." I glared at him but forced myself to take a deep breath and calm myself down. "If you stay with Nico, there will be war between our family and the entire Cosa Nostra." My eyes rounded at the implication and guilt that threatened to consume me, but he wasn't done. "Our siblings won't be safe from the fall out Arianna, there's a real chance that one or more of them could get hurt in the process."

"And if I don't stay with Nico," I hissed, "He'll be dead!"

"And the entire Cosa Nostra will be at war with us for it."

I groaned, falling back into the cushions. "Then what the fuck are we supposed to do?"

"Outsmart Papa at his own game," Carmine said plainly. "Father won't expect you to choose Nico over him. He's demented into thinking that you'll be revolted by the life you have with The Don and will gladly choose to come home rather than stay married to such a dangerous man. My guess is he will spin whatever lies he believes will convince you to go along with his plan. But if you tip off Nicolas to the plan, we can outsmart him, before this war claims anyone else."

"You're talking about killing Father."

"If we remove him from the equation, the Cosa Nostra and the Rosetti's can live in peace together with me leading the family. You can be happy in your marriage to a man you clearly are falling for, and our bloodline connection will ensure a long and prosperous life for our siblings and our children to come."

"You make that sound so easy," I quipped, overwhelmed.

"It can be, if we work together. If that's what you truly want," He held his hand up to the room we were sitting in. "If you're happy as Mrs. Capasso and want to live this life for all it's worth, I will help make sure Nico stays alive and in power for you to do that."

"And what about Cristian? And Amelia and Anita?" I questioned, "What happens to them if you kill Father."

"Amelia and Anita can choose love," He answered honestly, "They will never know the fear and despair that I couldn't save you from, Sunshine. The barbaric blessing ceremony and arranged marriages end with yours."

"And Cristian? Will he allow you to usurp Father and keep Nico in place after he put him in the hospital?"

"Yes," Carmine answered instantly. "Because Nico was within his right and had more than enough chance to kill our brother last night for what Father did. Father knew that which is why he instructed Cristian to show up at the warehouse without reason last night. He set him up, trying to force your hand to his plan. He knew you'd choose family over Nicolas if your husband was responsible for the death of your brother. Father willingly sacrificed our brother to best the Don."

"Then why didn't he kill him?" I asked aloud, even though I already knew the answer.

"You, Ari," Carmine confirmed. "Nicolas spared him for you. Because regardless of what he wants everyone to think, I think your husband is just as ensnarled in your web as you are in his." I rolled my eyes with a groan as Carmine rushed on, "That's not a bad thing, Sunshine. It means you have a real shot at happiness here."

"I don't want anyone else to get hurt," I stated.

"I know, me either."

I stayed quiet as I processed everything that he had told me until I was left with only one option. "I have to tell Nicolas." I stood up from the couch, looking down at my brother. "I have to warn him."

He nodded his head, standing up and sliding his arms around me. "You have my support, Ari, not that you needed it."

"Yeah," I whispered, lost in thought, "Let's hope it doesn't get either of us killed."

CHAPTER 19 – NICO

"**D**o you think he's telling her about Cristian?" Matteo asked from the chair across from me at my desk.

I tilted back my third rocks glass of liquor since I left Ari and Carmine to talk in the salon twelve minutes ago.

Twelve.

When I had instructed her that she only had ten.

"Probably," I grimaced, fighting every single thing inside of me that was trying to make me storm into the salon and kick Carmine off the yacht. Was she angry with me? Hurt? Was she planning on packing her things and trying to leave me as I sat here and worried?

"What do you think she'll do?" He sipped his liquor, feigning calm much better than I was.

When Carmine made an unexpected visit, I expected him to show up, guns blazing. But he didn't. He came aboard to discuss what happened last night at the warehouse with Cristian. He assured me that neither he nor his brother knew of the weapons until last night, and by then, I was already upon them.

I believed him, hating that I did. I didn't want him to be telling the truth, because my plan had always been to eliminate the entire Rosetti line, starting at Emilio and working my way down, sparing only Arianna if it was advantageous for me to do so.

But then the unexpected blessing ceremony occurred, and then Arianna's injury and Emilio's treatment of Carmine at the wedding completely changed the game in my head.

And I fucking hated that.

"She'll either kill me or align herself with me once and for all, forsaking her own blood."

"Do or die," He murmured into his glass with a shake of his head. "Which way do you think it will go?"

"Fuck if I know," I admitted. As close as Arianna and I had managed to get in the last few weeks, her brothers and sisters were her entire life. Her only family essentially, and I didn't know if she'd turn her back on them for me.

For us.

Matteo's response was halted as my office door swung open and a frazzled Arianna stood in the opening. "I'll see myself out," Matteo nodded to me, "Hide the knives," He whispered to me setting his glass down on the desk before bowing to Arianna on his way past, shutting the door behind him.

Arianna's brown eyes glowed with emotion as she stared at me, unmoving from the door. "Were you going to tell me you beat Cristian to a pulp last night?" She asked, but there was no anger behind the question.

"Yes," I responded instantly because it was the truth.

"You should have told me right away when you got back. First thing," She swallowed and walked into the office, stopping in front of the desk. "You should have trusted me for once in your *God damned life*." She closed her eyes and shook her head in sadness. When she opened her eyes to look at me again, tears swam in them. "Why won't you trust me?"

"I do." I rose from my chair, but she held her hand up, halting my movement before I could round the desk and get to her. I swallowed down my angry rebuttal to it, trying to allow her feelings to be validated, even if they were wrong. "I do trust you, that's why I was going to tell you later." I slowly rounded the desk as she looked at me through her unshed tears, and I hated how it made my chest constrict physically like I couldn't take a deep breath. "Is it so wrong of me that I wanted to enjoy my time with you, for just a little while, before I brought more darkness between us?"

She dropped my gaze and looked at the floor, letting the tears free to splash against the wooden top of the desk. With each drop of sadness, something inside of me cracked and fractured until I was nearly desperate to make them stop.

"My father plans to kill you," She whispered. "He's already met and made a deal with a new man to marry me off to once you're dead." My hands fisted at my sides as rage boiled through my system. More tears fell from her inky lashes as her brow creased, but still, she wouldn't look at me. "Carmine came to warn me so I could decide who I would align myself with." She took a deep breath and looked up at me, letting the tears trail down her full cheeks. "If I chose you, my siblings would suffer the rage of the Don because of who our father is." She tilted her head as her shoulders sagged in defeat. "But if I chose them, I was sentencing you to death."

I couldn't stay still a moment longer as violent rage vibrated inside of my body. I slid both hands over her cheeks, holding her face and wiping away her tears with my thumbs. She grabbed onto my wrists and pulled herself even closer to me as her small frame shook with anguish. She closed her eyes and whispered, "But I chose you."

Euphoria raced through my veins as an overwhelming pride consumed me, looking down at my perfect wife.

She was a goddess, the perfect partner to the Don, and far more than I ever expected her to be in such a short time. I had always hoped that we would be able to live amicably someday when I agreed to the marriage. I never imagined I'd gain my better half out of it though.

"I love you," I responded, surprising both of us but meaning every word. "I can't explain it to you, Arianna, in words. But this," I leaned my forehead against hers, "between us, is more than I deserved when I deceived my way into your bed that very first night. I never anticipated that I would be aligning myself with my very own soulmate."

Her shoulders shook again as more tears fell from her perfect eyes before they fell shut as I kissed her sweet lips. She dug her nails into my neck, anchoring herself to me fully as I growled into her mouth as she opened it for me.

I feasted on everything she offered me, and still, it wasn't enough. Nothing was ever going to be enough when it came to my little goddess.

"There's more," She whispered, breaking apart only far enough to untangle one of my hands from her hair before sliding it down her body. My cock stirred, thinking she was planning on sliding it under the hem of her dress boldly, but she stopped at her abdomen, turning our hands to lay flat against her lower stomach. I pulled back so I could see her face as she looked up at me with her watery eyes and chewed her bottom lip. "I'm carrying your child."

My ears rang as the blood in my head whooshed violently through my brain, trying to process her words and what they meant. "You're pregnant?"

She nodded her head, fear evident on her perfect face. "I lied the day I took the test back at Armarow. It was Molly's urine that Dr. Travis tested," She rushed out. "I wanted to be able to find out in private, so I could process what it meant for not only us but for me as well. I planned to take the test later that day, but then you sprang the trip on me, and I didn't get the chance. And then I let fear get the better of me, and avoided finding out for sure, even though my period still never showed up," She rambled, "But this morning the morning sickness started to hit. And the fatigue has been plaguing me for days." She shrugged her shoulders in defeat once again. "I couldn't deny the proof any longer, so I took a test, and it was positive."

"You're pregnant," I repeated like a moron.

"Say something else," she whispered; her fear evident. "You wanted this so badly before, but things have changed between us."

I didn't say anything else, even though I knew she needed me to. Because I was a second away from sobbing like a baby from the rollercoaster of emotions raging through me.

So I used my actions to tell her everything I could without words.

I sank to my knees at her feet, wrapping my hands around her petite hips and laying my forehead against her stomach, breathing her in and composing myself. Her fingers tentatively drifted through my hair as she trembled beneath my touch. "You're giving me the biggest blessing known to mankind, Little One." I finally forced out between my parched lips. "There is no greater gift that a woman can give to a man than her love and to create life within herself for him." I cleared my throat, "With him."

She nodded her head, sobbing and smiling down at me. "I love you, Nico," she whispered. "Even if you forced me to in the beginning, I couldn't stop it from happening. I couldn't stop fate."

I rose to my feet and kissed her like my life depended on it. Absorbing every moan and gasp as we clung to each other. When our fervent kiss slowed, and we both caught our breaths I picked her up and placed her on my desk, so we were almost face to face. I wanted her eyes even with mine as I pledged my commitment to her.

"Your father won't take you from me, because even in death, you'll always be mine. I promise you, here and now, I will kill him for even daring to try."

"I chose you, Nico, and I chose our baby. But I don't want my siblings to suffer. Carmine wants to align himself with you. He wants what you offered him on our wedding day," She shook her head. "I don't want my litter sisters to ever endure what I had to at my father's hands, because I got lucky with you. I beat the odds and found love, but I know they won't be so lucky."

"I keep my word, Ari, and I will make Carmine king of the Rosetti family. I promise you."

"I believe you," She sniffed and took a deep breath, "But I need you to show me the proof by trusting me with this, and everything else from here on out. No more secrets and veiled answers. Let me be your partner in life Nico, please."

"You will never be just my partner, Arianna, because you are so much more than I will ever be. But we'll start with this, just how you asked, and go from there."

My men congregated around the large room in my penthouse, lounging on the furniture and drinking my liquor. I called the meeting with my top men after Arianna's warning last night about Carmine's visit.

Emilio Rosetti was making moves to have me assassinated.

His daughter had warned me, sentencing her father and anyone else from her family who stood in the way, to death because she was growing life inside of her belly.

My life.

Our child.

She was glowing, even if no one else in the world knew she was pregnant yet. After our breakthrough last night, I took her straight to bed, making slow sweet love to her like she was delicate, and then held her all night long while she slept. I lay there, imagining every worst-case scenario that could occur to her and our unborn child with the weight of war weighing down on my shoulders.

Then this morning before her eyes were even open, she threw herself from bed and raced to the bathroom thanks to morning sickness. I held her hair back, avoiding her swats to chase me off as her small body was wracked with heaves until she was still again. Then I carried her back to bed and doted on her until Molly took over.

Apparently, Molly had some tricks up her sleeve to help her mistress because, within an hour, Arianna was back to normal and eating breakfast in a pretty pink sundress looking none the worse.

Now, late in the evening in the penthouse I kept for business matters that brought me to the city, she sat at my side facing off with my men and showing them where her allegiance stood.

"Before the end of this month," I addressed the group, silencing the chatter that they had been carrying on until they all looked at me, "Emilio Rosetti will be dead."

Raised eyebrows and devilish smirks passed the faces of my men as Luca spoke up, "I'm assuming something else has happened since the other night when we spanked Cristian for the weapons." He looked at Arianna after his statement with a slight grimace, but she didn't flinch. Carmine had assured her that Cristian would heal from the broken bones I gave him the other night. And I had assured her that I would mend the relationship when all of the fighting was over.

"I've been informed that a plan has been put in place, by Emilio himself, to have me assassinated. He's already made a deal with Matthew Rizzio to take Arianna as his wife once I'm dead." Angry murmurs filled the room as my men digested that information. "Obviously that won't happen, because even when I'm dead, I'm relying on all of you to protect my wife and care for her as your own."

"Of course, Capa." Luca nodded firmly before turning to Arianna. "Your father will no longer dictate your life."

"Good." She nodded back with a gentle smile. "Because I'd really hate to have to haunt all of you after I jump off a balcony to avoid him again."

Soft laughter answered her joke and she relaxed into her chair. "So, what are the plans then," Luca asked.

"First line of attack will be to starve the man out. Any and all lines of resources into West Shores will be ceased tonight. No drugs, no guns, no money, and most of all, no workers. I'll give the order after this meeting that anyone seen inside of West Shores assisting Emilio Rosetti will be immediately deemed a traitor of the Cosa Nostra and executed on the spot."

"Why not just execute the bastard himself?" Harris asked, always bloodthirsty.

"Because he's gone into hiding," I sneered. "As soon as he got word that I knew about the weapons being stored in the warehouse, he sacrificed his second born son to my wrath and went underground. So the plan to interrupt all of his avenues of cash flow will not only anger him, but it will anger any associates he has left when he suddenly cannot provide what he needs to, per their agreements. And I will eagerly fulfill the missing parts of their operations to ensure they all remember who the biggest wolf in the game is."

"Make your enemies' enemies your allies," Luca smirked wolfishly, "I like it."

"Carmine Rosetti is on my side, as I've previously discussed. I don't know how he's managing to stay under the radar in Emilio's home, but to my knowledge, he's safe there. I will pull him out the second I feel his safety is at risk being there though."

"And the others?" Harris asked, "His cunt of a wife specifically." Men snickered around him, and he grinned. "It's no secret that Mina Rosetti was responsible for making my life difficult thirty years ago. I'm just wondering if there's room for me to get a little justice out of her for it." He joked nonchalantly.

I felt Arianna's bristling reaction to his statement, but she didn't give any outward expression of distaste. "Mina Rosetti will be handled how Arianna sees fit. I'm leaving it up to her." I answered easily.

Arianna gazed up at me in speculation, but once again, kept her thoughts to herself.

"So, what's the second part of your plan?" Luca turned the conversation back to the important parts and I was glad for it. I would have hated to have to break Harris' jaw in front of his peers for making my wife uncomfortable.

"After we've tightened his belt so fucking tight around his own throat, he'll have no choice but to come out of hiding to mend some of those connections. When he does that, we'll take him."

"And what will you do with him then?" Luca asked with a brow raised and a smirk pulling on his lips.

"Let's just say his death will not be a quick one," I affirmed, "I plan to take my time with him, make an example out of him for anyone else who thinks that going against the new Don is a viable thing. Because it's not. I'll eradicate each traitor one at a time until all that exists are loyal men in my streets. I reward loyalty well, and in the end, those rewards will be far larger with the fat cut out of the family."

Everyone nodded and agreed with the plan, enjoying the prospects of bigger cuts for their dealings with the Cosa Nostra for being loyal to me.

I raised my glass and toasted the men gathered, "Then let us drink to our good fortune and the end of an era dictated by men unworthy of leading."

The veiled theory was there for them to read easily enough. My father had ruled with an iron fist, but only in the ways that were most lucrative for him personally. Many good men struggled under his powerful rule, simply because he was greedy.

Hence why he was such a good ally with Emilio, he leached himself onto the Rosetti fortune that Arianna's grandparents had made, and in return, Emilio ran unchecked for far too long.

Doing things like allowing his daughter to be raped by a priest and tormenting his other children in the name of power.

Fucking pig. It was time to take him to the slaughterhouse.

"Do you think Emilio will come out himself when his dealings start falling through?" Matteo asked me after all the others had left. Arianna retired to the primary bedroom to get ready for bed, the fatigue was evident on her pretty face, and I was left to wrap up the meeting with my second.

"I think he will. He's too greedy to leave it to his sons to handle and Emilio knows that the cartel and others won't deal with anyone but the top. So he'll surface eventually."

"What will you do in the meantime?"

"We'll retire to Armarow again in the morning and wait him out. I don't want Arianna in the city any longer than she needs to be. It's bad enough that I can't continue our honeymoon with her currently because I need to be able to come and go as needed, but I won't keep her chained in this tower amongst the rot and smog of the city."

He raised his eyebrows in surprise and smirked, "You act like she's a delicate flower."

"She's as strong as an oak tree, Matteo," I challenged. "But the tiny baby she carries in her stomach is a delicate flower and I won't risk either of their safety."

His mouth fell open as I gave him the news I'd held to myself for the last twenty-four hours and I tried to ignore how good it felt to tell someone. "Arianna is pregnant?" He clarified.

"Yes. Six weeks or so. Dr. Travis will confirm when we return to Armarow."

"Wow," he shook his head, with a shit-eating grin on his face before walking over to me and slapping his hand on my back. "I can't believe you're going to be a father." He shook his head again. "I can't think of anyone more deserving than you, but still, I didn't think I'd see it in my lifetime. Unless you knocked up some side piece like Edna."

"Oh fuck off." I shrugged him off as he laughed at his own joke. "I assure you; I would have killed Edna before I allowed her to carry the Don's baby."

"But you're happy about Arianna carrying your child?" he asked for clarification.

"Ecstatic," I confirmed. "I started trying to get her pregnant the first time I had her. That was always my intent. And if I have any say in it, this will be the first of many babies she brings into the world for me."

"Well fuck," he smirked again, "I'm happy for you."

"Good, because you're going to be staying here in the city in my absence for the immediate future. Which means you'll miss seeing the rest of Molly's new wardrobe."

He rolled his eyes, dropping the smile. "You're impossible, man. I've already told you, nothing is going on there."

"Right," I nodded, walking away from him in search of my wife. "And I'm the pope."

"Nope, just a high priest here to deflower virgin Mary," He called out as I left the room, and I flipped him off.

Chapter 20 – Arianna

I slid the silk nightgown over my body and looked into the floor-length mirror that lined one side of the master closet. I turned to the side and slid my palm over my flat abdomen, imagining what it would look like once it started swelling with life.

"You'll be breathtaking with a baby bump," Nico's warm voice called from behind me a second after I felt his presence.

"For someone who claims not to have a clue what runs through my head, you sure do read it pretty well," I sassed, looking over my shoulder at him before looking back in the mirror. My breasts were swollen and sensitive and I was exhausted, but other than that, I had no other visible signs of pregnancy yet.

"Hmm," he hummed sliding his large body against my back and cradling his own hands over mine against my stomach. "Maybe I'm getting better at reading you after all."

"Great, there goes my grand plan to overthrow the kingdom." I joked and he smirked before lowering his lips to my neck, cutting off anything else I was going to say.

"Come to bed, Wife, you look positively dead on your feet." He said, before scooping me up into his arms and carrying me into the bedroom. This was the first time I stepped foot in his penthouse, and I hated the jealousy I felt looking around the room, knowing he entertained other women here.

"I can't wait to be back at Armarow." I mused as he set me down on the bed that Molly expertly turned down just how I liked.

"Tomorrow, love." He kissed my temple before standing up and loosening his tie. "We'll retreat to the country tomorrow morning, and you'll have nothing but fresh air and happiness to fill your days with."

I laid back on the pillows, adjusting myself until I was comfortable, and watched him start to unbutton his shirt. "What about you?" I questioned, "Will you fill your days with happiness in Armarow? Or will you leave and come back to the city every chance you get?"

He pulled his shirt off and tossed it down on the bench at the end of the bed and then toed off his shoes and started on his belt. My body heated instantly watching each inch of his magnificent skin reveal itself to my hungry eyes. "I don't have any plans to be away from you overnight if I can help it." He answered, drawing me back to the present.

"Hmm." I hummed, suddenly fighting a dry mouth as he pulled the button and zipper down on his pants. Once again revealing his bare skin beneath. "Do you have a problem with underwear?" I queried, "Not that I mind the view, but I'm just curious."

He smirked that devilish snarly grin as he dropped his pants down his legs and stepped free, tossing them onto the bench with the rest. "I enjoy getting from point A, to point B, as quickly as possible. Underwear is just one more hold up to getting what I want." He knelt on the bed, and I watched with rapture as his cock swelled where it hung under his body, like a weapon readying itself to be used against me.

"And what is it that you want exactly? What's the prize at point B?"

"You," He growled, leaning down over my body until his face hovered over mine and his cock jolted against the silk fabric of my long gown. "With your legs spread and screaming my name as I bury myself inside of you over and over again, filling up your pretty little pussy."

I bit my lip to halt the moan that wanted to burst free from his words alone and smirked up at him. "I'll only be your prize if you take the kid gloves off tonight and fuck me like we both really want you to. I won't break, and neither will this baby."

His nostrils flared and his green eyes darkened, but his body still hung suspended over mine. "Pull your dress up and show me your pussy."

I instantly gathered the skirt of my nightgown in my hands and lifted my hips, pulling it up to pool around my stomach as he instructed. "Like this?" I toyed with him, biting my lip seductively and batting my eyelashes at him.

"Perfect." He growled, "Now spread your legs and show me how badly you want me, Little One."

I pushed my knees wide and watched his eyes trail down to my exposed center and then as his tongue swept over his lips like he was preparing to taste his favorite meal.

"Play with yourself." He instructed, causing my bravado to fall. He saw the moment of uncertainty fall over me and he was right there to catch the weight of it and push it off. "Run your pretty little fingers over your clit before sliding one inside of you." He lifted himself to kneel between my spread legs and sat back on his heels as he watched me intently. He put his hands on the inside of my knees and pushed them wider until I was flat on my back with my ass popped up off the bed, open and exposed. "Do it."

My fingers slid down my body to my wet center and I rolled them over my clit, the way I used to do under my blanket at nighttime and my eyelids fluttered closed as pleasure rushed through me.

"Tell me how it feels." He ordered huskily and my eyes opened, taking in the veins that bulged along his neck and arms where they held my legs open. "Tell me what your thinking about."

"It feels so good." I admitted, "But I keep comparing it to the feeling of your tongue against it that first night." I moaned, cupping one of my breasts in my hand and playing with my nipple through the silk fabric. "The wet bumpy texture of your tongue was like something I'd never imagined before. It felt so good."

His eyes were flicking between what I was doing between my legs and what I was doing to my breast like he couldn't decide which he wanted to watch more. "Pull your gown down," he grunted, nodding to my chest, "Show me your tits."

"Yes, Sir." I moaned and smirked to myself when his jaw clenched tight again. I shimmied down the top of my gown until both breasts fell free and instantly rolled the nipple I'd been playing with between my fingers, pulling on it and twisting before moving to the other one. "Do you like to watch me play with myself more than you like playing with me yourself?"

His impressive control slipped, and he let go of one knee to slowly push a finger inside my now-soaked entrance. I bowed my back, pushing down on his hand harder, and moaned. "What do you think, Wife?"

"I think you like both." I purred, "But I think you like making me come more, Nico."

His eyes squinted into slits as he lowered his face to my pussy, pulling my hand away from it and pinning it to my neglected breast. "Play with your nipples while I play with your pussy, baby girl. Don't stop until you coat my face with your orgasm. Then we'll see which I like more."

"Fuck yes." I groaned, pinching and rolling my nipples as he swirled his tongue over my clit, dragging it down and pushing it into my entrance before swirling it back up to my clit again. I hissed, arching my hips forward to push against his face more and he grabbed onto my thighs, pinning them to his head and squeezing as he pushed me towards the flames of pleasure. "Don't stop." I panted, pinching harder on my tits before palming them and pushing them together. "Please don't stop, baby."

"Call me that again." He hissed, eyes alive and glowing as he shook his mouth over my clit, sucking on it powerfully.

"Baby." I moaned, "Just like that baby."

He groaned and pushed two fingers inside of me, curling them forward towards the pleasure spot I hadn't known existed before I met him, and rocked me on and off his hand. "Come for me, Little One. Come on my face and coat your pussy for my cock."

"Fuck!" I screamed, curling up and riding his face as I shot off into an orgasm of epic proportions and he hummed, lapping at me through it until I was flopping on the bed like I was being electrocuted.

"Good girl." He praised, kissing the inside of my thighs and then my stomach, lingering there and whispering something into the flesh.

"Did you just speak to our unborn child after you ate me out like a whore?" I asked in shock.

He smirked, crawling up my body until he hovered over me again and winked. "I told him to plug his ears because his mama was about to go to church and pray to God with naughty words."

I rolled my eyes, snorting at his playful banter, and then paused, "Wait, '*he*'?"

He grinned again with that devilish snarl before lowering his lips to my neck and sucking, biting the flesh, and marking me. "Our firstborn will be a boy. Then we'll have a couple of girls to keep him on his toes." I groaned as pleasure and fear bloomed from his touch and words. "Lastly we'll have a few more boys just to round out the family."

"Jesus Nico, you make it sound so easy."

"It is, baby." He purred, lowering his hips until his cock slid against my wet clit, "Just spread those pretty thighs for me and I'll give you all the babies you desire."

"Keep doing that," I dug my nails into the back of his neck as I lifted my hips to create more friction against his cock, "And I'll let you do whatever you want to me."

I didn't realize it at that time, but that had been the wrong thing to say.

That evil smirk graced his lips seconds before he rolled off me and landed on his back next to me on the bed. "What I want, is for you to crawl over here and learn how to take my cock down your throat." I felt my eyes bug out of my head in surprise, but he wasted no time in letting fear or self-consciousness get the better of me. He pulled my arm until I landed between his powerful thighs, looking down at his Adonis body and massive cock that lay heavily against his abdomen. "Come on, baby, you're going to look so pretty with those lips wrapped around me," he said, running his thumb over my bottom lip, pulling it from between my teeth.

"I don't know what to do," I said honestly, flicking my gaze down to where his cock jerked and leaked.

"Start by touching it. Wrap your hand around it and slide it up and down."

I licked my lips, took a deep breath, and forged on, feigning bravery. But my hand shook as I slid my fingertips over the shaft, lifting it from his abdomen.

I was surprised at how soft the skin was, matched by the pure strength of its hardness at the same time. When I wrapped my hand around it, I didn't come close to touching my fingers together and looked up at him from under my lashes.

"You're so big," I whispered.

"Wrap both hands around me, sweetheart." I did and watched as he swallowed quickly before his cock jumped in my palms. "Slide them up and down." I tentatively, let my hands glide over the skin and watched his face, reveling in the pure erotic show playing out across his features as he stared at my hands like I was doing the most pleasurable thing in the world. When in reality I was hardly fisting him.

"Tighter or lighter?" I asked.

"Tighter." He wrapped his hand around mine, squeezing it and sliding it up and down around him with me. "Now spit on the head of it, and rub it in." He instructed and my eyes rounded at the ridiculousness of his command.

"Do it, Arianna," he commanded, "Use the thick stuff from the back of your throat and spit right on me."

"Oh, my God." I groaned, rolling my eyes, but lowered myself down until my mouth hovered right above him and I did as he said, feeling obscene.

"That's a good fucking girl." He growled. "Rub it in and make it all wet." I did as he said and he groaned, laying his head back on the pillow as his hips thrusted pushing his cock through my tight fist.

"How does that feel?" I whispered, letting him fuck his cock into my hands as I watched with rapture.

"Like I'm close enough to touch heaven but I can't quite feel it." He mocked, licking his lips with his eyes closed before stilling his hips and looking at me. "I want you to run your tongue over the head of me. Like you're eating an ice cream cone on a hot summer day and it's melting."

"Why is that so sexy?" I keened needily. I leaned forward and tentatively ran the tip of my tongue around the top of him, expecting an overwhelming taste to assault me, but it didn't. He tasted salty as your lips did on a hot day, but it wasn't overpowering. "Mmh." I hummed licking up the side of the mushroomed head of him like an ice cream before swirling it around the entire thing.

"Fuck." His hips jerked and he tightened the bed sheets in his fists, which emboldened me to explore more. I stroked him with my tight fists as I continued to tongue the head, dipping lower with my mouth and licking the shaft of him between strokes until he was writhing beneath me on the bed.

"That's enough." He growled, "Climb on top and put me in that tight fucking pussy."

"But I thought you wanted your cock down my throat?" I grinned evilly before squealing as he grabbed my hips, pulling me up his body in a surprise attack. He tore the gown up over my head and left me bare in his lap as he wickedly flexed his hips and pushed the head of his cock against my entrance.

The mixed wetness of us both made it silky and enticing.

"Ride my cock like a good girl, and maybe I'll let you choke on me after."

"Mmh." I smirked, lifting my hips as he held his erection tall under me as I lowered onto it, "So romantic of you." Before I was done, he pushed up into me in one slow torturous thrust until I leaned forward with my hands on his chest, circling my hips to accommodate his invasion. "Fuck."

"That's it, baby." He praised me, staring at me with tenderness and need burning bright in his green eyes. "You take me so perfectly; I can't remember what it was like before I had you now. You've completely replaced everyone else."

"When was the last time you had another woman before me?" I asked, tilting my head back and moaning as he flexed his cock inside of me, putting more pressure on the sensitive flesh.

"Why would you ask that?" He watched me closely, lifting me on and off of his cock.

"Because I want to know."

"It doesn't change anything, Arianna."

"Yes, it does," I argued, imagining worst-case scenarios the longer he went without answering me.

"I'm not going to talk about other women when I'm inside of you." He answered authoritatively, and that spurred the anger in my gut.

"Fine." I lifted myself quickly until his cock popped free of my body and fell to his stomach before I lowered myself to grind my clit up the length of it. "Now tell me."

"Fuck." He growled, tightening his hands around my waist as I rocked back and forth against him.

"Tell me and I'll take you back inside of me." I leaned down and kissed his chest, trying to tempt him into giving me what I wanted.

"And if I don't?" He challenged.

"Then I'm going to lay on my back and finish myself off with my fingers before falling asleep."

"Liar." He contested, rolling us over in one swift move before flipping me onto my stomach and pulling my hips up into the air. "You aren't the boss." He hissed in my ear as he laid his strong body across my back. "I am."

The air left my lungs as he impaled me with his thick cock, pushing my legs wider to accommodate his knees before pulling out and slamming back into me. "Oh, fuck yes!" I screamed, laying my palm flat against the headboard and pushing back onto him, arching my back deeper for the angle of penetration we both craved. "Just like that."

"My cock will always be better than your fingers are, Little One."

"Tell me the truth anyway." I hissed, throwing daggers at him with my eyes over my shoulder. He spanked my ass, twice in quick succession, drawing screeches and then moans from my lips before he reached around my body and strummed his fingers over my clit. "Please, Nico."

"Why do you want to be upset?" He asked gently at my ear as he kept fucking me and playing with my clit. "You have to know you won't like the answer."

"I know." I gasped, reaching down and running my fingers over his on my clit, rubbing it together, "But I need it."

A long pause filled the air, leaving only the sound of his body joining mine to cut through the silence before his sigh tickled my shoulder where his lips lay. "The morning you came to Armarow."

My brain misfired as I tried to focus on what he said as he expertly played with my body, but before long, realization dawned on me. "Wait." I gasped, shaking my head. "You fucked me my first night there."

"I know." He sighed again, sounding almost resigned by it.

"Jesus." I hissed, yanking my body away from his as I grasped what that meant. "You fucked another woman the same day you took my virginity?" I turned to face him on my knees. He was magnificent, kneeling with his hard cock jutting out from his body and a light layer of sweat coating his tattooed skin. "Hours before you fucked your future wife."

"I didn't know I'd be fucking you at all Ari. Not until I got to Armarow and met with your father about the ceremony. But I'll be honest, even if I had, I wouldn't have changed what I did that morning. You didn't mean anything to me back then, you were just-." He stopped, sighing and running a hand over his face.

"Your broodmare," I barked.

"Yes." He answered honestly and that smarted even more. "I never lied to you about what my intentions were, to begin with, Ari." He lowered his tone, to quell his anger that tried to rise to match mine. "That was before things changed between us."

"Got it." I nodded, crawling off the bed as my skin pebbled from the cold fury running through me. "That was probably the worst possible answer I could have gotten." I shrugged, "No, I guess it could have been worse if you told me you'd fucked someone right before the ceremony. I suppose I'm lucky it was hours before." I fumed then froze, turning back to face him where he sat on the edge of the bed. "Wait." I held my finger up at him, "Is that why you weren't there at the dinner? Were you absent because you were fucking someone else, instead of meeting me and being a decent human being?" My voice rose.

"I already told you; I was there that night; you just didn't see me." He replied evenly.

"What does that mean?"

"It means I watched you on the security cameras from my office the entire time you were outside of your room. I just didn't join you at the table."

"Why not?" I snapped, "Didn't you care how fucking scared I was? How terrifying the entire process was? Don't you realize you could have alleviated some of that for me by just being a decent person and showing up for a meal with me?"

"I couldn't join you, Ari, because, from the first second that you stepped outside of the bedroom I was so fucking overwhelmed by you, I couldn't fucking think straight." He replied, straightening off the bed and slowly closing the distance between us. "I was trying to play an expert-level game of chess, and I couldn't let you near me or I'd blow the whole fucking thing the second your perfect brown eyes landed on me. I would have fallen to my knees at your feet right then and there and given you anything you wanted."

My jaw snapped shut as I tried to tell myself he was lying, making up the story to appease me. But as he stopped right in front of me, I knew deep in my gut that he was telling the truth. "Would falling to your knees have been such a bad thing?" I whispered, "Think of all the anger and hurt we could have saved each other from those first few days."

He watched me keenly before lifting his hand to the side of my face and running his thumb over the apple of my cheek. "I couldn't allow that to happen before I knew what kind of person you were, Arianna." He tapped his finger on my chest, "In here. It was so important to me to come out on top that I had to play the game right. And bowing to you in front of your father at that moment would have been the end of us having a real chance at happiness. He would have manipulated it and infested it with his motives."

"I know." I sighed sadly, hating that he was right. "Doesn't mean I have to like that some other woman's vagina juice was on you when you took my virginity."

"Vagina juice?" He quirked a brow at me and smirked, "I've used protection with everyone else but you. You're the only woman I've ever wanted a future with. And do you think I don't shower?"

"There have been times that you've smelt worse than others, so it's hard to tell." I joked, feeling the tension freeing up in my shoulders.

"You're trouble." He tightened his fingers into my wild hair and pulled my head back to look up at him. "And I fucking love it, most times."

"But not now?"

"No." He replied, "Not when it's left me with a hard cock, and you absent of the orgasm you were chasing."

"Hmm." I hummed, sliding my hands up his bare chest to circle the back of his neck as he lifted me into his arms. "But you still love me, right?"

He walked until my back pressed against the glass wall overlooking the city beneath us and the sharp contrast of the cold surface against my overheated body sent shivers through my system. "More than anything else." He sighed "And don't think I don't already know that you'll use that against me in our life together."

I licked my lips as he pulled his hips back and lined back up, sinking into me with slow perfection until he was buried all the way. "Just think, when there are a couple of mini-mes running around as you plan, you won't ever be free of that feeling of being wrapped around someone's finger."

He pulled his hips back and then slammed into me again with a wicked grin on his rough lips. "That sounds delightful. I think I'd better practice making them so I'm good to go right after you give birth to this one."

Nico was working around the clock to find my father. He went into hiding right before Carmine's warning to us about his plans.

I spent my time alone in the peace and tranquility of Armarow and played out possible outcomes of the whole sordid mess constantly. Some involved Nico causing my father's death. And some involved the father of my unborn child meeting his demise at the hands of my father.

And I was physically pained by only one of those two possibilities.

I wasn't even the least bit ashamed to say that if anything bad happened to Nico, I'd be devastated, yet I wouldn't blink twice if my father passed.

My father had made his bed where I was concerned, and I wouldn't lose any sleep over him once he was gone. My mother was also a wanted woman. Which was news to me when one of Nico's men asked about what would be done with her when it was all said and done. Something about the way he said it, paired with the statement about her ruining his life years ago, felt ominous.

I didn't like my mother, but I also didn't particularly hate her either. There were times when I was growing up that I'd catch small little glimpses of the once young girl who was married off like cattle, forced to go through the blessing ceremony, and then used to reproduce heirs to my father's will. And when I would get those small snippets of humanity from her, I pitied her.

Empathized with what she had gone through.

But they were so fleeting and inconsistent that the feeling of compassion for her now after everything else happened, didn't come.

But when I found myself resolved to let her meet her fate at the hands of Nico's men, I remembered how I carried life inside of me and a tiny part of my soul ached for my baby to have a grandparent.

Both of Nico's parents passed away, first his mother when he was a young boy, and then his father a few years ago. He had half-siblings, from women that his father dated even before his mother died, but from the small bits of information that Nico gave me when I asked, he didn't maintain a relationship with any of them after he cut their mothers off with the passing of his father.

He didn't like to talk about it much and I didn't press him. He loved his mother, and the way his father treated her while they were married burned deep in his gut. I understood his dislike for those involved in that treatment, even if they were innocent kids themselves at the time.

I had my own siblings who would be in the baby's life if I could help it.

Anita and Amelia would both melt over a baby to spoil, I just had to keep them safe through all of the darkness headed our way, thanks to our father.

"Wife," Nico's warm voice snapped me out of the torturous thoughts that were consuming me as he entered the library where I was resting. I looked up at him as he neared the chair I was reading in and instantly felt on edge from the dark look in his eyes. "You have a phone call."

He held out a cell phone to me, "Who is it?"

"Carmine," Nico said, offering nothing else.

I took the phone from him and put it to my ear, "Carmine?" I felt Nico standing above me but didn't look at him.

"Hey, Sunshine," My brother replied and I could hear the smile in his voice. "How are you doing, kiddo?"

"I'm fine, how are you?" I asked as anxiety crawled up my spine. "Why are you calling?"

Nico put his hand on my shoulder, rubbing the tense muscles and lending his physical support.

"I have some news, and I wanted to share it with you personally," Carmine said and I could sense the gloomy turn to his mood. "Father knows that Nico has issued his death warrant. And he knows you've aligned yourself with your husband, over him."

"How?"

"There's a mole in the Don's close circle, though I don't know who."

"Damnit." I cursed, and Nico's hand tensed on my shoulder before he slid around the front of me and picked me up before sitting down in the chair with me on his lap. I put the call on speaker and held it between us. "You're on speaker and Nico is here, so repeat that, Carmine."

My brother sighed and then chuckled, "Package deal, got it." He joked. "My father knows of your intention to kill him, and he knows that Arianna has chosen to stand by your side, instead of his. Your ship leaks."

"Where is he?" Nicolas asked, ignoring everything else. It wasn't news to him if I had to guess.

"He won't say." Carmine sighed. "He doesn't trust anyone now that Arianna has proven his own child will turn their back on him."

"Are you safe?" I asked, "Does he know you're helping us? What about the others?"

"He's still trusting me with the day-to-day shit, so I'm guessing he has no idea that I'm the mole in his own home. The others are clueless to what I'm doing, so they're safe."

"They're not safe Carmine, he knows my only weakness was you guys. If he wants to get revenge for everything, he'll hurt one of you to get it. Look at what he did to Cristian." I cried, as panic set in.

"Easy, Sunshine." Carmine cooed, and Nico ran his hand up and down my back. "I'm keeping tabs on everything. I'll keep them safe."

"We need to find him, Carmine, the sooner he's taken care of, the sooner everyone can breathe easier." I dropped my hand to my stomach, cradling the little babe that was now almost eight weeks along. Time was flying while I lived on the edge of uncertainty.

"I know, I'm going to figure it out. I just have to do it the right way, so I don't blow the whole fucking thing." Carmine replied.

"Carmine," Nico interrupted, "We don't have time to leave him alive and unchecked. Arianna is pregnant. I won't allow her and our child to be his target."

We hadn't told anyone yet about our news, aside from Molly and Matteo. And I stared in shock at my husband as he told my brother without talking it over first.

"Wow." Carmine whistled through the line, "Congratulations you two."

"Thanks," I replied gently, feeling better for having someone know our news, but also fearful of letting it out into the universe.

"This stress isn't good for her, Carmine." Nico replied coolly, "So maybe from now on when you call me, you'll take that into account and just fucking tell me what you have to share as I told you to do a dozen times."

Carmine chuckled lightly, "Noted, Capa. I just wanted to make sure Arianna got the whole picture and wasn't left out of the decision-making. Considering it involves her."

"Yeah, well now you know better." Nico snapped, "Don't call back unless you have news that will actually help us." He hit the end button and I stared at him in shock.

"That was rude." I deadpanned, "I didn't even say goodbye."

"Something tells me he'll be calling back soon." Nico rolled his eyes, tossing the phone down on the table next to the chair. "How are you feeling?" He asked, running his fingers up the back of my neck and into the hair at the bottom of my head, massaging the tension away.

"Mmh," I moaned, "Shh, no talking. Just rub me." I closed my eyes and let his touch melt me until I leaned against him heavily. "I've been lonely lately." I stuck my bottom lip out in a pout to add humor to it to try to alleviate how the statement made me feel.

I felt pathetic.

And needy.

And whiney.

And emotional.

And very un-me.

"I've been busy trying to find your father." Nico replied gently, "But my first priority is always you. So tell me what you need."

"Just you." I laid my head against his shoulder, tucking it under his chin. "This is nice."

"It is, Wife." He leaned back further in the chair, reclining me in his arms so I was more comfortable as he continued to massage my scalp. "It's almost dinner time, we'll retire to our room for the rest of the night after we eat. I'll be so close to you; you'll be tired of me by morning."

"You could be buried inside of my body for the next twenty-four hours straight and I don't think I'll tire of you, Nico," I purred, enjoying the way his body tightened underneath mine.

"I think I'd like to try that," he chuckled, kissing my temple before pulling me up to sit upright. "But first let's eat, so I know you have the energy to take me deep into your body."

"Hmm, that's not the worst idea in the world." I winked and stood up. "You can tell me what advances you've made in all your time away from me lately while we dine."

CHAPTER 21 – NICO

Arianna sat across from me at the small table in the kitchen nook where we ate dinner most nights. The dining room was currently being renovated, with new paint, wallpaper, lighting, and furniture all hand-picked out by Arianna and the design team from Dubai.

But something told me we'd continue to dine in the kitchen even after it was done. My wife had a knack for chatting with the staff as they worked and she hated being isolated from the busy people, even if she had me for company.

She was a people person.

It was one of the things that had drawn me in the first time I saw her in Milan all those years ago.

"What room will the nursery be in?" she asked quietly when only Molly and Chef Alec remained on the other side of the kitchen, discussing the menu for the following day.

"Whatever room you want it to be," I replied, sipping my wine to clear my pallet before digging into the next course.

"What room did your mother use as the nursery when you were little?"

"One of the ones across the residence from their room," I shrugged, "I couldn't tell you which one exactly."

Her brows furrowed as she wiped her mouth, signaling that she was finished with that course. Manny appeared out of nowhere and cleared our dishes and Alec started plating the next course.

My staff worked more efficiently since Arianna's arrival, and I didn't doubt for one second that it was because they wanted to impress and spoil her for her kindness and generosity to them at every turn.

"You didn't have a room in the same wing as your parents?" she asked, not dropping the topic like I wished she would.

"No."

"How about when you were older?"

"I didn't move into the primary wing until I took over the entire Cosa Nostra, Arianna."

"Why?" She shook her head in confusion.

"Because my father was a smug son of a bitch, but he loved his wife," I shrugged, "And he refused to share her with anyone, even me."

Her eyes rounded and her pink lips parted. "That's terrible," She whispered.

I shrugged, "I didn't know any different."

She looked away from the table and her eyes misted over slightly as she stared out the dark window to the patio. "Our children will know different, Nico," she whispered sadly, "They'll know unconditional love and warmth." She closed her eyes, and a tear ran down her cheek before she took a deep breath and looked back over at me. "We have to learn how to be more than our parents were. We have to end the cycle."

"We already are, Arianna." I leaned across the table and took her hand in mine, even though my body ached to take her out of her seat completely and hold her in mine. "We already love our baby more than either of our parents ever did us. We're already changing everything. Together."

She gave me a watery-eyed smile before taking another deep breath and leaning back as Manny set down two plates before us, clearing his throat gently. "Tortellini with pesto." He informed with a bow and a smile to his mistress who returned it.

"One of my favorites," She patted his arm affectionately. "Thank you, Manny."

He backed away with a nod to me and we both started digging in, choosing to leave the sadness of the conversation behind us as we ate the delicious meal. "This is good," I commented as she took a giant mouthful and then giggled around it.

When she was done chewing. "Don't look at me like that, I'm starving."

"Good," I smirked back. "It's nice to see you eating for once."

She rolled her eyes and took another bite. "I feel like all I do is throw up and eat." She smirked, "Well, that and sleep."

"And fuck." I added, enjoying the way she blushed and looked over at the kitchen where our staff was actively ignoring us.

"Nico." She hissed and shook her head. "None of those things are under my control anymore. It's all his fault." She tapped her belly with a shrug, and I grinned.

"Takes after his dad then." I agreed, enjoying how she took to calling our baby a boy over the last few days, instead of fighting me on my wishful thinking.

To be honest, I was going to be ecstatic with either a boy or a girl, it didn't matter. But I had a feeling it was a boy.

Arianna rolled her eyes and took another large bite, seconds later she coughed, covering her mouth politely. She grabbed her glass of water and took a sip before coughing again as her brows pinched together.

"Are you okay?" I asked, laying my fork down as she wiped her mouth with her napkin, swallowing and coughing again. "Arianna!" I snapped as anxiety tightened around my spine. "What's wrong?"

Molly, Alec, and Manny all stopped what they were doing as Arianna looked at me with panic in her eyes and grabbed her throat.

"Fish." She strained as tears pooled in her eyes again.

"Molly!" I bellowed, looking over at the woman a second before she tore off through the kitchen towards one of the kits I had stocked throughout the house in strategic places. "Easy." I shoved my chair back, toppling it over as Arianna gripped the edge of the table with white knuckles. I threw the table away from us, scattering the food and wine all over the floor as I knelt in front of Ari. "Deep breath, baby." I put my hands on each side of her face as she looked around in panic. "Focus on me, sweetheart. Look at me and focus. If you panic, it will get worse," I reminded her.

After she told me of her extreme allergy to shellfish, I did extensive research on the condition, trained my staff to identify allergens and how to administer treatment to her, and stocked the house with every medication known to man for just this situation.

"My throat's closing," She rasped, coughing and trying to clear the blockage in her throat out of instinct but it was in vain. Her face reddened, the swelling in her mouth worsening as Molly skidded to a stop next to us, throwing the kit on the ground and tearing it open.

"Here," She handed the pen to me, and I ripped the cap off and pushed Arianna's dress up, baring her thigh, and stabbed her with it.

Arianna hissed and scrunched her face up as I injected the medicine into her leg. She grabbed my shirt in her small fists as it burned through her muscles.

"What's happening?" Matteo barked, running into the room with Saul and Dio following in. It was only then that I noticed the alarm system going off around the house.

It was the medical alarm I'd implemented to go off as soon as the EpiPen kit was removed from its base.

"There was fish in her food." Molly cried, tears running down her own face as Arianna struggled to breathe.

"How?" Matteo barked to the Chef who was tearing apart tortellini strewn across the floor from Arianna's plate with his bare fingers.

"I wouldn't," Alec shook his head in pure fear and disbelief. "I don't keep any shellfish in the house. Not since that first night with the lobster bisque." He looked at me where I still held onto Arianna, waiting for the medication to take effect. "I swear I didn't put anything in her food."

"Figure out what it is, and then we can find out who did it," I snapped, looking back to my wife. "It should be helping by now," I snapped, cursing as I noticed the blue hue on her lips. "Fuck!" I roared, tearing the kit open for another round.

"I'll get the car to the door." Matteo ran from the room to the garage, men filed out after him to start the convoy we would need to get to the hospital in record time.

I stabbed another round of medication into Arianna's thigh as her head started lolling front and back as a gurgling rattle began to escape from her lips. Molly held her against her chest, talking calmly into her ear and stroking her hair, begging her to keep breathing. As soon as the medication was done being administered, I scooped Arianna up in my arms and tore through the house to the front door.

"Manny!" I yelled as I ran, "Find out who did this!"

"Yes, Sir," He nodded, working with Alec to dissect the food for evidence of what was used against my wife.

Matteo skidded to a stop in my SUV and four more joined the lineup, parking ahead and behind the truck in a convoy. I jumped inside with Arianna in my arms and Molly slid in beside me before the trucks roared out of the driveway.

"Stay with me, baby," I whispered, staring into her glassy eyes as she lay in my arms.

"The medication should have kicked in by now," Molly cried with panic. "Why hasn't it kicked in?"

"I don't know," I admitted defeatedly. "I promise I'll find out though." I kissed Ari's forehead, wiping away the sweat that stuck to her brow as she clung to me.

Matteo and the other guards drove like professionals, getting us to the trauma center in record time.

But by the time I ran into the Emergency room with Arianna in my arms, she was unconscious. "My wife has been poisoned," I told the doctors waiting for us when we arrived. "She's in anaphylactic shock, I've given her two rounds of Epi but she still can't breathe. She's pregnant."

"Mr. Capasso," one of the doctors tried to get my attention as medical professionals surrounded Arianna on the gurney, attaching monitors, starting IVs, and administering medications, "We're going to take care of her, but you should leave while we do it."

"No." I pushed his hand off my arm, "Do what you have to do but I'm not going anywhere."

"Sir, we need to intubate her." He tried again. "It's not pleasant to watch."

I turned on him, and he backed up a step as I started screaming. "Somebody tried to kill my wife! I'm not leaving her side!"

"Yes, Sir." He agreed finally, turning to his team and barking out orders.

I flattened my back against the wall at the end of her bed and watched every single thing they did to her. It felt like hours passed as they tried different things to counteract the reaction going on inside of her body, poking her and stabbing her with medications over and over again. The monitor on the wall showed her heart was beating, but I wasn't dumb enough to think that meant she was okay.

"Save her," I croaked through my dry throat when I felt like I couldn't take another second of it. "Please, no matter what. You have to save her."

No one in the room acknowledged me, save for the head doctor I screamed at when we came in. And even he only looked at me over her frail body and sighed.

Someone tried to kill my wife.

And as I watched that bump on the monitor go up and down with each beat of her heart, I vowed to decimate anyone involved.

"Apa," A voice called from the doorway of Arianna's dark hospital room hours later. She had been moved up to the ICU after the medication combination the doctors finally found worked to reverse the swelling in her body.

But she was still intubated and sedated, so her body could continue to recover. The doctors said they ran her blood and found no traces of epinephrine in her system when she first came in. I injected her twice with her pens, but none of us could figure out why it hadn't shown up in her bloodstream twenty minutes later.

I hated not having answers to simple questions. It left me feeling useless and dejected.

I looked at the doorway and saw both of my brothers-in-law waiting behind Matteo in the hallway.

No one came into the room without permission, hospital staff included. Dr. Travis personally vetted the elite staff allowed in with the Chief of Staff before anyone touched her after she left the ER.

"Let them in," I said tiredly, tightening my hand around Arianna's from my seat next to her bed.

Carmine and Cristian walked in silently with looks of horror on their faces as they stared at their little sister laying in a hospital bed, still barely clinging to life.

"Will she be okay?" Carmine asked quietly as he took a seat on the other side of her, picking up her hand in his.

"She should recover," I responded, looking back down at my wife.

"And the baby?" Cristian asked from where he stood at the foot of the bed.

"Holding on through it all," I sighed, "Fucking miracle if you ask me."

"Ari's strong." Carmine watched me closely as I finally paid either of them any attention. "Doesn't surprise me that her babe is too."

Cristian pulled a chair up next to his brother and rested a hand on Ari's calf. "Do you know how it happened yet?" The cuts on his face were bandaged together and the swelling was far less than it had been, but he still looked like shit.

I shook my head solemnly, "I will before the sun rises in the sky. Even if I have to do it myself."

"I think our father was behind it," Carmine admitted. "I have no proof, but it makes the most sense."

"Agreed."

"I moved Anita and Amelia to a safe house." He sighed, "I can't risk him wiping us all off the face of the earth."

"What about you two?" I nodded to them. "You'd seem like bigger targets than your little sisters."

The oldest Rosetti shrugged, and the younger one smirked sadistically before stating, "I survived the wrath of the Don. I'd like to see him try."

"Sir." Matteo interrupted from the doorway. "We have news." Behind him, Saul and Dio stood ominously with death in their eyes. They took it personally that someone attacked Arianna in her own home right under their noses, and I intended to let them use that anger in her favor to figure this whole mess out.

"Send Molly in," I replied, nodding for Carmine and Cristian to exit the room before leaning down and kissing Ari's forehead. "I'll be right outside, Little One. I love you."

I hadn't left her side since the entire thing began, but I needed to eliminate the threat to her safety, and I didn't need to do that in front of her in case she could hear us. I didn't want anything at all upsetting her.

Molly walked in and took my seat, picking up Ari's hand and nodding to me.

She had her.

The young girl's loyalty to my wife was fierce and there was no better feeling in the world than knowing that Ari had someone unapologetically in her corner beside me.

"I'll be right back. Dio and Saul will be at the door." I walked towards the hallway when her gentle voice called me back.

"Make it hurt, Nico." Molly looked down at my wife, but I knew it was her that spoke. "Whoever did this to her." She turned her gaze up to me with misty eyes, "Make it fucking hurt in repayment."

"I will, Molly." I bowed my head and walked out, feeling shaken by her viciousness. She was always calm and gentle, but she was as rattled by this whole thing as I was. And if she needed violence to settle her equilibrium, I'd give it to her.

An empty room sat across the hall, and I followed Matteo, Carmine, and Cristian into it, where we could all still see into Ari's room.

"It took nine guys reviewing the security footage from the last two weeks, but we found who did it and sequentially found the mole leaking information to Emilio," Matteo said, linking his phone to the tv and pulling up a picture of a woman in one of our maid's uniforms. "Her name is Valentina Shaw. Though she went by the name Valentina Harlow when she applied for the job as a maid at Armarow. She was vetted, but the alias wasn't picked up."

Rage burned inside of me as I saw the face of the woman responsible for hurting my wife and unborn baby. "Show me."

Arianna's brothers tensed beside me as we watched clips of the security footage from the kitchen as Alec prepared dinner. He was mixing the pasta dough out on the counter when Molly walked in, followed by the provision staff that brought groceries to the estate a couple of times a week. Alec walked away from the food and took the list from Molly as the staff unpacked the items and started putting them away.

One of the provisions staff was the woman from the picture.

Valentina.

She took a couple of different loads of groceries through the kitchen to the pantry, and each time she looked around the kitchen and then into the mix sitting unattended on the counter. On her last trip by the dough, she flicked her hand over the top, pausing for only a fraction of a second as, and poured something, into the dough.

"Play it back," I said, and Matteo rewound the tape, zooming in on the mix itself and playing it frame by frame as the woman walked by.

In the opening of her sleeve, a glass vial stuck out under her hand and as she flicked her wrist, a clear liquid poured into the dough.

I watched it over and over again, in forward and reverse, trying to figure out someone could take three and a half seconds out of their life, and come damn fucking close to killing Arianna because of it.

That was it.

Three and a half seconds from start to finish before all traces of the liquid inside the dough were gone.

After the provisions were done, Alec returned to the counter and finished preparing the dough to be pressed and rolled into tortellini for our dinner.

"Was the chef in on it?" Carmine asked.

"No," I answered instantly, "He bloody adores your sister." I shook my head. "His meal was just the weapon that woman used."

"There's more," Matteo said grimly, drawing our attention back to him from the screen. "When the guys were watching the kitchen footage, they came across this."

He switched video clips, and we watched his new footage.

The kitchen was busy, early morning prep was happening all around the space as maids and butlers filed in and out of the space. "When was this?" I asked.

"The day you and Arianna returned to Armarow," Matteo answered. "Watch the top left corner."

Seconds later the same maid walked into the room with a stack of linens in her hands, opening the door to the cabinet in the butler's pantry to put them away.

The same cabinet where Arianna's medication kit was stored.

I walked closer to the screen to see better as the woman stood behind the cabinet door, obscuring what she was doing. "Switch cameras."

Matteo flipped to the other camera from inside the pantry, catching the same scene on the screen. This time, when she hid her actions from everyone else in the kitchen behind the door, we had a clear view.

She opened the lid to Arianna's med kit, careful not to dislodge it from the brace it was attached to that triggered the alarm. Then, after a quick peek over her shoulder, she removed the two pens from the case and replaced them with exact replicas.

"She replaced them with duds," Matteo answered the unasked question. Then, two other clips popped up next to each other on the screen, showing her doing the same thing with other kits around the house on the day we returned to the estate. "She ensured that Arianna wouldn't get the care she needed after she poisoned her."

"Jesus fuck," Cristian cursed, "Do you have any idea how lucky she is to be alive, having not only been exposed to her allergen but to have lived twenty minutes without medication to reverse it?" He paced the room. "She had an anaphylactic episode once when we were kids, and it was the scariest thing I've ever lived through." He shook his head horrified.

"Where is the girl now?" Carmine asked.

"Detained," Matteo answered, shocking us all. "She was trying to flee the village when Davide Bussa came upon her."

"Molly's father caught the woman?" I asked for clarification.

"A mass alert went out to all of the staff after identifying her, disclosing the assassination attempt on Arianna. Moments later he saw her running between buildings, still in her uniform. He tackled her and alerted security to her whereabouts."

"See that he's compensated," I responded firmly, "Largely."

"Yes, Capa." Matteo nodded. "The woman, Valentina, is secured back at Armarow. How do you want it handled?"

"I'll do it. Personally." I sighed, rubbing my hand down my face, trying to figure out how to be with my wife and avenge this vicious attack on her life at the same time.

"I'll stay," Carmine said, noting my troubled mind. "Take Cristian with you to handle the maid, And I'll update you immediately if something changes."

I mulled that over in my head, torn between not trusting anyone near her anymore, and the burn inside of me calling for bloodshed and answers. While we assumed it was Emilio Rosetti, we needed to know for sure before I wrote off the possibility that it was someone else.

"Dio and Saul will stay with you," I finally conceded, trusting in Arianna's favor of her brothers. "Matteo and Molly too."

"Fine," Carmine nodded, "I'm quite fond of Molly's charm." He winked, missing the glare that Matteo sent at the back of his head before walking back across the hallway to his sister's side.

"Don't kill him for flirting with the poor girl," I ordered Matteo, drawing a curious look from Cristian. "Let him flirt and distract Molly from the peril she's feeling inside right now if he wants to. It won't hurt anything, and it might even help the poor girl."

"Whatever," Matteo snapped, following after the man like he was afraid to leave him unattended in Molly's presence. I slapped Cristian on the back and walked out, pausing briefly to look at my still-slumbering wife before heading toward the car.

"Let's go before I change my mind."

"I think I'm going to quite enjoy being on this side of the Don's anger," He smirked, falling into step next to me.

CHAPTER 22 – ARIANNA

*T*welve Years Old

The bright-colored leaves crunched under my boots as I walked through the elaborate grounds. I was told to stay close, not to wander off and be bothersome to anyone, but I never knew what those boundaries of space and behavior were until I already crossed them.

It was like a game my father liked to play to keep me on my toes.

Don't do anything wrong.

But I'm not going to tell you what's right or wrong until the game is over.

Nor will I tell you the punishment until I give it.

It was the worst kind of torture sometimes, out of all his sick games. That was saying something because torture was kind of his favorite thing.

At least where I was concerned anyway.

Being twelve was hard.

According to my father, I was no longer a child, I was a business asset. One to be bartered with and traded as property for him to obtain something he wanted more than me. Which could be just about anything else in the world because the man didn't even like me.

I don't think he ever did.

To test the fate I was already destined to anger, I walked around the estate, wandering farther than I normally would. Because, why not?

I was going to be punished anyway.

Might as well explore a little bit, even if I was cold as ice. The frilly white dress my mother made me wear to the old castle did little to ward off the fall chill, but I wasn't going to let that stop me.

The trees were the brightest I'd ever seen before, and I wanted to stare at them forever. We didn't have trees like this in the city.

They were breathtaking.

As I wandered through an elaborate garden of Armarow Estate, I envisioned what it would be like to live amongst nature beyond the mystical castle walls. Would it be magical and exciting? Or would it feel lonely and isolated like everywhere else I went?

I bet it'd feel magical.

The adventure of the rolling hillsides sprawled out as far as the eye could see would lead me on such grand adventures. I just knew it.

I ached to live here amongst the polite staff and kind village people we met on our way in.

It was such a stark difference to the city, I ached to drown myself in it.

"Hit it."

I froze with a foot raised in the air as the voice drifted to me through the trees. Slowly I lowered my boot to the ground and ducked to look through the dense trees.

"You hit it," A different voice snapped back to the first. It sounded like a couple of boys, just beyond the first layer of trees.

I looked around me, looking for the best way to get away from the trees undetected, because something burned in my gut that told me I'd found the boundary of distance and behavior, and if I went any further, I'd cross it.

And I didn't feel like being beaten today.

I turned and quietly stepped around the majority of the crunchy leaves trying to avoid the sticks to retreat when I heard a pitiful noise come from within the trees that stopped me cold.

Meow.

Hiss.

"Fucking just stomp its head in already, this is getting boring," A different voice complained as a cold shiver crawled up my spine.

They were hurting a cat.

Before I could even think twice, I stupidly pushed my way through the tree line and stumbled into a clearing where the voices came from. The trio of teenage boys didn't notice me, but as one of them raised his booted foot over the head of a tiny kitten I yelled. "Stop it!"

Three matching heads of dark hair and bright blue eyes snapped in my direction and fear exploded through my brain.

Run.

It was the first thing that came to mind, but it was too late.

I turned back towards the trees and made it only a step and a half before a set of hands tangled into my hair and yanked me away from the safety of the foliage and threw me to the ground in the center of the clearing. I landed in the dirt next to the cat that was tied by a collar to a stake in the ground, fighting with its life to get off.

"Well, well, well," The oldest one sneered down at me as they circled me. He was the one who had grabbed me and threw me to the ground. "Who do we have here?"

The other two looked just as menacing as they walked around me, their heavy boots stomping in the dirt.

"Is she the queen of England?" the middle one joked. "You'd think so by the way the staff has acted leading up to her visit."

"Maybe she's the court jester." The youngest one mocked me. "She looks funny."

But the oldest one is the one I kept my eyes on as he stood at my feet with his arms crossed over his chest. He was older than Carmine, if I had to guess, I'd say eighteen. Maybe older.

The other two were somewhere between sixteen and fourteen.

All three were older and way bigger than I was. And I didn't know what to do.

I should have kept my stupid mouth shut or run back to the estate to get help.

Hissing from next to me reminded me that the cat was still trapped though, and they would have stomped it to death with their boots if I had stayed quiet.

I had been left with no choice.

"My name is Arianna." I tilted my chin up like I wasn't afraid for my life in the very second. "My father is-."

"We know who your father is," The oldest one snapped, cutting me off. "Do you know who ours is?"

He knelt into a crouch in front of me and I slid back an inch to get away from the crazy I saw in his eyes. "Dominic Capasso?"

To be honest, I had no idea who the boys were. But if I had to guess considering we were at the Don's house, they belonged to him.

"Bingo." The oldest one said with a snarl. "And you're the one that they brought in, to ruin everything."

"What are you talking about?" I whispered, understanding his open disdain for me a little better now, though I didn't know what I'd done to cause it.

"Little Rosetti, darling, here to marry the big bad wolf and ensure none of us ever see the throne," He heckled, and then spit at my feet. I recoiled from the offensive move and scurried further back from him.

"I don't know what any of that means." I tried to keep my voice calm and serene like I did when my father was in an uproar. Sometimes it helped keep his fists to himself. Most times it didn't though, but it did usually delay the inevitable.

The oldest one sucked his teeth and stood back up, looking down at me menacingly before gazing over at his brothers who flanked me. "What do you think the wolf would do if we stomped his pretty little fiancé's face in like the cats? Do you think Dad would have to start the whole process of finding his beloved son a wife all over again?"

My mouth fell open in absolute shock seconds before my brain started working.

And I used my brain power to push out the loudest scream of my life from my lungs. The noise ripped from my lips like a violent volcano erupting but the impressive act only lasted seconds before the oldest one lunged at me, covering my mouth with his hand and pinning my head to the ground.

"Shut up," He hissed, pushing my face into the dirt and stone, cutting my cheek up, "Shut the fuck up or I'll slit your throat."

I fought against the weight of him as he climbed onto my back, pushing his knees against my spine. Agony bloomed through my lungs as his weight made it impossible to take a breath in. I couldn't scream again, even if his threat hadn't scared me silent. I couldn't even catch my breath to stay alive.

He was going to kill me by suffocation.

The threats of knives and boots were irrelevant.

"Dude, get off her," The youngest one said after a beat of time. "You're not actually serious, are you?"

"Yeah, man," the middle one, shoved the eldest's shoulder, but it didn't dislodge him. "Dad will fucking kill you for interfering with his plans."

"Don't you two get it?" the boy on my back snapped as my vision darkened. "If he marries someone, he'll have kids and then they'll take everything next in line. We'll be so fucking far off the throne we won't even see it anymore."

"We'll never get it anyway, Diego." One of them yelled, shoving the one on my back again, but I was so close to unconsciousness I couldn't decipher the difference in their voices anymore. My nails dug into the dirt, bending backward as I fought to get away from the pressure on my lungs. "Dad will never acknowledge us the way we want him to, he's too old-fashioned. Just get off her."

"No," Diego, the eldest replied, pushing harder against the back of my neck and head until I could feel the warmth of blood mixing with the cold dirt under my face. "I think I want to upgrade from killing off strays and see what it feels like to kill a human."

"Diego!" One of the other brothers yelled again before suddenly the weight on my back intensified a millisecond before it let up completely.

I gasped for breath, sucking in dirt and debris as I tried to sit up off of the ground, but my body protested like my limbs were still pinned.

I caught sight of the youngest brother running away from the clearing as a scuffle ensued behind me, but I was still so focused on breathing I didn't dare look over my shoulder.

"I thought I told you fucking bastards to learn your place," A deep baritone voice I hadn't heard before chided before the middle brother went flying through the air, landing along the tree line in a wad of limbs and screams.

"Fuck you!" Diego screamed, as I finally got my arms to work and pushed myself over onto my back to see what was going on.

A man as tall as a tree and as wide as a truck stood over the boy that had decided to kill me because of someone called the wolf and was currently squeezing his hands around his throat. Diego's face was molten red and purpling more by the second as he swung his fists towards the bigger man's face and arms, trying to dislodge his hold, but they simply bounced off like he didn't feel them at all.

I watched in horror as my attacker's body went limp before the newcomer finally released his throat and let him fall into the dirt. The middle boy had scurried away at some point, unnoticed, and now it was just the three of us in the clearing.

And I feared the big man even more than the three others combined.

As if sensing my fear, he turned and finally looked at me where I cowered on the ground, covered in blood and dirt. His green eyes were so vibrant that they glowed through the dim forest lighting.

"Are you okay?" he barked at me, and I flinched, scurrying back on my hands and rear end. He groaned, rolling his eyes and sighing before wiping his hands on his black suit pants and walking towards me. "I won't hurt you." He held his hands up as he got closer.

I shook my head in fear, unable to force words out of my dry mouth. He crouched down at my feet and slowly brought his hand up to my face, using only the back of one finger under my chin to turn my face so he could see my battered cheek.

"Is this all they did to you?" His green eyes darkened, and his jaw clenched when I stared at him dumbly, "Did they touch you anywhere else, Little One?"

"No," I whispered, finally understanding what he meant. "They just threw me to the ground."

He nodded his head once and then dropped his hand from my chin, "Let's get you back to the house."

"Are you the wolf?" I asked as he helped me stand up. He looked way older than the older brother of the trio, but not old like my dad. He looked like the men my father paid to guard us though; tall, strong, and powerful. "They talked about me belonging to the wolf, but I don't understand what they meant." He didn't respond, but pushed the tree limbs apart for me to walk through and I froze, finally remembering what started this all to begin with. "Wait! The kitten."

I turned back to the center and searched the dirt floor for the orange banded kitten that had been trapped as a sacrifice, as I had, but it was gone. I lifted up the rope tied to the stake and found the end frayed and untied.

He got away.

"Is that why you were here to start with?" The man nodded to the rope in my hand.

"They were going to kill the baby," I said sadly, dropping the rope back into the dirt and looking around for the little thing. "Do you think it'll be safe from them?" I looked back up at him, hopefully.

One side of his lips pulled back in what I thought was his attempt at a smirk, but I couldn't quite tell. His dark features were so serious and hard to discern. "You narrowly escape your death, and you're worried about someone else's life? A cat's?" he questioned before sighing and nodding for me to go through the trees he still held open.

"My life has already been written out for me," I shrugged. "Nothing will change what is already planned."

He stayed silent as I walked out through the trees, wincing slightly as my tired body bent to get through the limbs.

"I'll have the groundskeeper look for the cat and protect it. What did it look like?" He finally said as he fell into step beside me. I tried to figure out who he was as we walked; he was well dressed and sharp looking and he looked a little like the trio of boys who had terrorized me, but their eyes were opposite colors. And they didn't act related.

The trio were the Don's sons, but who was this?

"It was an orange, tiger cat," I finally said, shaking off the family tree trying to paint itself inside of my brain.

Cousins, maybe?

"I'll do what I can." He replied gruffly.

"You never answered my question." I turned and looked at him as we got to the mouth of the trail leading to the patio. He stopped walking like it was the end of his path and I was supposed to go the rest of the way alone. "Who are you? And what about him?" I nodded back to the forest where the unconscious boy hopefully still lay.

He put his hands in his pants pockets and rocked on his heels, looking at the house before us. "I'm nobody."

"You're the wolf, aren't you?" I challenged. I didn't know who this 'wolf' was, but it sounded like the boys were intimidated by him, and that matched the vibe this man was giving off. The man I supposedly belonged to.

He sighed like I was annoying him, something Cristian did all the time when I berated him with questions, and then looked down at me. "Don't worry yourself with Big Bad Wolves, Arianna." He replied cryptically. "It never ended well for Little Red Riding Hood." He nodded towards the path once more. "Go inside before you freeze to death. Make sure you tell your parents exactly what happened out here."

"They wouldn't care either way." I looked down at my feet and made them start moving towards the castle and away from the man who intrigued me and scared me all in the same breath. "And you got my fairy tale wrong." I turned in a circle a few feet down the path, holding out my mud-streaked dress and soiled skin cocking my head to the side, and giving him one last look. "I'm the forgotten daughter who lives in the attic with the mice."

I walked further down the path but turned when his voice trailed after me. "Doesn't she become a princess in the end?"

I chuckled and shrugged my shoulders. "Highly unlikely. Unless you believe crazy old women can turn pumpkins into carriages and mice into horses." He didn't respond and it felt silly to stand fifty feet apart and continue a conversation, so I gave him a slight little wave with one hand and turned back towards the estate.

When I looked back at the top of the stairs to the house, he was gone. And I wasn't sure why, but I missed his presence.

And it felt as if I imagined the whole bizarre thing like a forgotten glass slipper.

CHAPTER 23- ARIANNA

The weight of darkness that had been holding me under finally started to slip, letting my brain fight through the fog of my mother's tonic.

I must have been bad because it was an especially strong dose this time.

"Hmm." I hummed, fighting the weight of my eyelids like they were the heaviest things in the world.

"Arianna," Nico's deep voice vibrated against my temple seconds before his warm lips pressed a kiss to it. "Open your eyes for me, baby."

"Hmm." I hummed again, unable to get my tongue off the roof of my mouth as I cracked one eye open. His perfect face was blurry when he leaned down right in front of mine, and confusion rattled my slow brain.

What was he doing here?

Where were my parents?

Why was I high on the tonic, if Nico was here?

"Come on, Little One." he said again. "Open those pretty eyes for me. It's been so long since I've seen them."

I forced both eyes open, using up all my strength, and then blinked a few times to clear the blurriness from them. "Nico."

His rugged face lifted with a breathtaking smile of relief as he held mine in his hands, rubbing his thumbs over my cheeks. "Welcome back to the land of the living, darling." he said, kissing me gently and then laying his forehead against mine and breathing me in.

"What happened?" I lifted my hand to his chest and ran my fingers over the smooth fabric of his shirt, grounding myself as panic tried to seep in through the cracks in my memory.

"You had an allergic reaction at dinner," He replied, pulling back to look at me. "Do you remember it?"

My brow furrowed as I tried to recall what led up to that moment, and then it all flooded back.

Panic.

Anxiety.

Suffocation.

"The baby?" I gasped, clawing at the blanket laid over my body to get it off. I couldn't move it from under his hip where he sat on the edge of the bed and struggled. "Is he okay?"

"Shh," Nico cooed, pulling the blanket free and then lifting the gown I was wearing so I could run my hand over the bare skin of my abdomen. "He's perfectly fine. Doctors have been monitoring you both the whole time we've been here."

I deflated back into the pillows with my hand cradling my stomach as tears burned in my eyes. "He's really, okay?" I questioned, hesitant to believe it.

"I promise, he's just fine." He covered my hand with his and then covered me back up, keeping me warm from the cool air of the room.

A hospital room.

"How long have I been here?" I wondered out loud as his thumb drew small circles around my belly button.

"Two days," He sighed. "You were almost lifeless by the time I got you here." He swallowed and worked his jaw back and forth before closing his eyes and pressing his forehead to mine again. "I died over and over again watching them work on you, baby. I never want to feel that way again."

"I'm sorry." I patted his cheek and kissed him gently. "How did it happen?"

He shook his head, keeping it against mine. "Your father hired a woman to assassinate you." I recoiled from him as the weight of his statement hit me. "She infiltrated the staff at Armarow and laid in wait for the perfect moment to strike. She tainted your meal with a concentrated form of your allergen and then switched all of the rescue pens out for duds." His jaw popped from how tight he clenched it as his anger rose. "I gave you two doses, and nothing was happening so we rushed here. You were completely unconscious and blue by the time you were finally given medication. You were dangling by the thread of life, Ari."

"I can't believe he did that," I said sadly. "I mean I can, but." I shook my head, not needing to use any other words to express my feelings.

Nico knew.

"Carmine has moved Anita and Amelia into a safe house. We've interrogated the woman that attacked you and have information about where your father will be in two days." He said firmly. "We'll strike then."

"You and Carmine?"

"Yes. He and Cristian were here. He stayed with you and Cristian helped me get the information we needed out of the woman."

"Cristian helped you torture her, you mean?" I shuddered, and then flashbacks of the dream I had came back. "Wait." I gripped his shirt in my hand again as I played the dream back, trying to decipher if it was real or not. It felt like a misty image on the edge of my sight that I couldn't quite get to come into focus. "The cat."

"What cat?" Nico asked confused with a scowl. "We're talking about your father, Little One."

I smiled up at him as the mist cleared, revealing the dream to me completely. "You called me that the first time I met you." His brow knitted deeper as his confusion grew. "In the woods at Armarow. You saved my life."

He sat back and watched me closely. "I thought you forgot about that."

"I did," I admitted. "I didn't remember it at all. I had a weird sense of déjà vu the first time I walked the grounds of Armarow, but I couldn't find the place where it came from. But then I had a dream, I think."

"A dream?" He cocked his head.

"A memory?" I shrugged, running my hand over his cheek. "You were so young." I sighed wistfully. "And handsome," I smirked as he groaned and brushed it off.

"Gone are those years."

"Wrong." I removed my hand from my stomach and held his face in both of them. "I think you are absolutely breathtaking now, just as you were before. You're strong, and wise. Weathered to the life you live but not in a negative way." I smoothed my finger over the frown lines formed between his brows as he watched me cynically, "You could stand to smile more often, but I think our little babe will help with that."

He smirked and then sighed, taking my hands in his and kissing both as he took a deep breath. "That was the day that our fathers agreed to the marriage contract. You were a fucking baby, and I was already a grown man."

I glared at him, "I was three months away from being a teenager. And it doesn't matter, because even at that age, you were still my prince charming."

He snorted and shook his head, "I'm still the big bad wolf." Running his hand through my hair. "You're still the perfect little Cinderella."

"Finally the princess you always thought I was. Even with a scar." I fingered the white line I knew that marred my cheek from something I had blocked out of my memory. But now I had the answers I'd always sought after. "Wait." I paused, thinking back to that terrifying day. "Were those boys your brothers?"

"My father's sons. But no brothers of mine." He sneered.

"By a woman that wasn't your mother." I clarified. "The woman he stole from you selfishly but still didn't stay faithful to you mean?"

"Something like that." He agreed. "My father sired eight children that he claimed in his lifetime. But he was only ever married to my mother."

"And when he died you-," I paused, raising my eyebrows questioningly.

"Eradicated that infestation." He answered evenly. "Those three were the only ones to live on the grounds at Armarow. Their mother was a maid when she met my father and then she wormed her way into living in the estate because she continued to spread her legs for my father and bear him more children." He scoffed. "They didn't deserve anything they were given over the years. They were menaces; torturing animals, and disrespecting the staff. More than once maids would up and quit with bruises around their wrists and necks from one of the trio getting rough with them. I couldn't stand it. And short of beating their asses each and every time, I had no power to punish them for being degenerates."

"So you waited until you were the Don and then you removed them."

"I destroyed them. And their whore mother." He declared. "She was particularly vile, ridiculing my mother constantly and undermining her at every turn like having to live with her husband's whore wasn't punishment enough." He stood up off the bed as the tension became energy inside of his body. "I made her regret every single thing she did to my mother before her death."

"The whore or your mother's?" I asked for clarification but already knew the truth.

"Yes," Nico answered evasively, giving me the answer without outright admitting it.

"Noted."

"Don't act like that is appalling, Little One," He stalked back to the bed and leaned down over me. "because I'll do so much worse to anyone who ever crosses you."

"I know you will," I confirmed and took a deep breath, deciding not to shy away from his dominance and darkness. "And I love you for it."

"Do you?" He questioned, running his thumb over my bottom lip. "Or does it scare you?"

"It excites me," I replied, nipping his thumb with my teeth and sucking it into my mouth. I knew I was the opposite of seductive in a hospital gown and two-day-old body odor, but I also knew my husband was as addicted to me as I was to him. "It makes me crazy with need."

"Arianna," he growled, lowering his hand to my neck, laying the weight of it against it but not squeezing. "Be careful or I'll give the entire hospital staff a shock when I fuck you right here, hard enough to make you scream for mercy." I swallowed and smirked up at him, tiredly admitting defeat. "It's been two days since I've felt your body against mine, love. I'm a very triggered man right now, so I recommend you don't tempt me."

"Yes, Sir." I laid back on the pillow and winked at him. "How about you get me home and I'll let you make slow sweet love to me that you love to do, even if you won't admit it and damage your bad boy exterior."

He tilted his head back and chuckled loudly before smiling down at me again. I could see the fatigue in his eyes even as he stood tall and strong over me. The last few days had weighed heavily on him, even if he wouldn't admit it. "Let's work on getting you home and then we can go from there."

"Whatever you say, Wolf," I smirked cheekily and he shook his head in exasperation.

"You're trouble, Little One."

I lay on the couch in the den with the television playing in the background but wasn't paying attention to it. Tonight was the night that Nico planned to strike against my father, killing him and handing over the entire Rosetti fortune to my brother, Carmine. It would effectively end the terrorizing reign of Emilio and Mina Rosetti and ensure that my four other siblings were never in danger again.

But there was so much at stake, leaving me nervous and unsettled as Nico prepared for battle.

"Well a girl could get used to this kind of life."

I snapped my head around towards the entrance and squealed with delight as my sisters walked in.

I leaped from the couch and grabbed onto them both, hugging them tight as something powerful passed between us. Like we could all feel the weight of today while also trying to enjoy the presence of each other.

"What are you guys doing here?" I pulled back and looked at them both. Amelia looked beautiful in a pair of dark skinny jeans and a cream-colored sweater and Anita wore a pair of burgundy corduroy pants and a sage green shirt. Not once had any of us been allowed to wear pants outside of the house.

Part of my parent's control, forcing us to wear modest dresses anytime we stepped out the front door.

"We're here to keep you entertained." Amelia shrugged, "Your husband thinks you're going to go stir crazy today." My eighteen-year-old sister was one of those souls that were old, regardless of her age, and it showed when she talked so casually like that.

"And *we* were going stir crazy," Anita added with a smirk. "Carmine locked us up tighter than even our parents did."

"It's for our safety." Amelia rolled her eyes and then gazed at me. "How are you?" She looked down at my stomach with a pointed glance. "Is there something you'd like to tell us?"

I pulled them with me to the couch and sat with one on each side. "Who told you?"

"Believe it or not, Cristian," Amelia answered. "I think the quiet one is actually really excited to be an uncle."

"He blabbed and Carmine smacked him for it." Anita joked. "Why didn't you tell us though?"

"It's only just happened and with everything else going on-" I droned. "I just didn't get a chance."

"Are you excited?" Anita asked.

"Extremely," I responded instantly, taking their hands in mine. "I got lucky with this marriage, guys. It's unlike anything I could have imagined."

"He definitely brainwashed her," Anita whispered around the front of me to our middle sister like I wasn't three inches away. "How do we break the spell?"

"Oh, stop it." I swatted them both. "I won't lie and say it's been all rainbows and butterflies. We actually hated each other in the very beginning, regardless of-" I froze, looking at Anita. "Never mind."

"No, no." Amelia rushed on, "You have to finish that sentence. I have to hear it."

My parents never spoke of physical relationships between partners. We never had the sex talk or learned anything about our bodies past what our older brothers joked about when they thought we weren't listening. Or what Google could come up with if we happened to crack the wifi password that changed more often than the weather.

"We have a strong, *connection*. That's all." I tried for politeness.

"The sex is good." Amelia nodded, "Got it."

"Ew." Anita curled her upper lip and leaned back.

"See." I glared at Amelia who just raised an eyebrow amused. "We decided to make a truce. Neither of us actually chose the marriage, but we were forced into it for different reasons, and after fighting almost nonstop and both of us being miserable, we just decided to... get along." I shrugged. "After that, things got *better*."

"And now you're knocked up with the heir to the Cosa Nostra and suddenly our father wants you dead for foiling his plan to murder your husband and marry you off to someone else instead once he realized he wasn't going to be able to use you to control the Don. In return, our brothers and your husband are going to murder our parents and turn us all into orphans." Amelia droned on like she was listing off a grocery list. "Did I miss anything else?"

"Nope." I popped the 'p' dramatically. "That about sums it up."

"Good." Amelia clapped her hands and stood up. "Then let's just focus on keeping you happy and relaxed for the next few hours so it can all go off without the men worrying about your delicate condition and then we can all go on with our lives."

"You don't have to be so rude about it." Anita gasped, dropping my hand and crossing her arms looking up at our sister who made it all seem normal. "You guys may be okay with being orphans, but I'm not." My heart hurt for my little sister as tears lined her lower lashes. She crossed her arms over her chest and leaned back into the couch. "I know Mom and Dad weren't the best parents to you guys, and I wish I understood why. But they weren't bad to me."

"I know, bug." I sighed, pulling her into my arms. "But if you knew even a fraction of what they did to all of us, you'd be less inclined to allow their favoritism to shadow your mind."

"I know." She wrapped her arms around my waist and hugged me. "I'm just torn."

"That's fair," I admitted. "How about we just don't talk about it, good or bad? The guys are going to do what needs to be done, regardless of how we feel. That's the joy of being the Don." I reminded her. "So how about we just have a day together where we don't worry about everything."

"Okay." She nodded, "I have really missed you since you've been gone."

"You sound surprised by that." I snorted and Amelia smirked down at our little sister.

"Well, you were so cold-shouldered before the wedding." Anita grimaced. "It was kind of like you were already gone before you moved here."

"Duh, Anita." Amelia snapped, "Because they drugged her to keep her quiet."

"Amelia." I hushed.

"They what?" Anita asked leaning back to look at me. "They drugged you?"

I looked down at my innocent little sister and found myself wondering what she knew and what she was just naïve of. "Don't worry about it today. Let's just enjoy our day." I kissed her hair and looked at Amelia. "Right?"

Amelia looked sad but she nodded her head, putting her brave face on and agreeing with me. "Right."

CHAPTER 24- NICO

My wife was breathtaking.

Single-handedly the most beautiful woman in the world.

She sat at the kitchen island with her sisters, helping the chef prepare desserts for their evening movie marathon that Ari had planned to distract themselves from what we would be doing at the same time.

The woman that had tried to kill Arianna eventually confessed who her contact was within the Rosetti security detail, revealing who gave her the instructions to follow. Turns out, the man was soft on the devious woman, and with a little assistance from her, we were able to schedule a meeting with him tonight.

The guard thought he was meeting up for a status update and a quick fuck behind some dumpster in the city. When in reality he'd be captured and forced to lead us to my sniveling father-in-law.

Who was conveniently scheduled to meet with the man who he planned to marry Arianna off to before he decided to kill her instead.

Valentina never got a chance to alert the Rosetti's that the attempt on Arianna's life had been foiled, so to their knowledge, we were still two steps behind them.

When in reality we were right on their heels.

Emilio was meeting with Matthew Rizzio, Arianna's would-be future husband, to assure the lad that things were going swimmingly in his plans to kill me and offer his daughter to him.

According to Carmine, Matthew had been obsessed with Arianna for years, making him the perfect target to marry a 'tainted' bride off to after my death.

Emilio didn't plan to tell Matthew that he was actively trying to kill his daughter before killing me and was probably just sucking him dry for what he could until the truth revealed itself.

Matthew would find out tonight how wrong he'd been to plot against me with Emilio though.

I'd kill him for his willingness to think with his dick and not his brain. Giving free rein to his desire to have Arianna instead of his fear of the Don was going to cost him his life.

And I was going to enjoy taking it.

Almost as much as I was going to enjoy taking Emilio and Mina's.

I didn't like leaving Arianna behind, but Armarow was impenetrable, and the army of men I was leaving to secure her was more than capable of protecting her. I needed to end this whole sordid affair with her parents so we could move on with our lives.

The darkness that loomed over us since finding out that Emilio was using his children to gain footing in the Cosa Nostra had worn out its welcome. It was time to feel the fucking sunshine again.

I walked into the kitchen, sliding my hand over the slope of Arianna's neck as she cut up strawberries for a cake and pressed my body against hers. I didn't care if her sisters watched, I was going to give my wife a proper goodbye before going off to war. "I need to leave."

She stiffened slightly before setting her knife down and turning to face me. Her eyes spoke thousands of words, though she didn't allow any to cross her lips.

It would be futile to tell me to be careful or to try to convince me to stay behind while my men handled it.

I was the Don.

I was the Capo.

I was the one who would end it all tonight and solidify the power transfer I deemed fit.

Arianna wrapped her arms around my neck and pulled me down, kissing me with that silent passion I could read in her eyes. My own hands wrapped around her slim waist and pulled her tighter against me, reveling in the way her body melted into my touch.

Not long ago her body's reaction to me was the only way I could tell what she was feeling.

I had no idea what she was thinking at that time, but I knew what she was feeling.

And over time, I've learned to read my wife's body language to decipher what she was thinking as well. Cementing the bond between us.

"I love you," I spoke against her lips when she finally sank back down onto her heels and slid her hands down my chest.

"I love you, too." She whispered, staring at the spot on my peck where her teeth had permanently branded my skin beneath my shirt. "Hurry home to us." She finally lifted her eyes to mine. "We need you here."

"There isn't a force on this earth that could keep me from you now, Little One. Man or heavenly included. You are mine."

"Yes." She smirked but the act didn't reach her eyes. "Go. Before my pregnancy hormones cause me to beg you for something you will not give me."

"I'd give you the world," I whispered against her lips. "Starting tomorrow."

She chuckled, finally letting it bloom into a sincere act, and sighed. "I'll hold you to that."

"Good." I kissed her forehead and then stepped away, "I'll see you when it's done."

I nodded to her sisters who looked on from the other side of the counter and they smiled back. The youngest one, Anita, watched me with something deeper than her sister Amelia, causing the hair on my neck to stand up briefly before Molly and Matteo walked into the room, pulling me out of the trance.

"Ready?" Matteo asked as Molly skirted around him with her head tipped down.

I glanced at him and nodded to his shirt with a smirk. "You missed a button."

He quickly noticed the undone button of his shirt and swiftly corrected it, glancing at Molly once who was staring at her feet so hard I would have worried she was asleep if not for the way her fingers wound themselves into her skirt over and over again.

"Leave them alone," Arianna warned with a glare. "Goodbyes are hard."

"Hmm." I hummed, winking at her. "But hellos are so much more rewarding." She smirked and I pushed Matteo back out the door before he tried to jump the maid one more time.

When we got into the car and headed out with the cavalry, I glanced over at him, but he wouldn't meet my eye.

"So Molly has let you in, finally?"

"Not talking about it."

"We have nothing else to talk about on the trip there. We might as well talk about the woman you've been crushing on forever." I chatted.

He rolled his eyes, "You sound like an old hag, gossiping in a hair salon." I tipped my head back and laughed, surprising him and the other men in the vehicle. "Arianna's done something to your head." He grumbled, looking back out the window.

"Yeah," I shrugged, "She has. The same thing Molly will do to yours if you're lucky." I replied as he let the silence stretch on as we neared our target.

"**Y**ou good?" Matteo asked later when we sat at our rendezvous point, waiting for someone to get their eyes on Emilio before we moved in.

"Yeah," I replied, looking through the binoculars into the estate that Matthew Rizzio had just purchased.

He didn't know it, but he had purchased it from me, conveniently giving me insider information on the comings and goings of the property. I knew the men that worked the estate for decades prior to the arrival, and they stayed loyal to me even after the transition.

I didn't know how much it was going to come in handy until today though.

A car pulled up next to us and I glanced over my shoulder as Cristian got out and walked to my side. "Any update?"

He shook his head, adjusting his black suit. "Carmine got a call from Emilio an hour ago to meet him here. That's it."

"Seems suspicious that Emilio would give his whereabouts out to anyone that far in advance," I said, squinting as speculation filled my gut.

"I agree." He responded, looking over to Matteo and then down to the grounds. "Think it's a trap?"

"I think Emilio is too good at being a snake to not have a backup plan. I just don't know if sabotage was his original plan or not." I grumbled, hating the uncertainty.

"What are we going to do?" Matteo asked.

"Wait for confirmation that he's even here," I responded. "And then we'll feel it out. Worst comes to worst we'll blow the fucking house up with him inside of it." I shrugged. "But that's plan B because I want to see the look in his eyes when I kill him."

An hour later, we had our answer when Luca radioed from his position across the property. "Head Rosetti has arrived, with second Rosetti in tow."

"Got it. Wait for orders." Matteo responded and then looked at me. "What do you say, boss?"

I used the binoculars and watched the car roll down the expansive driveway and stop at the front door, with its army of vehicles. Emilio stepped from the back of his SUV and Carmine got out behind him, following his father into the house.

Seconds before he stepped inside, he looked out over the tree line, not sure where we were, but that we were there, and nodded his head once.

"No trap." Cristian interpreted for us.

"That he knows of, anyway," I responded, dropping the binoculars.

"Or that he's willing to tell us about," Matteo grumbled from next to me, eyeing me closely.

He didn't trust Carmine and Cristian, and I got that. They were the blood and flesh of the man we were hunting after all.

But I trusted Arianna, and she trusted them.

So I'd have to give them the benefit of the doubt until they showed differently.

"Let's move." I nodded to Matteo and then to Cristian. "You'll ride with me."

He gave me a curt nod, understanding that if I had to, I'd use him in a trap, yet allow it which showed good in his favor.

Before I even took a step forward toward the car, gunfire and explosions rang out all around. Mayhem ensued, screams tore through the night air as my men and I fired into the darkness, using the glowing flash of bullets coming our way to trace back to the guns firing the rounds.

No!

Men fell to their knees and continued firing until their bodies no longer functioned. Death swirled all around me as we persisted to fight.

A bullet tore through my shoulder the same second that Matteo landed on the ground, bleeding from a wound on his head. "Retreat!" I bellowed out, trying to save as many of my men as I could.

It was a trap.

But the trap had come to us, instead of us walking into it.

Gunpowder burned my nostrils as more explosions blasted earth and metal from the cars into the air, raining more weapons down upon us as they fell. "Let's go!" Cristian screamed, grabbing my arm as I shot off rounds toward one of Emilio's men, hitting him in the head and dropping him. "We have to go!"

"Get out of here, kid," I yelled over the roar of gunfire. "Save yourself."

I looked at him over my shoulder as a black-clothed figure walked up behind him and smashed the butt of his rifle into the back of his head, knocking him out cold, seconds before someone did the same to me.

As darkness started to overtake my vision I groaned, falling to the earth as my wife's name laid on my lips one last time, "Arianna."

CHAPTER 25- ARIANNA

"Your pacing is making me seasick." Amelia snapped at our youngest sister as she walked back and forth in front of the tv. "You've been doing it for twenty minutes now and I'm going to knock you out if you don't stop."

Anita didn't even acknowledge her as she paced back and forth, chewing on her nail. I caught Molly's eye as she too watched my younger sister with a pensive glare.

Something was wrong.

"Anita," I called, slowly rising to my feet from the nest of blankets I'd made on the couch. She didn't respond but just kept pacing. "Anita." I barked out louder and she jumped, falling still and looking at me. "What do you know?"

"I don't-." She shook her head with eyes as wide as saucers before turning them over to Amelia who stood up on the other side of the room and stared at her. "I'm just worried."

"You don't have any skin in the game," Amelia remarked, walking around our sister with her arms crossed. "You have no reason to be worried this much. Even Arianna isn't in panic mode like you are."

"They're our parents Amelia!" Anita cried and then covered her mouth and looked at me with wide eyes.

"Oh, my God." I paled, feeling all of the blood draining from my face as I realized our younger sister was on their side. "What's going on?"

Anita shook her head, before dropping her hands and clenching her jaw, steeling her spine in defiance. "I'm staying out of it."

I crossed the room in a split second, hardly beating Amelia to our sister. I grabbed her shoulders and spun her around to push her back into the wall. "You have two seconds to tell me everything you know before I start beating it out of you!" I threatened. "If you think I'm kidding make no mistake, Sister, I'll resort to bodily harm to protect my husband and our *brothers*!" I yelled, reminding her it wasn't just Nico versus our father. Our brothers were there and involved too.

"Anita!" Amelia yelled, shoving me away and pushing our sister to the wall herself. "He is the Don! Do you have any fucking clue what his men will do to you if you betray him?"

"Worse than what he's going to do to our parents?" Anita shrieked.

I grabbed my forehead in despair as anxiety clawed at my heart and found Molly. "Dio!" I screamed at the top of my lungs, passing my stubborn sister desperate to protect Nico.

Dio and Saul ran into the room with other soldiers, "What is it?" Dio asked, taking in the scene.

"Call Nico," I demanded. "Anita knows something but won't say. I think it's a trap." I hurried, shaking my hands at him as he fumbled with his phone, "Call him!"

He held the phone to his ear as Saul dialed his own, staring at me as they rang and rang.

"No answer." Dio cursed.

"Matteo either."

"Fuck!" I screamed, feeling a full-blown panic attack take over my body.

I ran back to my younger sister and slapped her in the face, shocking her as tears welled in her eyes. "Tell me what you know! Papa and Mama will not think twice about leaving you here to suffer the wrath of the Cosa Nostra for this! It's your only chance at saving your own life!"

"I can't." She cried, shaking her head back and forth as Amelia continued holding her against the wall. "It's too late. It's done."

"The fuck it is!" I snapped. "Tell me!"

"They were going to ambush them!" She screamed in my face as she sobbed. "I overheard Diego telling one of the others about it before Cristian took us to the safe house."

"Diego?" I shook my head in confusion. "Who's Diego?"

"Her guard." Amelia groaned. "A man with a soul as black as his hair. He hates the Don, I've picked up that much from my few interactions with him."

"Wait." I paced, on the edge of hyperventilating, and looked at Dio and Saul, "Diego as in Dominic's illegitimate son?"

"Fuck." Dio whispered as the pieces fell into place.

"You know him?" Amelia asked, releasing our sister.

"He tried to kill me when I first came to Armarow when I was a kid." I paced. "I didn't remember it until recently. Nico cut Diego and his brothers off after Dominic's death."

"What was the ambush plan?" Dio demanded from Anita, making the young girl wilt under his dominant anger. "Tell me now!"

"They were going to wait until my father arrived and then strike against the Don and take him and his men inside the house."

"Then what?" I asked, even though my heart already knew the answer.

"They're going to kill him." She whispered as more tears fell down her cheeks. "Like he was going to do to Papa."

"We have to get there." I turned to Dio.

"We can't." He shook his head, as men started scrambling around the estate, readying to disperse to the meeting point to try anyway. "We have strict instructions from the Don on what to do if he's taken or killed. We're to remove you to safety and lock down until the Cosa Nostra can secure your safety."

"No!" I screamed in frustration, pulling my hair. "I don't care what he said! He could still be alive! My father won't kill him quickly! He's sick and demented, he'll drag it out and torture him."

"We have our orders, Mrs. Capasso." He replied sadly, but Saul didn't look so easily convinced.

"Please." I turned to him and begged. "There has to be a way." Tears flowed down my cheeks as I begged for my husband's life. "We have to do something."

"Get changed," He nodded his head, "We'll formulate a plan on the way." He turned and barked out orders to the men, telling them to ready themselves for extracting the Don.

I stood there in shock for half a second before Molly grabbed my hand and pulled me from the room.

"We need to get you dressed and on the way." She said, running up the stairs. "I know how we can save Nico and Matteo."

"Thank God." I cried, rushing into my closet as she changed into her traditional maid's uniform that I had insisted she stopped wearing thanks to its drabness. She had a plan. "Please let us be in time." I prayed quietly. "Please, please, please."

W e tore off from the convoy as they circled around the property, staying farther out than Nico's original rendezvous point that was attacked.

We had finally gotten word about twenty minutes away from the estate of Matthew Rizzio that my father's men attacked Nico's group where they waited.

There were no survivors left at the site, but Nico, Matteo, and Cristian weren't there.

Which meant that they were taken and possibly alive still.

I had to stick my head out the window and throw up when we got the news as nausea and panic forced all of the desserts I'd binged on earlier up. But I refused to stop with the plan.

The other two groups of Nico's men didn't attack once the Don was taken because they knew it would mean certain death for him. Instead, they waited and formulated a wider approach to the estate that would leave them better undetected. Add in the hundred men I brought from Armarow with me, the force was strong to face off with whatever my father had.

"Tell me what you're going to do again," Saul ordered from the front seat.

It hadn't been easy to convince Dio to go along with us and allow me to go in with the extraction group, but he finally caved. And then on the way, we crafted a plan thanks to Molly's insane ability to listen to gossip and small talk as a service member.

It was a good plan, and given that the estate used to be Capasso property, Molly knew the inner workings of the secret passageways that were nearly identical to Armarow.

"I'm going to the front door and acting like I belong there," I repeated. "Like I am meeting my father."

"Right, and then what?"

"And then I'm going to distract my father long enough for you to make your move," I confirmed, taking a deep breath as the estate came into view. "This has to work, right?" I asked Molly as she squeezed my hand in her lap.

"I'll be there as fast as I can." She reassured me and I nodded, knowing she wouldn't let me down.

"Okay." I took a calming deep breath as the gate appeared and armed men jumped out of every dark shadow, circling our car as Dio came to a stop and rolled down his window.

I wiped my nervous hands down the front of my pants and put my poker face on as men peered in the windows, using their flashlights to see everyone in the car.

Part one of the plan.

Get inside the estate gate.

"I have Arianna Rosetti here to see her father, Emilio," Dio said coolly.

The guards looked between themselves and back to me before one radioed to someone else, relaying the message.

Which meant that my father would know I was here, and that he was getting a chance to kill me as well as my husband. I knew he was conceited enough to take the opportunity.

Seconds later the head guard nodded his head once to Dio and the gate slowly opened, allowing us into the estate.

"Go time," Saul whispered as we approached the front door. He looked over his shoulder at me and nodded. "Stick to the plan, and we'll get you out as soon as we can."

The door opened as another armed guard from my father's team stood staring down at me, halting me from replying before I slid from the car with Molly getting out behind me.

The men stared down with scrutiny but remained silent as Dio and Saul got out.

One of the guards with a machine gun in his hands looked at my body-guards and sneered. "You're Capasso's men."

Dio shrugged his shoulders like he was relaxed and conversating in a bar, "Aren't we all Capasso's men? He is the Don after all."

The guard scoffed and spit on the ground at Dio's feet, "We'll see for how long."

"Are we going to stand here all day and chitty chat or are you going to allow us inside to talk to my father?" I stepped in, keeping my head high and my brow raised indignantly.

"You can go in," the guard said, "Capasso men stay here."

"Whatever." I flicked my wrist, nodding to Molly to follow me. "The testosterone around here." I scoffed, pretending to be annoyed.

When in reality I was shaking like a leaf inside. I didn't know what I would find inside, if Nico was still alive, or if I'd make it out alive either.

But I knew his best chance involved me distracting my father long enough to carry out the rest of the plan.

I just had to stay brave.

As soon as we cleared the front door, more armed guards signaled for us to stop. One of them pushed me against the wall and started patting me down. My skin crawled the longer his hands touched my body and nausea boiled inside of me anew when they wandered over my breasts and between my legs, feeling for far more than weapons.

I waited the appropriate amount of time before shoving him backward and glaring at him. "Nothing in life is free, boy. If you want to cop a feel, hire a hooker," he snarled at me but I turned my attention to the guard getting ready to grab Molly and search the same way I just had been.

But I couldn't let that happen.

Part two of the plan.

Get Molly inside and alone.

"Molly, be useful for once and go get me a drink," I snapped my fingers impatiently as she looked between me and the guard, playing her part perfectly. "Now!" I argued, ignoring the glares from the men. "I'm sure if you rub your two brain cells together you can find the kitchen." I waved her off demandingly and then turned my attention back to the guards. "Where is my father, I'm growing quite bored of you all."

The men glared at me, but they ignored Molly as she bowed once demurely and then walked off into the house towards where the kitchen was.

"This way," The one that had fondled me said, walking to the right and down the hallway. I followed after him, daring one glance under my lashes at Molly as she cleared the foyer and rounded the corner to the kitchen.

Yes! I cheered in my head as step two checked itself off my list perfectly.

My heels clicked across the marble floor behind the guard with two more flanking me as we reached a double set of doors. As the man grabbed the door handle a muffled scream pierced the air from behind the hardwood and the hair on my neck stood up.

Please just let him be alive.

I prayed on repeat in my head as the doors opened and revealed a large ballroom, littered with men and chaos.

I quickly scanned the room for my husband and found him on his knees chained to the floor by a metal collar around his neck and his arms pulled out to his sides, chained to a wooden contraption. He was shirtless and bleeding from what looked like a gunshot wound to his shoulder and multiple slices across his abdomen and chest. His face was bloodied, and one eye was swollen but he tracked me with the other. I shivered from the volatile anger burning me through that one green iris. "Ari," he growled, angry with me for defying all of his orders and showing up tonight.

"Ah, the diamond of the Rosetti line." My father's sniveling voice drew my attention across the space to where he sat on what looked like a throne on a raised dais.

Go time. "A throne for the court jester?" I questioned, tsking my teeth snidely at him. I needed to goad him, without sending him so far over the edge that he killed me prematurely. I turned my attention to Matthew Rizzio, a man I'd met a handful of times before and instantly disliked. He stood on the floor in front of the dais like a commoner in a royal court. It was pathetic really. "And here I thought this was your home. Good to know you're just a little bitch in the game too."

"Shut up, girl," My father sneered.

I found my brothers knelt by the wall, bound by chains similar to Nico's with their mouths gagged. They wore battle wounds but didn't look too bad off. The angry glare in their eyes matched my husband's though.

Matteo on the other hand, was a different story.

The man lay on his side on the ground, bleeding heavily from a wound in his head, and judging by the size of the pool of blood underneath him, he hadn't moved in a while.

I wasn't even sure he was alive, but I forced myself not to react.

I glanced around the room again and found the other man I'd been searching for when I walked in, finding him standing behind one of the posts holding Nico's wrists wide. "And you." I shook my head disappointedly. "You're probably the most pathetic one out of every man here, Diego." Nicolas's half-brother's eyes darkened as he realized I recognized him and talked down on him. "How on earth have you gone from attacking twelve-year-old me in the woods and failing to kill me, *miserably* might I add, to being the pathetic babysitter of my twelve-year-old sister?" I rolled my eyes. "Oh how the mighty have fallen, wouldn't you say, *brother*?" He took a step towards me as his anger hit a boiling point but my father snapped his fingers, gaining his attention, and waved for him to stand down. I laughed mockingly before walking to the center of the room and facing my father, tossing my hands out at my sides and quirking a brow at him. "Well, well, well, Papa. You've orchestrated quite the little show here this evening."

My father smirked and stood up from the chair, slowly walking down the steps toward me. "And you've done me such a great honor by joining me for the festivities, Daughter." He cocked his head. "We have almost the entire family here. Like one big reunion to see the end of the Capasso rule."

"Is that what this is all about?" I rolled my eyes. "But you're missing two very vital parts of your little family tonight, Papa. Or have you forgotten that *I* have your other two daughters?" I paused and watched his eyes darken fractionally. "Who will you use for bargaining chips if not for your virginal child bride daughters after you kill the rest of us off?" I tsked.

"I will not need to make deals once I am Don." He snapped, letting his short temper show as his face reddened.

"Oh!" I nodded dramatically, "So, that's the plan. You kill Nicolas, and then you just suddenly do what? Take the crown? Stand upon the throne and stomp your foot and demand that everyone does as you say?" I chuckled, "You really are as dumb as you look." I turned back towards Diego before he could react, "I take back what I said." I hooked my finger over my shoulder towards my father. "He's the most pathetic." I waved at him, "You're off the hook."

My father took a menacing step forward as his jaw clenched and I fought my body's fight-or-flight reaction to him. I'd suffered so much over the years because of the man, and it was hard to just turn off that fear.

But I refused to show it.

"Money can buy you a lot of things in life, Papa. Obviously." I spun around with my hands out, showcasing the room we stood in surrounded by men he paid for. "But you know what it can't buy?" I questioned, facing him again.

His lip twitched but he remained silent. "Respect," I whispered. "You see, no one on this entire planet has ever respected Emilio Rosetti, no matter how much ass-kissing they've done for your money. And they never will, even if you manage to take the entire Cosa Nostra over. Which let us be honest, there'd be no good men left by the time that happened because they'd all rather kill themselves than answer to a sniveling, weak, cowardly, little man like you," I hissed.

I watched his hand move in a high arc across the space, anticipating it and bracing for the crack of it against my cheek. It didn't help alleviate the pain of his hit, but it did give me time to process it and overcome it before I lifted my head from the side where it was thrown.

"You listen here you little whore!" my father screamed in anger, "You don't know a fucking thing about how business is run. All you've ever been worth was by what lay between your legs. And now that this animal has had you, you'll never be worth anything again!"

When I stood up straight and stared at my father, I ran my tongue over my teeth and tasted the blood from a cut on the inside of my lip and then smiled, showcasing the gnarly grin. "Oh, come on, Papa. You're getting weak in your old age, even Mama can hit harder than that."

He lunged, falling right into the trap I set forth for him, and grabbed me by the hair, hauling me across the room to his throne.

Part Three of the plan.

Get physically close to my father and separate him from all of his guards.

I heard Nico and my brothers all fighting their bindings as I was heaved down onto the steps, only catching myself an inch from bashing my face off the marble before my father dragged me up them with his fist still in my hair. My scalp burned and tears filled my eyes but I stayed on track.

I looked over at Nico and ached to heal the pain in his eyes as he tried tearing his body limb from limb to free himself to aid me.

When we were at the top of the steps my father shoved me down into the seat he had vacated and stood over me, with one hand wrapped around my hair and the other on my shoulder, holding me down in the chair. "Now, if you think I'm so weak, you've just convinced me to show you how powerful I can be. And you know who's going to suffer for that?" He sneered, "The wolf."

I bit my cheeks so hard to keep my mouth shut as my father waved his guards to bring Nico forward into the center of the room.

Deep breaths, Ari.

I repeated as I felt myself start to panic. If my father killed Nico right in front of me, I'd never recover.

But it was all part of the plan, which brought me back to that.

Part four of the plan.

Trust Molly's knack for finding her way through dark secret passages.

Nico's bloody face stared right at me as he was shoved to the ground again and forced to face my father.

"You've outgrown your place, boy," My father sneered from above me like he was casting down judgment upon Nico like a king in olden times. "You had the whole world at your fingertips when you took over as Don, but you just couldn't fucking follow the path your father laid out for you."

"My father was a coward." Nico growled, "Much like you."

My dad's body vibrated with anger, tightening his hold on my hair until I winced before schooling my features. "You'll see what a coward really is when I make you watch these men have their way with your wife!" My father shoved me down the stairs, catching me off guard as I tried to protect my head and my stomach the best I could. "Perhaps I'll allow your brother first crack at her." My father said, and I whipped my head up from where I landed on the floor, finding Diego's cruel smile aimed my way as he stalked toward me.

Nico lunged, fighting the binds that held him, as did my brothers from their spot against the wall. But none of them could get to me in time.

Diego's hand wrapped around my throat as he pushed me onto my back, looming over me while I punched, kicked, and clawed at him. His hand tightened around my throat, cutting off all the airflow, and memories of my childhood assaulted me, tormenting me with the panic I had felt the last time this man had tried to suffocate me.

I kept fighting him, even as he overpowered me and my vision darkened at the edges.

No.

I screamed inside, where was Molly?

Part five of the plan.

Try not to die.

CHAPTER 26 – NICO

M y shoulder dislocated from the force I pulled on my wrist, trying to dislodge the chains. Diego crawled on top of my pregnant wife and strangled her, but not once did she stop fighting him off. Agonizing pain tried to blur the things happening around me as I fought to get to her, but I wouldn't let it blind me.

I had to get to her.

Before I could get free though, the wall behind Emilio exploded open, raining down shards of wood and plaster over the entire room. The gunfire cut through the ringing noise in my ears from the initial blast and I screamed Ari's name as smoke filled the room, blurring my view of her twenty feet away.

I coughed, fighting with the binds again, roaring as my shoulder tore even further out of the socket, desperate to get to her. The sounds were deafening but I never stopped yelling for her. It went on and on; gunfire, explosions, screams. Never relenting for what felt like ages, as I stayed chained to the floor, unable to move or fight.

"Stop." Cold hands pushed through the smoke as they slid up my neck and into my hair. "Stop fighting."

"Ari!" I coughed around the smoke, dipping my head slightly as a bullet whizzed past my ear. Shouts filled the room, followed by screams of men who were dying and falling onto the marble floor all around us.

"I'm here, baby," she said, finally getting close enough for me to see as the smoke from the explosion started clearing. "I've got the key, stay still." She hurriedly worked the lock free around my neck and then off each wrist, releasing me and jumping into my arms, clinging to me like a koala. "Oh, my God." She cried. "Are you okay?"

"Get down," I growled, throwing us to the floor and shielding her body with mine as more bullets whizzed past. "Are you fucking insane?" I snapped at her, angry for her risking her own life and that of our babies to show up here.

"Yes." She yelled back, glaring at me angrily when I peeked down at her. "Fucking insanely in love with you, you big jerk."

"Capa!" Dio's voice rang out and I looked up, seeing him and Saul flanked by no less than fifty armed men standing around the room. "Where's Ari?" He yelled when he found me.

"Here." I sat up, getting my weight off of her and pulling her to her knees. I ran my hands over her entire body, noticing the purple handprints already blooming around her throat and the cut on her lip. But other than that, she was okay.

Alive.

"Carmine!" Ari yelled, fighting my hands off of her as she looked around the room. "Cristian!"

"We're here," Carmine yelled back, coming forward and brushing off the debris from his body. "Are you okay?"

"Yeah." She cried, nodding her head before hugging them both. "I'm so sorry."

"Shh." Carmine soothed her, "We'll talk about all of that later."

"Capa." Saul interrupted and knelt over Matteo's body. Molly held his head in her lap, sobbing as she looked around in a panic.

"Is he alive?" I asked, pulling Ari under my good arm and tucking her face away from the gruesome sight.

Molly nodded and looked up at me with tear-filled eyes. "Barely."

"Get him out of here," I ordered Saul. "Get him to the trauma center and keep me updated. Take any other wounded with you."

"Yes, Capa," He nodded, sliding Molly out of the way to pick Matteo's large body up and carry him from the room.

"Go with him," Ari said, pulling Molly in for a hug. "We'll be there shortly. Thank you for everything."

Molly nodded, looking torn between Matteo and Ari but eventually gave in and chased after the man that had been smitten with her for years now.

"Sir." Luca walked up, holding his rifle in his hands and looking around the room. "There's some business to attend to."

My men that stormed the room had the surviving Rosetti men lined up against the wall on their knees. Some were bleeding from fatal wounds and some looked like they'd rather be dead already.

At the beginning of the line, Emilio and Diego knelt next to each other. Emilio had a bullet hole in his leg, bleeding far faster than he deserved, and Diego had a couple in his chest giving him a musical rattle to each breath he took.

"Stay here, Little One." I kissed her temple but as I went to walk away, her arms tightened around my waist and she clung to me.

"Don't ask me to let go of you." She whispered hopefully. "I can't. Not yet."

"I'm going to kill many men for you Arianna," I replied, trying to express the gravity of what was about to occur.

"I want to pull the trigger on my father." She whispered with her eyes so wide.

"No," I responded instantly.

"Nico." She whined. "I've earned this." She squeezed tighter, putting pressure on my broken ribs and making me hiss, but she didn't let up either. "I survived twenty years of torture because of that man. I've earned this."

I stared down at her, trying to come up with a reason to deny her what she wanted, but came up blank.

"I don't want that darkness on your shoulders, Little One."

She just shook her head and looked over at her father where he knelt yelling and begging for mercy. "This will finally blow that darkness off of me, baby." She looked back up at me. "This is how I get free."

I clenched my jaw, hating that I knew she was right because I never wanted her touched by any of this world, but conceded. "One bullet. And then we leave."

"Deal." She sighed and smiled at me.

"Luca." I held my hand out over her shoulder and he placed a loaded pistol into it. "Watch how it's done," I told Ari, pulling her over to where my father's illegitimate son knelt next to Emilio.

Even staring death in the face, the bastard smiled with his sick and twisted grin. "You should have taken the opportunity I gave to you when I allowed you to leave Armarow with your life the first time, Diego," I noted, staring down at him. "But now, not only will I end your life here tonight for your part in all of this. But I'm going to hunt down your sick brothers and your whore of a mother and any other relatives you have left, and I'm going to give them an even worse death than the one you've awarded yourself tonight."

His face turned purple with anger as I lifted the gun to his temple and pulled the trigger, blowing his brains out the back of his skull and all over the wall. I nodded to Luca and the others started executing the others in line, ending the Rosetti revolution on its knees.

Emilio still knelt, begging and pleading to his daughter for mercy as we stood before him, and I watched her for any sign that indicated she wasn't prepared to handle the weight of the task.

But it never came.

Instead, she lifted the gun out of my hand and held it up, aiming it at his chest and pausing. "None of us will miss you, not for a single second." She said and then pulled the trigger, emptying the entire magazine into his chest and stomach before clicking the gun multiple times with its empty slide locked back, like she didn't realize she was out. Emilio fell to the floor, dead before his body landed against the marble with an ominous thud. Her chest rose and fell with exertion but she never lowered her still shaking hand.

"Give me that, sweetheart." I covered her hand with mine, forcing her to let go of the gun. "Let's go," I whispered, pressing my lips to her temple and turning her away from the carnage laid out before her. When we got to the doorway I stopped and looked back, nodding to Luca. "Burn the entire estate to the ground."

"Yes, Capa." He responded, smirking down at Arianna as her brothers met up with us again.

"I'm sorry I didn't let you have him." She said to Carmine, "You two deserved that as much as I did." I couldn't tell if it was regret or shame that made her tilt her head to the floor but I wasn't having it. And neither were her brothers.

"It doesn't matter, Sunshine," Carmine said, pulling her in for another hug. "As long as it's over."

"He had it coming from all of us," Cristian affirmed, throwing his arm over her shoulders and kissing her temple. "Let's just all move on from it. Together."

"Together." She smiled up at them and then over to me. "I like the sounds of that."

EPILOGUE – ARIANNA

"Would you get off it, woman? I'm more than capable of feeding myself." Matteo grumped from the room he was staying in on the east wing as I rounded the doorway.

"Knock, knock," I announced loudly, holding out the basket in my hands as he and Molly looked up from where he sat in a chair next to the bed.

Molly rolled her eyes on the stool at his feet with a bowl of soup on a tray and the spoon held out for him like a toddler.

"Am I interrupting?" I joked with a smirk.

"Only if you aren't here to call her off." He complained.

"You know," I set the basket down on the end of the bed and crossed my arms over my chest. "You're no better at being a patient than Nico is."

"I wouldn't know, since he gets to leave the house," Matteo complained and Molly swatted his leg.

"Is being here with me taking care of you all that bad?" She asked and I bit my lip to keep from chuckling at the trap she left out there for him.

He groaned and laid his head back on the chair with a sigh. "That's not what I meant." He lifted his head and relaxed his features. "I'm sorry. I'm just not used to being so *useless*."

I snorted and then waved my hand in front of my face embarrassedly. "I'm leaving. I just brought you some treats from Mrs. Bussa." I winked at him. "I tried one and they're delicious so you should shape up or Molly might take her mama's sweet baking away."

"Yes Ma'am." He replied, thoroughly chastised and remorseful. "Thank you, Arianna."

I nodded and winked at Molly, "Your mama asked if you were coming to dinner tonight, it's been a while since they've seen you." I said pointedly.

"I know." She sighed.

"Give her a call. I think she thinks we're holding you hostage in a tower up here."

"I will." She smiled. "Thank you."

"Mmh." I hummed, "Tood-aloo, love birds."

They both groaned as I left the room cackling at their discomfort. They weren't together, but I didn't doubt that both of them would be angry if the other started seeing someone else though. It was just a chapter that they needed to walk down on their own, in their own time, and in their own way.

I just quite enjoyed teasing them about it along the way. To be honest, I liked having them both living inside of the estate in the east wing full-time for the last few months.

Matteo's recovery had been slower than Nico's simply because Nico was shot in muscle and bone, whereas Matteo's bullet literally went into his brain. He was a walking miracle to even be alive; let alone be able to walk and talk like he used to. But he did suffer from lingering migraines, muscle spasms, and neurologic miscommunications that made it a concentrated effort for him to move certain muscles from the damage the bullet caused. He saw physical and occupational therapists every day. They came to Armarow and were helping his brain remap the signals that were sent to his body to operate it, and he was recovering.

It was slow, and he was frustrated, and it put a strain on a new connection that he had begun with Molly before the shooting. But they were going to figure it out, that was obvious to anyone that saw them.

They just had to figure it out for themselves.

I went searching for my husband, already knowing where I'd find him this time of day, so I headed to the basement where his state-of-the-art home gym was laid out.

When the sliding glass door slid open, loud, chaotic music thumped with a heavy bass, swirling around me as I entered.

He had his back to me sitting on a bench doing some impressive move where he pushed a dumbbell the size of my torso high over his head with one arm and then slowly lowered it back to his lap.

My husband was drop-dead gorgeous and worked hard to stay in tip-top shape, even nursing a shoulder injury from being shot and then from separating it trying to get out of his chains. It didn't slow him down a bit, it just made him angry, and he turned that anger into dedicated muscle energy and spent a lot of his time working out to soothe it.

Because he didn't trust himself to let loose around me anymore.

And I fucking hated it.

He wore only a loose pair of black shorts with sneakers and sweat covered his torso and arms, making my mouth water with a carnal need that hadn't been satisfied in months.

Five long months to be exact. That was how long it had been since the shooting and since he started treating me like a delicate flower again, refusing to give me the passion I needed.

Don't get me wrong, the slow tender love Nico 'The Wolf' Capasso could put down was otherworldly and I never came up for air feeling unsatisfied. But I did end up feeling like half of me was missing.

After every slow sensual lovemaking that he gave, he'd sneak away to the gym where he could get the violence he craved out of his system until he could relax.

But enough was enough.

"Wife." He said from the bench with his back still to me. The mirror he faced gave me away, but he never lifted his eyes from his own form to notice me. He didn't need to. He sensed me just like I did him when he came near. "You're staring again."

I snapped my eyes from the delicious muscles of his strong back to find his eyes finally locked on me in the mirror. I stood behind him, running my hands over the swell of my baby bump, nearly salivating and he caught me.

"You shouldn't look so yummy if you didn't want admirers." I cocked my head to the side and smirked at him. "Why are you hiding from me today?" I walked in front of him and pressed my back against the mirror, blocking his view and interrupting his set. But he just kept pressing the iron over his head with his eyes locked on mine.

It was freezing cold in the room, thanks to the world-class air conditioner, but my body was an inferno of desire that even my small sundress couldn't provide relief from.

"I never hide from you," he replied, finally setting the weight down and leaning back against the inclined backrest, spreading his feet and looking even more god-like. "You're always right here." He tapped his temple. "Even when I try to keep you out."

"Do you still try to keep me out?" I questioned, twirling the tie that held the bust of my dress closed around my finger. His eyes followed the motion before trailing back up to mine.

"No. It's pointless to even try."

"Do you have any idea how much I love you?" I asked and his brow furrowed as he regarded me, but he didn't answer. "Or how much of my life is consumed by you?" I leaned up off the mirror and walked forward until the hem of my dress brushed over his knee. "There's no hiding myself from you either, Nico, yet somehow you're still avoiding my needs."

His scowl deepened and he sat forward on the bench. "What needs of yours am I not meeting."

"The one to make me feel like a woman," I responded, sliding my fingers up the sides of his neck and looping them around the back. "The need to feel like you've never wanted anyone else in the world more than you want me." His nostrils flared and he dropped my stare, choosing to look off at something behind me. "The need to feel like you wouldn't survive without me anymore."

"I do." He snapped, finally letting that anger free that burned inside of him.

That violence, that I craved.

"You used to," I rebutted, hooking my thumbs under his jaw and forcing his head back to me until he had no choice but to face me.

To face this.

"I don't know what you expect me to do."

"I expect you to fulfill my needs," I hissed, letting my own frustrations rise to match his. The passion burned in my belly, and I felt his body tense under my hands. "Give me what I need, Nico."

He wrapped his hand around my throat and pulled me forward until I straddled him on his lap with my toes hanging above the ground and our noses nearly touching. Neither of us let go of the other's neck. "And what about my needs, Wife?"

My skin prickled at the implication. "Am I not meeting every single one of yours? What need do you have that I'm failing to give you?"

"My need to keep you safe!" he snarled. "My fucking need to protect you and this baby from any fucking harm that could come to you." He dropped his free hand to my stomach and our baby responded by kicking against it. "Don't you fucking understand what watching you walk into that house was like for me?" he yelled and then clenched his jaw shut so hard his molars cracked.

It was the first time he'd spoken about that night to me. He never told me what they did to him before I got there, and he only ever listened when I would talk about what I felt facing off with my father and his brother.

"Tell me," I whispered, pressing forward on the hand around my neck until our noses touched. "Tell me everything so I can understand it."

"It destroyed me, Arianna. It broke the last part inside of me that believed in good." Nico swallowed and the muscles in his neck tensed under my fingers. "I saw your death a million times in the short span of ten minutes that you were there. I saw my brother raping you and your father beating the life out of you. I saw his men destroying our baby while I was chained to the floor like a fucking dog. I saw the light in your beautiful eyes fade as your soul left your body and what little part of me that was still human died in that same moment, Arianna." He pressed his forehead against mine and took a couple of deep breaths, his chest rose and fell against mine and his entire body vibrated. "You don't understand what will happen to me if you're taken away. If our children are taken from me." He closed his eyes and his strong shoulders deflated. "I won't exist in this world as a human without you, Little One. The floor will open up and the devil himself will call me home if you leave me." He whispered in agony, "I can't take that risk."

"I'm sorry." I shook in his arms as tears fell down my cheeks. "But that is exactly how I felt when I realized you were in danger." I took a shuddering breath, and he dropped his hand from my neck and wrapped both arms around my body. "When I realized my father had you, and that you were going to suffer unimaginable pain at his hands, I felt like my skin was being pulled from my bone. Every single nerve in my body was on fire with this need to do something, to save you somehow." I pulled back to look at him, "I had to do something."

"You sacrificed yourself for me." He shuddered. "If your plan failed, we would have both been dead."

"Better to be together in death, than be alone in life." I replied. "You are my heart; without you, it does not beat. I do not thrive. I do not exist."

He slammed his lips down on mine and tangled his hands in my hair as he tilted his head and kissed me with fervent need. "That is exactly how I feel."

He finally said as he untangled his hands from my hair. "And I don't know how to feel that and protect you from the intensity of it at the same time."

"I don't need your protection, Nico. I need what no one else can give me. You're love." I rocked my hips, pinning his cock between us as it hardened. "Give me your love, baby. Show me."

"Fucking hell." He growled and then tore the tie at my breasts open, shredding the dress into pieces before he ripped it off my body.

"Yes!" I cried as he dipped his mouth and sucked on one of my hardened nipples, twirling his tongue around the tip and biting it with his teeth. "Fuck!" I screamed, tilting my hips and offering him more of my breasts as I rubbed his cock between our bodies. "Just like that, baby."

"This is how you want me?" He growled at my breast, moving to the other one while he pinched and pulled on the one he had just bitten. "You want me rough with you?"

"Yes." I kept rocking my hips, nearly orgasming already from the high libido that pregnancy gave me paired with the carnal desire he was building inside of me.

"You want me to take you like I did the night of our wedding." He hissed, "When I bent you over the back of that chair and slammed my cock into your body without a care for anything else in the world but how good your pussy felt wrapped around me. Because you hated me for it when I did it." He slapped my ass before ripping my panties to shreds and throwing them to the side with the scraps of my dress. "But God, you milked my cock so good." He groaned, "I pushed you down and made you take every fucking drop of me."

"I'm coming." I panted, rocking faster and clawing at his neck as I threw my head back. "I'm fucking coming!"

He sucked on my nipples and extended my orgasm out until I fell forward in his arms, gasping for breath and shivering from how hard I came.

"Don't fade on me yet, Little One." He said, standing up and carrying me over to the large orthopedic bench that Matteo's therapists used to work his muscles out. It was essentially a twin-sized bed and sturdy, thankfully as Nico threw me down on it and pushed my legs up towards my shoulders. "I'm going to fuck this pussy so hard."

"Yes," I whined, spreading my knees apart further and staring up at him as he pushed his black shorts down and freed his hard cock. "I want to wear your marks on me."

"Reach down and spread that pussy open for me." He commanded, stroking his cock and licking his bottom lip as I circled my clit a few times with my fingertips before spreading myself open just like he said. "Good girl." He praised, lining his cock up. "Look at me when I sink into you."

I lifted my eyes from his cock to his face and stared at him as he pushed his thick erection in, slowly stretching me until he was buried deep. His eyelids fluttered closed, and he bit his bottom lip in a way that made me gush around him. "God, you're so thick." I groaned, pinching my nipples to add to the stimulation.

His eyes locked on the motion and his lips twitched as he pulled out and slammed back in, watching my fingers tease his favorite part of me.

He had loved my tits before I got pregnant, but even I was impressed with how full and juicy they were as I grew life inside of me, and he was utterly obsessed. "Pinch them." He grunted, thrusting quickly as he held my knees wide so he could see and didn't push on my belly that was stubbornly in the way. "Harder."

I did as he said and moaned from the sensation as he slammed into me over and over again. "You feel so good," I whined, tossing my head back and forth as I grew closer to yet another orgasm. "God, I missed this." I mewed deliriously. My eyes closed and seconds later a burning pain branded the side of my breast following a smacking sound.

"Eyes on me, Wife." He commanded. "Watch me while I make you come."

"Yes!" I screamed, shattering around his cock as he did just that. He was relentless, slamming into me and giving me what I asked for.

Demanded. I demanded this of him.

"On your knees." He demanded, pulling out and helping me roll over until I knelt with my legs spread wide on the edge of the table. My ass hung off the edge and I faced the mirror as he lined back up and sank deep inside of me. "This fucking pussy." He growled, tightening his grip on my hips as he thrust.

The angle was so deep like that, forcing the head of his cock against my g-spot over and over again while we watched our bodies in the mirror. It was erotic and sensual, and I was a goner for the appeal of it all.

"You have to come." I gasped, clawing at his arms until he wrapped one around my body and grasped my neck in his hand, anchoring me down. "I can't take anymore." My eyes closed and my head lolled back onto his shoulder as his other hand circled my clit before he slapped it. "Nicolas!"

"I'm coming." He grunted, growling in my ear as I screamed through the blinding pleasure of yet another orgasm. "Take it, Little One. Take my come like a good little girl. Take it all."

"Oh, my god." I moaned, falling forward onto my elbows as his cock twitched and jerked inside of me, buried deep. "I'm dead." I panted, unable to do much else.

"Shh." He soothed me, pulling my locked-up knees out from underneath me and turning me to lay on my side before laying down next to me, cradling me and my belly in his arms. "Did I hurt you? Are you okay?"

"I'm perfect," I replied dreamily, smiling into the slick skin on his neck before biting it.

"Promise?" He grunted, pulling his flesh from my teeth. "Is the baby okay?"

"He's fine." I sighed and the baby confirmed that by rolling over forcefully between us and stepping directly on my bladder. "Though I may pee all over you and the table if I don't get up soon."

He chuckled and kissed my temple. "Now that's where I draw the line."

"Hmm. Then help me up."

He stood up and lifted me off the table onto my tingling legs and held me until I was steady. "Put this on, your dress is ruined." He lifted his tee shirt off the back of the bench, and I lifted my arms over my head as he put it on me. It covered me well enough to make it upstairs to our bedroom where I could change. He slid back into his black shorts looking like my most favorite snack in the world.

We walked out of the gym together, with his arm over my shoulders and smiles on both of our faces. "I needed that," I whispered as we went up the stairs to our wing.

"Yeah, so did I." He smirked down at me. "But I'm too old to give it to you like that every time. So you'll have to settle for every third or fourth time."

I tilted my head back and laughed, pinching his side and allowing his mirth to warm me. It'd been so long since I'd seen him genuinely relaxed in my presence. "Every other and we have a deal."

He grunted and kissed my head, holding open the bedroom door. "Fine, but only if you promise to soak your body in a hot bath after each time. I don't want you getting sore."

"Hmm." I hummed, tapping my fingertip to the end of my chin like I was contemplating his proposal. "Deal." I smirked and held my hand out for him, as he closed his palm over mine, I quickly added, "If you join me for the bubble bath each and every time. Or no deal."

He pursed his lips and rolled his eyes. "I'm an incredibly busy man and you want me wasting my time away in a bubble bath to appease my stubborn wife?"

I raised one eyebrow at him and put my hands on my hips as he turned the tap on in the tub before pouring my favorite bubble bath in. When he looked back over at me, I took the shirt off over my head and leaned up to get as close to his ear as I could and whispered. "If you join me, I'll do that thing with my tongue you like. You know, where I lick your balls and try to tie them like a cherry stem with my tongue." I purred and ran my hands over his bare shoulders.

"Minx." He growled, grabbing my ass with both of his hands. "I would have agreed anyway, but now that you've sweetened the pot, you have a deal."

"Worth it." I winked at him and stepped into the steaming water, lowering my tired body down into it with a hiss and a sigh as he sank in behind me and pulled me against his chest. I listened to nothing but the hiss of the bubbles as they popped while his hands massaged my arms and shoulders until I was a pile of goo in his hands.

"Marry me." He whispered into my ear.

My eyes popped open as surprise confused me. "I thought we already were." I scoffed, "For almost a year now."

"I know." He kissed my neck, gathering my hair to one side for easy access. "But I want to do it the right way this time." He kissed me. "I want to woo you." He kissed me again. "I want to romance you." And again. "I want you to have the wedding you didn't get last time and the honeymoon we got robbed of. I want a redo."

"I don't need to redo it, Nico." I turned in his arms and faced him. "I have you, and that's all that matters."

"I know, but I want this." His green eyes were serious as he stared at me. "For our first anniversary, right after the baby comes. Let's do it again, the right way."

My heart melted for the man who once told me he'd use my body for his own pleasure as it was his right as my husband in a tactic to dominate me.

Gone were his attempts to overpower me and control me with fear and authority. Now we were partners, lovers, and companions and he was everything I ever wanted without even knowing it.

"I'm so lucky to call you mine," I whispered dreamily. "Yes. Yes, forever and a day."

The End

WHAT'S NEXT

Thank you for joining again with another book. I hope you loved it as much as my others.

What's next you ask?

As promised, for quite some time now, **Book 3 of the Shadeport Crew Series** is coming out this fall. Zeke Evans and Laila Manning will finally get their story.

Zeke, second in command of the Shadeport Crew, has always been everyone else's confidant and right-hand man. But then the tortured and broken Laila Manning moved in across the hall in the barracks, and his protective and endearing side grew until he could no longer keep it hidden from her. It will take a strong, dedicated man like Zeke to empower and protect Laila from her past traumas and he's so utterly perfect for the job. He just needs to be convinced of it. So stay tuned for their story.

Plus, keep your eyes open for a sexy new MMFM why choose, chock **FULL** of spice to keep you warm as the weather turns cooler this fall as well.

As a reminder, I'm now offering signed paperbacks on my website, amm ccoybooks.com. They always come personalized and stuffed full of cute swag so go check them out now.

Already own a paperback that you wish you had gotten signed? No problem! I have bookplates too that make any paperback a custom one!

I hope all of you good girls and boys have a fantastic summer and read all sorts of filth and fun.

Until next time,

Ally

Made in the USA
Middletown, DE
09 October 2023